THE YEAR'S BEST AFRICAN SPECULATIVE FICTION 2021

THE YEAR'S BEST AFRICAN SPECULATIVE FICTION 2021

Edited by

Oghenechovwe Donald Ekpeki

Caezik SF & Fantasy

in partnership with

O.D. Ekpeki Presents

ISBN: 978-1-64710-128-2
First Caezik/WordFire Edition (Paperback). November 2024.
1 2 3 4 5 6 7 8 9 10

An imprint of Arc Manor LLC
www.CaezikSF.com

An imprint of Jembefola Press
www.odekpeki.com

CONTENTS

WHERE YOU GO

by Somto O. Ihezue

Maradi, Northern Nigeria

It follows me. Rain tapping against the window. In a bath, water trailing down my skin. I do not step into puddles. I cannot will myself to believe the still spread is nothing more than liquid over solid ground.

When the last sandstorm left town, it took Athjar's eyes with it. Hands thrown over my ears, I still heard them, his screams. I've never heard anything like it. As night fell and the desert winds with it, I pulled Athjar from the sands. In his face, I did not find his eyes. I knew when I saw his skin—cut in a hundred places like he'd been caught in a knife brawl—that I should have left him buried. *Needle sands* is what the locals called them. It is why we drape in the thickest of wool, from the ends of our hair to the tip of our toes. Their cuts came with a blistering infection, and with the nearest clinic two valleys away, I watched the fever take Athjar. With his passing, I am all that's left of those who came here to Maradi, searching for answers.

Today the winds are kind. Kind enough to leave the goats behind when they send hay scattering through the streets. I fasten the straps of my eye-gear and a memory walks in. Hair braided in sand, mind half lost, I had bartered Dike's ring for a sand coat, a pair of silver-rimmed goggles, and information about *The Collecting*. I remember the flickering of the gaslight, I remember my shadow leading the way into the makeshift shrine that served as a storehouse and a bedroom. Sometimes, in my dreams, I see it, the grin spread across the diviner's face as he pushed the goggles into my hands. With lenses scratched all over, I wouldn't see a dune rattlesnake if it was slithering right in front of me.

I turn a bend in the road, and I arrive. Like every other house in Maradi, the building is a pile of metal scraps, sandbags, and everything else. I ramble up to my one-room spot on the fourth floor. There are no railings on the stairs. If I slip and fall to my unquestionable death, the feral cats from the sewage will rip me to pieces before anyone finds me. So I lean against the wall. Inside, the table—the only piece of furniture I own, greets me. Kadiri would never have liked it here, neither would have Abike.

Botswana—21 years, 7 months, 2 weeks, 5 days before ...

It was Kadiri's second year at the oncology center. A cyst the size of a berry had been found lodged in a corner of her brain.

"The doctors said she has less than a month now," I said, staring down at my hands, then up to the cobwebs in the ceiling, and down at my hands again.

"No, they—they don't know that, they don't know how strong she—she is—"

"Abike, I'm sorry, I'm so sorry." I reached for her, and as I pulled her into me, her sobs came down hard, rocking both our bodies.

After the Oil War ravaged half the continent, from Djibouti down to the Table Mountains, Abike who had lost her sight, her family, and her home, became one of the last living members of the Ailopin people. When she came to us at the Botswana Sanctuary for Continentally Displaced Persons, no one had thought she'd make it. We thought wrong. She grew up sauntering all over the savannah with my daughter, Kadiri. The two were never more than a whisper apart. They'd squeeze into themselves, learning the texture of each other's hair. When the last of the Zebras migrated with the rains across the Chobe National Park, the girls would find them, weeding out ticks from their hide. In return, the zebras carried them on their backs, flying across the grasslands; bodies sailing in the wind, the echo of their voices carried for miles and miles as they ran reckless and wild.

A week before the Maitisong Festival, Kadiri died. Abike didn't cry. Not when the body was brought in from the morgue, nor when we laid her in the ground. She was being strong for both of us. Kadiri liked to stand in front of my mirror, she said it made her look like a painting. I shattered it. I took her things: the carvings on the wall, her seedlings in the old Milo tins; I shoved them into a box and threw it down the stairs. It stayed at the bottom of the stairway for weeks. I had lost Dike five years into our marriage and Kadiri had become everything to me. With her gone, I couldn't, I just couldn't.

"I'm leaving Botswana." I had rehearsed the line for days.

"When? Why?"

"Soon, dear." I lifted my head to pull the tears back in. "I'll probably head home to Nigeria, I'm not sure."

"When do we leave?"

I realized I'd been holding my breath all along. "Abike, I got in touch with your clan's people. They are so eager to see you," I said, drawing in a lungful of air, my hands reaching into hers.

"What? No!" she yelled, pulling away.

"I don't know where I'm headed, and I don't—I don't know—Abike, I'm not okay. Do you understand?" My voice was starting to break under the weight of the sobs I was stifling. "I'm not right for you, not the way I am now. You deserve better." The confused creases had still not left her forehead. "You belong with your people, your family."

"You are my family."

"Abike, please listen—"

"Where you go, I go, Mama."

That was the last we spoke of it. Together, we left Botswana. From the spice markets of Morocco to the Serengeti, we traveled the continent. Before long, she started to fledge. As a young girl, I too had fledged, but I was nothing compared to Abike. At the pyramids, she ran her hands across the hieroglyphics, translating texts lost to the ages and startling the tourists. In the Congo Basin, the birds had flocked to her as she called them by name. She had all these stories, stories before her time, before mine. There were times when I stared at her in wonder, and she'd turn to me and say, "I see you." I was the one with the eyes, yet Abike made me see.

Then it happened. She dropped in front of me, fingers clawing at her neck, face paler than paper. Frantic gasps escaped her lips as she reached for her voice.

"Ma—Mama." That was the last thing Abike said before disintegrating into a puddle of water. I never stepped into a puddle ever again.

...❖...

It stayed in the headlines for years. The papers read: *On the 23rd of June 2052, Lagos, capital city of United West Africa sank into the Atlantic.*

No one had expected it, but no one was surprised. After The Great Tsunami leveled Tokyo, we knew what was coming. But that wasn't all. As the granite walls of Cathedral Church of Christ tumbled into the depths; as the Third Mainland Bridge caved beneath the blue of the ocean; the last of the Ailopin, men, women, and children across the world, vanished. Panic came next, but not for the Ailopin. The collapse of Lagos and the consequent drowning of millions had trumped the eerie disappearance of an almost extinct clan. People thought I'd gone mad when I spoke about it. The only ones who believed were those who had seen it and the spirit tribes. We were calling it *The Collecting*.

Ire-mmili, South-Eastern Nigeria

From the Congo, where I had lost Abike, I took the first train back to Nigeria, and then on to my hometown, Ire-mmili. It had been years since I last was there. Botswana had been home for many years, with Dike, Kadiri, and Abike. My spirit sisters had been waiting. They knew I'd come.

"Ókpúkpú Ókpúkpú ànyì nnō. Welcome home, bone of our bone."

"Ìhè ná áfù gī ná áfù ànyì. What aches you, aches us," they said, taking me in.

Under the dancing stars, I was brought to the Hall of Daughters where my braids were loosened and soaked in the first milk of a mule.

"You have known suffering, now know rest," an elder chanted as she washed my hair in the milk. My sisters gathered, chanting alongside the elder who now came kneeling before me.

"See, see your mothers," she said as she lined my eyes with tanjèlé. "See the bones that bind you."

One by one, they came to me, sharing in my grief, siphoning as much as they could bear. In Ire-mmili, pain was shared, but there were limits. Pain brought with it a darkness, one that not only marked the soul, but replaced it. So, when my sisters took of my grief, they took with them fragments of the darkness that was starting to consume me. I never thought they'd perform the ritual, not for me, not after the things I had done.

Long before men could speak, back when the sun rose in the north, our first mother Oshimmili had clawed her way through the dirt and into the world. Where her hands tore through the soil, a forest sprouted stretching as far as the eye could see—the birthplace of the Ire-mmili. The initiation rite of spirit sisters was performed deep in the heart of the forest, before our mothers and their mothers before them, and beneath its leaves, we laid our departed. Seeing as I had not been keen on an initiation that included a hot knife slicing flesh from between my legs, I had gotten rid of the forest.

Clad in nothing but my strength, I had ripped out tufts of my hair, meshed it in my blood and bound it to the silver of a crescent moon. With a voice like a child possessed, I tossed my ritual into the fire I had started and cried: "Till the blood in my veins runs still, no tree shall hold root on this soil! Never again shall it know the green of grass or the songs of sparrows!"

For my abominations, I was dragged through the streets and whipped. I remember the giant snail shells clanging off my neck, announcing the coming of the spirit killer. Right there, as I sat amongst my sisters, I could still feel the hot poker searing into my back, marking me with the seal of banishment. Now all was forgotten, all except the forest. It still lay desolate, and there was no undoing it. They'd have to kill me to break the curse.

With the help of my sisters, I combed the spirit wild for years, searching, for a sign, a lost soul, anything. We weren't the only ones looking. There were others who had lost people to *The Collecting*.

Soon, we stopped talking about it. It was easier that way. Like everyone who had fled the coastlines for the mountain ranges and desert towns, I left Ire-mmili and headed north. It was there I met Athjar. His husband was an Ailopin and had disappeared just like Abike. He didn't like puddles either. He was part of a cult that had gotten word about a diviner up in Maradi who could help. I joined them.

Present day, Maradi

I raise a glass of water to my lips, careful not to stare into it. A knock comes on the door. It comes again, louder this time. The landlady's niece, she's come to remind me my rent is due. I do not answer. I bring the glass down to the table, and it tips over. On meeting the floor, its shards fly past my feet, spreading to the corners of the room.

"I know you're in there, witch!" her voice comes, heavier than her knocks. "I am going to call Big Auntie. She'll send you packing this time!"

I listen as her angry footsteps disappear down the stairs. A towel in my hand, I kneel over the pooling mess. When a piece of glass cuts into my knee, I do not feel it, not until I see the blood. As the pain sets in, I examine the wound, hoping it is something I can stitch up myself. Thin streams of blood trickle down the gash and drop into the water, sending ripples across it. In the circles, I see myself, what is left of me. Taking the towel, I press it hard against my reflection, and my hand goes right through.

"What the—!"

In crippling terror, I pull back at my arm; it stays, like it's caught in a snare. I pull again, harder, fear tearing through my body. Whatever is holding onto me, its grip tightens, dragging me in.

"Help! Somebody help!" I call out toward the door. The landlady's niece should have returned. "Help! Please, help me!"

No one comes. My shoulder goes in, and I know my head is next. Terrified that I could be inches away from falling into a chasm of water, or something worse, I shut my eyes and gulp in a lungful of air. Water does not meet my face, only warmth. I peel open my eyes, and far in the distance the lighthouse of Apapa stands, piercing the sky. The rays bouncing off its huge torch spill into the atmosphere, lighting it up.

"Lagos," I say under my breath lest I scare it off.

It is all here, its sky-liners, the overhead railroads, most in ruins, but here. And there's the color, like the rains of September came and never left. Algae, like carpets of green, crawl over the buildings in the most intentional manner. Vines, branches, and foliage loop and weave through windows and down rooftops. A breeze whistles in the trees, and comes for me, combing through my hair. Swaying down to the grass, it runs through it, and like a hall of children they whisper, "*shhhh.*" This place, Lagos, it feels like something alive.

Unsure, I walk. With each step, the grasshoppers dart off the waist-high grass. The hares follow, peeping cautiously before hopping off like toads wearing fur. I come upon a stream. Its water is a mirror. I see the scales on the trout and the smooth corners of the pebbles at the bottom. Squatting for a drink, I spot someone by the water's edge, their legs crossed in meditation. There are markings spiraling the ground around them. I inch in for a closer look, and they jerk awake, eyes piercing mine.

"Sorry I—sorry, who are—what is this—this—" I barely stutter through before they come speeding at me. I do not see their feet leave the ground. Walking backwards as I make to run, I trip over a rock, my body thudding hard to the ground. I sit up, and my assailant pushes into me, their hands wrapping my body.

"Mama, it's me."

In a raging desert storm, wind and sand thrashing at me, I could pick out that voice. Pulling her face up to mine, I look at the strange thing. Behind the intricacy of the dye patterns on her face, behind the cowries and corals lined in her hair, I see her staring back at me.

"Abi—Abike?"

"Mama," she sobs, wiping the tears starting to stream down my cheeks. "Praise Father! It worked this time. I've been trying for so long."

"Nwa'm," I say as the pieces of my heart find each other. "Nwa oma'm. My beautiful child."

I squeeze her into me. The prickly scent of herbs in her hair, the night shade of her skin, the energy burning within her, it overwhelms me, and I take it all in.

"What is going on? Why—how are you here?"

"You are more beautiful than I imagined," she says, ignoring my question as she takes strands of my hair in her hand.

Bringing my hands to her cheeks, I stare into her eyes. "You can see me?"

"Yes, Mama, yes." She laughs. "Father healed me."

She goes on and on about this Father, how he made her stronger, faster. How she never fell ill or stopped to catch her breath. I do not hear half the words she says, I do not care about any of it. She is here with me, nothing else matters. I bring my forehead to hers, she smiles, the kind of smile you give an old friend.

"You look the same as the day I lost you." I hadn't seen it at first, not with all the tears clogging my vision, but her face has not aged a day.

"Really?" she asks, her tone riddled with amusement.

"Yes. You've been gone for so long and—"

"How long?"

"You don't know?" She shakes her head from side to side, rather slowly, like she wasn't sure she wanted to know. "Abike, it's been over two decades."

"What?" Her eyes sink. "And all that time, you've been alone?"

"Abike, it's fine. Look at me." I lift her chin "It's all right. We are together now."

She pushes into me again, gently this time.

"Wait till you see Kadiri." Her mouth, pressed against the fabric of my clothes, muffles her voice.

"What—what are you talking about?"

"Kadiri, Mama, she's here," she says, gesturing to the bushes.

I watched Kadiri thin out on a hospital bed. Her hands clasped in mine when the light left her. I laid her in the garden behind our home, next to Dike. Looking towards the bushes and seeing no one there felt like losing Kadiri all over again.

"Abike, honey, there's no ..."

Then I see it: *Mmēghárị ányà, Illusion sorcery.* It wafts around her like a scent, a scent you could see. I've seen it too many times before; it's impossible to miss.

"Ow! Mama what are you doing?"

Tasting the strand of hair I pulled from her head, I realize it would take ten of my sisters to craft a curse this potent, and even more to break it.

"Abike, Kadiri is not here." I shake her vigorously, perhaps hoping to shake her out of it.

A rustle comes from the bushes. It is a boy. Others follow, appearing from behind the trees and nearby buildings. Soon, we have an audience. It's uncanny, but they all look quite like Abike. It's not the dye on their faces, nor the jewels in their hair. It isn't the exquisite Ankara material they are draped in either, their cuffs and shoulders lined in glistening gold. It's something else. *The Illusion!* It wafts around them too. To craft sorcery of this scale, one would require an unending source of power. Something is not right with this place—with these people.

"Abike, what have you done?" the boy asks, his eyes scanning me. "And who is this?"

"She is my mother."

Mother? Questions erupt from the gathering. *Did she say mother? What has she done now?*

"You know better than to go against Father," the boy continues, a frown setting on his face.

"Father would be furious," someone from the crowd chimes in.

"Father? What Father?" I can scarcely mask my irritation any longer.

The ground beneath our feet starts to rumble as if to answer my question. Heading in our direction, giant rhinoceros trample through the grass. If the gathering weren't as unfazed as they are right now, I'd have grabbed Abike and run. When the beasts halt and the dust settles, the riders come into view. The rider in the lead dismounts, and when his feet hit the ground, it does not make a sound. He is tall, taller than the guava tree in our garden back in Botswana. With his face long and thin, his eyes half closed, vacant, he reminds me of a professor I had at the university. The spongy afro sitting on his head is the white of cotton. He makes his way to us, a staff engraved in carvings, clenched in one hand. Beneath his robes, his left arm and legs stay shrouded. The people pour to their knees, heads to the ground. He and I are all that's left standing.

"She must leave." He does not look at me when he speaks to Abike.

"Father, please," Abike pleads, rising to her feet.

"You have disobeyed me again and again. Why?"

I step in between them. "*Ehh,* I don't know who you are or what—"

"I have lived ten thousand lifetimes before the first of your kind crawled through the mud. Do not presume to speak to me." His voice is empty. No pitch, no expression—empty. "You are not welcome here."

"Fine, but I'm not leaving without my child." I grab hold of Abike.

"*Your* child? You flatter yourself, witch," he says, mockery tainting his voice. "Abike is not yours, she never was, and she never will be."

"And who are you to dictate what is and what isn't?" I let him hear it, the anger in my words.

"Alápa-dúpé. I am Alápa-dúpé. Abike is born of my blood."

There is utter silence.

"So, where were you?"—I crack open the quiet—"when your people were massacred and scattered across the continent? When I took Abike, nursed her, protected her? Where were you?"

"Protected her? You can barely protect yourself." The mockery is louder now. "I am protecting her, protecting all of them from that insanity of a world. Here she is safe. Here she gets to survive, to thrive."

"You stole my daughter, you psycho! And these people"—I look to the gathering—"you took them from their homes, their families." Though I have no idea what he looks like, I imagine Athjar's husband is somewhere in the crowd listening. He never had a picture of him, said he needed him to exist only in his memory.

"I have had enough. I do not need to explain myself—least of all to you. You know what is out there?" he says, turning to the gathering, "the wars, the suffering. They have massacred your brothers and sisters, and they'll do the same to you. Your strength, this paradise, your immortality, is a blessing possible through me."

"Alápa-dúpé, forge of the Ailopin, mind wielder, the fall of rain, and tempest of Olodumare," I say, bringing his gaze back to me. "Yes, I know very well who you are."

I'd heard the stories, some more terrifying than others. They said he was an ancestor who killed his *Chi* and stole his seat. It is said he once struck a village of his own people with madness and made them feast on themselves.

"I also know that just like every other ancestral deity, the end of your lineage, is the end of you." I catch it, the subtle narrowing of his eyes. "That is why these people are here … they fuel you. Without them, your existence, your power, is a myth. Their immortality is not a gift; it is a guarantee that you get to live forever."

Murmurings escape the crowd. Those close to him draw back.

"Choose your next words wisely." He inhales, clasping his hands around his staff.

"Or what? You'll murder me like you did millions of Lagosians?" I see him now. I see as he unravels.

"Murder? Millions? What are you talking about, Mama?"

"Oh, you didn't tell them, how you drowned the other tribes and citizens of Lagos, so you could keep your exotic birds in this little exotic cage." Talks of drowning and murder fill the air. "You say our world is a disaster, an insanity, do you know what you did when you destroyed Lagos? The imbalance and strife you wreaked? You are the evil in the world!"

"A spirit killer accusing me of murder. That's a bit of a conundrum, don't you think?"

I can feel him flipping through my mind like it's some picture book. "Get out of my head!"

"Go on, tell them. Tell your daughter how you bound those spirits and set them ablaze. How you sentenced them to a fate worse than death. Tell her."

To a people like the Ailopin, murdering spirits, souls who had perished once before, was evil unheard of. A second death is utter erasure from every existential plane. It means they never get to see the ones they left behind, the ones they love, not in an afterlife, not in reincarnation, not ever. It is a punishment meted out on people who had led the most despicable, abhorrent lives. And without batting an eye, I had done the same to my own ancestral spirits. I watch the fear and confusion on the faces of the Ailopin people slip away. I watch disdain take their place. But it is irrelevant. Their hate is theirs, and they can keep it. All that matters to me is Abike.

"Then you know what's coming for you." I catch his gaze and I hold it.

"Witch!" He charges at me, staff raised, lightning sizzling through it.

I charge back.

When we meet, he brings the staff down, probably intent on splitting my skull. I grab it midair. The lightning runs from the staff, right into me. I do not waver. His eyes widen in disbelief, and in that distraction, I pull the staff from his grip. Bringing it to my knee, I break it in half.

"You filthy peasant!" Hitting me across the head, he sends me crashing meters away. I pick myself up, and collapse back to the ground, throwing up a mouthful of blood. My head feels like it is coated in steel. From the corner of my eye, I see him draw near.

"You dare stand against me? I, who saw the birth of the sun!" A spear materializes in his hand as he speaks. "No one will mourn you."

"Father, no!" I turn to see Abike holding him back from me. He tosses her aside like a rag doll.

"Don't you touch her!" With my scream comes a force, stronger than the sandstorms of Maradi. Just like he did me, it takes him, sending him headfirst through a stone pillar, and right into a building, which immediately collapsed with him in it. The once-clear clouds blacken as I soar to the sky. Lightning and hail pour from above, and whatever is in their path, comes undone. The trees crackle to a crisp as the buildings crumble and fall.

"The blood of seas course through me. They who stand against me, stand against many," I say, as the strength of my sisters pours into me.

I had known I would not last a minute in combat against Alápa-dúpé. So before he came charging at me, I channeled my sisters. Ours was a bond that transcended time and space. Their power courses through me like a river, consuming me. It is unlike anything I have ever felt. I am one, and I am three hundred.

"Mama! Mama!" I hear it through the storm raging around me, like a candle flame in the dead of night. "You need to stop! You'll destroy us all!"

With my life force starting to ebb away, I do need to stop. Power of this intensity, though tempting, is never meant for one to keep. Through a witch's scream, I let go of it, and before I fall to the ground, Abike catches me. Being in that power, everything else was shut out, all I had was rage. Returning to myself, I see clearly now. Burning foliage litter the grounds, and the buildings lie in far worse state than before. The life I once felt in this place feels gone.

"This, this is why you are not welcome here," Alápa-dúpé says as he pushes a boulder off himself. "Humanity kills everything it touches."

"No, I—I did not mean for any of this to happen."

"But it did," he says, pointing to the people. Scattered across, some are injured and being helped up by others, some lie unconscious. "Abike"—he turns to her—"you know what you must do ... for all our sake."

Exhausted, I am still in her arms, my hands latching on to her. She looks at me, her eyes are red shot, but they hold no tears.

"This is goodbye, Mama."

"No, Abike, no." I tighten my grip on her.

"Mama—"

"Listen, listen to me, I cannot live in a world where you do not exist, I will not. Please come with me. We can be together again. We'll be happy and ..."

I am back on the wet floor of my apartment. *Did she just send me back?*

"No, no-no-no," I cry, touching the water, the pieces of glass piercing my fingers.

"We have to leave now."

Startled, I jolt back, swinging around to the voice. I watch Abike step out of the shadows and stumble up to me.

"No, this is another one of his mind tricks," I say, shutting my eyes.

"Mama, it's no trick. I have bound our spirits. It was how I pulled you to me in Lagos. We can never be separated." She traces her hands up my head, cupping my face in them. "Where you go, I go."

"Oh, Abike ... your eyes." I caress her face. Her sight is gone once again.

"I see you," she says.

Bringing her forehead to mine. "*Nwa oma'm*. I see you."

"We must hurry. He will come for me."

"Let him come."

THINGS BOYS DO

by Pemi Aguda

Children can be cruel, you know?

The first man stands at the bedside of his sweating wife. He is watching their baby emerge from inside her. What he does not know is that he is watching their son destroy her insides, shredding, making sure there will be no others to follow. This man's wife is screaming and screaming, and the sound gives the man a headache, an electric thing like lightning striking the middle of his forehead. He reaches to hold her hand, to remind her of his presence. But he is surprised by the power of her latch, this strength born of pain, the way she crushes the bones of his fingers. He has to bite down to prevent himself from crying out.

And here is the baby; bloody and outside for the first time.

The baby opens his eyes, and the first man flinches at the sudden appearance of white eyeballs in the midst of all that slimy red. The baby is blinking now, and watching, but not crying—just watching?

"Um," the doctor says, frowning. "You have a son."

The first man leans down to catch the mumbled words from his wife's mouth. "Yes, hon. He's alive," he reassures her. The whites of his baby's eyes are impressed in his mind, behind the headache, like an image from biology class, so long ago. He looks up to the doctor who is still holding onto the baby, brows furrowed. "He's alive, right, doctor? Is everything fine? Isn't he supposed to cry?"

The doctor looks everywhere but at the first man. They fuss around, the doctor and the nurses, snipping, cleaning, moving.

"Doctor?" the man prompts.

"Mr. Man, you have a son! Congratulations! A living breathing boy!"

The second man huffs beneath the weight of his wife. The Ikeja General Hospital has sent them home even though his wife is still bleeding from the birth. "Sorry, no space," the head nurse had told him, her attention moving so easily to the next patient. "Take her home; everybody bleeds."

The second man's mother holds the door to their apartment open, one elbow cradling the baby like an expert. She trails them to the bedroom, where the man gently lowers his wife to their bed, still messy with signs of frantic packing for the hospital. Once his arms are free, the mother transfers the baby to him, as if she has been waiting to rid herself of the infant.

"Maami," he starts to say, but his mother leaves the room.

The baby is sleeping, and his eyes move around beneath his thin lids. The second man is repulsed by this movement, this unconscious shifting that strangely brings to mind the *Goosebumps* books he read and traded as a teenager, so long ago. The man is discomfited by this reaction to his child. He deposits his new son in the new cradle that smells like wood polish, then goes to find his mother in the kitchen.

"Maami, will you make peppersoup for her? Will that help?"

The mother is staring out the kitchen window, her fingers steeping in a bowl of uncleaned fish. "That baby is not yours, I'm sure of it."

"Maami, please. Don't start this rubbish again."

"That baby is not yours; I can swear on it! I know it. I feel it." Her hands move again, lifting a gill flap, gutting the fish with a soft snap.

The third man is startled when he walks into the dining room to find his wife dozing off while their baby quietly suckles at the feeding bottle's nib. The image he encounters is this: her neck tilted backwards and to the side so that the muscles seem contorted unnaturally, the tendons and veins pushing against skin. For a moment, he is sure she is dead.

She jerks awake when he tries to lift their son from her arms. Her hands instinctively tighten, then loosen. "Thanks," she whispers, her eyes drifting to close again. The man is impressed at how quickly she seems to have bonded with the baby they had accepted from the arms of a teenage mother—whose name they were not allowed to know—only three weeks ago.

The third man rocks the baby the way they'd been taught at adoption classes. Softly, softly, back and forth. The baby's eyes flutter open, and the man smiles down at his son, his first child, his baby. "Who's a good boy?" he sings, hoping that bond will grow between them too. "Who? Who?"

The baby does not smile, but do babies even smile? The third man now feels silly because of what seems like such a stern gaze from the infant, as if the voice he has put on is simply ridiculous, beneath him. How does one feel embarrassed in the sight of a three-week-old baby? He frowns at his child, noticing for the first time the flecks of grey in his pupils. Black and grey, like the stones he used to collect in boarding school—so long ago—from the pile of gravel in the school's parking lot, purchased for the new vocational labs that never got built.

"You're not a good boy," he whispers, no longer singing. "Are you?"

There was another boy, once. But that was so long ago.

The first man is alone with his toddler, again. His wife is in the hospital, again. Since the birth, six months ago, hospital visits and extended stays have become commonplace in their household. Money is running out. The first man worries about money; he worries about his job—all the time off he's been asking for; he worries about his wife; he worries about their baby.

But that's not true. He doesn't worry about the baby. The baby is fed and cared for by his extended family network in Abeokuta. His cousins and friends take turns to help out. What the first man is really worried about is himself.

The first man worries for himself when he is alone with Jon. Jon is what his wife insisted on calling their son. Short for Jonathan—that man in the Bible only known for being a very good friend to David. This fear of his son, for himself, it is a body thing; a visceral thing; a flinching, recoiling, chilling thing. What father is frightened of their own child, scared to hold him, scared to be looked at by him?

The second man's wife is dead, and now he is alone with Johnny, their six-month-old son. The barrage of love and support that immediately followed his wife's demise has slowed to a trickle. The bowls of rice and stew have stopped coming. His brother has gone back to Abuja. His cousin no longer stops by on the way to drop her kids off at school. The second man is alone. With Johnny.

His mother showed up at the burial, her nose in the air. But she did not make a scene. She did not hold Johnny, no, but she did not bring up more preposterous accusations about his wife's fidelity either, about the strange face of his son that she insists does not belong in her family lineage.

The second man watches Johnny roll from his back to his stomach on the multicolored mat; then to his back; then to his stomach. Back and forth. Back and forth. Back and forth.

The man backs away to the other end of the room, one foot behind the other. He sits in the armchair that still holds the cloying scent of his wife's shea butter. Back and forth, his baby turns, fists flailing, chubby legs kicking. The second man closes his eyes. The sight of his pivoting son makes him dizzy, askew, off-center.

The email is short: *I can't do this anymore. Adopting this baby changed me. I need to find myself again. And if I do, I'm not sure I'll want to return. Be kind to J-Boy. Be kind to yourself.*

The third man reads the email every morning before getting out of bed. He reads it again this morning. Then he checks for new messages.

"Fuck," he whispers when he reads the newest text. The latest nanny has quit. *I'm sorry, but I have to go back to the village to care for my family.* Bullshit, the man knows, it's all bullshit. This is the ninth nanny in the three months since his wife's been gone. The excuses are always unbelievable in their benign flavors.

The third man leans over the cradle beside his bed. J-Boy is awake. Does the boy ever sleep? "Why are you sending everyone away, J-Boy? Why?"

Because the common denominator is the boy, isn't it? The wife leaving, the nannies scurrying out the door, unable to articulate what they are balking at. Overcome, the third man slams his open palm against the side of the cradle. "Why? Why? Why?"

His hand is throbbing now, but the baby does not startle, does not flinch. He is just staring, still staring, as if he has expected this all along: this breakdown, this debacle, this undoing. Looking at his heaving father like, *well*, like, *hello*, like, *I knew this you would show up soon.*

That boy from so long ago. He was just another boy. The same way our three men once were just three boys. Just three boys doing things boys do.

The first man can no longer sleep at night. Not while it is just him and Jon alone at home. His wife has gone to live with a cousin in Seychelles; she needed bed rest and ocean breeze after the trauma of the birth. When he opened his mouth to protest what seemed to him like abandonment, she had looked at him so sadly, disappointed, shutting him up.

These days, he catches an hour or two of sleep when he can convince someone to come over, leaving his dwindling friends disgruntled because they thought they were coming to hang out with him, not feed his baby while he naps on the couch, drool glistening his beard. "I'm not your fucking babysitter," his friend Joy had said, plopping the baby on his chest, startling him fully awake.

The first man's nights are fraught with a fear of Jon that rises from the top of his stomach, acidic and pungent, like the beginnings of a burp. Tonight, he moves slowly toward the cradle, as if afraid of what he will find. But there, Jon's eyes are wide open, staring at the turning fan. The baby becomes aware of his presence, and his eyes move in an arc from the ceiling fan to his father's face. His eyes widen; his mouth trembles; he begins to wail.

The first man's fatherly instincts kick in. He stamps down his fear. He picks up the baby, pats his back. The wailing stops, but only because the baby's mouth has now affixed to his exposed shoulder. There is a sharp sting that sends the man's eyes backwards, upwards. How many teeth does this eight-month-old baby have? How can they be enough to cause such precise, penetrating pain? He gets a finger between and pulls the child off with a smacking sound.

He resists the urge to fling Jon back into the cradle; jaws clenched, he lowers his still son. There is no more wailing.

This is his life now: downgraded to managing social media for a small brand that pays peanuts but allows him to work remotely with permanent eyestrain. This is his life now: nappies that stink, formula that smells sickly sweet, and a baby that bites him too often.

He distractedly rubs against an old bite mark adorning his wrist. Then he wipes saliva off his shoulder, wincing at the rawness. Sitting in front of his laptop, he clicks to the Troubled Naija Fathers Forum he's found recently. *I think my baby hates me,* he types. The keyboard clacks echo around him. *He has taken everything from me. I am afraid of my baby. Is this normal?* Before he submits the entry, he remembers to make himself anonymous. Then the first man leans back into the chair, glancing briefly at his now-gurgling son. Is that a gurgle or a laugh? He turns back to his screen. The first man waits.

The second man feels seen when he reads the post on the popular forum. "Yes!" he wants to scream at his phone. What he does instead is move to another room, one where Johnny isn't present. He hunches over the device, somehow afraid that his son—not even one year old—will somehow prevent him from replying to this post.

YESSS!!! I feel the exact same way! I want to be a good father, but it feels impossible with this child. I hate to say it, but I feel like his appearance in my life has ruined me. My wife is dead, my mother won't talk to me. My friends avoid me now. I am afraid to be alone with my own child ... his very existence has undone me! Is this a medical problem? Something about a version of myself existing outside of me disrupting my balance? And is there a solution? Do I need therapy??? Sorry to ramble, but I feel so strongly about this!!! HELP US!

Then the second man hits Send. He does not make himself anonymous.

The third man, who has been eyeing the new post in the forum, clicks on the new and only comment.

He recognizes the name of the commenter immediately. His fingers snatch off the mouse and hover over it, as if electrocuted.

There is no such thing as coincidence.

No, no, no, the third man thinks. He has not allowed himself to think about this person, about what he represents, in so long.

Yes, children can be cruel, evil even.

So long ago, when three boys—who were not yet our three men—cornered their classmate, the new boy, the slight boy with asthma who wheezed at the back of biology class, the boy begged to be left alone.

"Please, let me go," he cried. He promised his pocket money, the chocolate bars, to slide all his dinners to them, to iron their uniforms, to lay their beds, to do their chores, to tend their portions of the school garden, to do all their assignments. He promised everything. "Just don't put me in there," he begged. "Please, that space is too tiny," he cried. "Please. Please."

But boys will be boys, right? The three best friends bundled him up and stuffed him in the locker at the back of the abandoned woodwork shop. He scratched at their wrists, at their shoulders, his head wagged back and forth, left and right; he pleaded with his white eyes, with the red veins bulging in them, with his wails; he clawed at their faces, thumped at their chests, scratched at their foreheads. But he was nothing but a whiff of a boy. They snapped the padlock shut, giggling, smacking each other on the back, in mirth, in solidarity.

How easily attentions shift. How easily boys can be distracted by other school activities, other friends, other weak students to tease. How easy it is to forget.

After they have confirmed what their bodies already know as true—through furtive private messages: *Is that you? The same one? From Ibadan High School?* The first man, second man, and third man wait till the dead of night. They wait till they think they cannot be seen, when Jon, Johnny and J-Boy are asleep; and then, with trembling fingers, they search the event they are all thinking about. The event. The Event of their boyhoods.

Over a decade later, the search results are not many, and he is faceless, but there it is: *Adebayo John—Gone Too Soon.* Adebayo John, who never did anything to them.

Watch as these men, who were once boys, look to their sleeping sons, now alert to the possibilities. The terror latches onto wrists, yanks them in. They look to their sons who have taken everything from them, who are still taking everything from them. The sons bound to them forever.

And two weeks or three months or four years from now, when these men try to rid themselves of their sons: abandon them with relatives, or on a park bench wet from rain, they will never be able to walk away. Because they can never be sure where a haunting ends and paranoia begins.

But right now, terrified by the possibilities, watch them behold their sons with hitched breaths, ticking pulses, raised hairs. And do you know, terror can feel like being trapped in a dark tiny place, with no space to move? Like a locker, like a coffin.

GIANT STEPS

by Russell Nichols

Hear those engines roar / rumbling
Feel those fires burn
Blasting off / blasting off / blasting off / blasting off
Step back.
Hear those engines roar / rumbling
Feel those fires burn
Bear the cross / bear the cross / bear the cross / bear the cross

The Blue Marble is shrinking as *Orion II* lifts off, ripping from the grasping tentacles of Earth's gravity, the world gets smaller, smaller, a blot on the cosmic sheet of infinite blackness, which closes in like a camera iris in a classic film's final shot.

Picture the planet's surface, where the wonders of the old-world buckle at the top of the hour under the weight of new wars; where down below, all those little people fall to their knees, desperate voices crying, crying out to their deity-du-jour for deliverance. There is no answer. Prayers unheard, wishes ungranted, for they've made their bed, and now liars must lie.

But not Dr. Jenkins.

Strapped in this single-person spacecraft, plugged into tubes for food, water, and waste, the thirty-three-year-old astrophysicist from South Carolina and soon-to-be first-ever human to step foot on Titan, never felt freer in her life. As the Richard Strauss tone poem, "Also sprach Zarathustra" rises in her ears, like the sun in her eyes, Dr. Charlene Jenkins turns away from her home world, never minding who she left behind. A long ride ahead—five years, two months, give or take—with gravity assists from Venus and Jupiter flinging *Orion II* like a slingshot to the destination. She hates that word, destination. Too close to destiny. Too far from reality.

"You cain't defy you and I, baby, this some destiny-level shit here," Dave used to say before he got clean, before Trane was born, before Gramma passed. Was that destiny too? Or did Gramma *refuse* to take her "med'sin"?

It's choice, not chance, that defines who we are, where we end up.

Or down.

Or 1.2 billion kilometers away on Saturn's largest moon, which may or may not be inhabited by giants, depending on who you ask.

"I don't believe in giants," Dr. Jenkins was quoted as saying by the *Honolulu Star-Advertiser.*

Not giants. Not the Nephilim. Definitely not the banduns Gramma used to tell stories about back in the day. No, she didn't believe in that nonsense. Not anymore.

The same can't be said for the world at large; a lonely world of blind believers, who see what they want to see. Take, for instance, the leaked images from NASA's Jet Propulsion Laboratory in Pasadena, California, which captured the public imagination—and common sense. Were these the lost 350 photographs from the Cassini-Huygens mission? The European Space Agency, on the record, said not a chance. But denial only added fuel to the viral wildfire as the mysterious pictures spread to all corners of the globe:

What looked to be "giant footprints" on Titan, on the northwest shoreline of Ligeia Mare, a hydrocarbon lake larger than Lake Superior. Twenty-four prints total, in a single-file pattern; each one sixty centimeters long, twenty wide, three deep, according to various imaging teams. These "footprints" could've been impact craters, land erosion, shadows from methane clouds. But cold, hard facts don't solidify in the minds of the masses, *Homo ignoramuses*, sheep in people's clothing who'd rather believe in Goliath than science.

"People lie to themselves," she told the reporter.

But not Dr. Jenkins.

She quit playing those mind games long ago, smart enough to know the human brain looks for patterns, seeks them out religiously, to deny the claustrophobia of utter insignificance. But who wants to hear that?

Definitely not the thousands of so-called "printers" who saw her quote online and flooded public eye-feeds with their own from Genesis 6:4—"There were giants in the earth in those days; and also after that, when the sons of God came in unto the daughters of men, and they bare children to them, the same became mighty men which were of old, men of renown"—who shared links to news stories about massive footprints discovered in China, Bolivia, and South Africa; who signed off messages with the sincerest of valedictions:

- Still don't believe in giants? Suck my giant dick.
- Stick to picking cotton, tar baby bitch!!
- DIE SPACE MONKEY

She's heard worse, seen worse, reflected in the green eyes of strangers and coworkers, men and women, those who resent her for making rapid strides against all odds.

"Initiating hypersleep," says Rigel, *Orion II*'s sentient computer.

Silent shaming rings the loudest. A look here, a look there, a look away. Ironed-on, Made-in-America smiles that say: *You're not supposed to be here.*

"Don't you go believing all that she-she talk." She hears Gramma's words echoing now, like rolling thunder, as she drifts into hypersleep. "The Lawd got you here for a reason."

She sees Gramma now, coming into focus, reclining on the porch of her saddlebag house in Fairfield County, humming "Way Beyawn' duh Moon" with a pop-up choir of crickets. Gramma was what southerners called "a force of nature," mythic in style and stature, with the head of a queen and heart of a bull, spilling stories for days.

Dr. Charlene Jenkins—back when she was just "Leenie"—was raised on these stories; homegrown hand-me-downs from her great-grandmother and *her* great-grandmother, coming from the

Lowcountry, namely St. Helena Island—a near-casualty of climate change that became one of the first UNESCO Bubble Cities.

"Leenie, come'yuh, lemme get them knockers out your head," Gramma would call out from her porch on those muggy summer days. Between Gramma's knees, Leenie fidgeted, feeling those rough hands pulling her pigtails and stretching her kinky hair like she always did to train it against shrinkage.

"Gramma, could you tell me about the banduns again?"

"If you keep still," Gramma said, bouncing her right leg, which used to be for dancing, but now had a strange habit of losing feeling. She was tired all the time, too. But she could talk from sunup to sundown about her kin: the Gullah-Geechee people, descendants of enslaved Africans who survived and thrived for centuries on the Sea Islands of South Carolina and Georgia. How back in the day, after the praise meeting, they would gather round to take part in the legendary ring shout.

A songster kicked things off, call-and-response style; a stickman played the beat, slow at first, then faster, faster; as the joyful congregation moved in a circle, handclapping, feet-tapping, shouting and shuffling, dancing on the devil till he begged for sweet mercy, Gramma would say.

"But every now and again," she said, looking around, then leaning forward to make sure no one else could hear, "some sanctified body would step in that ring there, wailing, flailing all furious-like. And lo and behold, that man, filled with the spirit, would up and start growing."

"Growing like a beanstalk?" Leenie asked every time.

"Child, bigguh than a beanstalk. Bigguh than anything in this whole world. Hold this." She handed Leenie her blue knockers. "Just kept growing and growing till they was big enough to reach for the clouds, then climb up to the sky and gone 'way."

"Gone where?"

Gramma lifted a hand to the heavens. "Off into the big black yonder."

Sitting there on the porch, Leenie cupped the knockers in her palm. Staring into the little blue orb, she pictured a faraway world. A land of banduns. A place where she might, for once in her life, feel free and feel big and feel like she belongs. Or find her mother.

"Put them knockers in the box 'fore you lose them," Gramma said.

She did as she was told and tucked her small world in a container with the other worlds. And it was these stories of free Black giants that inspired Leenie to learn all she could about the "big black yonder." In the process, she learned a bigger truth: Gramma, too, was a liar.

At the heart of every belief is a lie. A stretched truth. Facts distorted like the space inside a wormhole. Vows made to be broken. Like when somebody promises to return and never does. This, she learned, was the real world, so she did what disillusioned optimists do: Leenie grew up.

Never again would she fall victim to faith, be betrayed by hope, or led astray by love. Which is why, outside the Mount Wilson Observatory, when Dave popped the question …

… she popped him on the head. "What are you thinking?!"

"I'm thinking it's high time you and I settle down for real for real, do the family thing."

"Dave … I can't do that. I told you I don't want to be a wife; I don't want kids."

"What kinda woman don't want kids?"

"My kind," she said, closing the ring box and the conversation.

It wasn't him. Not all him. Somewhat him, but not all. He was a good man. Not educated in the conventional sense, not extremely ambitious, but a laid-back, lighthearted type of man. The type who knew to ask how she wanted to be touched and where, and allowed himself to be shown.

There he goes now, up on stage in the spotlight, wailing, while she's down in the shadows, clapping. But this is no ring shout. This was the night they met in New York at some underground jazz club with Dave on the sax. She watched his cheeks puff up; a man possessed. And, being a scientist-in-training, she wanted to test out a hypothesis: that a player who could maneuver his fingers and fix his lips to make that instrument scream, could do the same to hers. No strings, just a release. She initiated, he obliged. For seven years he obliged, tuning her body between the sheets. But as she moved up in status, he fell back on old habits.

An old habit, like history, repeats itself. What goes around comes around like a satellite. A record. Needles dropping. Heroin and insulin. Dave and Gramma, injecting and rejecting shots, respectively. Two peas in the wrong pods. Putting faith in false gods.

"Baby, that's all in the past," Dave told her the first week of his twelve-step program. And by the sixth week, he figured he could replace his defunct jazz band with a wedding band.

But what is marriage if not another drug? A lifelong dependence on a man-made substance that ultimately leads to abuse?

She'd heard that song time and time again. Lamentations of belittled women. Givers of life beaten down, swallowed whole by the vacuum of the fragile male ego. Born-to-be brides. Born-again wives. Ever-shrinking women with self-deflating voices who were raised to submit (from the Latin *submittere*: "to yield, lower, let down, put under, reduce"), to keep silent and to take up as little space as possible.

But not Dr. Jenkins.

She is not the one. She wouldn't follow in the fading footsteps of those who walk down the aisle and wind up getting walked over. Didn't matter how magical his fingers felt on the nape of her neck, how musical his lips felt massaging the length of her labia. She refused to sacrifice her identity on the altar of intimacy. She rejected a ring on her finger to see the rings of Saturn, because life is too short to live in the land of make-believe.

"Wake up, Dr. Jenkins," Rigel says.

And roused from hypersleep, she sees before her "The Ringed Planet," grander and more glorious than she ever imagined, a swirling pastel ball with bands of clouds running around it. But how is this possible? Reading her confused expression, Rigel declares: "We are now approaching Saturn. Destination: Titan."

She unstraps herself.

"It is advised that you remain strapped in, Dr. Jenkins."

No. Something's not right here. Why does the computer show a flight time of only four years, one month and seventeen days? Is she seeing things?

"Rigel," she says, her voice like gravel, "how long has it been since the launch?"

"This is the forty-seventh day of the fourth year," Rigel confirms. "The Jupiter assist gave us a bigger boost than—"

Right then, an alarm goes off as the spacecraft's autopilot tries to maneuver through tiny particles running from or being sucked into the delicate, narrow outer band of Saturn's F ring, herded by the shepherd-moon Prometheus. Stray pieces batter the composite shell of *Orion II* like sleet.

"A change of course is advised," Rigel says.

"No, no, stay on current trajectory."

"Dr. Jenkins, at this rate, you won't be able to sustain—"

"Stay on course, I said!"

Keeping her eyes dead ahead, the AR interface labels the various satellites in view, and right there, like a ripe Carolina peach bobbing in a deep, dark sea, the big, bright moon draws her nearer, as the warning alarm keeps ringing in her ears.

"Giant Steps!" Dave shouted the day he saw the viral Titan photos.

This was last fall in the living room of their downsized apartment in Berkeley. Dave was bouncing baby Trane on his right leg, a twelve-month-old girl with curious wide brown eyes, as Dr. Jenkins stood over them, projecting a hologram of images from her palmtab.

"No, Dave, these … these aren't footprints." She sighed. "I mean, they could be anything: impact craters, land erosion, shadows from methane clouds—"

"Nah," he said. "You not hearing me. See this right here? Look at this. See that pattern? Yeah, I'd recognize those opening chords anywhere. That's Trane." He tickled the baby girl. "That's you, huh? Huh, little star?"

Dr. Jenkins knew legendary jazz saxophonist John Coltrane was his idol, his influence, the namesake of their newborn. But he was taking this too far. Was he using again?

"Charlene." He set the girl down on the self-cleaning carpet. "Don't look at me like that."

"I'm not looking at you like anything."

He walked out, leaving Dr. Jenkins alone with the baby. She'd only held her a few times since giving birth. Now she watched the little girl lift herself to stand and start sort-of-walking. But she kept falling back, then smirking like she'd get in trouble for trying to defy gravity.

Gramma wasn't walking either by then. She was on bed rest, post-amputation.

"The Lawd ain't through with little ol' me," she proclaimed on more than one occasion. "I'll be back on my feet in no time, you watch."

Which Dr. Jenkins determined was a lie for three reasons:

1) "The Lawd" isn't real.
2) Gramma didn't have feet, plural. Diabetes hijacked her right foot. She had one left.
3) By the time she did leave that bed, she had to be carried out, never to tell a story again.

"Check this out here," Dave said, coming back into the living room with sheets of paper. "You'll appreciate this. I'm finna blow your mind right here. You know what this is?"

Before she could answer, he explained: It was a diagram of Coltrane's Tone Circle, a variation of the classic "Circle of Fifths" with a pentagram and vanishing point in the middle. "Been listening to these jazz and physics audiobooks, right?" he said. "And this Coltrane circle, it's drawing on the same geometric principles your boy Einstein was working with. Quantum theory, mathematics, relativity—all that heavy-duty scientific shit you went to school for."

"Dave, what does this have to do with anything?"

"I'm saying, it's all connected, everything's connected." He set the palmtab next to the diagram on the legless LeviTable and ran over to stop the little girl from climbing up the stairs. "Trane was out of this world, we know that. Straight-up transcendent. But I always thought to myself: What if that cat was, you know, channeling? Like possessed?"

She stifled a laugh to spare his feelings. "You can't be serious."

"Why not though? The way he improvised? Go listen to *Ascension* and *Interstellar Space*. Listen to *Om* and tell me I'm lying." He lifted the little girl's arms to help her walk. "What if, tucked under those 'sheets of sound,' Trane was tryna tell us the truth?"

"And what truth would that be, my dear? Aliens?"

"Could be. Or a warning. Instructions on how to be free, hell, I don't know," he said. "You the big, bad scientist."

Never copulate with a conspiracy theorist. An obscure scientific law she learned too late. She never told Dave about the banduns. The man believed everything he heard, never bothering to fact-check. In this day and age, you can't afford not to fact-check. Dr. Jenkins volunteered to fly 1.2 billion kilometers just to fact-check.

"Brace for impact," Rigel says.

A massive chunk of ice comes out of nowhere, slamming into *Orion II* like a fist. Knocking the craft off its trajectory. Dr. Jenkins, her heart pounding, looks around to find Titan, but the AR interface has shut off.

"Return to course," she commands.

"Shields down to seventy-five percent," Rigel says. "Life support systems damaged."

"Return to course, return to course, go to Titan!"

"Navigation offline."

"You ain't told him?" Gramma asked from her hospital bed and soon-to-be deathbed. "That man's the father of your child, for crying out loud!"

"He didn't tell me he was planning to get hooked on smack. How come he gets to do what he wants when he wants and I can't?"

"That's a cross you gotsta bear."

"But that's not ... look, it was his idea. *He* wanted to have a baby. Now I need to do what I need to do for me. I don't wanna be one of those kind of women—"

"What women is that, huh?"

"Never mind."

"Oh no, no, don't get all hush-mouthed now. What kind of women? You don't wanna be like me is what you saying. Tell the truth, shame the devil."

"Gramma ... I have big dreams."

"And what? You think I didn't?"

"You've lived in that same house since before I was born, weaving sweetgrass baskets, whipping up some Frogmore Stew, humming your *spurrituals*. You always said you wanted to get out of Carolina and dance on a big stage, and you could have. You really could have, but you never did. And now you're refusing to get a bionic foot."

"First off, don't worry 'bout my foot. And second, best believe I *chose* to be here. Everybody and they mama got to migrating, up and over to the big cities, fooling theyselves thinking they could outrun racism. But I wasn't fixing to leave my people like that. No ma'am, not me. I stayed my Black behind right here so I could raise you and this the thanks I get?"

"Gramma, this isn't about you. This is about me. I want to explore."

"'Clare to Gawd. So what, you think you Neil Armstrong? Hopscotching 'round the heavens like ain't nothing better to do? 'You wanna explore.' Shuh. How 'bout you go explore being a mother? That's some uncharted territory for that ass."

"I'm not supposed to be here."

"Oh. I'm sorry. Are you the Creator of the Universe? Didn't think so. So who is you to say where you s'posed to be, huh?" Gramma sighs, then scoots over in bed and pats the mattress. "Leenie, come'yuh. Come sit."

Dr. Jenkins shakes her head, staring at her single foot wiggling under the white sheets.

"Child, I know you scared. Seeing me all shriveled up like this, with one foot literally in the grave. Thinking 'bout Dave and his crookety self. You worried you'll be left to raise that child by your lonesome, I understand that—"

"The only thing I'm scared of is looking back on my life and realizing I was too scared to live. You raised me, Gramma. By yourself. You're the one who taught me to think bigger."

"Bigguh don't mean running from your motherly duties."

"I'm not running, I'm trying to grow!"

And as she said this, it dawned on her: Of the countless times Gramma sat on that porch, telling the story of the banduns, she never ever described these free Black giants as women. Leenie never pictured them as women. Never even thought to ask if any of them were women. The same way most people assume "Dr. Jenkins" is a man.

"I want to grow, Gramma. Like the banduns."

Gramma shook her head, chuckling to herself. "You so smart, huh? 'Like the banduns.' You even know why they was called banduns?"

Silence. Dr. Jenkins never thought to ask that question either.

"Means abandon," Gramma said. "As in: Your mother *abandoned* you to quote-unquote 'find herself,' and what happened? She fell off a cliff in them Himalayas."

More silence.

The space between them filled by the ever-expanding agony of unforgotten grief.

Dr. Jenkins wanted to say something. Something like "I'm not her" or "She only went out there to escape from that monster she married." These words wouldn't matter to Gramma.

"Know what your problem is, Leenie? Got your head all swell-up with facts and figures, only believing what you can see and prove, but child"—she tapped her ear—"you not listening."

"Listening to what?"

Gramma gestured as if to say, "My point exactly," and passed away three months later. Two months after that Dr. Jenkins was boarding *Orion II*. Not depressed or guilty or ambivalent like one might expect. She was ready.

"Go to Titan now!" she commands again.

"Shields down to fifty percent," Rigel says. "Navigation still offline."

She plugs the coordinates to the target site into the computer manually: 78° N, 249° W. "Initiate emergency landing procedures!"

"Initiating emergency landing procedures."

She *was* ready.

But right now, as the single-person spacecraft plummets toward Titan, she wonders if she made the biggest mistake of her life. Did she come on this mission to discover something? Or prove something? Maybe both. But why? Why this constant need to prove herself? Why couldn't she escape the long shadow of feeling less-than? Inferior? The feeling that no matter how high she climbs in her career, she'll always be looked down on, a speck of a speck of a speck in space-time and the eyes of society. And that the slightest misstep will cause irreparable damage, not just to her life, but the lives of others like her.

Who can live in those conditions? Under that kind of pressure?

The nitrogen-rich tholin haze wouldn't break her fall. The dense methane shroud of clouds wouldn't break her fall. Nothing would break her fall, save the moon's freezing surface. She pictures herself outside herself, like a methane droplet in a chemical downpour, falling, in a tragically slow descent toward the north polar region.

Falling …

"I want to make an impact," she said. "Why can't you understand that?"

"What I understand is, you going through a lot right now," Dave said. This was the night after Gramma's funeral, at Gramma's house, as they were packing up Gramma's belongings. "C'mon now, let's be serious."

Falling …

"I'm dead serious."

"How you talking 'bout going to space and your grandma's body not even cold yet?"

"This is my chance to do something that matters."

Falling …

"Oh, so this don't matter?" He moved his right hand in circles, like tracing an orbit, referring to him, her, and sleeping baby Trane. "We don't matter?"

She was about to say, "That's not what I meant," but right then, her eyes caught something in one of Gramma's sweetgrass baskets. It was the box. She snuck outside to peek at her childhood in private. On the porch, in the warm solitude of the starry night as male crickets called out for mates, she opened the box and inside, all those colorful knockers, all those small worlds, were still clustered together, though much smaller than she remembered. With her thumb and index finger, she held the orange one up to the clear new moon sky.

Falling …

The screen door creaked open behind her. Dave stepped out, Trane resting on his chest. He kept silent for a moment, observing; and when he did speak, his voice trembled, his words drifting out on the wavering wings of a half-whisper.

"Listen, baby, I understand you wanna go exploring, see what else is out there … I know you hate being boxed in. You been saying that since day one." He took a step forward, gazing up at the sky with her. "Now you tell me you wanna go to outer space to see if some moon can sustain human life. But here's a human life right here," he said, his long fingers on Trane's spine, like how he used to hold his sax. "Ain't she worth sustaining?"

The question echoes as if it came straight from the mouth of Ligeia Mare, which lies below her now, wide open and ready to devour Titan's first human trespasser. In the seconds before splashdown, she watches Trane, growing up so fast, bigger and bigger by the day, walking, talking, asking questions, learning to read, about to turn five, losing her baby teeth, printing her first bot buddy, wanting her own space.

Her own space.

A little girl on the porch looking up at the stars.

"Where are you, Mommy?" she calls out into the big black yonder.

But this little girl isn't Trane; it's her, Dr. Jenkins, in stretched pigtails and bright knockers, a little girl who actually believed prayer could bring her battered mother back home.

"Ain't she worth sustaining?"

That little girl, now grown, jolts as the damaged ship smacks belly-first into the still lake. She opens her eyes as *Orion II* converts into a hovercraft.

Floating.

"We've arrived on Titan, Dr. Jenkins," Rigel says. "Connect to the bioport for me to check for any injuries you may have sustained."

"Give me a second." She breathes deeply, to slow her heart rate. Five-second inhale. Five-second exhale. "Do you hear something? Like a hum?"

"Systems currently in standby mode for damage assessment and repair protocols—"

"No, not ... not in here," she says. "I'm going out."

"Dr. Jenkins, for your safety, it is advised that you first connect to the bioport for me to check for any injuries—"

"I'll be right back."

And moments later, she is outside the spacecraft, looking over the vast landscape that stretches out past the lake's edge, where the subdued terrain then takes over, saturated in a hazy sepia tint; something out of a dream. A deathly cold dream. Negative 180 degrees Celsius cold. Her only shield against the elements, the smart skinsuit compressed to her body; a banged-up body with bruised muscles and potentially internal bleeding that would deter anybody else.

But not Dr. Jenkins.

Below her, Ligeia Mare is still once again, like a mysteriously murky sheet of glass. What unknown creatures could be lurking in the deep? How many invisible hands might reach out to touch her, grab her, pull her under?

She replaces those thoughts with thoughts of her mother. And jumps.

She knew the viscosity of liquid methane was about a tenth that of liquid water, but the airy feeling catches her aching body off guard. She struggles to make her way, less swimming than gliding, to the shallows of the northwest shore. Crawling out of the lake and onto the land.

The surface feels somewhat solid, not all the way stable, like slush. She looks around to get her bearings and when she does, she sees it—right there, right in front of her: the footprints. She drags her wounded self forward and puts her gloved hand in the first indentation, deeper than originally estimated. When she touches it, she hears that hum once again, a familiar voice, like rolling thunder, humming "Way Beyawn' duh Moon," the looping soundtrack to those muggy Carolina summers, the song that helped Gramma survive and thrive, like other songs did for so many before her, and led Dr. Jenkins to being inevitably here, now.

She clutches her belly, buckles over in utter agony, her helmet hitting the frosty ground. Thinking about Gramma and her stories. And Dave and his sax. How truth, like space-time, is relative, and the beliefs we hold onto, the beliefs that keep us alive cannot, consequently, be lies.

That thought gives her the strength to lift herself to stand and start sort-of-walking. But she falls down, not used to the gravity being fourteen percent what it is on Earth. She stands again, and the atmospheric pressure pushes against her, which feels like walking in a swimming pool, but she staggers on. Following the marked path. One excruciating leap at a time. As she goes on, she discovers a different tune, a fact she can't prove, but a truth that can't be denied:

Dr. Charlene Jenkins does believe in giants. She was raised by one.

And as she comes to the end of the single-file footprints, she collapses on her knees and lifts her head, and the sight, suddenly, steals from her any semblance of speech, as if the same force beckoning the billions of rocks and ice and dust to bear witness to Saturn has seized the bulk of her words as well; and the sacred few she managed to salvage can be neither spoken nor swallowed, for they remain stuck in her throat, forming a lump as her eyes grow wider, wider, filling up with all the wonder in the world.

Hear those engines roar / rumbling
Feel those fires burn
Blasting off / blasting off / blasting off / blasting off
Step back.
Hear those engines roar / rumbling
Feel those fires burn
At a loss / at a loss / at a loss / at a loss

THE FUTURE IN SALTWATER

by Tamara Jerée

The god turned a soothing shade of black upon touching me for the first time and wrapped its eight suckered arms securely around my forearm. Cool temple air combined with its damp skin, and I shivered. I was not a strong child, but Cheypa, my parent, smiled down on me proudly for bearing the god's weight so well. The bulbous mantle of its body flattened as it sunk the needle of its beak into the soft flesh of my inner elbow. I winced.

Luo—the god spoke my new name into my mind, simultaneously pulling out the memory of my old name like blood from a vein. *I want to see the ocean*, it said, undulating and boneless. My heart sank at this first request. On the way to the temple, my parent had told me that their god's first request had been to acquire water from one of the inland freshwater lakes and pray over it until it turned to salt water. I wanted such a simple first task. My god's request would mean not only abandoning my ill parent but also walking for days in the dangerous heat, only to confirm the still-toxic state of the ocean water.

Two temple acolytes who'd been standing at the ready noticed my wince and hurried over to begin painting sacred scripts down my god-less arm. The black ink was chilled, as Ocean specified, and the brush tickled my skin. I suppressed another shiver, but my skin prickled.

"What name did your god give you?" the acolytes asked in whispered unison. They were intent on their job and spared me no glance.

"Luo," I answered.

All that remained was to paint my new name across my palm. The acolytes sat back and stared into the clay bowl of ink, divining the unique symbol that would represent my new name. As we waited for the symbol to manifest, sections of ink trailed down my arm, one cold word drifting into another. The two acolytes moved in a trance, hands and brushes a blur as they painted my name. The ink in place, they said, "An honor to meet you, Luo," and backed away with their clay bowl and brushes.

I looked at my palm in the dim temple light. Three circles: two concentric, the third intersecting both. Some ink had already passed through my skin and done its work to numb the site where the god's beak had pierced me. The god was silent now, but its arms undulated in reassurance. My parent smiled and patted the too-tight rows of braids they'd done the night before in preparation for the ceremony. We would not talk until we'd left the temple. Custom dictated that the newly named listen and talk only to their god while on sacred ground.

I glanced around the temple's main hall before we turned to leave, hoping to catch sight of the reclusive Temple Mother. I would not see her that day either. Few people had ever seen her. If she did not make an appearance for the naming rituals, there weren't many other important events she might appear for. Children liked to spread rumours that they'd seen her in the shadows, watching their naming, but then who didn't want to imagine the Temple Mother gracing them with her attention?

This time, as we passed through the hall of water that led to the outer doors, I looked up through the glass to watch the unpaired gods spiralling through the blue. My god had settled on skin black as the ceremonial ink itself, but the ones that swam around us flashed colors I'd only glimpsed on the garments of rich travellers visiting the market. Before we passed through the temple doors, my parent pulled their goggles down over their eyes and tapped my shoulder to remind me to do the same. My god shifted so I could bend my arm, and then we were out and into the blinding sun.

Following the quiet cool of the temple, I was unprepared for the assault of noise and heat and light. My parent could not afford a vehicle or riding animal, and so we would sweat on the walk home while rich travellers in sand skiffs and more modest traders with animal-drawn carriages sped past us on the dusty street. Sometimes I could successfully beg a trader to let us ride with them toward central New Limsa. Often ill, my parent didn't fare well in the strength-sapping heat. We waved at a couple of passing carts, but the most we got was the blank stare of their mirrored goggles, reflecting our sweaty, dusty figures back at us. Cheypa kept saying we would go to a glass weaver to repair my own cracked goggles, but that promise had first been made many moons ago, and the left glass was still cracked across its horizon.

The god withdrew its beak, slithered up my arm and onto my head to clap the end of an arm across the broken lens. When it slid back down to my shoulder, the crack was gone, and my goggles dripped water. Thanks to the ink, I did not feel pain when it anchored its beak into the flesh between my shoulder and collarbone, re-establishing our connection. *Thank you*, I said, but my gratitude felt inadequate. The god snaked its arms around my neck. An embrace. Its damp skin felt like a cool rag around my shoulders, a balm in the heat.

A woman with an intricately wrapped scarf on her head stared at me from the back of a merchant caravan. From her closely tailored clothes, I guessed she was from one of the cooler, central lakeside cities. Their caravans rarely traveled this far south toward the poisoned, heated ocean, and they did not understand the concerns of the previously seaside cities that were forced inland, away from their water. The lakesiders did not believe in the gods; rather, they did not believe our octopoda possessed fractions of Ocean's consciousness. Though they liked to come to New Limsa to trade fine goods with our unrivaled glass weavers, they didn't understand the Oceanic teachings behind the beautiful glass.

My parent stepped in front of me to shield me from the prying eyes of the lakesider, who had called more of her people over to come look at the strange child with an ocean creature around their neck. Near home, Cheypa's sandals scraped the street; they sagged against my godless shoulder. I scanned us into the small box of our ground-level apartment and the sand, as always, swept in with us. The door beeped, hissed shut. We crunched across the floor. I put my god in a shallow bowl we'd left out on the altar. The best water we had, our drinking water, was brown and not at all like the crystalline sparkle of the hall of water in the temple, but this was what we had to offer my god. I poured slowly so as not to splash any. The god, relieved to be in water again, squished its arms in close so they were all submerged. Cheypa gave me a smile as they passed and went to lay down on their cot in the corner of the room. They were always so tired. Even their time with their god as a child had not cured them of what the temple acolytes called their "weak heart fire."

We had one high narrow window in our apartment, and so despite the blinding desert light, it was always dim inside. The electric lights were expensive and thus saved for detailed work. New Limsa might have been known for its glass weavers, but that did not mean that most of our own people could afford much glass. Cheypa was not bothered by this, had said the dark indoors reminded them of their years of service in the windowless temple.

To the ocean. Soon, said the god.

I glanced at my parent, breathing shallowly on their cot. *Who will care for them when they're tired? Cook when they can't? Complete the ornaments for market?*

The ocean is always first. The god's black skin shifted toward grey.

Could you heal Cheypa's heart like you healed my goggles? Then I could go and not worry.

Your devotion is admirable, but Cheypa will not be forgotten.

We have no money to hire a skiff or even rent a riding animal. And no one would permit someone to take their animal near the ocean.

A pause. *Luo.* The god spoke my new name alone, and I averted my eyes. *The ocean is always first.*

I kneeled at the small altar so that I didn't have to speak. Ours was not as elaborate as those at the temple—platforms of glass in pools of water. One could wade in and almost imagine stepping into the wash of the clean ocean. In our home, we had a simple sandstone block with a glass cup of blessed saltwater on top. Each week, we tucked a new prayer slip into the small, corked vial at the bottom of the saltwater. At the end of the moon, we returned the saltwater to the hall of water, and drew a new cup.

I reached into the cup for the vial. Cheypa had said I could change the prayer by myself for the first time when we returned with my god. I removed the old slip of paper and took a new one to write, *Strengthen my parent's heart fire.* This was not a new prayer. I'd often asked Cheypa to pray for their own health. They'd been reluctant to do so but always wanted to make sure they acknowledged my input on household prayers.

This was not a new prayer, but now there was a god on our altar.

I took Cheypa water and started grinding spices for dinner. Put beans to simmer low over the gas fire. In minutes, the room was filled with aromatic warmth.

Cheypa dozed, their face dappled with sweat, carefully set curls frizzing back out into kinks. I was laying a cool damp cloth against their forehead when my god said, *They would not be alone. The temple would make sure of that.*

I did not look at the altar. I tasted the beans. Needlessly crushed more cardamom pods. The beans were already well-spiced.

I won't abandon Cheypa like Doni did, I said.

Doni had been the strong one in our family. Doni had abandoned us for the promise of a lakeside city shortly after receiving the ink of passage. We received less contact from her over the years. The last communication had been moons ago, about a joining ceremony with a lakeside. It wasn't an invite, only a statement. Not that Cheypa could have made the journey anyway.

I ate alone, sour now that I'd reminded myself of Doni. Cheypa still slept, and I did not want to wake them. I set aside their portion of dinner for later.

The god spoke again when I was settling into my cot. *Decades have passed since I've seen the ocean.* Their longing begged for an answer. My chest tightened. A splash in the dark from the direction of the altar.

I covered my head with blankets. Turned over.

Lungs, chest full of damp weight. My stomach churned. I stumbled out of my cot and fell to the concrete floor. Small morning light in the window. Cheypa's blankets rustled as they turned over in sleep. I crawled to the altar. Tried to take a breath.

The octopoda.

I stared.

The small light must be lying.

I fumbled for the light plate on the wall. It beeped at the touch of my hand. White-blue light hummed down.

The octopoda.

Water gone from the bowl. The godform. Grey, desiccated.

I pointed a shaking finger toward the mantle. Touch caved in papery skin. Bitter snap. Shivering breath in silence. My breath, my lungs.

And the ink on my skin—vanished. As if there'd been no ritual at all. No naming. The god had taken the memory of my old name, and the new one was gone too. I thought I could remember the way the sound moved, but the specifics were fading.

I was nameless.

I took the bowl from the altar. It was too light. Such a heavy light thing. A noise in my throat.

Cheypa turned over.

I crushed the bowl to my chest and ran, beeped the door open. As it hissed closed, I thought I heard Cheypa utter a sound that could have been my name.

Through the streets, dodging cartwheels and whirring skiffs. Sand stuck in the damp on my cheeks. Someone cried out, I stumbled, fell atop the god. The bowl rolled into the street. A hoof came down. Another. The clay bowl was crushed to dust.

"Let me help you." Brown hand in front of my face. A woman with an inked forehead, a new adult, stared down at me.

I scrambled up and tried to scoop the god into my arms. Its fragile skin crushed into my tunic like dust. Intact, though, was an arm. One. I gingerly picked it up.

The woman was staring. "Is that—?"

I ran.

Breathless, I slammed through the temple's heavy double doors. The clap echoed down the hall of water. Octopoda stopped their placid spiralling and hung in the water in shock. Temple acolytes were immediately upon me, hushing me: "This is the Temple Mother's meditation hour," and "Careful of the glass!" Delayed, I noticed the pain in my side from shouldering open the door.

My mouth was dry with dust and sand. So much of my octopoda had been crushed and whisked away by the wind when I fell. The thin membrane of some of the suckers on its remaining arm had started to crumble. "My god!" I said, holding it up for the others to see.

The temple acolytes stared at my skin, my hair, my clothes, all a dusty mess, uncomprehending.

"My god has—I think my god is—"

A splash sounded behind us, and we turned as one toward the central pool at the end of the hall. One acolyte thought to usher me forward, but now I did not want to move. Their grip was tight on my shoulder at one of the places where the god had pierced me yesterday, but now the site hurt like a wound.

A dark hand gripped the stone edge of the pool, then another. A black-clad figure hauled themselves from the depths. The Temple Mother. Long braids swung heavy with water. Lengths of fabric hung stiff and trailed behind her. Skin, hair, clothes dripping water, leaving a trail of darkened stone in her wake.

She appraised me with eyes the color of the lost, clean ocean. I had never seen someone like us with eyes like hers. Some of the rare, pale merchants had blue eyes, but none as blue as hers. None as blue as oceans. So struck by her, I almost forgot the desiccated arm in my grip.

Until she said, "I've never known a child to kill a god."

The Temple Mother took me to a small inner room and asked me to recount all that had happened. She'd taken the arm from me and cradled it like a child.

I could not tell if she was angry or not. Two candles on the table, lone sources of light, cast shadows across her dark face. She sat like a statue and did not blink. She'd not bothered to change her soaked robes, did not even seem to notice that they were wet.

The temple air still felt too cold. I struggled to hold her gaze.

"You refused your god its request?"

"I didn't—I didn't refuse, I just …"

"You told them you would not go to the ocean."

I looked down to my lap. "I told them I wouldn't leave my parent alone."

"That is refusal. You are not careful with your words."

I bit the inside of my cheek. Clenched my hands in my lap. "I'm sorry."

"I've never seen this. I've never known someone to refuse a first request. I've also never known a god to ask something so dangerous of a child. Ocean must have thought highly of you, but the force of your denial ruined this godform. I will not entrust you with another."

The candle flames flickered, smoked, steadied.

Without the god years, I would never get the ink of passage. I would never be considered an adult. No one would take me as an apprentice to learn their trade, and I would never be able to support Cheypa as I had planned. One decree from the Temple Mother and my future fell to dust.

"I will not entrust you with another," she repeated, "but you must restore this one. Losing godforms weakens an already frail Ocean."

"How do I heal them?" I asked. Eager, mouth dry.

"When Ocean was young, they were strengthened by sacrifice that melded the human and the divine. They are strengthened by expressions of love and beauty." The Temple Mother returned the dried arm to me. "You have altered the course of your journey so that I cannot predict its path. Now you must interpret these things. Ask Ocean for guidance."

I did not look at the arm. "But how can I ask if my god is … gone?"

"Ask *Ocean* for guidance. Not the smaller consciousness of the godform."

"I thought you were the only one who could talk directly to Ocean."

"I think Ocean will be looking to hear from you now."

The Temple Mother guided me to the meditation pool she'd emerged from only an hour before. Her cold hand on my back, she gestured to the pool. "Rest until you have answers."

I nodded, though questions spun my thoughts. She took the arm again. I sat at the edge of the shining pool. Swung my legs over and into the water. Let go and sank. The bubbles of my exhale tickled my face as I kicked to the pool floor. I swam a slow, lazy circle around the perimeter. I didn't need to breathe.

The shadow of the Temple Mother withdrew from the edge of the pool, and I was alone.

When Ocean spoke, they spoke in image. An ornate glass-woven vessel. A heart beating outside its body. The grey arm. Together in the saltwater of the vessel.

Cheypa sat upright on their cot when I returned. Their pouf of hair was flattened on one side. "Where is your god? Why are you soaked?"

"I was at the temple."

"That answers neither of my questions. And you left the light on while you were gone! Do you know what that will cost us?"

"I'm sorry."

"You will explain. Explain everything."

"I lost my god."

Cheypa put their hand to their chest and stood.

"I lost my god and I talked to the Temple Mother and then I talked to Ocean and now I have to make a sacrifice."

Cheypa shook their head and didn't stop.

"I can restore the god I lost."

"Ocean has not asked for a sacrifice in decades! And you are a child. What can you offer?"

The vision Ocean had given was clear. I told Cheypa. I said I didn't think it would hurt. I felt calm about the image of the heart.

"I will talk to the Temple Mother," said Cheypa, moving for the door.

"I want to try."

"You didn't want to go to the ocean, but you will take your heart out? I will surely lose you now." They returned to their cot. "Why does Ocean demand death?"

"It's not death. It's something else." I tried to find the right words for how the images had felt, but my mind fed me images of water arcing, leaping for the sky. I couldn't translate them, so I said again, "I want to try."

Not even legends existed about anyone putting their heart in a glass jar of saltwater. When I went to the glass-weavers' corridor in the market, none understood my request. "I need a jar that will hold my heart," I told them. Some showed me elaborate vases. The most practical among them offered me squat jars meant for storing food for many seasons. The last glass-weaver I found was at the end of the lane, her cart shadowed by a tall building.

Her glass creations spiralled like windstorms and surged up from their bases in waves of color. They were not containers or jewellery or windowpanes as the others had.

"What are they for?" I asked, reaching out and letting my hand hover near a spike of translucent green.

The woman's arm bangles clinked as she moved. She was younger than my parent but not a child. She wore the face ink of an adult who had only recently returned their god to the temple.

"Joy," she said.

"I mean, what do you use them for?"

She smiled and stepped around her cart so that the array of colored glasses no longer fractioned and magnified her face. "Are you here for a gift, perhaps?" But then she stopped. "You're the child from the street yesterday!"

I took a step back.

"No, no, don't leave. Are you okay?"

"I need to buy a jar."

"Did you come to the market with a parent?"

"My parent is too sick for the market." I glanced back at her wares. "Will you help me? I need something like a jar. Something that can shut. But also, it should be pretty."

She disappeared behind her wares again, carefully setting aside crates and wrapping and unwrapping the scarves she used to cushion each piece. She came back with a cool sphere and dropped it in my hand. Inside the glass, an orange seashell, forever suspended. I could almost close my hand around it.

I marvelled at the trinket, turning the glass in the light, peeking inside the sloping fissure in the shell as if something might still live there.

"Now for this jar? I don't have anything like that, but I could make it."

"I don't have much money, but I could work for you to pay for the piece. If that would be okay."

She looked me over again. "You seem young. Around the age you would receive your god."

I hesitated. "I did. Two days ago."

"Where is your ink? Where is your octopoda?"

"I made a mistake. Now I need something beautiful to make it up to Ocean."

"To provide for Ocean is payment enough. If you give me three days, I will craft for you a work of art."

"I will not go with you to the temple this time," Cheypa said on the morning of the ritual. They kept their gaze on their beadwork. "I can't see you through this. I can't see you do this."

"I understand."

"I don't know why the Temple Mother is allowing this. It's not tradition." They yanked at the thread and fed another clear bead along the line. "The lakesiders already think we're—" An untied portion slipped and scattered beads across the floor. Cheypa clapped their hands into their lap and huffed. I picked up the fallen beads and poured them into the cup of Cheypa's waiting hands. Their lips trembled. They squeezed their eyes shut.

"I'll be okay. I'll come back. I *promise.*"

Cheypa put their beadwork aside. I left with the glass-weaver's jar safely cushioned in my pack.

The entire way to the temple, I kept my hands over my heart.

A sensation like rising, like swimming up, like being buoyed by water, filled my chest. And there was my heart, beating, beating, beating with each step. Here was Ocean. Visions rose like bubbles to the water's surface, a mosaic of past and—future? A city by a clear ocean. I did not know if this was Old Limsa or Limsa-to-be.

The Temple Mother stood at the doors when I arrived. I'd never seen her outside. She did not sweat, only glowed in the sun. She did not shield her eyes with goggles, didn't blink, didn't squint. Her robes pooled around her feet in the dust, and her braids, as before, dripped water.

Locals bowed to her. Travellers stared. She acknowledged none of them.

I took her hand when she offered it, and we entered the cool dark of the temple. She told me I had nothing to fear, removed a bundle of cloth from her robes, and unrolled it at the edge of the pool, revealing three knives of different shapes and sizes. I went for the jar in my pack in order to avoid looking at them and held out the swirl of glass to her. She admired how its curves caught the candlelight; the blue of her eyes seemed even brighter when I saw them through the glass.

"The water will accept you now," she said.

I woke in the temple's central pool. My chest was light but not pained, and there was no evidence of incision. Cool water lapped my skin. The Temple Mother loomed statuesque at the edge of the pool. Between her hands, the glass-weaver's jar—and inside that, my still-beating heart. I sensed the black octopoda, restored, on her shoulder before it moved its arms, climbing down to wrap itself around the jar. *Depths*, it whispered to my heart, conveying Ocean's new name for me. I grasped the edge of the pool as I'd seen the Temple Mother do, and the water seemed to push me up, to lend me its strength. I splashed out onto land like a sea creature having just gained legs. The Temple Mother gave me the jar, and I was instantly steadied.

"Keep it close," she said, then reached again into one of the folds of her robe and withdrew a string of beads. I instantly recognized the style, the pattern. I could pick out a piece made by Cheypa in any market display. The pattern was the distinctive alternating black and red given to new adults leaving home for the first time. A blessing. The Temple Mother slipped the necklace over my head with the ceremony of a coronation.

"See them before you leave," she said. "We will care for them at the temple while we await your return." And then she bowed to me, fully kneeling so that we were the same height.

I walked into the desert, clutching the jar against my chest and occasionally glancing down to marvel at how the heart still dutifully beat. Cheypa's beads clicked against the glass with every step. The octopoda, carefully bundled in a sling of scarves, nestled against the glass.

Old Limsa's skeleton broke the horizon.

I pulled along a small cart that held our rowboat. We'd brought no provisions. Would not need them.

Cheypa'd been confused, had tried to give me dried fruits and hard flatbreads for the trip. They'd wondered where I would restock. How I could carry enough drinking water. I'd held their hands, and they'd stopped fretting and said, *You have eyes like the Temple Mother. You're beyond us. No longer a child. Not a human at all, are you?*

I would row across the ocean, and when it was clear, I would come back for Cheypa. I would carry them to the clean water and make them strong.

You're not Ocean, but you're next to the divine. Your presence is heavy and fluid like water.

I am Depths.

Cheypa'd backed away, tried to bow, but I gathered them in a hug.

During my human life, I never knew the sea as anything other than a grey-green mire, but now the possibility of what it could be flashed in my mind like a memory: rippling, ecstatic blue, like the lake-sider women's scarves in the wind. For that future, I had the strength to row forever.

THE THOUGHTBOX

by Tlotlo Tsamaase

The ThoughtBox sits planted to the wall next to the distribution box. It's a slim, expensive hand-sized model that you brought home (stolen) for our anniversary. I heave out a breath. Relief. You step into the kitchen beaming. You're happy. Happy is good. You have a gorgeous smile; I don't want to turn it into a sulk. You've just had a fresh cut, what some people call a fuck-boy cut. You're experimenting. Your eyes aren't their typical lazy, half-lidded, and red-eyed gaze, which means at least today you didn't come home high. At least tonight, you'll stay awake. As usual, you offer your hand to the ThoughtBox first. I glare at it as if it were your mistress.

I remember the first time you brought it home, pushed it onto our living room floor like it was a pet: "Now we get to hear each other's thoughts. Good for our relationship, don't you think?" You smiled so widely, I was afraid to say no. "Remember that night you were crying? I couldn't understand what you were saying. You wanted so badly for me to understand what you're going through. Remember, love?"

I remember. That night, lightning stroked the clouds, sunset tinged. I'd picked you from the airport, our aircar rattling, chugging on low fuel through a chockful of air traffic. I stared at the fuel meter, biting my lip, needing you to assist financially in fueling the car, but our journey home was overwhelmed with your incessant ringing cochlear phone: troubled clients, work issues—your earlobes burned the entire ride. *Tomorrow,* I thought. *Tomorrow I'll ask.* You'd returned from your two-week-long work trip strained and morose. When we got into the house, you dumped your bags on the floor, threw your clothes aside, and sank into a warm bath. I cleaned up after you, pushing time, waiting. Then I heard you yell out, "Where's my towel?" in a grumpy tone, which I handed to you like a hotel room attendant.

You'd trained me well. By the time you strapped your gown on, your plate of paleche and oxtail stew was waiting for you by your laptop tube, which you unrolled into A1 size, verifying the drawings for your family's design firm. It reminded me of our varsity days, of the traditional black-and-red storage tubes every artist student carried everywhere, and where we'd keep all our drawings during our studio days.

You were sitting at your desk when I approached you, trying to ease into the conversation because every breath in this relationship escalates into an argument, and I don't know how to maneuver breathing anymore. "How was the trip?" I asked.

On our wide desk, you stared at your hologram screen, tweaking through the formidable and anachronistic archibus software, hunchbacked, eyes tense. I once asked you why you always kept quiet when I talked to you or asked you questions, you'd said you were still thinking of a response until, after a forever-wait, I requested your response. It turned out you weren't listening at all. It's that passive expression you have. That doesn't reveal anything, not even to me. *I just don't want my emotions all over my face, love,* you once said. *For people to read me. Because that's how they destroyed me to begin with.*

And people reveal secrets about themselves by what they say, don't they? Because my emotions are always wet across my face, and you snort them, getting high off them. So I sat at the edge of the table and refilled your glass. "How was your trip?" I repeated softly. Silence. Waiting, I stared out our window: no trees, no expansive land, just a boundary wall. A rabbit warren, this place was.

That pensive stare. The glass on the table, I could slog you with it, break that skull and perhaps see your emotions bleed all over our floor. Taste your blood, see if it's human. I pinched the skin between my eyes. Something was terribly wrong with me. How could I think like that about you?

You reached for the glass and took a deep swig. "It was fine. Boring. Just training how to operate this new software for the clinics."

I leaned forward. "This it?" It looked like the old, way-back-when 3-D software that designers used to draw up mansions, strip malls, prison facilities. A mall. "When was the last time we went on a date? Did something nice?"

"I don't get to be like you, sitting around at home all day."

Your body was a state of calm, which is always the case when you dismember me and minimize what I do. But a chord snapped in me, sirens of pain flared up. I didn't want to shout, no, because you find it disrespectful when I raise my voice. A woman shouldn't do that. Shouldn't talk back to her boyfriend.

I get it that things are done differently in your family, but do you know how disrespectful it is the way you talk to me? you'd warned me once. *Where I come from, we value family, and when we are married, you must be up before my grandmother wakes, make sure the house is clean, and you must cook for my grandfather,* you'd continued.

I keep doing things for you, how are you *taking care of my heart or my family?* I replied weakly. And you just walked off. *Is that really a future I want?* I know I was having this argument alone in my head, recalling things. *This is the way things work, I need to grow up and accept that's what marriage will be. I can't marry into families and just shit on tradition. It's fine, I thought, I'm sure I can manage.*

"I don't just sit at home," I said, quietly. "It's actually hard work being self-employed, wondering where my next salary is coming from."

Your fingers scrolled through the hologram screen, and after a few minutes I asked if you heard me. "Ja," you said. "There's nothing I can say that won't make you angry."

I stared at the boundary wall, a bird sitting on its top.

"Did you get my messages?" I asked.

"What messages?"

You always do that. I'll call or send a message, but you'll claim you've never seen them, which is ironic given the endless business calls you rarely leave unanswered. You have this upgraded cochlear phone your boss has implanted into your ear so you're always wired, on the ready for 24/7 business calls. You made me get it once. I hated that thing, used to burn up my ear, disrupted my sleeping patterns. It makes you snore so relentlessly that I just want to snip your lungs off. I had the manufacturer take mine out, and sometimes I can barely hear out of my left ear. And I caught you once, in the mall, when you sent me to get your order papers in the aircar, I buzzed and buzzed your cochlear phone, and you just let the vibrations continue in your skull endlessly without answering. I found you standing in an aisle, watching the shop consultants cut a five-meter cord for you, the tinny red light blinking in your earlobe.

I'm not crazy, but I knew it then, that you actually ignore my calls. You have two of them, these little slim expensive devices implanted in both ears. And if I scrolled through their call records, I'd find my missed calls. My ignored messages. And I wonder, if you just watch the ID caller fill your vision, see my name, cringe, and swipe it aside. But I don't want to believe that, I don't want to believe that you'll ignore me during our difficult time, during a time you've put me in debt. I've never been in debt before until we moved in together.

I refilled your glass again and said, "The messages I sent you about—"

Your ears pinged red. A call. Your reflexes snapped; your eyes turned foggy. "Hello?" you answered so obediently, like a dog, leashed to the system. The conversation turned into you scanning through your laptop to remedy the problem that was being reported by the client on the other side. Sometimes I wished I was as important as your job. I felt terrible because I know you're busy and overwhelmed with work. I wouldn't function as a human if I were in your shoes. I just felt too lonely.

That night, I'd said to you, "You're too busy to be in a relationship. You don't hear me, understand me, or have time for me anymore." I wished you'd let me go, it'd be easier, but it'd kill me.

And that's why you brought that cackling ThoughtBox into our house.

"Now we get to hear each other's thoughts," you said, smiling. "I will be able to understand you now, love." You held me tightly, kissed me on my forehead, and murmured, "I love you, Ogone."

Snatches of advertising intermission woke me up that midafternoon. The Internet is part of our inhales and exhales, it's dissolved into the air like fine dust. The internet is everywhere, in the air we breathe, in the food we grow. Sometimes I wish I could disconnect from it, but

I'm still updating my mental mail and apps. I sit up, tilt the orange juice box into my mouth, and finish the last drop of our food.

"It's best for relationships to be transparent," you'd said. This thing you got as a gift from a client, but it's a lie I try to believe, because these things aren't supposed to be consumed by the public. It's a prototype restrained to office buildings of detectives and forensic anthropologists. The LED light is amber, which means it's updating or something, but it's still recording every thought in my mind regardless of proximity. Bluetooth, wireless, all the works, given the feed you made us consume on our bed that became mechanical nanobots circulating my nervous system, connecting me to this ThoughtBox. I sigh. The steam of my coffee rises into the air, and I blow on it before taking a sip. I look out the picture window of our two-bedroomed apartment and nature looks deadpan and beat.

"Ogone, he should have just gotten you flowers or a trip to the Maldives not a fucking AI snitch," my friend, Keaboka, says. Her hologram-narrow body sits on the edge of the kitchen counter during our call. I can make out the features of her open-plan office in the background, a traffic of white-collar employees moving about like uniformed buzzing sheep behind her gray cubicle. "ThoughtBoxes are used for forensic investigations and insurance companies to sniff out duplicity, not to hand out to your girlfriend so you can stalk her mind. How the fuck did he even get one?"

"He says a client gave it to him."

"*Mxm*. Bullshit."

"He just gets worried about me, all the way out here alone and—"

"Brah, you're not in the fucking bundus or in the middle of the desert. You live in a gated estate. What the fuck? Is he afraid the neighbor's daughter is going to steal into your house with a chainsaw and hack you to death?" She giggles, amused by her joke.

"I also get to read his thoughts."

"Oh?" She props up onto her elbows, her bob-shaped braids shake as her brown eyes brighten with excitement. "So, anything juicy?"

"He's stressed about work, his work trip up north, the incessantly irritating client, and his boss. This morning, he had a sweet thought. He was watching me sleep and he thought of how much he loves me, how he's planning to marry me—"

She jerks her head back. "Sounds scripted."

"Why would you say that?"

"It's just … too perfect. His thoughts could literally win an acting award." She chews on her lower lip, and I know she's hesitating to ask me something. "So how do you read each other's thoughts?"

"The ThoughtBox prints them out. I can opt for a mental listen or read them through a hologram screen. Of course, his thoughts sound like his voice."

She blows out her lips. "Ag, creepy. My boyfriend and I have a very organized relationship, thank you. He can have his side dish, I can have my own side dish as long as we respect each other."

I lean back on the stool laughing. "Now that's creepy."

"Can you … can you delete or edit thoughts before you listen or read them?"

My eyes flick away from her. "Ja, but that would appear as a deletion in the logbook. I deleted something once and he gave me the moody silent treatment for a week."

"Has *he* deleted something?"

I look down. "Ja. When I asked him about it, he was honest. He'd signed a nondisclosure agreement for a project his company started working on. And well, his thought revealed too much detail that would compromise his job."

"Brah, you're his girlfriend, not a fucking AI snitch." She shakes her head, rattling the beaded braids. "You really love this guy, huh?" She doesn't say it with envy or joy, she says it with pity, like I'm being naïve, so I quickly add, "I am *living* with him."

She taps her manicured nail on her table absentmindedly. "That's not what I asked. I just wish you hadn't moved in with him. No wonder why he's so chilled with shit. Other guys, sure, they'd get more serious, but he's … I don't know, taking advantage of you. You know you can be open with me, right?" She chews on her thumb's nail and adds, "Don't worry, we're not on loudspeaker, my colleagues can't hear what I'm saying, only you." The hands-free hologram calls were recently upgraded in such a way that only the caller and respondent could see each other and hear each other's voices. The sounds are muted to every other party. My hologram form that appears in her office is invisible to her colleagues.

I quickly add, "Our company could be in competition with that client's project, and I could subconsciously end up using the idea … unaware."

"Eish, ja-nee. Well, if you trust him. But, tsalu, it looks like there's more bothering you."

I turn the mug in my hands and stare at the ripples in my tea. How can I deliver this in such a way that makes me less stupid? Keaboka has been my best friend since childhood, but she just has this way of making me feel like I'm naïve and in need of hand-holding in making smart decisions.

I take a deep breath and blow it out. "He says he didn't get paid this month. So I've used the last remaining of my savings to pay the rent and this month's costs. I'm just trying to figure out how to make money."

Her eyes widen. "Hold up. Doesn't he *already* owe you money?"

I heave in a breath. "Ja, since last year."

"Dude—"

"I know, I know what you're going to say. Listen, I don't mind my boyfriend borrowing money from me, especially if he's stuck, you know."

"We're four months into the new year." She claps her hands the way only a Motswana can do in shock. "This guy though. He owes you money, and then he doesn't contribute to your 'cohabiting' expenses. Yet he's sleeping in *your* bed, eating the food *you* cook, walking through the house *you* clean, wearing the clothes *you* wash for him, hammering *your* vagina whenever he wants, *and* then showing all of this off to his relatives and friends because you're a 'kept' woman. Brah, you're enabling this asshole."

That's my blunt, no-filter best friend.

I place my mug down, hoping the air will hold me.

"You're investing your time and money into a guy who's just taking and taking," she continues. "He hardly gives you the time, he hardly helps you with anything. He doesn't pay for shit, then he makes you feel guilty for all these things—he's the only one gaining from this relationship."

"No, come on. His work and family situation is very unstable and … abnormal, but it won't be forever. Things will work out eventually. We're just waiting for things to tide over. He's overworking and he doesn't really have time, and the company he's working for hasn't paid him this year. He doesn't even have time to look for another job, it's not like it's easy—many of our friends are unemployed!"

"You always have excuses for him," she says. "If he's not getting paid then why stay? Why can't he just stay at home with you and hustle to make your own money? I swear he's just lying to you, but you, just—God, why do you always believe him? He probably knows he can get away with anything when it comes to you. I mean, what if he's actually getting paid and hiding the money from you?"

"No, no, no. He's not like that. These are facts we can't change. Things will look up at his job. They'll pay him, then I can recoup my costs."

"*We* gave him three chances." She lifts three fingers to count off. "One: he said things will be better if he moved out so you could spend time together. Two: when you tried breaking up with him a million times because it didn't work out, he promised he would make things better. Three: he promised things would be way better if you two moved in together. You're not living with a man, you're living with a devil baby who's so comfortable that his needs are met and not yours. He is not your child. *You* are not his parent. You need to start living for yourself."

My body turns cold, the whole world shakes, ripples. I'm cold. I'm feverish. It's not true. I am both the girlfriend and boyfriend in this relationship. No, but he loves me. He can't be that cruel.

"And last thing, I don't trust him," she says. "He's hiding or manipulating his thoughts somehow, so you don't see Satan laughing behind his face."

"I feel sick," I say. "He wouldn't do this to me. He loves me."

She turns her head quickly as if something caught her attention, though I can't see. She cranes her neck. "Oh shit, the boss is hobbling his fat ass over. Gotta go. Chat later. Please take care, choms!" She reaches out to the screen to end our call.

Her hologram figure fizzles like white noise, and soon all I see is the kitchen counter, dryer, and washing machine no longer obscured by her opaque hologram. The silence is ostentatious, it has a deafening voice clearly telling me how alone I am. I hate being this lonely, it itches all over me like an allergy.

I jump when an echo sounds: "Call ended," a neutral, bodiless voice responds. Our home system. He has our home calibrated to our minds. The heating and air-conditioning system. The coffee maker. The door automaton system. And right now, my design work, which I've mentally projected out from my computer as a 3-D object, which has taken up the entire space of my home office. I walk through one of the bedroom designs of a multi-residential project I'm working on for my company. I am an architect and property developer. I started this company with my boyfriend hoping it would sustain us in the future. Except, because of his overworked job, I'm doing all the work, reading through the contracts, vetting all sellers, analyzing market trends of plots and property markets, and injecting all funds from my savings. *You're his golden goose, you've sure made it too comfortable for him that he would never leave,* Keaboka had said. I laughed it off. But I'm now sitting here in the 3-D design, knowing that whatever decision I have over the interior décor, I still must run it past him, and how his hard criticism will chide me. I pinch my wrist. I hate the way he always looks at my creative work with a serious bored face and picks the one thing he hates. Always. Never mentions something good *and* something bad. Only bad. I do all the work and all he gets to do is decline or offer a signature after much begging to read through the contents.

Then I'm blamed for the decision making.

"You make the decisions, it's not like you're interested in my input or my ideas," he once revealed during an argument. "You made sure you had a higher number of shares, but anyway, you put in the money, so my thoughts aren't important."

"I'm sorry," I said. "I didn't mean to make you feel this way. It's just that ..." and I was too afraid to say it: that you're always too busy to spare a second to go over things. I knew it would lead to another sulky and moody event. Lately, even when I call him for his input, he's too busy. When I send him an alarm message, he hardly responds.

So I wait for him.

I wait for him.

God, I wait for him.

So he doesn't feel small,

left out,

closed out.

I slump against the wall, and I want to sob. I want to destroy everything that closes me in, including myself. I throw the cup of coffee against the visualization of my design. The cup just waddles through the hologram projection,

fibrillating the walls it skims through

until it hits a

real wall

and shatters.

WHO ARE YOU?

I knew it. You're deleting your thoughts. I know it's not just work-related ones, you're hiding something from me.

When I extracted the morning logbook after my workout, with a steaming cup of coffee now in hand, I coughed out the hot beverage onto the digital printout. The hologram reported a night's worth of deleted thoughts. Every single one. You were sleeping for fuck's sake. What was so revealing about work that you had to get up and delete them? This was becoming ridiculous. If it was me, you'd be despondent and moody for a month. But that's not it. The time stamps remained, showing that you were up at 2:33 a.m., a couple of hours after I went to bed. Your mind was overworking like a seething laptop processing heavy software until 4:17 a.m., which explains your sharp, moody behavior that morning. Snapping at me because you didn't get much sleep.

Well, I bought a File Recovery, installed it into my mind depository, despite how expensive it was, to recover mind files "that are accidentally deleted" goes the description. And, well, our thoughts are files. If you are telling the truth, that your thoughts are in fact work-related, I'll dump the file recover and I'll never go behind your back again. It's the least I can do for doubting you.

Twenty-four hours it has been since I mentally linked the recovery app to the ThoughtBox. I logged you out from the ThoughtBox as soon as you left for work, but there's not much I can do for the thought-reporting chip you shot into my neck. The requested files have been recovered. If you catch me going behind your back like this and I'm wrong, I'll manage your moods for at least a month; they can't last longer than that, right?

I've been sitting in a locked bathroom in case you come home. Using the hologram screen, a message floats before me: *Read through the terms and conditions and press accept to obtain the recovered files.* I'm on my knees now, leaning against the bathroom cabinet, and I'm too afraid to accept, too afraid to read the truth. What will I find? Will you still be the same man I fell in love with? I don't even read the T&C's, couldn't be bothered really. I close my eyes and jab my finger against the "accept" icon. A window in gray shades comes up with an .exe file that I must install, which a program in my mind depository can read. Once I run the .exe file, I flip the hologram window with my right hand, and it opens an MTM (mind text messaging) app that allows for free international conversations and shows a list of dated backup files, which are basically thoughts *you* deleted.

I hold my breath as the chat opens, obscuring the shower behind it. Fear trickles into my chest when a series of images and texts fill the empty space of the hologram. The first thing I see is a snapshot of someone's breasts, their thighs, and their insides, like I'm watching a medical procedure through a laparoscope that tunnels its way through them. I clasp my hand to my mouth. My whole world turns black as I try to slap away the images. Is this a joke? The conversations span back one year. I scroll through the messages between you and your correspondent Boothang69, who's in Shenzhen, China.

Her profile picture is a photograph of my face, intensely photoshopped. Except, it's a mask she's wearing. What sick-minded game is this? Why would another woman want to wear the face of the girlfriend? The masked girl is staring up at the camera, smiling, large eyes, a weave on. She's squeezing into her breasts, so they appear bigger, the cleavage showing.

I zoom into the photograph. Before proceeding, I grab her picture with my hand and throw it into the web on another window, hoping the scan will reveal her online identity. I watch the loading icon, a silver light zipping around a circle, and finally a picture comes up. Her name is Gorata Tau. She's studying for an MBA in China. I flip through her photographs. She's on the metro. She's in front of a street with fairy lights. She's smiling at the camera, and behind her is Canton Complex in Guangzhou with steely skyscrapers. I feel faint, my armpits sticky with sweat. I switch to the other hologram window to read the chats:

Boothang69: I love you, boo. Couldn't stop thinking about you. 2:44 a.m.

You: Send me a picture. I miss her, the warmth between your legs. 2:45 a.m.

Boothang69: How about a hologram connection like last time? 2:45 a.m.

You: Babe, you got me going crazy. If only I could feel your body. I miss you so badly. I need you back home. 2:45 a.m.

Boothang69: Ya know, soon I'll be there. Isn't she taking care of you? 2:46 a.m.

You: She's so stiff. She's not like you. 2:46 a.m.

Boothang69: You won't have to wait so long. One more year left. 2:46 a.m.

You're really cheating on me. I don't believe in a fight that some women get into with other women because the guy wronged you. Your partner is the one who committed adultery. What is the point of fighting someone outside the relationship, as if he can't find another one? Am I then going to hunt down every single woman you cheat on me with? No. This war is between you and me. I scroll down to last night's messages, which only confuse me more.

Boothang69: Babe. You up? 2:34 a.m.

You: Ja, aren't you in class? 2:39 a.m.

Boothang69: It's 8:40, the lecturer's running late. 2:40 a.m.

You: You feeling better this morning? 2:41 a.m.

Boothang69: Fuck, no! 2:41 a.m.

Boothang69: Where is she? 2:41 a.m.

You: Hibernating. Jesus, she's a lot of work. She's not acting according to our plans. 2:42 a.m.

Boothang69: WHAT?? 2:42 a.m.

Boothang69: Did you find out why she logged you out from the ThoughtBox? 2:43 a.m.

Boothang69: Hello? 2:46 a.m.

Boothang69: Where are you??? This is bugging me. 2:49 a.m.

You: Sorry. It's almost 3 a.m. She was just up for a glass of water. I was still talking to her. 2:50 a.m.

Boothang69: What? She can eat now??? Isn't that dangerous? 2:50 a.m.

You: No. The glass was empty. She sees it as filled with water. She "thinks" she can eat and drink, but her plate is always empty. 2:51 a.m.

Boothang69: Oh, that's a relief. 2:52 a.m.

You: I didn't want to tell you this because ur stressed with classes, but the monitoring-and-remote-controlling chip is not working ... I can't hear her thoughts. 2:55 a.m.

Boothang69: What the fuck! 2:55 a.m.

Boothang69: Since when? 2:55 a.m.

Boothang69: Why are you only telling me this now????? 2:56 a.m.

Boothang69: Oh, modimo. We're fucked. We're seriously fucked. We can't have her running around unsupervised. Do you understand how in serious shit we'll be??????? 2:57 a.m.

Boothang69: Why are you taking forever to respond? This is FUCKING important! 3:07 a.m.

You: I'm sorry, babe, I was on a call with a client. 3:13 a.m.

Boothang69: Jesus, we need to bury her. 3:13 a.m.

You: People around here know her. If she disappears again, I'll be their first suspect. I'd hate it if you got punished too. 3:14 a.m.

Boothang69: My aunt was taken in, incarcerated. She hung herself in a fucking toilet. I can't go to prison. I won't survive. 3:14 a.m.

You: I won't let it come to that. I'd rather take the fall than have you suffer. I love you, s'thandwa same. 3:16 a.m.

Boothang69: I told you we should've never given her an identity. Never. We should've hidden her, tied her in a basement or something. 3:16 a.m.

Boothang69: I don't trust her. What the fuck was she doing yesterday? 2:40 a.m.

You: She says she was working from home. The gardener said a professional-looking woman visited her. 3:19 a.m.

Boothang69: Why the hell are you so calm? I did this for you. 3:19 a.m.

You: I know, and I appreciate you for that. Babe, you need to relax. I have her under control. 3:23 a.m.

Boothang69: We can't get caught, ja. 3:23 a.m.

Boothang69: This shit is stressing me the fuck out. 3:25 a.m.

Boothang69: I can't sleep. 3:25 a.m.

Boothang69: If they find out who she is—Jesus, I keep seeing her face on the news. It's driving me mad. 3:25 a.m.

Boothang69: Where the hell are you? 3:28 a.m.

Boothang69: You're not taking this seriously. 3:35 a.m.

You: I'm sorry, babe, I was on another call. Just why does she have to be goddamn difficult? 3:38 a.m.

Boothang69: You and that fucking job. You're always busy! 3:39 a.m.

Boothang69: Fuck this. I'm getting on a flight tonight. 3:39 a.m.

You: Wait. What?! 3:40 a.m.

You: What about your dissertation? Your studies? 3:40 a.m.

Boothang69: Are you kidding me? There'll be no future with this bitch acting out. We need to sort her out. Clearly, you need manpower. 3:41 a.m.

You: I'm really sorry. I hate disappointing you. 3:41 a.m.

You: You still there? 3:47 a.m.

You: Babe, she's made a lot of money for us in the past year, which paid for your studies. Let's just run her for another year. Just be patient. 3:52 a.m.

Boothang69: No. I am coming home, finish and klaar. Get everything ready. 3:52 a.m.

You: Ok. 3:53 a.m.

You: What should I prepare? 3:59 a.m.

You: Hello? 4:07 a.m.

You: Um, have a safe flight. I love you. 4:17 a.m.

The floor is cold under my feet. The knobs of the cabinets have eaten into my back and my spinal cord hurts. I stretch out my legs, refusing to face what I've just read. The hologram glows in front of me and the bathroom darkens, clouds overshadowing the sun. These messages are from last night, which means she'll be arriving tonight at the latest. Why are they so concerned about me and my diet? What identity did they give me? Who is this woman? Why do they need me under their control? What the hell is going on? They want me to disappear. No. No. You wouldn't do that. I stare at myself in the mirror, your words with your mistress running through my mind:

I told you we should've never given her an identity.
She's not acting according to our plans.
We're seriously fucked. We can't have her running around unsupervised.
She can eat now??? Isn't that dangerous?
I keep seeing her face on the news.
If they find out who she is ...
If she disappears again.
Let's just run her for another year.

Who are they referring to that they're so afraid will find me? You keep seeing my face on the news, and it makes your mistress sick, but how come I haven't seen my face on the news? If I disappear again? Am I a missing person? Did you take me in?

I press my hand against the mirror, and I feel like a stranger. "Who are you? What have you become? What has he done to you?" I ask, staring at my reflection. I draw my arm back, strike it into the mirror. A sharp sound; glass cascades into the porcelain sink. "Who are you!" I shout at the mirror. I bang my arm again. "Who are you?" My face distorts into anger and confusion.

When I look down, night-like liquid spills down the white of the sink. I do not bleed like other people. My blood is not red. I have no menstrual cycles. I do not consume food nor liquids. *Who are you? Who are you? Who are you?* I look at my arm. A shard of glass has sliced it open. The skin is folded back, like an orange peel. I pull it further back, inspecting what lies beneath my skin:

In my arm, there are fiber cords and not veins.
There are tubes and steel but no bone.
So what is in the rest of my body?
Sensors,
processors,

actuators
in my limbs are responsible for my tactile reception
that my brain-search can identify.
I inspect the flap of skin:
this is lab-harvested biological tissue and muscles,
fused with technology,
with a venous network of nano-sized sensor-wires
meshed onto my endoskeleton
inside me, there are nanobots used for cell regeneration.
Aluminum alloy lies beneath this skin like bone.
I fold into myself on the floor. "Who are you?" I cry to the cloud-eclipsed sun.

I DRAG YOUR TONGUE

You didn't come home.

You stayed at work. Showered at work. Slept at your desk.

Twenty-four hours I've sat here waiting for you. You tell me you'll be home tonight.

For one year, you continued this other life, sending each other nude snapshots. I remember our friends during our game nights, lightly telling me over shots how I'm obsessed with you, that I have the peculiar OCD to tend to your every need. Maybe I crave pain. Maybe sadness feels like home. Maybe it's nice to blame you for something. It feels safer to be in your realm than outside. It's the only environment I know, from childhood to adulthood. I keep choosing people like you, as if you are all twins in love with your dominant role. Your wrongs make mine feel lesser, make me feel like the perfect human being. Hey, you abuse people. At least I'm better. I may flirt with a guy, keep him wrapped around my finger, but I'd never do anything as bad as that.

But this. The thing I learn about *you*. You have crossed the line and *that* is bullshit. Here's the thing that no one knows about your charm and your pull-the-crowd humor: *you're* the obsessed freak. Obsessed with pussies and demands. Mollycoddled by mummy issues. The sexting. The pictures. Naked bodies. Exchanging these illicit texts. The lies—the damning lies about who I really am. I unpack the Thought-Box, I autopsy it and rummage through the deleted thoughts. The bare truth in postmortem form lies on my living room floor. You're a bastard. And I need answers:

Who am I?

Who is that woman?

What is wrong with my body?

After everything I have done for you. You do this to me? I stare at it, the evidence of you begging her to send you a picture of her vagina, whilst telling me you love me. Not only me. But you're begging them. Many girls. Girls who want you to stop asking, who tell you to think about me. But you're persistent. Our neighbors—God, you begged her, wanting to kiss it. Even our friends. Bloody bliksem, no wonder they gave me strange stares when we were together. This is not only embarrassing. You've torn the dignity off my body. You've left me naked. And everyone knew. Everyone. Except me.

I search every nook and cranny of news reports online and offline just to find something, something that connects me to something honest and real. And there it is, a hidden report you've confiscated from our viewing; it's a nineteen-year-old woman who disappeared on her walk home from work. Three years ago. Three! When I enlarge the missing-person picture, it is me, except the name is different: Olerato Mosime.

Who are you? What is beneath that skin of yours? Can I flay you like I did the cats in my old neighborhood? See if you have bone or blood.

I don't want any explanations.

I don't want your voice and your lies.

I want you dead.

When you enter through the door, I'm not your shitty little submissive girlfriend. I knock you out with a fucking pan. The fucking pan you chided me for misusing. I want the pain in my heart to be a bomb in your body. But what is my plan? To kill you and then what? To kill you because you cheated? Because you two kidnapped me? Because you're planning to do far worse to me? Because you're both screwing around with me, trying to control me? And what have you done to my body? Why is my blood black?

I take your life because you took mine. No, you took three years of my life, wasted them, you fucker. And what about my family? My poor family who've suffered so many years. Anger, I've never felt anger like this. What have I become? I crumble onto my knees. Ashamed of myself. Embarrassed. This is not me. I am not cruel. How can I let this relationship turn me into this ugly thing? You customized me like a sex doll, only I had a mind of my own.

Lies or not, I dial.

The operator answers. "9-9-9, what is your emergency?"

"Hello," I wail, swiping blood and tears from my face. "Please, I need help. I was kidnapped three years ago. I just killed my kidnapper in self-defense. I need help, please."

THE PARTS THAT MAKE US MONSTER

by Sheree Renée Thomas

We didn't want your nail clippings or your blood. Your laughter, or tears, would do. That strange light you saw drifting where a shadow should be, was the promise mother made when she bore us. Where we lived, there would always be sun. Where we go, there would always be light. That star never scarred or scared us. Even in the face of our father, the sun's blistering gaze, we were the daughters of night.

On that first journey across the waters, we held each other close. When we shut our eyes we floated on azure sleep, lifted by wave upon wave, until the darkness behind our golden lids became lonelier still. Before they trapped us, we bathed in leaves, bark, stones, and spice. We sang no fear. We knew. Ancestors descend when needed. Spirits rise when called. It was the way of the world, the way day follows night and moon, mother said, it was moon who follows ocean's call. For it was the water that carried us in the womb and water that reigns supreme.

When they chased us from the village into the forest, when we fell into the arms of ghosts, we knew we would have to feed, our worries and our appetites, replanted in strange, disordered lands. With lowered eyes we watched the traders, whose skin was the color of clay, the wet earth that came from waters, the moon clay our mother and her sisters used to mark their territory. From the way the ghosts moved, the way they stared through us, barking out words that sounded like insanity falling, we knew. The clay moon ghosts believed wherever they walked, wherever their square toes landed, was their territory. We sang the song of our mother, sang the songs that came before. Force marched through a door of no return, we wore our chains like an elder's gold, carried our song inside, still waters flecked with shards of moonlight. Three days later we entered the dark maw of what the ghosts called ship. We lay in the bottom of the belly with the others. We lay in the noise and the filth with the mothers, and the sisters, and the daughters, listened to their dirge song of shrieks, moans, the twisting of tongues, the deaths of worlds yet born. We did not speak with words but with feelings. Ours was the language of survival, flight.

Mistress Godwin was a laughing girl, a mere child, barely a woman when we joined her. Her cheeks and eyes still flushed with the sounds of mirth. Disappointment had not yet clawed its way into her heart. Her breasts were hard blossoms yet to break earth. *Mistress*, we sang, *Mistress Godwin*, but she did not speak or smile. In this strange land, dead tongues no longer answered us. *God wins*, we laughed, *god wins*, we cried. The sound of our pleasure frightened the blackbirds in the trees.

When they found her, her skin had grown pale, her temples the color of sour milk. We only meant to take a little, but the hunger had long since overtaken us. We wanted to taste the sound of her laughter, to let the woman-child's joy fill the hollows that hid deep inside. Like the ghosts, we took too much, and just like them, we were not ashamed.

Thirst is thirst.

When the good mistress grew still and joined whatever cold ancestors that claimed her, we dropped the slop bucket in the field, left the dough rising in the wooden bowl, abandoned our chores. We drained the others and fled, taking their laughter with us. Into the wild forest, we ran, cousin to the bush that once betrayed us. We hid in wildness. We hid in plain sight. In hickory and peepaw and loblolly pine, in the light that has always claimed us.

We waited. Sparkling light where shadows should be. The blackbirds visited, kept us company in the silent years when even the first ones marked our hunting ground in the language of their fear. *Croatoan*, they later said, croatoan carved into the heart of a tree. But no tongue has found the right tones to name us. Twenty years later, finally, the blackbirds crowed good news. When the new beast arrived, it bore one hundred and twenty souls, but none like us were in its belly. We took what sustenance we could from the joyless ones who struggled to make the dry-bone land home. In time, their parched throats would rival our own, for the old gods of this land refused to send rain. And thirst is thirst.

Leaf, ghosts, earth, light. We suffered together. Finally, when we had grown so weak, our light only the spark of fireflies, twenty-and-odd men joined the colony. A few suns later, a woman appeared. Angelo. Angela. Their ebon skin and eyes stirred memory, the ghost of their laughter refracted light of our own. The sound, infrequent as it was, reminded us of home. And because we are our mother's daughters, we left the men and the lone woman who could be kin. After the journey across the big water, their bodies held such little joy, we were ashamed to drain them. We knew. Even in strange lands, old seeds release fresh roots. Eyes stinging with memory, we fled again, taking the silver shards of light with us.

We left temptation and the shadows and something close to sorrow. We buried thirst and the seed of ourselves deep within the forests. And the years passed through us. Past the cypress and the oaks. The memory of laughter floating around, dust motes in sunlight. With time, memory became our only home.

The old home was a memory time would not let us forget.

Some night-days we dream. Our thoughts are upside down.

We hang from our feet in the limbs of thick-boned trees.

The blackbirds come and sing to us. They say we have become the language of fear, the hushed gasps and breath around open fires. But the stories they teach are wrong. Darkness is not the only thing to fear. Sometimes the dark is hidden in light. Once girls, we have grown old here. Once girls, our hearts have become hard like the mottled bark of the strange trees that grow here. There are layers to this loneliness. We feel its bite. Its teeth are sharp. Hard things hold beauty, too. The world we live in is a fire. The people we love all burn. Ever hungry, our red-gum smiles hide the empty pit within. We know. Legends rise from all the broken places, emerge from the stories and the memories, the half-remembered and the ill-formed, all melded together, united in one. In this land we are like moons who have lost their water. We no longer hear the ocean's call. If water no longer speaks to us, are we still our mother's daughters?

The parts that make us monsters are not the teeth or the heart, but the mind.

The part that makes us monsters is bone and sinew, spirit and flesh.

We have not been ourselves here. We will not be ourselves here.

We are always ourselves here.

We are always

here.

SCAR TISSUE

by Tobias S. Buckell

The evening before you sign and take delivery of your son, you call Charlie and tell him you think you've made a huge mistake.

"Let me come on over and split a few with you," he says. "I haven't seen the fire pit yet."

Charlie—a short, compact man with green eyes and a shaved head whom you met when he delivered groceries the first few weeks you were housebound—brings over a six-pack. You walk out into the complex's community garden together. It used to be a parking lot, and the path through the mushroom gardens under the solar panels is still faded gray asphalt and leftover white lines. You're careful with your right foot; you still haven't gotten used to the way your prosthetic moves. It's easy to trip.

You and Sienna from 4B have a fire pit and stone circle dug out in your combined lots, and she's grown a privacy wall of rosebushes that surround the relaxing space. Charlie sits on one of the cedar benches as you fiddle with twigs to make a fire.

This beats the awkwardness of sitting down to talk right away. Your parents didn't raise you to be direct about feelings. Neither did the army, nor the warehouse you drove a forklift in. Charlie will, if you let him.

Making a fire gives you a moment to sort out all your feelings.

Or maybe it just gives you an excuse to delay talking about them.

Charlie knows all that. It's why he created an excuse to come over.

The beer is warm, but the bottle still sweats enough that it drips across the pale plastic knuckles of your hand. You switch the bottle over to your other hand.

"It's too late to back out now," Charlie says.

"I know."

"You need the money."

The fire starts to lick at the twigs and burn brighter. You awkwardly drop yourself onto the bench across from Charlie and look down at his tattered running shoes and the frayed edges of his gray jeans.

"Everyone needs the money." You swig the cheap beer that's the best either of you can manage. You can't wait to afford something from one of those smaller local breweries nearby.

"But ..."

You've been on disability since the forklift accident. The apartment's small, but Enthim Arms is nice. The shared garden out back, the walking trails. You can't use them as much as you'd like right now, but that physical therapist keeps saying June is when you might be able to make it to the lake and back.

It'll hurt, but you've never cared so much about seeing a mediocre quarry lake before.

"Advent Robotics will pay me more money to raise it than I made at the warehouse, and I can keep focusing on recovery while doing it." You raise your hand and flex it. A low-battery alert blinks on your wrist.

Plus, the bonus at the end will give you enough to afford something only the rich usually can: regrowing your forearm and your leg. Like a damn lizard. The biolabs that do that are so far out of your reach you normally wouldn't even consider it.

And you want it all back. You want it to be just like it was before the forklift started to tip over and Adam screamed at you to jump out, running toward you as fast as he could, ridiculously long hair flying, his clipboard clattering on the floor.

"So what's wrong?" Charlie asks softly, and you have to stare back at the fire to avoid the discomfort of looking at another person.

"I told myself I'd never have kids." You look up from the brown bottle and at the thorns that twist around each other in the vines that

Sienna has so carefully trained. "Can't see my way to passing on the shit my parents gave to me."

"Damn," Charlie nods, folds his hands. "Cory, you can't think you'll be the same people they were. The fact that you're scared about this, that means you're going to be such a better parent than they were."

"No." You point a finger over the neck of the beer bottle at him. "People say that, but that's some backwards-assed logic. Refusing to pass on the bad mistakes, understanding maybe you're going to screw up something you're responsible for, that doesn't mean you should go do it. I know I can't go climb a mountain without a rope, I'm going to fall. That was true even before the accident. Understanding that fact doesn't mean I'm going to be a great climber without a rope. It just means I realize I'm going to fall."

"Fair enough," Charlie says. "So you going to just send it back?"

You look at the blinking light on your right wrist.

"I don't know. Maybe."

You should ask how things are going. Charlie started a new job helping an artist down the street weld large, corporate symbolic art sculptures. Better than all the gig-economy stuff he'd been piecemealing together.

You should finally thank him for spending all that time chatting with you when he'd unload groceries, losing money every second he went the extra mile.

Instead, you drink and talk about the weather. Something inconsequential.

"Well, even if you do screw up, it's just a robot, right?" Charlie raises the bottle of beer in a salute.

Your son crawls out of the crate the next morning. It thrashes pieces of the box aside and mewls in confusion as it turns on.

Instant regret grips you as you try to grab him, and one of his arms smashes the coffee table. Shattered glass bounces off the tile, and you let go of his unyielding artificial skin.

"Hey," you tell the confused machine. "Easy!"

It crunches around in the glass, and you can hear its eyes snick in their sockets as it anxiously looks around your small apartment. The sound unnerves you.

When it opens its mouth, a gurgling electronic scream warbles out.

It's the most alien, unnerving sound, and it makes your whole spine tingle.

"Just relax."

It's taller than you. Heavier. The ultradense batteries mean that even as you try to physically stop it from flailing, you can hardly budge it.

Those ruby-red eyes with the LIDAR range detectors behind them lock hard onto you. You feel like you're in the sights of something and lick your lips.

The pediabotic trainers at Advent told you the first few minutes could be chaotic. You just need to make sure that you remain within its eyesight. Once you do that, it starts to imprint on you.

Like a baby animal.

Soothing tones and patience. You dance about as best you can to make sure it's aware of you.

"Make sure you have a name picked out and keep using it," you were told in the CARE training. "It's a mind in a pre-language, pre-memory state. The language matrix plug-in will be aiding it, though, and even human babies start recognizing names and language much faster than you realize."

It's one thing to watch a video of a robot coming to life with its new parents calmly welcoming it into their new, perfect multiroom home. You, on the other hand, are hopping around shit you left out and trying not to fall over as you stumble after the thing. This, you know, is a huge mistake.

"I even forgot your name!"

You're hunting about for something as the robot turns around and squalls at you.

"Rob, stop it, please."

And the mechanical screaming finally stops. Sharrad, upstairs, has been banging on the floor, upset at all the noise.

"It's OK, Rob. You're OK."

Rob cautiously approaches you.

"Hi."

The coffee table has been destroyed. You feel a knot in your stomach, scared the machine might hurt you.

"At this point in our manufacturing iterations, there's tremendous aversion to harming anything organic," the recruiters at Advent have explained many times. "Just like people have a deep instinct of fear around a snake, our robots have instinctive fears about hurting anything."

Rob gently crouches down in front of you and starts to pet your shoes, fascinated by the laces. He keeps picking them up and letting them fall back to the top of your shoes.

"OK," you laugh. "Now let's show you where your charging base is."

Rob should have the instinct to go looking for one when he's running low. The next important step is to make sure he can find it.

"Talk as much as you can. Language acquisition is key," Advent has explained. "Narrate everything you're doing as you go, and even when your foster robot is older, explain why you do everything you do. Context is key. The more you can do that, the better."

You spend the next two days teaching Rob how to find its charging port and stay still on it. It's constant and exhausting. The robot will stay charging for a while, but then get up and go chattering and exploring through the house. You have to keep moving it back.

On the third day you fall asleep on the floor as Rob warbles about and opens every single drawer and cabinet in the kitchen, working on fine-motor movement.

You wake up, panicked, to an unmoving lump next to you. You drag Rob over, the body limp in your arms, to the charger. "Please don't be broken," you say. You need this to work. Advent won't pay you anything if you kill the damn thing in the first few days.

Back on the charger, Rob starts babbling nonsense and making faces at you. Relief floods through you and you slump down to the floor.

Three days of no sleep and that meaningless proto-speak. You punch the wall with your prosthetic hand, and it crunches through the drywall. Rob sees that and startles. It punches the drywall as well.

"No!" you shout.

Rob curls into a ball on the charger and looks at you through raised arms. It's scared, and you did that. This is everything you feared. You remember your dad standing at the top of the stairs, that anger curdling you with fear.

"I can't do this," you say, curling into a ball on the floor. "I can't do this."

"You'll be surprised at how exponential growth in learning works."

Advent is all gleaming showroom factory floors. The human workers wear protective gowns, hairnets, and goggles. It's as much lab as it is factory, you think.

The recruiter walks you by glass windows looking into the factory. You stare at the pieces of robotics, impressed by the circuitry and technology everywhere, but having no clue what any of it does.

"At first, your foster robot will seem like no more than an infant, and that's because it is! But every time they get on that charger, they're not just powering up their onboard battery—they're taking in their experiences and uploading data to our servers to have it examined and encoded back to them, to accelerate their growth. Just like sleep and dreaming work for us, helping us to process our world."

You're told that in just months you'll see significant developmental gains. And then the really big leaps will start to come.

It'll take six months to fully mature your son.

Can you make it six months, taking care of a growing mind? Being *responsible* for a whole thinking being? Being a good parent? It seems like forever, and yet it's not that long of a temporary job.

"Some of us do it for twenty years," one of the recruiters laughs when you express this. She has professional highlights, perfect teeth, and shoes that cost more than your disability allowance pays out in a month.

She laughs too hard, you think.

But you say nothing and swallow anything acidic as she talks through the monthly payments and the bonus for a successful maturity.

"He's 'asleep' for now," you tell Charlie, the next time you take a moment to meet up around the fire pit. It's been hard to find the time while raising a brand-new robot. Sienna's annoyed, fairly, that you haven't been out to weed, and the fire pit needs cleaning.

You don't even bother to try and start a fire.

"You look exhausted." Charlie hands you a beer, but you shake your head. You need a clear mind. You've given up one of the few vices you have.

"It takes everything I have to just keep up. I can't go out much with him. Just too damn clumsy still. He's broken half of everything I own."

Rob has explored the backyard, the hallways. People stare at you when you go out, and you have to pull Rob away from something because his coordination isn't that good yet. They're used to seeing robots doing things for people, not a person babysitting a robot. There are only a few hundred robots being fostered at any given time.

And it's not babysitting when you're the parent, you guess.

"Ahmed said you're not at physical therapy anymore."

"I'll get back."

Maybe.

In four more months, you'll be free, and you'll have that maturity bonus. In four months, you'll be in a clinic watching flesh and blood regenerate.

You have to hold onto that.

Things can get back to the way they were if you just get through this.

"You gave it a name?"

"Rob."

"Rob?"

"I panicked."

"Rob the robot?"

A loud crash from the apartment, followed by a shrill shriek. "Shit, Charlie, I wanted to hear about that piece you're working on for the city park, but he's awake. You can head out by the gate."

"Dad?"

You wake up as Rob taps your chest, his red eyes open wide as he stares down at you. You blink and pull back the blanket.

"Dad?"

You can't escape him. It's 2 in the morning, but he's finished a charge cycle.

"Dad. Dad. Dad. Dad. *Dad.*"

You can wrap a pillow around your head, but it's not going anywhere. That word.

Dad. Dad. Dad.

It's new. Just in the last few hours before you went to bed. But he's using the newly acquired word for everything. He has two words now.

He points at himself. "Rob!" He points at you. "Dad!"

You get up and turn on the lights.

"Dad!"

You'd asked one of the scientists that the recruiter brought in for the Q&A session why robots needed raising. The recruiter had explained it, but you wanted to get it from the egghead, not the Parental Unit Liaison.

"The simpler the animal, the less parenting it needs," the scientist said. "Some are born with all the instincts they need."

But a robot meant to move and look like a human being, to help people in nursing homes or other similar cases, that robot couldn't just be programmed with a few repetitive functions.

To understand nuance, to get a theory of mind and understand context, one needed intelligence.

"You need to be raised, and in your own body. You're not just a mind in a jar—that's an old theory of consciousness. You're a grown being. A whole being. Your gut bacteria, spinal column, the society around you, all of that creates an entire person, as well as the experiences and time that it passes through. You can't just manufacture a thinking robot. We have to raise it."

And to do that, Advent has to pay for human caretakers.

You passed the screening process, particularly because they're interested in a variety of types of caretakers.

"It immerses units in a full scope of experiences, which makes our product lines more randomized, encompassing a wide range of interactions with people from different walks of life. Our robots pass that knowledge around, and it gives them a service-oriented edge."

Raise a robot that works well and makes it through job training, you get rewarded.

"Once we have a functioning unit, then we can copy and paste it," the scientist grins. "We have 2,000 different models and personalities you can interact with, now, for a variety of workplace functions."

At the park you teach Rob to throw a baseball. It's good for coordination.

"Dad, you're breathing heavy," he says as you walk back toward the apartments.

"It's just been hard. I've been inside for three months taking care of you. I haven't been doing my physical therapy."

"I know. You keep saying I was such a hard baby to take care of." Rob rolls his laser-red eyes dramatically.

You *are* struggling. You need to make sure to take the time and get outside for walks more. That quarry lake was the big target, wasn't it? You never did get there. It feels like your whole life has just been the apartment or the yard for so long.

Charlie hasn't called in a while. You saw online that he's won a prize for the art he worked on with the collective he's now joined. The sculpture is in a park near the courthouse. It looks like rusted iron spikes shaped like lightning bolts hitting the concrete pad it's bolted onto.

You tell Rob about that. He never really replies, just listens and asks simple questions. He's past the constant "why?" stage. That was last month, and it was hell. You've been chattering to him nonstop, now.

The pediabotic experts told you to keep doing that, so you tell yourself you're doing it to be the best caretaker you can.

You fall to your knees on the sidewalk halfway back to the apartment.

"Dad!" Rob is scared. He triggers an automated call for medical help, his body strobes emergency blue as he shouts at the people around you to come help. But seeing a nervous robot scares them, and they stay away from you both, not sure what's happening. "Dad!"

It's your heart. You can tell from the pain in your chest.

You're not out of breath. You're out of oxygen.

"He hasn't left your side," the nurse says when you wake up after surgery.

Rob squeezes your hand.

It hurts to sit up, to cough. They've split you in half and pulled out your heart, fixed it as best they could, and put it back in.

"Dad, I was so scared."

And you hug him, because that's what he seems to need. A robot can't cry, but it can be worried. Scared to lose the one person it's known since it was born.

"It's OK. Everything is OK."

Rob helps you home, and pitches in with some of the chores. Rob's like an older kid now, able to do basic things around the house in a pinch.

As you recover, the two of you start working on some home renovation. Holes in the wall from the first few days of Rob showing up. A new coffee table becomes a father-son project.

Your own father took weeks to get jogging again after his heart transplant. You just need a few days.

Progress.

"What was your father like?" Rob asks as you scrape wood with a lathe.

"Dangerous," you say. "He was a dangerous man. Particularly with a few drinks in him."

You tell him about the door your father threw at you and how it clipped your forehead. It bled for hours. You tell him about the time the cop showed up to your door, and your mom stood in front of you and smiled and flirted until he was satisfied nothing was wrong and walked off.

The longest moment of your life, watching the man in that uniform walk away into the night.

At least, until the moment that forklift pinned you to the concrete floor.

Every breath an infinity, every pulse a universe of pain as you faded slowly away.

"I tell him too much," you say to the Advent rep at the weekly checkup call.

"There's no such thing." He's gone over the logs, asked about Rob's behavior, the usual questions about how well Rob is integrating into life at the apartment. You've asked questions about whether assuming Rob was male made any sense because he's a robot. Robot self-identity is complex, they say, but they're talking to Rob, and he's OK with the label for now. There's a documentary on robot identity and human interactions you can watch if you need. "The conversation is good for their development."

"I've talked to Rob about things I haven't told anyone else."

The rep nods. "We find this common with men in particular. Your records say you've been through trauma, and you were raised without cognitive behavioral therapy to help you. I'll bet you were told as a boy not to cry, to hold those emotions in, right?"

He looks up at you.

The direct eye contact makes you swallow. "Uh, sure."

"Real men don't cry. Real men don't follow safety guidelines. They show strength. Willpower gets you through everything, right, no matter how hard? The fight's the thing." The rep is taking notes. "And that does work, until it doesn't. You can't fight your way out of trauma, or out of a worldwide economic depression. And then your whole mental model fails to match the world around you."

You remember how much worse it got when your father lost his job. His identity. He couldn't will a new job into existence when there were none.

You wonder what he'd call his son, living on disability, raising a robot like a bizarre Mary Poppins.

"There's a reason getting a dog, or some other living thing, can by extremely therapeutic," he continues.

"You're comparing having a child to getting a dog?" You're a little shocked, maybe outraged.

"Not at all, I have a kid, it's not the same," the rep says in a reassuring tone. "But the act of raising something isn't just about what you raise and take care of. It's about how you change yourself around the space they need within you, as well. You'll have emotions and vulnerability during that process. We talked about this during intake."

Yes, you remember that detail from the parenting class you had to take with Advent. The fostering program comes with free therapy, but you turned it down. You're tough. You're the dude who got trapped under a tipped-over forklift and gritted your teeth and got through it.

Everyone's complimented you on how strong you were to survive that, how tough you were to get through everything that came afterward.

How many times were you thanked for your service after doing a full tour?

You knew that you could do six months of parenting. You were tough enough. Even despite the day of misgivings right before Rob arrived.

But now you're wondering if you're tough enough to handle what comes after Rob leaves.

Rob throws a pamphlet at you. It rustles through the air, then softly lands against your chest, just as he planned. "What is that crap?"

"It's the medical clinic I'll be going to," you say. "I've been talking about this forever."

They could take your DNA and grow a new heart for you in a nutrient bath. They can regrow whole legs and arms.

"Have you ever thought about how I feel?" Rob shouts. "Do you even think about anyone else besides yourself?"

You're confused as hell. "What does this have to do with you?"

"You're a whole person, Dad!" Rob hits the countertop. Hard enough to make a point, make you jump, but not hard enough to break anything.

"What?"

"You're fine just the way you are." Emotion crackles in Rob's voice. It's a warble that flashes you back to that first moment he staggered around the apartment, crying in that electronic voice of his. "Not wanting artificial limbs—how the hell do you think that makes *all of me* feel?"

He holds up his arms in front of his face, and you look down at the one arm of yours that looks just like his.

"Rob—"

You're stunned at the argument that explodes between you. He's been holding things in. Things you do that anger him. No, that *hurt* him.

Trying to decide if regrowing limbs is somehow an admission that you aren't whole—that's been *your* struggle. Not his.

But clearly, Rob feels that this is his universe as well. You can no longer make choices just about yourself. They have to include him as well. He even hates his own name.

"I panicked!" you say, as he tells you people laugh at "Rob the Robot."

"My whole life, you've talked about walking to that quarry, Dad. You can't wait until you have just the right leg to go do that. It hurts when you use me as an excuse to avoid things."

Rob helps you over the last few boulders to get to the quarry's edge and then you both sit and look out over the mossy rocks near the edge to the brownish, silty water.

It's one of your favorite walks now.

The human body is a thing of constant change. Your skin is made out of cells that were just food a few weeks ago. You're a ghost of an idea that keeps getting passed on down through cell instructions.

You're not a mind in a jar. You're an ecosystem, a community of cells and organisms with a theory of mind bolted onto them. And they're all involved in a complicated dance that keeps the complexity going until that system of passing on instructions gets disrupted after too many copies and it all falters.

You think: We're often so scared of how we'll be different if we take medicine for our minds, or go to therapy, or make a major life change. How can we be the same person if we change so much over time?

The physical therapy hurt. It was a real pain in the ass after you'd taken so much time off. You threw up the first time you got back to the gym.

But Rob was there every day, proud as could be.

And you started taking walks together. It's his favorite thing to do with you. Walk and talk about life, whatever comes to your two minds. Rob has odd taste in TV and has even taken up reading. Mostly nonfiction, but he has some interest in mystery novels.

You have some plans to take a trip and hike a small part of the Appalachian Trail next year, when he gets some vacation after his first year of work.

That's something you've been terrified of. You'd never thought much about robot rights when you agreed to bring this person into the world. But there have been big advances in how the world treats robots, particularly since robot strikes out west forced people to realize that if you had to raise them to be complete minds, enslavement was horrific. Rob will have free will. He will make less than a human would—there's still a metal ceiling to break through—but he'll get vacations, pay, while he does jobs that would be tough for organic people. Deep-sea diving is what he chose.

Most importantly, you'll get to see him.

Because you never just stop being a parent.

"I want to give you something," you say. You hand him over the watch your grandfather gave you when you left for college.

"You know I can tell time internally, right, Dad? Do we need to get you another checkup?"

"It's—"

"I know what it is." Rob puts it on, metal against metal. "Thank you."

When it's time to leave, he asks several times if you're OK to walk back to the apartment alone.

"I'm OK," you reassure him.

He slings a duffel bag with everything he owns over his shoulder and heads out.

Charlie's at the door to the complex when you get back.

"So you got your freedom back!" He waves a six-pack at you, then does a double take when you raise your arm to wave back. "What the hell?"

"Oh." You look at the arm. It's all burnished metal, then scrimshawed with Rob's art. You two spent days building the custom arm together, thanks to Rob taking high-end robotics maintenance classes during his charging cycles.

The leg is even more customized. An object of expression and a personal statement by the both of you. And now that you're out of physical therapy, the upgraded artificial limbs are kicked up and finely tuned, thanks to Rob tinkering with your neural interface.

"It was set up for a standard off-the-line synapse reading," he'd explained while tinkering, making you twitch every time he played with the settings. "Now that you're getting better at timing and control, I can help you more."

A week ago, you went to a tattoo artist and got a sleeve of three-dimensional gears and diesel engine pistons on your other bicep to make the organic match the inorganic.

People at the park stare at you. Sometimes mothers pull their kids back, in instinct.

For a second you're worried that Charlie's going to do something similar, but he looks closely at it. "That's fucking sweet, man! I love the engine details!"

"They're based on some of the equipment that Rob will be using. Come on in."

You put your organic arm around Charlie's shoulder and pull him along. You've invited him over to ask him about his art, to see how things are going for him in his new career as a sculptor.

There's better beer in the fridge.

After Charlie leaves, you lie in bed and look at a picture of you and Rob standing by the quarry with big smiles.

You put a hand to your chest. Under it is a new scar since a second heart surgery. A fresher scar. Under it is a cybernetic heart, a mechanical pump that whirs softly underneath. *Faster, better, stronger.*

When you look at the picture of your son, who has just left a home that now feels empty without him in it, that heart surges with love.

ANCESTRIES

by Sheree Renée Thomas

In the beginning were the ancestors, gods of earth who breathed the air and walked in flesh. Their backs were straight and their temples tall. We carved the ancestors from the scented wood, before the fire and the poison water took them, too. We rubbed ebony-stained oil on their braided hair and placed them on the altars with the first harvest, the nuts and the fresh fruit. None would eat before the ancestors were fed, for it was through their blood and toil we emerged from the dark sea to be.

But that was then, and this is now, and we are another tale.

It begins as all stories must, with an ending. My story begins when my world ended, the day my sister shoved me into the ancestors' altar. That morning, one sun before Oma Day, my bare heels slipped in bright gold and orange paste. *Sorcadia* blossoms lay flattened, their juicy red centers already drying on the ground. The air in my lungs disappeared. Struggling to breathe, I pressed my palm over the spoiled flowers, as if I could hide the damage. Before Yera could cover her smile, the younger children came.

"Fele, Fele," they cried and backed away, "the ancient ones will claim you!" Their voices were filled with derision, but their eyes held something else, something close to fear.

"Claim her?" Yera threw her head back, the fishtail braid snaking down the hollow of her back, a dark slick eel. "She is not worthy," she said to the children, and turned her eyes on them. They scattered like chickens. Shrill laughter made the sorcadia plants dance. A dark witness, the fat purple vines and shoots twisted and undulated above me. I bowed my head. Even the plants took part in my shame.

"And I don't need you, shadow," Yera said, turning to me, her face a brighter, crooked reflection of my own. "You are just a spare." A spare.

Only a few breaths older than me, Yera, my twin, has hated me since before birth.

Our oma says even in the womb, my sister fought me, that our mother's labors were so long because Yera held me fast, her tiny fingers clasped around my throat, as if to stop the breath I had yet to take. The origin of her disdain is a mystery, a blessing unrevealed. All I know is that when I was born, Yera gave me a kick before she was pushed out of our mother's womb, a kick so strong it left an impression, a mark, like a bright shining star in the middle of my chest.

This star, the symbol of my mother's love and my sister's hate, is another way my story ended.

I am told that I refused to follow, that I lay inside my mother, after her waters spilled, after my sister abandoned me, gasping like a small fish, gasping for breath. That in her delirium my mother sang to me, calling, begging me to make the journey on, that she made promises to the old gods, to the ancestors who once walked our land, to those of the deep, promises that a mother should never make.

"You were the *bebe* one, head so shiny, slick like a ripe green seed," our oma would say.

"Ripe," Yera echoed, her voice sweet for Oma, sweet as the sorcadia tree's fruit, but her mouth was crooked, slanting at me. Yera had as many faces as the ancestors that once walked our land, but none she hated more than mine.

While I slept, Yera took the spines our oma collected from the popper fish and sharpened them, pushed the spines deep into the star in my chest. I'd wake to scream, but the paralysis would take hold, and I would lie in my pallet, seeing, knowing, feeling, but unable to fight or defend.

When we were *lardah*, and I had done something to displease her—rise awake, breathe, talk, stand—Yera would dig her nails into my right shoulder and hiss in my ear. "Shadow, spare. Thief of life.

You are the reason we have no mother." It was my sister's favorite way to steal my joy.

And then, when she saw my face cloud, as the sky before rain, she would take me into her arms and stroke me. "There, my sister, my second, my own broken one," she would coo. "When I descend, you can have mother's comb, and put it in your own hair. Remember me," she would whisper in my ear, her breath soft and warm as any lover. "Remember me," and then she would stick her tongue inside my ear and pinch me until I screamed.

Our oma tried to protect me, but her loyalty was like the *suwa* wind, inconstant, mercurial. Oma only saw what she wanted. Older age and even older love made her forget the rest.

"Come!" I could hear the drumbeat echo of her clapping hands. "Yera, Fele," she sang, her tongue adding more syllables to our names, Yera, Fele, the words for one and two. The high pitch meant it was time to braid Oma's hair. The multiversal loops meant she wanted the complex spiral pattern. Three hours of labor, if my hands did not cramp first, maybe less if Yera was feeling industrious.

With our oma calling us back home, I wiped my palms on the inside of my thighs and ignored the stares. My sister did not reach back to help me. A crowd had gathered, pointing but silent. No words were needed here. The lines in their faces said it all. I trudged behind Yera's tall, straight back, my eyes focused on the fishtail's tip.

"They should have buried you with the afterbirth."

When we reached the courtyard, my basket empty, Yera's full as she intended, we found our oma resting in her battered rocker in the yard. She had untied the wrap from her head. Her edges spiked around her full moon forehead, black tendrils reaching for the sun. She smiled as Yera revealed the spices and herbs she collected. I pressed fresh moons into my palms and bit my lip. No words were needed here. As usual, our oma had eyes that did not see. She waved away my half empty basket, cast her eyes sadly away from the fresh bloody marks on my shoulder, and pointed to her scalp instead.

"Fele, I am feeling festive today, bold." She stared at a group of *baji* yellow-tailed birds pecking at the crushed roots and dried leaves scattered on the ground. They too would be burned and offered tomorrow night, at Yera's descension. And we would feast on the fruits of the land, as my sister descended into the sea.

"I need a style fitting for one who is an oma of a goddess. My beauty."

"A queen!" Yera cried, returning from our *bafa*. She flicked the fishtail and raised her palms to the sky. "An ancestress, joining the deep."

Yera had been joining the deep since we were small girls. She never let me forget it.

"Come, Fele," she said, "you take the left," as if I did not know. Yera held the carved wooden comb of our mother like a machete, her gaze as sharp and deadly. Her eyes dared me to argue. She knew that I would not.

Together we stood like sentinels, each flanking Oma's side. The creamy gel from the fragrant sorcadian butter glistened on the backs of our hands. I placed a small bowl of the blue-shelled sea snails, an ointment said to grow hair thick and wild as the deepest weed of the sea. Yera gently parted our oma's scalp, careful not to dig the wooden teeth in. Before I learned to braid my own hair, Yera had tortured me as a child, digging the teeth into the tender flesh of my scalp. Now her fingers moved in a blur, making the part in one deft move. A dollop of gel dripped onto her wrists. She looked as if she wore blue-stained bracelets—or chains.

I gathered our oma's thick roots, streaked with white and the ashen gray she refused to dye, saying she had earned every strand of it.

"This is a special time, an auspicious occasion. It is not every year that Oma Day falls on the Night of Descension. The moon will fill the sky and light our world as bright as in the day of the gods."

I massaged scented oils into the fine roots of her scalp, brushed my fingertips along the nape of her neck. I loved to comb our oma's hair. The strands felt like silk from the spider tree, cotton from the prickly bushes. Oma said in the time before, our ancestors used to have enough fire to light the sky, that it burned all morning, evening, and the night, from a power they once called electricity. I love how that name feels inside my head—*e-lec-tri-city*. It sounds like one of our oma's healing spells, the prayers she sends up with incense and flame.

Once when Yera and I were very small, we ran too far inside the ancestors' old walled temples. Before we were forbidden, we used to scavenge there. We climbed atop the dusty, rusted carcasses of metal beasts. We ducked under rebar, concrete giants jutting from the earth, skipped over faded signage. We scuttled through the scraps of the metal yard at the edge of green, where the land took back what the old gods had claimed. I claimed something, too, my reflection in the temple called Family Dollar, a toy that looked like me. Her hair was braided in my same simple box pattern, the eyes were black and glossy. She wore a faded skirt, the pattern long gone. When I flipped her over, to my surprise, I discovered another body where the hips and legs should be. The skirt concealed one body when the other was upright. Two bodies, two heads, but only one could be played with at a time. I tried to hide my find from Yera, but she could see contentment on my face. So I ran. I ran to the broken, tumble-down buildings with blown-out windows that looked like great gaping mouths. I ran into the mouth of darkness, clutching my doll, but when I closed my eyes, searching for the light, Yera was waiting on the other side.

That is when I knew I could never escape her. My sister is always with me.

Before the Descension, our people once lived in a land of great sweeping black and green fields, land filled with thick-limbed, tall trees and flowing rivers of cool waters, some sweet and clear, others dark as the rich, black soil. Our oma says when our ancestors could no longer live on the land, when the poisons had reached the bottom of every man, woman, and child's cup, they journeyed on foot and walked back into the sea, back to the place of the old gods, the deep ones.

But before they left, they lifted their hands and made a promise. That if the land could someday heal from its long scars, the wounds that people inflicted, that they would return again. In the meanwhile, one among us, one strong and true, must willingly descend into the depths to join the ancestors. This one, our people's first true harvest, will know from the signs and symbols, the transformations that only come from the blessing of the ancestors, when the stars in the sky above align themselves just so. Yera is that first harvest. She has wanted this honor her whole life. And from her birth, the signs were clear. Her lungs have grown strong, her limbs straight and tall, she does not bend and curve like the rest of us. My sister has the old gods' favor and when Oma Day ends and the Descension is complete, she will join the waters, and rule them as she once ruled the waters of our mother's womb, she will enter them and be reborn as an ancestress.

The ceremony has not yet begun and I am already tired. I am tired, because I spend much of my time and energy devoted to breathing. For me, to live each day is a conscious act, an exercise of will, mind over my broken body's matter. I must imagine a future with every breath, consciously exhaling, expelling the poison because my brain thinks I need more air, and signals my body to produce light, even though my lungs are weak and filled with the ash of the old gods. Unable to filter the poison quickly, my body panics and it thinks I am dying. My knees lock, and I pull them up to my chest and hold myself, gasping for breath like our oma said I did, waiting in my mother's womb.

Oma gives me herbs. She grinds them up, mortar and pestle in her conch shell, and mixes them in my food. When I was smaller, she made me recite the ingredients daily, a song she hummed to lull me asleep. But as I grew, the herbs worked less and less, and my sister did things to them, things that made me finally give them up. I have given so much to her these years.

And I have created many different ways to breathe.

I breathe through my tongue, letting the pink buds taste the songs in the air. I breathe through the fine hairs on the ridge of my curved back and my arms, the misshapen ones she calls claws. I breathe through the dark pores of my skin. And when I am alone, and out of my oma's earshot, out of my wretched sister's reach, I breathe through my mouth, unfiltered and free. My fingers searching the most hidden, soft parts of myself and I am *light air star shine, light air star shine, light—*

In the suns before Oma Day, I spent a lot of time sleeping. My breathing tends to be easier if I sleep well, and so I slept. My lungs are filled with poison, which means there's no space for the light, the good clean air. I have many different ways to expel the poison, and meanwhile my body goes into panic because my mind thinks I'm dying, so between controlling the exhalation, telling my mind that I am not dying, inhaling our oma's herbs through her conch shell, I am exhausted since I do this many times a day. And then there is Yera. Always my sister, Yera. I must watch for her. I know my sister's movements more than I know myself.

This night, on the eve of Oma Day, which is to say, the eve of my sister's descension, I can feel Yera smile, even in the dark. It is that way with sisters. As a child I did not fear the night. How could I? My sister's voice filled it. Outside, the *baji* birds gathered in the high tops of our oma's trees. Their wings sounded like the great wind whistling through what was left of the ancestors' stone-wall towers. They chattered and squawked in waves as hypnotic as the ocean itself, their excitement mirroring our own. And I too was excited, my mind filled with questions and a few hopes I dared not even share with myself. Would I still exist without my sister? Can there be one without two?

As more stars add their light to the darkness, I turn in my bed, over and over again like the gold beetles burrowing in our oma's soil. I turned, my mind restless while Yera slept the sleep of the ages. For me, sleep never comes. So I sit in the dark, braiding and unbraiding my hair, and wait for the day to come when my world would end again, or perhaps when it might begin.

The past few days I've been aware that braiding makes me short of breath, and I realized that I am very, very tired. Last night I was going through my patterns, braiding and unbraiding them in my head, overhand and underhand, when I remembered what the elder had once said to our oma. That she had done a lot in her life, that she, already an honored mother, had raised *felanga* on her own, and it was all right if she rested now. And I thought that maybe that was true for me, the resting part, which is perhaps why today I feel changed.

"Hurry, child. Hunger is on me."

Our oma calls but even she is too nervous to eat. Her hair is a wonder, a sculpture that rises from her head like two great entwined serpents holding our world together. My scalp is sore. My hands still ache in the center of my palms, and I am concentrating harder now to breathe. I rub the palm flesh of my left hand, massaging the pain in a slow ring of circles.

Yera has not joined us yet. She refused my offer to help braid her hair. "You think I want your broken hand in my head? You know your hands don't work," she said. I remember only once receiving praise from her for my handiwork. I had struggled long, my fingers cramped, my temple pulsing. I braided her hair into a series of intricate loops, twisting off her shining scalp like lush sorcadia blooms. Yera did not speak her praise. Vocal with anger, she was silent with approval. Impressed, Yera tapped her upper teeth with her thumb. Oma, big-spirited as she was big-legged, ran to me. She lifted my aching hands high into the air as if the old gods could see them.

Now dressed in nothing more than a wrap, Yera's full breasts exposed, nipples like dark moons, her mouth is all teeth and venom. "You have always been jealous of me."

"Jealous?" I say and turn the word over in my mouth. It is sour and I don't like its taste. I spit it out like a rotten sorcadian seed.

She turns, her thick brows high on her smooth, shining forehead. "Oh, so you speak now. Your tongue has found its roots on the day of my descension?"

Inside, my spirit folds on itself. It turns over and over again and gasps for air, but outside, I hold firm. "Why should I feel jealous? You are my sister, and I am yours. Your glory is my glory."

I wait. Her eyes study me coolly, narrow into bright slits. The scabs on my shoulder feel tight and itchy. After a moment, she turns again, her hands a fine blur atop her head. She signals assent with a flick of her wrist. Braiding and braiding, overhand, underhand, the pattern is intricate.

I have never seen Yera so shiny.

I take a strip of brightly stained cloth and hand it to her. She weaves it expertly into the starfish pattern. Concentric circles dot the crown of her head. Each branch of her dark, thick hair is adorned with a sorcadian blossom. We have not even reached the water and she already looks like an ancestor.

"Supreme," I whisper. But no words are needed here. I pick up the bowl of sea-snail ointment and dip my fingertips into the glistening blue gel. My stained fingers trail the air lightly.

"Mother's comb," Yera says and bows her head. "You may have mother's comb. I won't be needing it anymore."

I smile, something close to pleasure, something close to pain. My fingertips feel soft and warm on her neck. They tingle and then they go numb.

Yera's mouth gapes open and closed, like a *bebe*, a flat shiny fish. Her pink tongue blossoms, juicy as a sorcadian center. Red lines spiral out from her pupils, crimson starfish.

"Sister, spare me," I say. "Love is not a word that fits in your mouth."

The sorcadia tree is said to save souls. Its branches helped provide shelter and firewood. Its fruit, healing sustenance. Its juicy blossoms with their juicy centers help feed and please the old gods. To have a belly full and an eye full of sweet color is not the worst life. As I leave our oma's house, the wind rustles and the sorcadia in Oma's yard groans as if it is a witness. I gaze at the sorcadia whose branches reach for me as if to pull me back into the house. Even the trees know my crimes.

Silver stretches over the surface of the sand. Water mingles with moonlight, and from a distance it looks like an incomplete rainbow. Our oma says this is a special moon, the color of blood, a sign from the ancestors. The moon is the ultimate symbol of transformation. She pulls on the waters and she pulls on wombs. When we look at it we are seeing all of the sunrises and sunsets across our world, every beginning and every ending all at once. This idea comforts me as I spot our oma in the distance. I follow the silver light, my feet sinking in the sand as I join the solemn crowd waiting at the beach.

There are no words here, only sound. The rhythmic exhalations, inhalations of our people's singing fills the air, their overtones a great buzzing hum deep enough to rend the sky. Before I can stop myself, I am humming with them. The sound rises from a pit in my belly and vibrates from the back of my throat. It tumbles out of my dry mouth to join the others around me. Beneath my soles the earth rumbles. That night my people sang as if the whole earth would open up beneath us.

We sang as if the future rested in our throats. The songs pull me out of myself. I am inside and out all at once. As my sister walks to stand at the edge of the waters, I feel as if I might fly away, as if every breath I had ever taken is lifting me up now.

A strong descension assures that straight-backed, strong-limbed children will be born from our mothers' wombs, that green, grasping roots will rise from the dead husks of trees to seed a future. The others dance around this vision. When one descends, all are born. When one returns, all return. Each bloodline lives, and with it, their memory, and we are received by our kin.

Music rises from the waves, echoes out across the sand, a keening. The elders raise their voices, the sound of their prayers join. I walk past them, my hair a tight interlocked monument to skill, to pain. The same children who laughed in my face and taunted me are silent now. Only the wind, the elders' voices, and the sound of the waters rise up ahead to greet me. The entire village watches.

Oma waits with her back to me, in the carved wooden chair they have carried out to face the waters. When I stand beside her, her fingertips brush the marks on my shoulder. Her touch stings. The wounds have not all scabbed over yet. She turns and clasps my hands, her eyes searching for answers hidden in my face.

"Fele, why, why do you do such things?"

Our oma's unseeing eyes search, but I can find no answer that would please her.

"Yera," I begin but her *tsk*, the sharp air sucking between her teeth, cuts me off.

"No," she says, shaking her head, "not Yera. You, Fele, it is you."

They think I don't hear them, here under the water, that I don't know what they are doing, from here in the sea. But I do.

I wanted Yera to fight back, to curse me, to make me forget even the sound of my own name. I am unaccustomed to this Yera. This silent, still one.

"Fele!" they call. "She has always been touched." "I told her oma, but she refused to listen." "One head here with the living, the other with the dead." "Should have never named her. To tell a child she killed her sister, her mother. What a terrible curse."

They whisper harsh words sharp enough to cut through bone. But no words are needed here. I have withstood assault all these years, since before birth. This last attack is borne away by the ocean's tears. They say my Yera does not exist. That she died when our mother bore us, that I should have died, too. But that was then and this is now and we are another tale.

It does not matter if she is on land or that I am in the sea.

We are sisters. We share the same sky.

Though some spells, when the moon is high and the tide is low, and my body flinches, panics because it thinks it is dying, I journey inland, to where the ancestors once walked in flesh, the ones we carved into wood. I journey inward, and I can smell the scent of sorcadians in bloom, the pungent scent of overripe fruit, and feel my sister's fingers pressed around my throat, daring me to breathe.

Tiny *bebe* dart and nibble around my brow. They swim around the circles in my hair and sing me songs of new suns here in the blueblack waters. Now I am the straight and the curved, our past and our future. Here in the water, I dwell with the ancient ones, in the space where all our lives begin, and my story ends as all stories must, a new beginning.

BREATH OF THE SAHARA

by Inegbenoise O. Osagie

Today was Sabbath, but my brother had to take the mare on some excuse that he needed to run to the mines before heading for the temple. This was enough reason for me to miss worship with no compunction. The temple was at the heart of our large village; after a horseless walk in the biting cold, I'd be too weary to mumble a prayer. But missing worship by myself, staying alone in my cabin, my ears would ring until I'd find myself rambling round the room trying to shut one side of my heart to the other.

Even if all the villagers congregated at the temple, there was one person who would guiltlessly remain tethered to her bed—Esohe Okhah. If one needed a tangible rationale to miss the temple, other than the weightless indisposition to stand for a lifetime in a vast rotunda, Esohe could coin out a hundred. Her family's cabin was only a few walks away. Whiling away the time with her would make the hours whirl out faster.

Outside, the villagers all headed north, families striding together or on trotting horses, some with eyes yet bordered by sleep vestiges. It was still early dawn, the kind with the cleanest air, before the poised harmattan dusts would begin swirling. I meandered between horses, half-hoping no good-natured faithful would offer to transport me. I dodged faces, focused on the flanks of horses.

Close to the Okhahs', I saw Nata, Esohe's father, riding his old mule. I quickly dropped my eyes. If I looked straight up, I was sure to find his eyes piercing me—the girl who was luring his daughter away from the divine tenets. (If I too had a father, he would have thought the same of Esohe.) Yet, I was relieved knowing I wouldn't be encountering him at the house and enduring the monologue of how errant today's youngsters had become.

Esohe was a morning sleeper who had seen the first white clouds fewer times than a cock had crouched to pee. I whistled at her window, loud enough to eclipse the shrill of the larks and penetrate the cedary window. Footsteps loomed from the other side of the cabin. She emerged, holding a chewing stick and cup, dressed in her cottony cloak.

"I thought you said you'd be going to the temple," she said.

"Mudia had to take the horse."

Seeing Esohe dressed on a Sabbath morning was rare. But I did not want to make a fuss of it, especially since she was already acting like it was a habit.

"You're going to worship?"

"It's been a long time," she said.

"We'll ride together then."

"You can ride her alone." She gestured at her mare in the shack, whose neck was stretched up toward the teasing leaves of a crooked coconut tree. "I'll go on foot."

"Foot?"

"You'll be faster riding alone." She laced and unlaced her fingers. "It's already late."

She started to say something but stopped. She was fumbling for words; it was not hard to see.

"You dressed up to deceive your father," I said. "You have no intentions of going to the temple."

The contrived cheer from her face waned out. She knew I could perceive that something was off. We'd done things together for eons.

"I'll tell you the truth," she said. "I've made plans to visit the sanctum today. Now is the best time, it's first Sabbath, the sanctum will be empty."

Visit. That was our code word, but we *visited* only at nights.

Before she said it, I had sensed it. Lately, she had been rambling about the sanctum of the Order of Zephyrs; would poke it in the face of an unrelated discussion. I had been waiting for her to build the courage to voice it, only I never expected she'd schedule a *visit* to the sanctum on a Sabbath. But thinking about it now, no other day than today could be better.

"What if we have the same intentions?" I leaned against the hardwood wall of the cabin.

"I'm going to the sanctum to seek more knowledge of the pantheons. You're least interested in that." She began walking toward her horse's shack. "We could ride together. You'll dismount at the temple." She untethered the mare.

I was tempted to burst out, shout at her, hit her on the head and remind her of how she'd be useless without me. Esohe was a deft thief, but without me, she wouldn't last a heartbeat before being seized by one of the sentries. "I know the inner sanctum of the Zephyrs is adorned with gold. If you dare to steal alone, I guarantee you'll be seated in the prisons by dusk."

"I have no intentions of looting!" She was frowning at me. "I never knew the sanctum has gold."

I decided to return home. I rose without sparing her a look.

After I'd walked a short distance, her voice sprang forth behind me. "Alright, Obehi, please come back, we go together."

I was still chafed that she could think of venturing without me, and I made sure she saw it on my face.

"You've thought about this?" I asked. "What's your plan? How do we get past the lock?"

She reached into her boot and slipped out a roped key. "I'm a thief." She smiled. "We enter, grab, and dash out."

The Order of Zephyrs were our link to the gods. They were the closest to the gods. Stealing from them might have divine consequences.

Esohe must have sensed my thoughts, because she said, "The Order do not care a tad about gold."

She was the most avid and informed pantheon scholar I knew of, spent most of the night fixed on her papers. If she affirmed that the Order couldn't care less about gold, robbing them was a reasonable risk. A handful of such pure nuggets could make a person rich enough to say no to an extra penny for the next ten years.

...❖...

The streets were almost empty, with a few youngsters loitering, and some senile faithfuls slowly riding their old horses to the temple. I imagined some of these faithfuls grimacing at us. Esohe didn't have the best reputation in the village. "Money thief," some persons have named her, and of course, some of the reputation must be rubbing off on me, but having a marred reputation was better than being a penniless saint hounded by the tax collectors.

I'd known Esohe since before we could walk, from those evenings when children convened in circles at the moonlit square to listen to folktales. She was a story lover, especially those stories related to the pantheons, the Order of Zephyrs, or pilgrimages to the Sahara, but she was also a known irritating pedant; even as a child, she intruded in the storytelling to uncourteously correct any factual flaw in the tale. She had grown to be a savant in matters of the pantheons—which might have made her overfamiliar enough with the gods to breed a little impiety—and would have been a great story weaver, but no parent would allow their child sit near a *notoriety* like her.

We slowed to a walk when riding past the temple to avoid causing a distraction (doing that would give the guards a reason to stop us and ask questions), and we heard the faint mumblings of the faithful villagers. The early sun spilled over the dome of the enormous temple, whose spire glistened softly.

We trotted into the third quarter of the village, so empty and quiet it hummed; clean streets and green air, perfect alleys between uniformly separated buildings: the relics store, cabins inhabited by the households of the sanctum keepers, temple marshals, holy faithfuls who had never missed a prayer in their lifetime. We trotted past the village court, hedged by towering squirrel-nested trees rustling in the gentle breeze. The air became serener as we approached the sanctum, its dome gleaming like varnished porcelain. As we rode nearer, my chest tightened, and I willfully shoved away the fear, but I kept my ears open for the slightest uncharacteristic noise. Esohe, as always, continued riding resolutely, and I comforted myself with some of her boldness.

We stopped, tethered the mare to a nearby palm tree, and scanned around us. When certain no eyes were on us, we circled the sanctum to arrive at its entrance. Esohe fetched the key from her boot and slotted it into the lock, pushed the door open to an unending line of downward-sloping stairs. Any attempt to peer to its end and I might topple over. We climbed down side by side, the air growing damper and dimmer with every step, my legs growing wearier. Faint echoes of our steps began to reverberate from the round walls.

Hung on the walls were stingy lanterns that shed their light on a small sphere, barely illuminating the etched glyphs on the wall. After the stairs was an underlit narrow passageway, sidewalls lined with alcoves that contained reliquaries. Stealing relics would be unwise, as an attempt to sell them could raise suspicion, and they weren't even gold. The gold adornments, I supposed, were in the innermost sanctum. I remained expectant as we journeyed the passageway. We might be a hundred feet below the surface.

"Where is the gold?" Esohe asked when we were out of the passageway into a less sweaty space. In the encompassing quiet, I heard faint steps shuffling from behind. I froze. The steps didn't continue, but it wasn't a trick of the ears. I waited for a voice, closed my eyes, tried to breathe, waited for the next steps. The quiet lingered and the steps didn't come. I turned to look.

It was no keeper, no sentry, not anyone I would have guessed in a thousand trials. Standing there was a Zephyr, shrunk like the hind legs of a sickly calf, floury skin clothed with silk, tiny bristly hair on its head. Today was the first Sabbath of the month; all the Zephyrs were supposed to be in the temple. I was engulfed with a different kind of fear. I bowed slightly and was not sure why, reverence or shame.

With tilted head, the Zephyr looked at us giants, its petite eyes barely reaching our waists. Around the creature's narrow neck, wrists, and ankles were rings of gold that managed to glitter in the dim. Esohe remained still, staring.

When trouble comes, don't give it a chair. The Zephyr probably had not gotten a good look at us; now was the time to dart out. I reached to touch Esohe's stiff hands. She, too, was staring, entranced, with head tilted as the Zephyr's.

"Let's leave," I said.

She remained stiff, not seeming ready to flee. I started to walk past but halted at her voice.

"We came hoping to see the sacred relics," she said to the Zephyr. "And to pray," she added as an afterthought.

Esohe might be daring enough, but I wasn't getting hanged with her. "I'm leaving, and you should too." I strode off while she remained there.

I paced back through the passageway, gathered my frock at my waist to hurry up the stairs, and when outside, I continued straight ahead, occasionally looking behind, hoping to see Esohe. The worship would be over soon, and the villagers would start pouring out of the temple. I continued walking until hooves and footsteps became audible and I was amid a handful of villagers before I turned and headed for my cabin, still hoping to bump into Esohe.

Esohe was a sage friend, I had never thought her otherwise, and though I had never deemed her wisdom infallible, I had also never thought it so lowly. Wisdom was also knowing which way to run when pursued by danger. I prayed she had recovered from her hesitation early enough to have hurried out before the keepers returned.

I didn't leave the cabin for the remainder of the day, didn't even head to the drying lake to refill the pails. I lounged on the chair at my porch and studied the face of every passerby, if they bore news of any abominable trespass, the kind so treacherous like a young thief caught in the sanctum on a Sabbath. The haunting ill-defined face of the Zephyr couldn't leave my mind. The Zephyr was supposed to have been in the temple. Zephyrs were wind lovers, even if the wind shrank them; breathed through their skin so that it became loosened enough that it turned floury. They only came to the surface and gratified their wind lust on first Sabbaths, at the temple. I stayed out on the porch till the orange sun became haloed by its lush shadows, hoping to see Esohe riding toward the cabin.

Before it became too dark to see, Mudia, my brother, trotted home in coal-stained clothes, holding by the tail a dangling rabbit he had found shackled in its cage. Far behind him was Esohe astride her mare, slowly riding.

Mudia, after tethering our horse at the yard, headed for the kitchen, howling that he was unbearably hungry and needed to grill the rabbit immediately.

Esohe had the same mien she bore after every other *visit*.

After she came inside the cabin, I said, "You could have landed us in trouble. Perhaps you have already." I tried not to yell at her. "Where have you been?"

"The only thing I landed us in is this." She upturned her goatskin bag, and gold and silvery utensils, bowls, spoons, cups, fell on the floor with a clatter. "I dug more after you left. I never knew of such gold; we should have raided there long ago."

I quickly shoved them back into the bag, looking behind to check if Mudia had come into the room. "Where did you find these? How?"

"I located the dining room. It happens our Zephyrs don't eat with mere earthenware."

"The Zephyr will report you to the keepers."

She waved a hand. "Oh, fear not." She cocked her head. "Aren't you happy?"

"I'm worried."

"Don't worry. This is all on me."

"Yes, of course. I'm worried about you."

She chuckled. "That's charming, but there's nothing to worry about. The Zephyr won't talk, nobody will notice, there's still a lot in there."

"This has to be buried and not unearthed until it's clear you're in no danger."

She shrugged.

I reminded myself of the day's events, her folly, what could have happened, what could still happen. "It's best we no more *visit* together," I said. "I've never been this close to death."

"Aren't you curious of what information I got from the Zephyr? We had a long talk."

"I'm not."

Esohe remained with us for dinner. I couldn't eat much of the bushmeat. Mudia had rushed the grilling and the meat was too sinewy for my teeth. He and Esohe munched most of it, chewing noisily, and for a moment the usual friction between them seemed to have dissolved (my brother had never liked Esohe and was strongly against our friendship). I gulped the most of the palm wine. After the meal, Mudia staggered to the bed and quickly started snoring.

Esohe requested I accompany her home.

We walked alongside while Esohe held her mare's rope, leading her. It was already dark, and Esohe had begun to ramble some things that made me conclude she was near drunk or sleepy or both. In this possibly drunken state, she was so intent on telling me of what information she learnt from the Zephyr, while my mind drifted to the loot at my cabin, imagining if it was possible for Mudia to awake and stagger to the high shelf where I had placed the bag. Merely seeing the bag could implicate him. Esohe had asked I keep it for the night; she could encounter her ever-suspicious father at home, who might try all means to see what was in the goatskin.

"Where did you find the sanctum's dining room?" I asked.

"I'll draw you a map tomorrow."

After a while, I said, "At least you got gold."

"I have no use of gold."

"Yes, just the money in it."

The streets were thick with flickering fireflies and a bit auburn from the few lambent torches tilted from the walls of stone cottages. Occasionally, we ambled past circles of children playing games that made them lace their ankles against each other's.

"Give my share to Mudia."

I stopped walking. "You said?"

"My share, give it to Mudia," she said. "Even if he doesn't like me."

"You—did you hear yourself? I mean you did all of the work."

"I don't need it. I was honest when I said I never knew the sanctum had gold. If you'd been listening to me, you'd know I have bigger worries than gold."

Her words prickled and unsettled me. "What are you saying?"

For a while she said nothing, her face solemn. She started to talk but stopped, and for a moment I feared it had something to do with the loot.

"I am like those of the Order."

If she had said this at another moment, I would have indulged her with a feigned laugh. But now, even though she was muttering gibberish, laughing might only worsen things. So I said, "Is that what the Zephyr told you? That you too are a Zephyr?"

"I went to the sanctum hoping to find a panacea that retarded the shrinking or assuaged the wind lust. I've known I'm a Zephyr for some years back. But only recently have I noticed my flesh and bones shrink under the gentle yet irresistible air. The Zephyr at the sanctum said I've reached the growth peak. I can now only shrink, and I will only last a few weeks if I don't vacate the surface and come dwell in the deep sanctum with them."

The Zephyrs came from the Sahara, sent by the gods to be an intermediary with us humans. I still expected her to burst into a laugh at her facetious joke of being a Zephyr. "You were birthed here. You have lived amongst us your whole life."

"Yes, I'm not from the Sahara. Not all possibilities are contained in the parchments. The Zephyrs come from lands far beyond the Sahara, where they are deemed abnormal and cast away. They find us in search of safe harbor."

There was no glimmer of cheer on her face.

"But you don't have the gifts of the Zephyrs," I said. "You can't foresee the rain, the storm, a good planting season."

"Obehi, I know the wind. I feel her, her movements. That's all required to foretell a good planting season."

We were almost at her cabin. "I don't know what—"

"You can't voice this to anyone. Not even Mudia."

I nodded, still trying to put my head together, still half-expecting her to break into a chortle at how she caught me. "But you were born here."

She nodded and exhaled loudly. I stopped walking and watched her stride to her cabin, leading her mare, and then I saw her silhouette, atrophied, shriveled, clearly noticeable despite her cloak.

That last image of her stayed with me the whole night. I rushed to her cabin the next morning. Nata, her father, was gratingly whetting his carpenter's knife at the porch and, on seeing me, did not bother to keep straightened brows to hide his resentment.

"I've come to return this." I showed Esohe's goatskin. I had buried the gold at my garden before dawn.

When I entered Esohe's room, she was still in her smock, pooled on her bed like liquid. Her breasts were almost flattened, no stomach bulge, brown skin already turning clayey. Everyone now would conclude her ill.

"Don't look at me like that," she said. "I'm neither cold nor sick." She grinned. "In a different circumstance, you'd be reverencing me. I don't need the pity."

"If you really are a Zephyr," I said, "you have to show yourself to the keepers. You need to move to the sanctum."

"I can't. Nobody can know of my shrinking. What I need to do now is leave the house before my father sees me." She rose and pulled on a tunic that was now twice her size.

"Your father may know what to do."

"My father is the most devoted faithful. If he knows his daughter is of the Order, he'll be disoriented. He will panic beyond reason, and in the end he'll feel obligated to reveal me."

I sat on the edge of the bed. "What do you intend to do?"

She stared at me for a while. "I do not know."

"I know of a place that may help, before you decide."

"Where?"

"There is a forgotten dried-up well beyond the grazing field. It's not nearly as deep or enclosed as the sanctum, but it can shut out some of the surface wind."

"A well?"

"It's a suggestion, that I hope makes you rethink and decide on the sanctum."

The gentle morning harmattan air had already started streaming through the wide-open windows, every draft a pernicious acid dissolving Esohe's skin, seeping through all her pores to wear out her bones, the flesh of her insides. She was already unbelievably thin. I imagined each outer layer flaying off.

I marched to the windows and shut them. "You're going to the sanctum! I'm telling your father!"

She pushed the windows open. "Please let me relish the air."

"You're shredding yourself apart."

She sat on the bed beside me and leaned against a bedpost. "The sanctum is not a lasting solution. I'll still fade out, albeit slower, until my last grain becomes one with the wind. Anyways, it is a comely place, houses a lot of writings that could occupy me till my eyes become too small. But have you ever thought of how the village would react on finding out the disreputable Esohe, infamous thief who was never caught in the act, is of the Order."

She glanced at me.

"I guess right now you're already thinking the Zephyrs are not that holy after all; it's all a sham, the worship, the gods. Imagine if everyone harbors such thought. It would only be a little while before they start to worry about the meagre tithe they offer to cater for the Zephyrs. There are not very many places where Zephyrs are accepted. Revealing myself would be disastrous to my kind."

"You don't know that. What is certain is, at this rate, you won't last a week."

She rose. "My father has ridden off. Why don't we start heading for this well. Before the streets become full. I don't want to be the spectacle of the village."

I could barely feel Esohe's presence beside me while we walked abreast. I tried to avoid faces so no concerned person would enquire if I was helping her to the sickhouse. We traipsed across the area of the field far away from where villagers grazed their horses. After, we continued into the vast uninhabited thickety grove, blades of sere grasses scraping our feet.

The well was not as deep as I had thought, wouldn't shut out enough of the wind's breath, and it was speckled with grass tufts on its wall and bottom. We stood at its edge, peering, and I supposed Esohe, too, was thinking of snakes. We wound a rope round a nearby stump and unfurled it into the well. And slowly we descended in.

Stooped at the bottom, uprooting the tufts, Esohe said, "I hope I don't die of a serpent's venom before I fade into nothingness."

"I hope you decide to live in the sanctum before either of those happens."

Esohe didn't ask, but I visited her in the well thrice a day, bringing food. She was shrinking at all sides, becoming misshapen, like a weathering termite mound, face receding into a lump, mouth tightening into a tiny pout, hair curling into distinct frills, and I could feel the powder of her skin, as though a mere stare could puff it off. Soon, she couldn't eat much; could barely finish a scone or cup of gruel and began to prefer only boiled plums.

"Are you just going to let yourself fade out?"

"Same way old people let themselves grow old."

"If you show yourself now, you can still save some days of your life."

"At the expense of invalidating the Zephyrs and those that will come after."

"Your father stopped by my house. He's worried."

She had begun to lose her voice. I was seated on the well's bottom, just beside her, yet her words eluded me. The lemon oil I had sprinkled in the well could scarcely dwarf the underlying stench. But Esohe said she could barely smell a whiff; she was gradually losing that too.

"My father will have to conclude me missing."

"It won't be easy for him."

"I know."

After a while, she said, "The more I shrink, the more her voice becomes clearer; the wind, no longer a misty bluster."

"I wish I could hear too."

"Yes, I wish you could. It's distinct, beautiful." She smiled, a little stretch of her pout. "The wind's thanking you. The departed Zephyrs, they wish there was a way to repay the favor."

"The air I breathe is enough. Tell the wind that."

"I think she heard you."

She asked me to take her to the surface to spend a moment; that even the Zephyrs in the sanctum came outside once a month, on the first Sabbath. She urged, but I tenaciously refused. The Zephyrs were almost a hundred feet below ground, and she was scarcely over twenty, still savoring a good portion of the wind's breath daily.

"I'm sorry," I said. "Here, I'm your keeper; it's my duty to make you last as long as possible. A moment on the surface will cost you much. Very soon you'll have all the air you can get."

Esohe was never much loved on the surface, so her absence was not felt. Only her father made noise, knocked on doors, questioned every villager walking on the street, beckoned neighbors to join him in a search, and I imagined them weaving out intricate excuses to decline. He continued stopping by my house. People claimed they saw the two of us walking together, he said. Yes, I affirmed, but I left her at the field.

I was Esohe's only friend; I had to join her father in the search. The two of us scoured the grazing field and beyond until we had to conclude she couldn't be anywhere near; of course, there was no place to be beyond the field. But whenever he glanced at me, I saw suspicion spread over his face: *What in the gods name have you led my daughter into?*

I began to carefully watch my path when going to visit Esohe in the well. I visited only once per day, with little food that would last her.

I would nestle her to myself to shield her of the scarce yet poisonous air and tell her of the latest happenings in the village, not sure if she could hear. I told her Mudia was worried and sometimes joined her father and me in the vain search. I sang in low tunes to her and moved my body with hers. Some days, I spent the full day with her. The well quickly became dark, the nights were longer, and so we constantly lived under the golden hue of lamplight. I read to her, scoured for all the books I could find, and would read aloud. But in my alone time, I read records on the lives of Zephyrs, searched for what could make them last longer. There was no other way; only the sanctum.

One night, when I was caressing her with olive balm so that the white-brown of her fading skin shone like metal, I brought her close to my ears and said, "No one deserves to spend her last days in a well."

I pressed her closer to my ears, yearning to hear her speak, but she said nothing.

"I can take you out of this well. I can take you to the sanctum, I don't care who sees us. No one would recognize you. I'll tell the keepers I saw you near the borders."

I felt her vibrations against my face, her gentle spasms, but I wasn't sure if that was an approval.

"Everyone should spend her last days with her kind," I said, "in a becalming comfort."

I pressed her to my face and breathed her in, tried to fill up myself with her, to absorb her aura, render it everlasting.

"Who is your kind?" she spoke, her voice a gentle breath against my cheeks.

I held her closer to my cheeks, and she muttered again: "Who is your kind?"

"One who is like you."

Later, after a long quiet, I said, "One with whom you share love."

"Yes," she muttered.

I continued caressing her floury skin with my balm, watching her sparkle in the dimming light.

"Please take me out of here."

I stroked her face and for a moment saw flashes of her former features; the subtle contours of her face before the wind had consumed her flesh. When the jar of balm was empty, I tucked her in my cushioned goatskin bag, and together, we climbed out of the well.

On the surface, the night was far gone and tranquil. We rode together on my mare, and I trotted with prudent thuds. It was a long and raucous journey through the grove, but soon after, my clip-clopping became the only sound of the village.

I periodically felt my bag to know if she was still in there, but I never looked into it. After a continuous ride without halting, the thoroughfare leading to my cabin became visible. I rode until I was at my door. The house was empty and humid. Mudia was at the mines.

Esohe was almost half her size since we had left the well and could easily nestle in my hands. I laid her on the bed and swaddled her with my fleecy shawl but felt her resistant spasms. I uncovered her, left her bare, unclothed, and lay beside.

All through the night, I felt her morph against me, into grains, into noiseless air, nothingness. I breathed in and let the rest of her fill the space of the room. I listened for the moans of the escaping winds.

On the next Sabbath, I worshipped in the temple. I went before dawn so that I could stand just before the pedestal of the Zephyrs and have a complete view. The Zephyrs were more alike than I thought, the same shapeless features, many of them having the same heights, and I had to squint to see some of them. I focused on the indistinguishably minute ones all through my worshipping, those who resembled the last phase, who would barely last a day if left on the surface.

When Mudia and I were riding back home, we sighted three men standing by our door. Tax collectors, I feared. As we got nearer to our cabin, the raven-like judicial signet clipped to the collars of two of the men became visible. The third man was Nata.

The night before, Nata had stopped by and directly asked me: *Where is my daughter?* I couldn't tell him where Esohe was. I didn't know, she could be anywhere in the Sahara.

"What are they doing here?" Mudia asked.

The two judicial men strode to us before we could dismount. "Obehi Ehichoya, we have orders from the court to place you in custody."

They let me dismount. Nata blankly stared at me from a distance. What arrest-worthy evidence could he have given the court, to prove my involvement in his daughter's disappearance?

"What has she done?" Mudia was screaming. "This is absurd! She has nothing to do with Esohe's disappearance!" I wished he would stop. Neighbors were already assembling.

The men ignored him and manacled my wrists with cold metal and led me to their carriage beside the house.

The aridness of the harmattan didn't reach into my cell. Its stone walls were edged with fungus. It was dank at night and fusty during the day but always reeked nauseatingly like old moist hay. There were two other women in the cell, who were older and less interested in conversation than I was. I did not recognize them and deemed them foreign prisoners apprehended in the village.

They didn't stay long. They were led out four days later, the same day I was informed of my trial. It was scheduled for the first week of the following month. I imagined now that the news of how I was involved in Esohe's disappearance must have pervaded the village; her only friend, how pitiable.

I spent most of the time mapping out how to defend myself in court, what could her father have said against me. Perhaps he had enough corroborators who claimed to have seen me with Esohe beyond the grazing field, contradicting my claim. If that was all, then I could easily defend myself before the tribunal. But the intuition that there was a greater evidence kept gnawing on me; the court wouldn't issue an arrest on a fragile foundation. Most nights, I didn't sleep; I retraced my steps, searched for loopholes.

The seven chiefs were present for my trial, hatted and seated on plush armchairs behind the king's hand, who had a red left eye. Beside the king's hand sat his clerk, already holding his quill, and at the door stood the staid custodian. At the left end of the court was seated Esohe's father, Nata, his face grim as ever, staring straight at the blank wall opposite him. I, surrounded by nothing, stood at the middle of the court, a small distance away from the king's hand. I was still trying to find a loophole and concoct a matching defense.

After acknowledging the chiefs, the king's hand looked at me and then lowered his head to the papers on his table. "Obehi Ehichoya, you have been accused with burgling the inner sanctum of the Order of Zephyrs on the first Sabbath of the past month. How do you plea?"

The sanctum. The charge kept resounding in my head. Treason against the gods. I'd be sent to the gallows. I stared at the king's hand. My legs began failing me.

"How do you plea?" he asked again.

"I do not wish to contend."

After the spectacle of me at the gallows, Mudia would certainly be sent away from the mines, and he might not find any other work to do. I wished I had told him of the gold buried in the garden; he might have been able to find a buyer at another village where no one would suspect the gold's origin.

The king's hand ordered Nata to speak.

Nata rose. "It's no news of my missing daughter, Esohe. After searching the village with no result, I opted to check inside my house. My daughter is a lover of the pen; she writes everything down on her papers. I ruffled through her papers in hope for a clue, and I happened upon a heartbreaking discovery, which I cannot keep to myself, or I would suffer the ire of the gods. In my daughter's papers, I found the layout and writings of how she intended to steal the key of the sanctum and sneak in on the first Sabbath of the past month. I have handed the papers to the court. Obehi Ehichoya, I know, is my daughter's closest companion and cohort."

"Obehi Ehichoya," the king's hand said, "several villagers have been consulted, and a few who were not at the temple testified to have seen you riding with Esohe Okhah on the first Sabbath of the previous month. Is this true?"

"Yes."

"To where were you headed?"

"I rode with Esohe to the sanctum, but I left with empty hands, took nothing."

The custodian strode to the clerk, whispered in his ear, and returned to the door. The clerk leaned nearer to the king's hand and muttered to him; they conferred for a while and turned heads to the door. The king's hand nodded at the custodian.

The pounding of my head heightened. The chiefs stared at me with gathered eyes as though they wished to impale me with their gaze and spare the hangman of his duty.

Shadows loomed at the door. A jacketed man, dark as tar, strode in, cradling an open oaken box. The custodian directed him to a chair beside Nata. He held to himself the box, which must of course contain the loot. I had buried the gold deep enough, but it wouldn't be hard for a determined seeker to find.

The king's hand ordered the jacketed man to speak.

The man rose and held the box to his chest. "I am thankful for the unplanned reception. I am a keeper of the sanctum"—only now did I notice the moon-shaped signet on his collar—"I am here to speak for one of the Order, who is here with me." He dug into his box and gently brought out what could have been a shapeless bough wrapped in wool. Though mostly immobile, it could manage few noticeable jerks. It was a Zephyr, looking so holy. I instantly peered at it, searching for familiar features, anything to match my last memory of Esohe, any familiar spasms. Its woolen garment made it look much less shrunk than the Esohe who had perfectly fitted in my bag.

The keeper continued. "I will speak out the words of the Zephyr to the hearing of the tribunal." He gently raised the Zephyr to his ear.

The keeper held the Zephyr to his ear for a long while, then began, "The Zephyr, on behalf of the Order, expresses discontent on how they were not apprised or consulted of a case that relates to the sanctum, their dwelling. Had the matter not slipped from the mouths of conversing keepers, such a case would have continued without the Order's knowledge."

"It was agreed upon to leave the Order undisturbed," the king's hand said. "They need not hear of such a profane act."

The keeper listened again to the Zephyr, now for an overstretched period, during which the atmosphere grew denser. My legs were wobbling. I was standing in empty air. There was nothing to wedge myself against.

"On the first Sabbath of the previous month, the Zephyr chose not to go to the temple. A while after the others had left, two young women appeared in the inner sanctum, for reasons unknown at first. But on further study, it became clear to the Zephyr that they had come to revere the dwelling of the Order."

The chiefs turned their heads to me, and I held their gaze. I prayed within. I'd never thought of praying since my arrest, not to the gods, not to the Zephyrs.

"Perhaps, out of overzealous faithfulness," the keeper continued, "believing their worship and petitions were more acceptable if presented from the sanctum rather than the temple. The lengths to which some faithfuls can go to secure the favor of the gods can be as unimaginable or absurd as illicitly entering the sanctum to worship. It should be the temple's duty to address the villagers, advise them of the limits, so they don't go overboard with their faith."

I peered at the Zephyr, wishing I could hold it to my ears, thank it for the freedom, hear its voice, if it would be similar to Esohe's, ask it about Esohe: *Can she be possibly here? Is she still living, in the winds? Is she happy? Does she have any words for me?*

A Zephyr was too pious to tell a lie. If it said we had come to worship, then we had come to worship; our gods defined truth.

After a conferment among the king's hand and palace chiefs, the trial was adjourned to the next day. The keeper replaced the Zephyr in the box and strode out with it.

I was sentenced to four months in the fusty and dank cell for unlawful entering and was fined twenty pounds of coins; the village could not afford the faithfuls yearning to access the sanctum. I always went early to the temple on first Sabbaths to stand at the front row and see the indistinct Zephyrs on their pedestal and focus on the most familiar, those of the last phase.

In the following years, I journeyed with the pilgrims to the Sahara. The breath of the Sahara was sublime, gently slid through my every pore and slipped through my fingers like dreams, swirled from the flowing skies and from beneath the seas of cascading sands, eager to embrace me with its delight and impress its mark. Sometimes, when it was as quiet as empty, I heard it, her subtle distinct voice amidst her undulating sighs.

THE MANY LIVES OF AN ABIKU

by Tobi Ogundiran

I. THE TETHERING

I lay on that stone slab beneath the stars, weak and delirious. I could feel the life bleeding out of me, even as the chilly mountain wind kissed my nakedness. From somewhere to my left came Mama's distraught gasps: the cry of someone who had lost a child one too many times.

Baba Seyi appeared in my line of vision. "Cruel child," he said. "Do you know what you are?"

I opened my mouth to speak, but the fever had stolen my voice.

"You are an *abiku*, a spirt child," he said. "You have come to your mother three times before and have died before your seventh year. You relish her pain and suffering."

How could he say that? How could he say I relished Mama's suffering? I pitied her. I wanted to hold her, to tell her all would be well, that this was but a normal childhood ailment.

But I knew better.

"You will torment your parents no more." He raised a bone knife and carved into the back of my hand.

I found my voice then, screaming as Baba Seyi carved three deep incisions into the back of my hand. He chanted dispassionately as he carved, fixing his lazy eye on me with a penetrating gaze.

Heat flared through my body. Heat so consuming that I feared I would melt into the slab. But I didn't, and when Baba Seyi finished carving, I felt my fever break, felt the life return to me.

"Is it … is it done?" Mama asked.

"It is," growled Baba Seyi as he faded into the darkness. "This will be the last time. The markings will hold her …"

Not long after, I started to see Rewa.

"Who are you talking to?" Mama asked.

"No one," I said too quickly as Rewa snickered behind me.

Mama squinted. She wasn't so easily fooled. "I think it's time we went to see Baba Seyi again."

"No!" I wailed. "Not the mystic, please Mama!"

Mama took my chin in her hands. "Look at you. You have that far-away look in your eyes. Don't lie to me, are your friends calling at you?"

By 'friends' she meant other spirit children. By 'friends' she meant Rewa.

Rewa floated just above Mama's head, doing cartwheels and pulling faces. I wanted to wince. "Mama," I said, "no one is calling at me."

Mama searched my eyes for a few moments before finally deciding I was telling the truth. She sighed. "Fine. But you'll tell me if you … see them, won't you?"

"Yes."

"Good." She stood up and went into the kitchen.

I slowly exhaled. Rewa finished cartwheeling and dropped in front of me, dipping into a courteous bow.

"See what you've caused," I hissed. "Don't talk to me when she's around."

Rewa plucked a blood grape from the bunch and tossed it into her mouth. For someone who was a spirit, I'd always wondered how she could contact the physical realm. "Your mother's too much of a problem."

"If you behave when she's around, she won't notice you."

Rewa scoffed. "Look at you. Playing the good little daughter. You shouldn't have to answer to them. You have no idea what you are." She jabbed a finger in the direction of the kitchen. "You lived millennia before *she* was born."

"The only life I know is this one. Whoever you claim I was—"

"Are."

"—before, I don't remember."

Rewa gave a sour look. "How would you, when you ..." She shuddered, gesturing at my markings.

When she raised her eyes, I saw something dark there.

"I have half a mind to kill her."

"Don't! Don't you dare!" I cried. "Or ... or I swear I'll go to Baba Seyi."

Rewa's eyes were murderous. "You dare threaten me?"

"No—no—" I spluttered, remembering she did not respond well to threats. "It's just—please don't kill her."

Rewa scowled at me, jumped off the table, and vanished into the floor.

II. A WALL OF MANY FACES

Sometimes the walls developed faces. One moment they were the uninspired blandness of old wood, coated with soot from the coal pot, and the next there was a face staring at me, bulging out of the wood, a crude androgynous relief carving. Sometimes the faces stared unblinking, watching my every move. Sometimes they tittered. Once or twice the faces morphed, twenty or so of them, fusing into one hideous gargantuan aberration of a face. Strangely, strangely I did not scream.

I wanted to, though.

When I asked Rewa who they were, she said they were my family.

"My family?"

"Yes." Her voice dripped with characteristic disdain. "Your *true* family. But obviously you don't remember them."

I looked at the tittering, whispering faces. "What are they saying?"

"Wondering how long this fallacy will last. When you'll realize this isn't where you belong."

I bristled. "Well tell them this *is* where I belong. And my life is not a fallacy!"

Rewa tutted, touched my face. "You've forgotten yourself. This is not even your real face—it's a mask." My fingers reached for my face, tracing the spot Rewa's fingers had been seconds ago.

I looked at the faces on the walls. "Why are they hiding in the walls? Why don't they appear like you?"

Rewa shrugged. "I'm special."

Just then Dotun poked his large round head into the room. "Hey *abiku*."

"Don't call me that."

He flashed his stupid, annoying grin. "I'm not the one with spirit friends." He entered the room, closing the door. "Where is it?"

"Where is what?"

"My cantikle. Don't play dumb. I know you stole it."

The cantikle was a brass-and-wood device which he had won from a toymaker a few weeks earlier. It had a wooden griot sitting atop several rows of rune tiles which could be selected to make the griot sing different songs. Almost like a real griot telling a story.

"Dotun, I didn't take—" Out of the corner of my eye I saw Rewa produce the cantikle from the folds of her skirts, a wicked grin on her face.

"Hey, hey!" He snapped his fingers in my face. "Over here. You were saying?"

"I ..." I found it hard to concentrate with Rewa threatening to press a rune tile. The bloody faces were tittering behind Dotun. "I will try to find it."

"See that you do, *abiku*."

"Do you want me to handle him?" Rewa asked once he had left the room.

"Handle him?"

"Make it so he doesn't bother you again." She gave me a sly look, moving the stiff arms of the griot as though playing with a puppet.

Did I even want to know what she meant by that? "No, Rewa," I said. "Just leave my family alone. Please."

Rewa looked at me for the longest time. And when I looked back in her eyes, I realized for the first time that they were the wrong shade of black.

...❖...

III. EXTRACORPOREAL

I did not feel the bed underneath me when I woke up. I did not feel the coarse bedspread scratching at my skin. At first, I wondered what was wrong, and it took me a while to realize it.

Then.

Then, I looked down ... and did not see myself. My first instinct was to scream, but some morbid fascination held me back. I could feel my hands as I stretched them to my line of vision. I *knew* they were there—I just couldn't see them! Panic welled up in me. I leapt off the bed ... and found myself floating, buoyed as if I were weightless, as if I were some stray redwood leaf tossed about by a chilly northern breeze.

I screamed.

But that too sounded wrong.

My voice echoed, strange and hollow, like the clang of a gong in an old well. The effect jarred me, so disconcerting that I snapped my mouth shut. The world had a strange hue to it; where before my room had been a cacophony of colors—the sheets a mosaic patchwork of different fabrics, the old timber of the walls dark and subdued, colorful raffia embroidery on the walls—now everything, *everything*, waned to bluish grey, like the uninspiring hue of a rainy dawn.

And I felt cold. Too cold.

I heard chatter and laughter from the dining room. I drifted, grasping with hands I couldn't see, towards the sounds. The same strange hue permeated the dining room, but the scene was a familiar one: Baba sat at the head of the rickety table, gently blowing on spoonfuls of steaming *ogi*; Mama sat opposite him, her headgear a wild elaborate thing perched on her head like some great bird of prey. She watched Dotun with mild fascination as he wound up his cantikle. I did not have time to wonder how he'd gotten his cantikle, because sitting opposite Dotun, in my chair was—

Me.

No. Not me. *Rewa.*

"... and then he said, 'See that you do, *abiku.*'" Rewa was saying in a voice which sounded uncannily like mine.

Dotun gasped, looking askance at Rewa. "I didn't."

"Yes, you did."

"Now, now," said Baba, gesturing with his spoon. "Haven't I told you not to call your sister that?"

Dotun lowered his eyes and fiddled petulantly with the rune tiles. "She stole my cantikle."

"I was trying to surprise you. I made some changes."

Dotun finished winding the device and released it. The griot sprung to life, gesticulating and mouthing as she sang. Bright sparks went off from her tiara, lighting up all of their faces with awe.

"Wow!" said Mama. "Where did you learn to do that?"

Rewa shrugged. She caught my eyes and grinned a wicked grin. "Oh, you know. Lekan has been showing me some things."

"I'm proud of you," said Baba, reaching out to pat Rewa's head.

I floated there, stunned. Lekan was a pyricc—the only pyricc in town—who had been showing me how to imbue light into things without light. I went to him when I could spare time from my chores, which was not often, and as a result I hadn't even been able to summon light, let alone *imbue* things with it.

But he had shown me, not Rewa. He had been teaching me. *Me!*

This was my life, and this impostor was stealing it.

In that moment, blind fury rose up like a gorge within me, and I forgot all about my fear of Rewa. I threw myself at her, but I was a leaf in a breeze, and my movements were clumsy and uncoordinated. I careened off to the side like a stone from a sling, knocking my head against the blackened rafters. White lights exploded in my vision, but my anger washed the pain away.

My family sat below, oblivious to my efforts, ignorant that the girl sitting at the table with them was an impostor and not their daughter. Oblivious to the fact that their real daughter floated above them in the astral world.

Rewa shot me triumphant looks as she slurped her *ogi*. Dotun wound his cantikle, face screwed in concentration as he selected rune tiles. I willed my anger into a fine point and shot down at Rewa like an arrow. She had only a moment to realize what was happening before I smashed into her. We crashed to the floor in a tangle of limbs.

My parents sprang to their feet, rushing to Rewa's aid. Rewa sat there, flabbergasted. The look of surprise on her face was pleasing to look at.

She didn't think I could touch her. *I* didn't think I could touch her.

Before she could recover, I launched at her again, grabbing her hair and yanking it back and forth. She screamed, and I relished it.

"Give me back!" I yelled, dragging her hair. Mama gasped in horror as Rewa's head snapped dangerously to the back. Rewa's claws dug into my skin, but I held on in a viselike grip, yanking her out of my disturbed parents' arms. I wondered, vaguely, what they were seeing: their daughter being yanked about by an unseen force. But this wasn't their daughter. The earlier they realized it, the better.

And then ... Rewa became that which I feared the most. She flung me with such force that I landed on my belly with a loud *oomf.* I staggered to my feet and watched in horror as she morphed into a tall, spindly thing. Long arms and legs too numerous to count sprung out of her torso in sickening succession even as she stretched and elongated. Her face was the worst, never still for more than a moment, changing, changing, as though she couldn't quite decide what she wanted to be.

I looked to see what my family thought of this metamorphosis and saw that they were frozen in position.

"I had to see for myself." Her voice was something forbidding, textured. "Had to see why you love them so much. Now, I think ... I can understand."

I was pinned to the floor, watching the many faces of Rewa flit before me.

"And you know what? I think I want them for myself."

"You can't have them."

Rewa bent till she was eye level with me, her hideous face bare inches from mine. "Who is going to stop me. You?"

I felt a leaden sense of despair steal over me. I couldn't stop her, and she knew that. I looked at my parents, at my brother, frozen. I thought of my life with them. The camaraderie. I thought of the way Baba bounced me on his knees, the musky, faint coconut smell of him. I thought of Mama, and how she sang to me when she braided my hair to keep my mind off the pain. It wasn't all bliss and sweet memories, but they were my family and I loved them. I couldn't—didn't want to—lose them.

"No," I said with more conviction than I felt. "You won't succeed. They'll know you aren't me. They'll—"

Rewa laughed. "Oh, but they won't. Like I said, we all wear masks. And yours fits perfectly over my face." And with that she started to shrink, her numerous limbs retracting as she deflated back into my likeness.

In that moment my markings started to tingle, a low incessant itch which slowly morphed into something unbearable. White-hot pain flared up the skin of my arms—*my arms, which I could see!*—And I watched with morbid fascination as my arms materialized before me, as the markings twisted and curled along my forearms like snakes. I watched as my hands moved of their own volition, as they wrapped around Rewa in a strong embrace. I felt something yank me from behind my navel and then I fell into darkness. Down, down, down …

Even before I opened my eyes, I could feel that I was back in my body; I could feel the sheets beneath me, the coarse threads digging into my skin. Good gods, those sheets had never felt so good. I opened my eyes to find my parents peering at me, their faces sick with worry.

"Mama," I croaked, "please take me to Baba Seyi."

IV. CATHARSIS

Baba Seyi came in the dead of the night to carry me away. I sat on the hard-cracked earth in the town square, beneath the gnarled iroko tree, and waited for him. I had called him—or rather begged my mother to call him. I wanted to get rid of Rewa once and for all.

I waited in the town square because it was not safe for him to be in a human dwelling.

It wasn't safe for the humans, of course—not him.

Rewa hovered somewhere around me, invisible. She only became invisible when she was angry, and oh—I could feel cold malice radiating from her.

"You're making a terrible mistake," she hissed. "You're going to regret this."

Rewa never made empty threats, and the flavor of this threat was something chilling. But I ignored her. This time I was determined to get rid of her. This time I would open myself to Baba Seyi and his … devices.

He came at the hour of the owl. One moment the barren landscape of the town center stretched unbroken in all directions, and the next there stood Baba Seyi, jutting out in stark contrast.

"Girl," he said, beckoning, "come with me."

I stood up on gangly feet and dusted my skirts. I started towards him, and Rewa flickered before me, her black eyes alight with murder. I faltered.

"Quickly now," he snapped. The crack of his voice broke through my paralysis and sent me cantering towards him. He seized me with a bony hand—I barely had time to register the dryness of his touch before the world bent in over itself and the air squeezed out of my lungs. I felt myself flatten, thinner than a sea reed.

We stood high up on the mountain, outside his shack.

He let go of my hand and shambled into the shack, leaving me with the howling wind and biting frost. My heart fluttered as my eyes settled on the stone slab jutting out of the mountain like some giant phallus, remembering how Baba Seyi tied me to it before cutting the markings into my hand. Six years had passed since that fateful day, and yet the memory was as fresh as ever.

I stood there for a few moments, fighting the fear that threatened to spill out of my throat like bile. Moments later, Baba Seyi poked his head out of the shack and beckoned me in.

The guttering fire from the fire pit cast an interesting pattern of dancing shadows and warm light on the rough walls. An assortment of oddities hung from the ceiling, rotating on strings: a stuffed raven; yellowed clacking bones; old, blackened carvings; a large water drum stood in the corner. I hesitated by the door, watching with great trepidation as Baba Seyi set his walking stick to the wall and unfastened his tie-dyed cloak, exposing a gaunt torso.

"Why did you call me?" he asked.

I could feel Rewa bristling with anger. "To … free myself."

He looked at me, his lazy eye boring into mine. "Freedom is a many-faced god. There are a great many things I could free you from. Do you want to be free of this shell that you've worn to house your spirit? Do you want to die, *abiku*?"

What? No.

Yes, Rewa whispered.

"No. Baba. I want to be free of … Rewa."

"Mm-hmm." He tore off a bunch of leaves and threw it in his mouth, chewing it methodically for a few moments. "Why do you want to be free of her?"

Why did I want to be free of her? Because she was demanding. Selfish. Destructive. A bully. "She scares me," I croaked. But I knew that was not enough. "She is bad … for my family."

Baba Seyi looked at me. "Hmm. So you've decided to stay."

"What?"

"The last time you were here, I bound you to your flesh to keep you from dying. You have remained with us only by the spells holding you, and that, effective as it is, is not enough. It is why you are still visited by your spirit companions. But now you have lived with your family and have grown to love them. So much so that you've come to the decision to remain with them."

He paused here, and I had the feeling he was waiting for me to say something. "Yes, Baba." I thought of my parents, of Dotun. I thought of the look on their faces when I gained back my body. It was a look I never wanted to see again. "I have."

He nodded, contented. "Take off your clothes."

I did not hesitate. Gooseflesh erupted over my skin the moment I peeled off the last layer of clothing. Baba Seyi placed me behind the fire before shuffling over to the large drum. He thrust a hand into it and came up with something brown and sticky—clay. And then he began to mold, chanting an earth song as he coaxed the clay into a shape.

I didn't know how much time passed. It felt like a minute, but it well could have been years. Time this high up the mountain was irrelevant. But after some time, Baba Seyi stepped back to reveal a clay image, eerily lifelike. It felt, oddly, like looking into a mirror; from the position of uneasy repose to the small mounds that were my breasts. The image was me in every way, except for the face, which was smooth and featureless, a blank surface.

"Where is the face?" I asked.

"You see, I wondered how Rewa was able to steal your body," said Baba Seyi. "You are, after all, not the first *abiku* I have dealt with. They all have spirit companions, but you … this Rewa seems to have a much more potent hold and connection to you. And then I realized: she is your *ibeji*."

I was stunned. "My twin?"

"Yes. You have taken turns in coming to this world, each living for a short while, before dying to allow the other come. Except for now. You have ... overstayed, and she is quite displeased."

It made sense now. I remembered asking her how she could manifest in a whole body while the other companions were just faces on the walls. She had only shrugged and said she was special. But then I also remembered her saying she wanted my family for herself. But didn't I know? Hadn't I realized, in the back of my mind, that she looked exactly like me?

Baba Seyi nodded at the clay image. "I will attempt to invite her into this vessel."

A sister. I would have a sister. The prospect excited me. I turned to see what Rewa thought about it, but she was nowhere to be found.

"I—I can't see her." But that wasn't right. Rewa didn't always make herself seen, but I could always feel her and now ... there was a Rewa-shaped space in my heart where she always dwelt.

Baba Seyi frowned. He sniffed the air and started to clap his hands and chant, stomping his feet into the ground. He stopped suddenly, his eyes growing wide. "No."

That one word was a spear through my heart. Before I could open my mouth to ask what was wrong, Baba Seyi took my hand, and we appeared in the town square beneath the iroko tree.

Baba Seyi was hurrying in the direction of my house. "Quickly, girl!" he called over his shoulder.

I darted after him, a million thoughts hurtling through my mind. Through the chaos of it all I kept seeing Rewa's black eyes, kept hearing her spiteful hiss: *You will regret this.*

I expected to find the exterior of the house in disarray; the roof on fire, the walls caved in—anything to denote Rewa's wrath. But everything was just as I left it. Nestled between the fishmonger's hut and the seamstress's, it stood serene. Deceptively serene.

Baba Seyi hovered by the door, unable to enter. I brushed past him, calling for Mama, Baba, Dotun. Anyone.

I found them at the dining table. They sat transfixed, staring at the gesticulating griot of the cantikle, watching as bright sparks shot out of her fingertips to bathe the otherwise dark room in a wash of colours. Where before, the griot's movements had been fluid and graceful, now they were the choppy and strained movements of arthritic joints. She had a painful expression on her face.

Rewa sat in my chair, dressed in my best clothes, her dark eyes alight with malice. I did not want to think how she was there, how she was real.

"Rewa, please—" I started, but she held up a hand.

"Shush, now," she said in a sugary voice, "we're watching the performance."

I truly saw the faces of my family members then. They wore slack, nearly vacant expressions and their eyes—oh, gods, their eyes!—were white.

The griot's song sounded strangely detuned and warbled, and when she finally cut off mid-rendition, the silence that came after filled the air like a blanket of despair.

"Ah," said Rewa, wiping a tear from her eye, "wasn't that beautiful, Mama?"

I watched, numb with horror as Mama turned her head ever so slightly, settling her white eyes on a spot just above Rewa's head. She nodded.

"Rewa …" I croaked. "What have you done?"

She drummed her tiny fingers on the table. "I have taken your place."

"You—you don't need to take my place. You're my sister"—her eyes snapped towards me and I rushed on—"I remember now. We're twins."

She narrowed her eyes at me. "You remember?"

"Yes!" I cried. "We had a pact! I wasn't supposed to stay this long. I—I left you, and I know that is bad, but I understand everything now, because I would feel bad if you did the same to me."

A genuine look of hope appeared on her face. She pushed herself off the chair and rushed to hug me. "Oh, I'm glad! You finally remember. You have no idea what it was like waiting and waiting for you to come back to me." She pushed me back and searched my eyes. "I thought you were going to send me away, that's why …" She looked over her shoulder at my family who sat immobile, staring blankly into space. "Wait. *How* do you remember?"

"I—it doesn't matter," I said quickly. "We made you a body so you could come and join me here. But it looks like you have found a way."

She gave me a mischievous smile. "I always find a way. Oh, we're going to have so much fun together. Just like old times!"

I gave her my widest smile, darting a glance to my family.

"We'll find another family to torment."

My smile faltered. "Another family?"

"Why, yes."

"I thought you wanted to stay with this family?"

"I've changed my mind," she said, leading me to the table. "Besides, where's the fun in that? We were never meant to stay in one place."

"But ..."

She stopped to look at me. "Do I sense hesitation, sister?"

"No."

A knife materialized in Rewa's hand, which she pressed into mine. She nodded at Mama. "Kill her."

"What?"

"Kill her," she repeated, watching me closely.

It was a test, I knew. And it was one I would fail. Even as I struggled to find an alternative, to say something, Rewa yanked the knife from my hands and plunged it into my Mama's neck.

"What, you think I'm an idiot?" she said calmly as my mother buckled and thrashed like fish out of water. "You have been a very bad girl, Sola, and you will pay the price."

The door opened, and my siblings—my real siblings—filed into the room. They were the lesser of us and had fashioned bodies for themselves out of anything they could find: straw, wood, cooking pots and pans. Their faces were wood, the same wooden faces that had spied and tittered at me from the walls of my room. Grotesque aberrations of human forms, they moved in unison.

"Bad Sola," they chanted in voices of metal and wood and straw. "Bad Sola. Bad Sola."

Hands reached out to grab me as Rewa yanked out the knife and turned to attend to my father, cackling with pure delight, her thin sonorous chant of "Bad Sola" adding a musical texture to the droning of my siblings. It felt like a dream. A bad dream from which I would soon wake up, shivering and sweating but otherwise safe, safe in the knowledge that nothing could hurt me, that my mother was alive—

Something grabbed me. I looked down and felt the sudden urge to burst into maniacal laughter; a soup ladle, the same ladle Mama had used to pour soup into my plate, was now the arm of one of my siblings. It curled around my wrist in a viselike grip while the sibling in question twisted his wooden face into a malicious smile.

I smacked his head with my other arm, screaming in pain as my fist connected with the hard wood of his head. Hands snaked out to grab me before I could recover, pinning me to the spot. Gods, they were strong. Too strong. They lifted me off my feet and bore me to the table, still chanting. My father sat drooling, and when I saw that Rewa had carved out his eyes, I fainted.

The pain woke me. Hands of spoons and wood held me to the table as Rewa carefully sliced the knife through my skin, cutting out my—

My markings!

"Be still, now, sister," she said when I started to struggle. "I am going to free you."

Free me, no! I didn't want to be freed. The markings were the only thing keeping me tethered to the world. Without them ... I would be spirit again.

I screamed as Rewa plunged the knife into my skin, meticulously hacking away at the flesh. "Please, Rewa—I swear I'll do anything—*please*—"

Rewa was deaf to my pleadings. She hacked, her eyes alight with malicious glee.

One of my siblings, who had fashioned for himself a body out of my mother's cloak, leaned in. "Finish it," he said to Rewa.

Just then, the roof caved in with a resounding crash, and in swooped the largest owl I had ever seen. It landed on the table just above me as my siblings scattered about. It turned its head to look at me, and I could see myself reflected in the huge glassy orbs that were its eyes. The left eye was a little slow. A lazy eye.

"Baba Seyi," I breathed.

"Go," he growled. And when I lay there stunned and transfixed, he spread his great wings and screeched, "GO!"

I fell off the table and bolted out of the house, Rewa's formidable shriek of fury chasing me down the street.

I reached the town square when I noticed my feet were no longer touching the ground. The world took on that bluish-grey hue I had now come to recognize, and I rose, as if buoyed by an invisible wind.

No.

I flailed, grasping for something—anything—to keep me tethered. As I turned around, I saw my body lying facedown in the dirt, saw my bloodied arm where Rewa had hacked away at my flesh.

Lying next to it was the torn patch of skin with my *abiku* markings.

The world fell away, breaking off like little flakes of burning parchment, until all that was left was the void.

V. REBIRTH

First there was darkness; the cold, numbing darkness of the void. Then voices—whispers really, a thousand sibilant words slithering over my skin like snakes. Then warmth.

—I am alive. I am me, festooned in a cocoon of water—

Then I am born. I see a face, teary-eyed and exhausted, the face of a new mother.

A LOVE SONG FOR HERKINAL

AS COMPOSED BY ASHKERNAS AMID THE RUINS OF NEW HAVEN

by Chinelo Onwualu

I slam the car door with more force than I mean to. It's childish, but I don't care; I want Ashkernas to see how angry I am.

But my sister pretends not to notice.

"Don't worry about the supplies, Herkinal!" Ash calls with the false cheer she adopts when I am upset. "I'll get Haba to bring them in."

I don't bother telling her that I had no intention of helping in the first place. Instead, I storm past her and unlock the door of the front lobby. And there they are, all six of them, lounging on the leather settees across from the registration desk—as they have for the last two weeks.

They no longer bother playing the penitents with me; they know it won't work. They only put on their act for Ash—whose indulgence they are aware is all that keeps them from the void of the lower depths where they belong. They look like typical wood sprites—except they're not. Something has corrupted them, and now they are like walking trees carved out of ice, their faces abstract sculptures. They radiate a cold that's almost solid, and even if my sister and I didn't have the Sight, we would still be able to feel the unpleasant clamminess that they bring to any space.

I know this because we haven't had any guests since they arrived. I've lost count of the number of people who've walked in here looking for a room and then found some excuse to leave as quickly as possible. They're killing our business and for some reason, my sister doesn't seem to care.

"Aren't you supposed to be in room 306?" I bark at them. It was Ash's idea to have them act as ACs for the tokoloshe who'd been complaining that his room was too hot, but they've yet to make their way to the first floor, talk less of the third.

They begin a chorus of laments, but I tune out their tired excuses and begin prepping the front desk for the day. We both know they're lying. Hell, I'd known they were lying when they'd first arrived, telling a woeful tale about how the Accident destroyed their ancestral forests far to the north. I seethe, remembering Ash's cheerful dismissal of my protests at the time.

"There's a reason for everything, even if we can't see it," she'd said, flashing that brilliant smile of hers. "Don't worry, it'll work out."

The old Ashkernas would never have let such obvious dupes pull that nonsense with her. Granted, I was the brains and she was the body, but she'd always been sharper than she let people think. I would plan the scams, and she would execute. Brick and Lace, they'd called us then. The Sisters of No Mercy.

The front door dings as she enters, loaded down with foodstuffs and cleaning supplies. I pretend to review the guest register, ignoring her as she huffs towards the kitchen in the back. The spirits erupt in a chorus of effusive greetings when they see her, and she beams in response. I notice that none of them offer to help her, though. I kiss my teeth at the farce, which the spirits pretend not to hear.

"Haba!" Ash calls from the kitchen. "Habakuk! Come help Mommy with these things!"

The little girl sidles out from wherever she's been hiding. It's a disconcerting habit of hers. One moment you think you're alone, then you turn around and there she is, staring at you with those odd yellow eyes of hers.

I've never really taken to her. She looks nothing like either of us—small-boned and ebony where we are both full-bodied and warm earth. And where other six-year-olds chatter and laugh, she seems to hoard her words, only wheezing quietly when one of her secret schemes has come to pass. Our grandmother would have called her an ogbanje, a spirit child with one foot in our world and another the afterlife. One who torments her mother with multiple births that all end in death. Except she's Ash's first and only child, and it was an easy birth.

As usual, her clothes are filthy, and her hair is a knotty mess because she won't allow anyone to touch it. I eye her suspiciously; what has she been up to now? I suspect I'll find out in due time—when the complaint reaches me.

As if reading my mind, she hunches her shoulders as she passes me, skittering to the kitchen like some sort of furtive insect.

I sigh. The Accident changed so much for us. Though, I suppose it changed things for everyone. I turn on the supernatural scroungers across from me.

"So, you people just balanced yourselves here for the whole day? You didn't do anything again?"

"Madam, it's not like that ..." They cringe and apologize profusely, and I let loose a tirade of insults on them. It won't dislodge them from their perch, but it'll make me feel better.

I know he's bad news the moment he walks through the front door. I don't need the Sight to tell me that. From the middle-aged pot belly that speaks of more cheap beer than sense, to the expensive suit several sizes too small. Then there's the overly shined leather shoes, the oversized gold watch, and the heavy cologne that assaults me long before he gets to the desk. I know.

He surveys our small lobby with a disapproving sniff, as if he's used to more luxurious digs. I stiffen. The Spirit Inn isn't much, but it's clean, and I've worked hard to decorate it with locally made handicrafts. Some people just have no taste. On top of that, he's untouched. I wonder how he found the place; the untouched shouldn't be able to even read our sign. Then, the girl slips in from behind him. As she hurries to join him at the desk, she glances at the settee and shivers, and I understand.

She's at least half his age, if not younger. Her makeup has been carefully applied to make her seem older, but her face has yet to shed its childhood fullness. She's dressed like a Runs Girl: her skin artificially lightened, her fall of human hair expertly styled, a bodycon dress that seems to have been sprayed on, and high heels that could double as weapons they're so sharp.

I force my mouth into a chirpy smile. "Good evening!"

"This AC is something else," the man booms. I catch the wisp of grey discomfort that he squashes down with green lust and yellow arrogance. "Una fit off am small."

"With this heat, is it not better like this?" I fake a laugh, and the man joins in.

Of course he only wants one night. Of course he wants our most expensive room. As he fills out the registration form, I take a closer look at the girl. No doubt about it, she's touched, but she doesn't seem to share the Sight. I wonder what her gift is. Her aura is the dark blue of sadness, but that's not unusual for girls in her profession.

I call Big Goliath to show them to their room. Just as the old man shuffles forward to lead them up the stairs, the girl's aura turns the black of despair.

I sigh. This is going to be a long day.

The Accident shook something loose in all of us, I like to think. Some say it happened because the gods were bored, and having nothing better to do, decided to answer all our prayers. Others believe that the world was split into alternate realities, and that somewhere, there exists other planes where the Accident never happened, and all our lives went on. Whatever the reason, one morning we woke up to chaos.

Nearly every country beyond the African continent had vanished. Millions of people, all of them rich or powerful or corrupt, had also disappeared. Millions of African migrants, in fact anyone with a discernible trace of African ancestry, found themselves relocated to Africa, scattered in countries across the continent. The Diaspora was now home. The "West," as we understood the term, no longer existed. In the vast upheaval that followed, our political, financial, and social systems fell to dust, taking with them the systems of inequity that they had upheld.

In Nigeria, our government imploded, and teachers became the most powerful people in the country. They started by instituting a policy of universal income that eradicated poverty. Healthcare, education, and housing were now free. Then they created truth squads that rounded up the ignorant and forced them into critical-thinking camps. The heroic rebels fought back, of course. After all, shouldn't the ultimate freedom be to be able to be as violent, obtuse, and reactionary as you want? To be able to hold opinion over fact, even if it maintained your own oppression? But as re-education took hold, those protests died too. Eventually, religious institutions fell apart, and we all returned to the enlightened worship of the Old Gods. Many of us took on new names, divorced from the ethnic heritages that once divided us. We renamed our land New Haven.

Amid all this, an unexpected thing happened: some of us developed what could be called … abilities. Flight, teleportation, telekinesis—if you could imagine it, then somebody somewhere had it. One policeman I knew was able to alter people, so that after they met him, they could only speak the whole truth. He is now our Chief Justice.

For my sister and me, it was the Sight. The ability to see and to interact with the world just beyond our plane. After the Accident, our cons no longer made sense. What good did it do to lie to someone who might be able to read your thoughts? Even if your scam was successful, how far could you run from someone who could teleport? And so, when we found ourselves living in an abandoned hotel with no more need to work or scrounge—Ash nearly bursting with child—well, we did what we always did best. We adapted.

I decide to keep the front desk open through the night, though I usually close it by 9 p.m. and leave the late shift to Big Goliath. We rarely have more than a few guests at a time, and at night most of them are out doing their business. If there's any trouble, he always knows where to find me. Tonight, I sense that something big is about to burst; it might be more than the old shapeshifter will be able to handle alone.

By 10 p.m., I am sitting in the back room with a cup of Kenyan black tea, which Big Goliath has thoughtfully provided me, and trying to decide when would be a good time to check on the girl and the man in the suit. I haven't heard from either of them since they checked in. That's not unusual. Some clients are eager to show off their wealth, ordering our most expensive meals and overpriced drinks. Others are more focused on getting down to business as quickly as possible, sneaking out when their deeds are done. The man in the suit had struck me as the former—an inveterate boaster desperate to seem more important than he actually was. That he hadn't ordered so much as a bottle of water worried me more than I cared to admit.

I catch a movement in the corner of my eye and whip around.

But it's only Habakuk crouched on her haunches in the corner and blinking up at me. I have no idea how long she's been there.

"Amadioha fire you, you this child!" I roar at her, but there's no real anger to it. My mind is too preoccupied. "How many times have I told you to knock before you enter here?"

The little girl is unfazed by my empty show of temper. I don't know how she does it, but she always seems to know when I am truly angry and when I'm just being dramatic.

"Mummy is asking if anybody is still eating today, she wants to close the kitchen."

I sigh. I suppose now is as good a time as any to head upstairs. I send Habakuk to call Big Goliath and when he arrives, we start towards the penthouse on the fourth floor.

I hear the low wailing as soon as we clear the landing. It seems to echo and thrum, settling into my bones like a bass backbeat. I know it's not physical and I hurry to the penthouse door, knocking harder than I mean to. The man takes a little too long to answer. When he does, he's clothed in nothing but a towel, a thick carpet of hair running to grey across his sagging chest.

"What is it?" he bellows, but I note his aura is blue with fear, though tinges of a red rage still shoot through it. Whatever happened, it's over now. A dark feeling of dread settles in the pit of my stomach.

"Good evening, sir." I stretch my face into as much of a smile as I can, straining to look past him into the darkened room. "We are about to close the kitchen. Is there anything I can get you?"

"I'm okay," he snaps and turns to close the door, but Big Goliath places a hand on it, forcing it open. The man narrows his eyes at the surprising strength of the old man, but the shapeshifter keeps his expression mild and slightly vacant.

"What of your guest, sir," I ask. "Would she like anything?"

The man's expression goes dark and he steps toward me, pushing his bulk out in front of him. I suppose the move is meant to intimidate, but it has little effect on me. I've taken on worse than this little man. His stomach presses into my chest, but I don't budge and neither do my smile or my gaze. This clearly unnerves him.

"She's okay also," he says, shrinking into himself and taking several steps back. He tries closing the door again, but Big Goliath still has it open. His anger is gone now. It's all fear. No, it's terror.

"If you change your mind, please let us know!" I say in my cheeriest voice. The man nods quickly and only then does Big Goliath take his hand from the door, allowing him to close it.

"Did you see her in there?" I ask him. The room was too dark for my human eyes, but the shapeshifter's preferred form is a massive dire wolf, and he has always had good night vision. He shakes his shaggy head, and my foreboding deepens. She could have been in the bathroom, I tell myself—though I didn't hear any water running, and the old plumbing of the toilet was suspiciously quiet. I place a hand against the wall next to the door. It feels like I'm dipping into a bucket of ice water, the cold climbs up my arm into my shoulder, and the low wailing intensifies. I drop my hand.

Crap.

"Are you sure she didn't just leave?" Ash asks as she spoons generous helpings of okro soup into a bowl for Big Goliath. The shapeshifter joins Habakuk and me at the kitchen table and happily tucks into his massive mound of pounded yam.

The inn is officially closed, and we are gathered in our living quarters for the last meal of the day, but I have little appetite. I watch Habakuk struggle with the thick slices of yam slathered in salted palm oil on her plate until I can't take it anymore. Irritated, I pick up my knife and cut her yam up into more manageable chunks.

"She didn't 'just leave', Ashkernas," I snap. "I've been at the desk all day, I would have seen her. Also, she's been touched. I would have felt her."

"Well, maybe she's gone invisible, like that boy who came with his family last month," Ash continues, taking her place at the other end of the table across from me. "Remember how we spent the whole day looking for him, and in the end, he was just asleep on the chair in the room?"

"This is different. Use your sense, can't you tell something is wrong?"

She cocks her head, frowning. "I feel cold ... and a wind? You're sure it's not those poor boys in the lobby?"

I sigh and silently repeat the Serenity Prayer. Then I shove my chair back and stand. "You know what? It's okay. I'll find out what's going on by myself. You, just sit down and relax. If I need somebody to clean that girl's blood, I will call you."

"Herkinal, it's not like that now!" But I ignore her and stalk out of the kitchen.

I emerge into the lobby to find that the wood spirits have finally moved. They are standing by the front doors, but they don't seem to be leaving. Instead, they are stock still, their faces turned towards the big staircase that leads to the upstairs suites on the other side of the room. It's almost as if they are waiting for something.

The entire room has gone deathly cold, so cold that I can see my breath in front of my face. I shiver and duck behind the registration desk to grab the sweater that I usually keep draped over the back of my chair. If I hadn't raised my head at that minute, I would have missed him. But I did, just in time to see the man in the suit sneaking across the lobby, clutching a bundle under his jacket and trying to make his way silently to the door.

"Oga!"

He spins around, terrified, and almost collapses when he sees me. His aura is a chaos of several emotions all overlaid with a miasma of guilt, like an oil slick over a pool of sewage. "Are you checking out?"

"Y—Yes, of course!" He laughs nervously. "I didn't see anybody at the desk, so I was just going to go and find you."

I don't bother with the niceties this time. Not when I've just caught him trying to chop and run. As I calculate the bill, I "remember" some line items, such as the AC surcharge, the mosquito-spray payment, and an early checkout fee, that I neglected to mention when he first checked in. He has the grace not to argue them—even when I make them as outrageous as possible. He pays quickly and starts towards the door. Beyond him, I see that the wood spirits have fixed their hungry gazes on him.

"Oga, what of your guest?"

He stops, startled. "Who? Oh, yes … she—she's still sleeping."

"Up till now? Wasn't she sleeping before?"

"So somebody can't sleep inside your hotel again? See, you better not disturb her, okay? Allow her to rest and she will check out in the morning." The man tries to draw together the tattered remains of his earlier bluster, but he does a poor job of it.

I consider calling out to him again, but I note the edge of a high-heeled shoe peeping out from under the bulge of his coat. I watch him hurry to the door, the spirits shifting in anticipation with every step he takes towards them. As he passes over the threshold and out into the night, they latch onto him one by one until they are a tangle of frost around his whole body and he is barely visible beneath them. The man pauses just outside the glass-fronted doors of the inn and draws his jacket closer around him, hunching his shoulders as if against a cold wind that only he can feel.

In the short time that they were in our hotel, those spirits sucked in every ounce of warmth and good fortune that came near us. Though they are barely out the door, I can already feel the cloud of anger and ill will that had surrounded me for the last few weeks lifting.

His will be a bad death.

"A bad death for a bad man." I'm not surprised to see Habakuk by my side standing on the low footstool we keep behind the desk. Even on her tiptoes, with her fingers gripping the counter, her eyes just peep over the counter.

We share a look.

"Go and call Big Goliath."

The cold on the penthouse floor has deepened. Big Goliath and I make our way slowly down the hallway, dreading what we'll find in the room. The wailing from before has coalesced into a mournful wordless keening—a dirge that brings tears to my eyes. We open the door to the room and switch on the light.

It's empty.

Beyond its size, the penthouse suite is fairly standard in its décor and furniture: in the middle a king-sized mahogany bed flanked by two matching bedside tables; voluminous curtains that are always closed to hide how small the windows are, a center table, and two armchairs instead of one. The contents of the minifridge in the corner are untouched—as are the cheap liquors we keep in expensive-looking carafes on top of the sideboard. The bedding is lying in a crumpled heap on the floor, as if pulled off in a hurry, but other than that the room is as clean as a surgeon's blade, and just as cold.

The noise is louder in here, though still oddly muffled. Then I notice that the door to the bathroom is closed. That's strange enough, stranger still is the blue light leaking from under the door, as if someone has lit a hundred fluorescent lamps inside. Except I know there's only a single naked bulb hanging from the ceiling in there. The cold seems to seep into my bones and my skin erupts in goosebumps. Behind me Goliath growls, and I turn to see he's shifted into his dire wolf form, which he prefers for combat. His fur is standing on end. Somehow that makes it worse.

I open the bathroom door.

I'm hit with a wordless scream, filled with more agony than anyone can endure. As if all the grief of every age and time were contained in it, as if every nerve was being flayed with cold. It continues without respite, without end, and I want to double over. There is so much pain in it … yet there's no one here. In the glow of the blue light, I can see that the tub is clean, the toilet hasn't been used, even the sink next to it is still spotless, the bathroom mirror, though …

For one thing, it's the source of the awful blue light. Faint wisps of smoke curl languidly from its surface, like a bag of dry ice. My reflection is oddly distorted by the mirror's warped surface and looking into it feels wrong … so wrong that it makes me nauseated. I want to turn away, but something catches my eye. I fumble for the torchlight I wear clipped to my belt in case of the frequent blackouts and shine its light directly into the mirror. Even then, I can only just make out the girl trapped inside, a paper doll encased in a thick block of ice. And she is still screaming.

My hands are shaking so much I can barely get the mug of hot tea to my mouth. Ashkernas has joined me on the couch in our small living room and has wrapped her arms around me. She is rubbing my back and rocking me gently as if I'm one of her strays—for once, I don't mind. I still feel cold, even with our heaviest wool blanket over my shoulders. We've shut down the whole penthouse floor, citing repairs. I can still hear the girl's screaming, even though it's only inside my own head.

"May all the gods punish that man," Ash murmurs.

"I'm sure they will," I say, recalling the wood sprites. Big Goliath lumbers into the room with the teapot and carefully refills my mug. His brown eyes are filled with understanding, and I almost want to cry. Instead, I burrow deeper into the blankets. Next to me, Ash suddenly stiffens.

"Where's Habakuk?"

We find her in the bathroom of the penthouse suite standing on top of the closed toilet cover and leaning over the bathroom mirror. Her head is in her hands and she's tranquilly staring into it. She looks up as we burst into the room.

"I was talking to the girl in the mirror," she says.

As Ash lifts her off the toilet, I notice the room's temperature has returned to normal. The mirror is clear and its sick blue light is gone. More importantly, the room is silent.

"What happened here?" I ask her.

"She was afraid of the bad man," Habakuk replies. "The bad man wanted to do something to her, but she ran away and hid. I told her he was gone, so she can go home now."

I crouch until I'm eye level with my niece. Her yellow gaze is clear, untroubled. There's no trace of the girl's anguish in her.

"And did she? Did she go home?"

Habakuk nods. "I showed her the way." Then she beams, and it's the first time I think I've ever seen her truly smile. "Her name was Aisha."

The next morning, I'm sitting on the veranda in the back of our living quarters, looking over the empty garden lot. I've been meaning to plant something out here ever since we moved in, but I've never gotten around to it. Maybe now's the time. It's a Market Day so the world is quiet. The front desk isn't due to open for a few hours yet, the morning sun is warm on my face, and I drink it in.

I don't have to open my eyes to know that Habakuk is next to me. I'm not sure why I've never been able to sense her before, but now she shines like a yellow-gold coin glinting in the light. I open my eyes, and she's freshly bathed, water droplets beading like diamonds in her dark hair. I reach out and touch the soft, springy mass of it.

"This, your hair, won't you allow anyone to make it?"

"You are the only one who can do it well. I was just waiting for you."

We exchange a look.

"Go and bring me a comb."

A CURSE AT MIDNIGHT

by Moustapha Mbacké Diop

I was at my window that night, soaking up the dazzling rays of moonlight, a tender breeze relaxing my exhausted soul. Make no mistake, the view was not extraordinary. There was just a soothing simplicity in seeing the shriveled mango tree, along with chickens bickering over poor worms and other insects that swarmed below it.

This had always been my favorite spot to think, or just be. Although right now, I just wanted to be diverted from the pain, its ribbons of fire twirling around my abdomen, which felt gaping and empty at the same time.

"The painful token of childbirth will not leave your body alongside your baby," my mother had said with her guttural voice, altered by years of smoking tobacco with her old, cracked pipe. "You better get used to it, Magar. The pain will be here for a while."

For some reason, the women in my bloodline always have difficult pregnancies. Being married for almost ten years, I myself had almost given up hope of getting pregnant, but last year, the miracle happened. The pregnancy had been riddled with complications, and I was still recovering, three days after giving birth to my son.

I turned and looked at him, my mouth curving into a weary smile. He was sleeping, my sweet boy, liberated into this ruthless world after causing me so much worry. However, just looking at his angelic face, hands tightly clenched in his sleep, I realized that all the pain, mood swings, and fearful tears were worth it.

With a deep sigh, I fiddled with the sachet I was holding in my right hand, my thoughts going to my mother's words when she gave it to me.

"Don't play the little toubab with me, Magar, not this time," she had said the day we came back from the hospital. She held out three twigs taken from a broom, a chunk of charcoal, and rolls of black twine. "Keep this close to your boy, especially where he sleeps at night."

My mother would often use that word—toubab—to taunt me, since it referred to people of European lineage, or anyone speaking decent French, really. Neither she nor my little sister, Astou, had gone to school, but I was able to finish college and was teaching math at a public school nearby.

I had told her, "Yaye, you know I don't believe in this stuff. We'll be just fine without it, I assure you." But I should've known there was no use arguing with Yaye Awa Diedhiou when spiritual stuff was involved.

In the small town we lived in, people still visited her from time to time, asking for protection charms and ritual baths. Her ancestors had been the spiritual protectors of our kin, and I was sure she knew more about the old arts than she let on. After she retired from the army, she came back here to fulfill her role, like her mother did before her.

Yaye Awa had expected me to do the same, but I didn't want to have anything to do with all that hocus-pocus. Astou, on the other hand, was thrilled to play the chamberlain, and meticulously organized the appointments that Yaye Awa assigned. My mother would pass on a few bits of knowledge in exchange, and, of course, would never miss an opportunity to tell me how delighted she was that my little sister was her worthy heiress, unlike the good-for-nothing toubab that I was.

"My house, my rules," she had concluded, forcing the charms into my hands with a stare, challenging me to persist in my rejection.

Nope, I was not suicidal. Therefore, I accepted the offering, already planning to throw it in the trash can, hoping she wouldn't notice.

Now, without a second glance, I got rid of it before taking my phone to call my husband. Ismaïla emigrated to the United States before we were married and had been working there ever since, returning to Senegal only twice a year. This time, he was coming back for the special occasion, and I wanted to hear from him before he got on the plane.

We spent a few minutes talking, even if it was mostly me listening to him repeat how excited he was to meet his son. I couldn't help but smile, knowing how much he had wanted this to happen, but he still managed to stay patient and caring with me, as much as he could despite the distance. I knew his parents (uptight, conservative people that they were) wanted him to marry a second wife. I was concerned that he might not be able to resist them forever and could already hear my sister's dry laugh.

"*Senegalese men are all the same,*" she'd say. "*Your charms are withering, or you're not laying children by the minute? They just find a younger, prettier co-wife.*"

Putting aside those silly thoughts, I hung up after he wished me a good night, asking me to kiss his son for him, but the weariness looming over me became more difficult to ignore. I changed into an old shirt and baggy sweatpants before going to bed and covered my loose cornrows with a head scarf.

Tomorrow will be an ecstatic day, I said to myself. Ismaïla was coming back after five long months, and he would finally meet his son.

The tepid lilac sheets, courtesy of my thoughtful sister, were a blessing for my sore muscles. Wrapping myself even tighter, I inhaled the rich smell of gowé incense that impregnated the sheets. Soon enough, the steady song of cicadas and the purifying breeze shrouded me in a peaceful sleep.

I abruptly awoke in the middle of the night, my heart pounding so fast I felt as if I'd just run a marathon. Not a sound was to be heard, apart from my ragged breath. Lost amid this terror coming out of nowhere, I turned to check on my baby.

An abomination stared at me, crouched right where my baby was supposed to be.

A body, furred and bulky like that of a gorilla, giving off a pungent smell of wet excrement and rotten corpses. A face, slowly losing the humanity it usurped, with red and wild eyes fixed on mine. A mouth wide opened, filled with sharp, irregular teeth which sunk deep into the flesh above my right clavicle when the creature pounced on me, and scarlet rivers of blood splattered across the sheets.

I howled, tears of shock filling my eyes.

Answering my distress call, the door opened violently. Yaye Awa was in her night outfit, an old shirt like mine and a wrapper. She pointed her old rifle at the creature drinking my blood as I lay paralyzed with terror. It stared back, turning away from its gruesome meal, but with steady hands and unflinching eyes my mother fired, and hit it straight in the stomach.

Thick blood oozed from its wound as the creature screeched and jumped away from me. At a speed near-invisible to the human eye, it escaped through the window, leaving me bloody and horrified.

My mother leaned through the window, peering over a courtyard immersed in darkness as she tried to see where it went. Giving up, she ran to my bedside and began to examine my wound.

"Thank God, that bastard didn't cut too deep," she said, tearing up the sheets and using the shreds to apply pressure on the wound.

"Yaye, where is my baby? What the hell was that thing?" I asked in a tremulous voice.

My sister walked in, rubbing her eyes and rearranging her loincloth back in place. At the sight of all the blood covering me, she slapped her hands over her gasping mouth.

"Bring the green sunguf from my chest," Yaye yelled. "Quick!"

Without a word, Astou ran to the living room where my mother received her clients and came back a minute later carrying a jar filled with some green powder.

"Brace yourself, daughter. This is going to hurt." She poured some powder into her palm, muttering words in dioula, her native tongue, before she sprinkled it over my wound.

I couldn't contain a cry when the substance met my exposed flesh, but the scorching pain was brief. The powder absorbed the coagulated blood and the demon's saliva, not closing the wound as you'd expect a strange magical powder to do, but drying it up and leaving a protective residue like green salt crystals. While Yaye was working her charms, Astou had removed the sheets and threw them in a corner of the room. When our mother was finished, she helped me change into new clothes, and before I knew it, a cup of water was slipped into my hand.

"Yaye, where is he?" I asked again.

"You didn't leave the talisman I gave you by his side, did you? Stupid, toubab girl," she sputtered.

"Please!" I cried. "Where is my son?"

"That thing who attacked you was a demon," she finally said. "A changeling, so to speak."

"A what?"

"You heard me well. It wasn't some rabid animal, but a djinné, traded for your son. Obviously it was a child too, or all of us would be dead already."

Her words sounded like complete gibberish to me, but part of me knew they were true. All the stories she used to tell us when Astou and I were little, that I was too afraid of, and that later, my logical mind couldn't see as anything other than old-woman tales. This was a nightmare come true. What kind of mother was I to let my son be abducted? In my own house?

"It still doesn't tell me where my baby is. Yaye, what if he's in danger?"

"Is this who I think it is?" Astou asked, ignoring me.

Yaye nodded, her flat nose wrinkling as if she smelled something particularly foul. "It's Ciré, that old hag. Heard she was messing with djinné now."

"Why would she take my son?" I shouted, fear now entangled with rage. "I don't even know this woman!"

Yaye took a deep breath, her black, deep-set eyes avoiding mine. "I might be responsible for this. She is the one person who hates me enough to try and hurt me or my family. And she might have the power to break through the barriers I raised around the house, allowing the djinné to enter while she took your baby. Around sunset, I did have a slight feeling that they might've been disrupted, but I didn't give it much of a thought. I am getting old."

She sighed. "Her beef is with me, Magar, and she's always liked to prey on the weak." She scowled. "To think that she and I were friends."

Without giving me time to react, she got on her feet and handed the gun to Astou. I was more than flabbergasted to see my baby sister handle it with an expert touch, her delicate fingers tinkering with it in a way far beyond my understanding. "Yaye taught me," she said with a little smile in reaction to my widened eyes.

"You gonna stay here in case Ismaïla comes back before we do," my mother said to her, "or in case that thing comes back."

Lord, I had almost forgotten about my husband. What was I going to say to him? New tears threatened to come forth at the thought of everything going wrong, but I kept them at bay. Tears would not bring my baby back, now was time for action.

Eyes heavenward, I fervently prayed to Allah for no harm to come to my baby, then I turned toward my mother, my fists clenched. "What are we going to do?" I asked.

The corners of her mouth quirked up in a devilish smile, and Yaye walked out of the room, beckoning me to follow her.

"I'm gonna change into something more suitable, and we are getting your son back. Nobody messes with my family. It's time to teach that hideous goat a lesson."

Less than ten minutes later, my mother and I walked out of the house, stalking the dormant streets. She was wearing a sweater and her old military pants, and I was dressed in sportswear. Yaye was almost sixty years old, but at this moment she didn't look a day over forty. In her right hand she held her old pipe, and over her shoulder was a satchel containing some trinkets, powders, and what she said was a ceremonial knife.

"Do you know where she lives?" I asked.

"I do. But I have to warn you, Magar. The road to her den is filled with deceptions." She grabbed my neck and hugged it. "I'll need you to be brave and to keep your head straight. For the sake of your son."

I nodded, a lump in my throat, as I followed her lead. Yet I couldn't help but resent her for what was happening. If I were not her daughter, wouldn't my son be at my side, safe and sound? Still, our priority right now was rescuing him, there would be plenty of time to begrudge her later.

Leaving our block, she took a fork to the left. There were fewer and fewer houses, and soon we had reached the forest edge. Different types of trees loomed over us, Flamboyant and Neem, threatening our very presence in these woods, making us feel unwelcome. The sounds of small animals grew louder, as if they were angered by our nocturnal intrusion.

Yaye looked unconcerned, but so soon after a creepy supernatural encounter, I was terrified by every dark corner, every shadow that my mind saw moving. Stumbling on an insidious root, I would've fallen on my face if it weren't for Yaye, who stabilized me with her hand.

"Watch your step," she growled.

Breathless, I took a second to catch my breath, leaning against the rough, hostile trunk of a baobab tree. How could my life have become this madness? I was a teacher, a mathematician, my husband a man who flew across oceans by plane—how could I now be a hunter of demons beside a woman whose magic I'd long since stopped believing in?

"Come on, girl," this same woman snapped, "or are you too tired already?"

As we walked, I remembered the story Yaye told us for the first time when our father was dying. With tears in her eyes, she spoke of the man who once trapped a female djinné, stealing strands of her hair, hence binding her to his service. Yet despite him being the master, he fell in love with the djinné and after a couple of years freed her from her bond. The djinné left him, returning to her realm, and he died of sorrow soon after that.

This was the place for magic, in stories to distract children from the imminent tragedy awaiting them! But here I was now, terrified for my son, the most precious thing in the world to me. I'd shed blood and tears to bring my child into this world, and now he was in the hands of an evil, unknown woman. An evil, unknown *witch*.

"What's your history with this Ciré anyway?" I asked as the trees closed in on us like a vegetal prison.

After a reluctant moment of silence, Yaye said, "She was my best friend, back when we were little girls. We played together, ran around like headless chicken, even passed initiation together. I believed nothing could tear us apart."

"What happened then?"

"Jealousy happened, Magar. I was better in every domain, a virtuoso in the old arts. I was in line to inherit my mother's role as our spiritual guardian, and she had twenty and one brothers who preceded her. I was the apple of my mother's eye, the pride of our ancestors, Mother used to say. But Ciré's parents couldn't even see her for the talented girl she was. Perhaps I'm partially responsible for what she became, considering the fact that I drifted from her, from everyone really, in order to find my own path."

"You feel sorry for her," I realized.

"I *did*. After that, from the way she interacted with me when we occasionally saw each other, I knew she blamed me for everything.

I received spiritual attacks, curses meant to cause a fatal disease, or make me barren. Of course, I shooed them away like mosquitoes, but now she takes my grandson? I can't afford to feel pity towards someone who harms the innocent."

Yaye didn't say a word after that, and it was only then that I noticed the sudden silence, far from the inimical murmur of earlier. This late-night trek did nothing to alleviate my claustrophobia, especially with moonlight unable to penetrate the canopy anymore. To elude the deafening darkness, we had nothing but our feeble flashlights. Uneasy, I was about to ask her if we had arrived when the ground gave way beneath me.

The earth swallowed me whole, like a starving grave, and I fell.

I screamed at the top of my lungs, calling for my mother, my deceased father, Ismaïla, anyone. The darkness itself was a monster, clawing at my soul and whispering unholy words to me, unspeakable phrases coming straight from the bowels of Hell. Feeding off my every fear and torment, the tunnel coiled around me as if it were a python, and I its prey.

I began to suffocate, mouth and nostrils full of decaying dirt, heart overflowing with dread, when something like a tree branch wrapped tightly around my waist and dragged me from the clutches of death.

It was Yaye's old pipe, planted in her palm and slowly absorbing her blood, thus becoming an extension of her arm.

But I could barely see any of that, because the moment I stopped coughing from all the dirt I had swallowed, the screams kicked in. I wailed like a wounded animal, and in that instant, I had no control over my own mind.

My mother held my head between her hands as she wiped my face with her sleeve. Then she slapped me, hard. "Daughter, get a hold of yourself!"

At last, I stopped screaming, my throat as sore as if caught in barbed wire. I clung to Yaye, desperately longing for a semblance of human touch after this near-death experience. She allowed me to, vigorously rubbing my back before I pushed her away, gulping down air like a drowned woman.

"I just gave birth to you a second time," she snickered as she helped me up.

I sniffed. "Yaye, you slapped me."

"Oh, but you're welcome," she said, all sweetness.

I couldn't help but smile, picking up my flashlight and turning it back on. The aftertaste of tainted soil stuck in the back of my throat, and I thanked the Lord that it wasn't the rainy season at this moment, or I would've ingested bacteria and all their cousins.

"What was that?" I asked. "The tunnel felt ... alive somehow."

"It was. She booby-trapped all the perimeter surrounding her house, and this pitfall was spiced up with djinné magic. But look. We're here."

She pointed her finger to a hut that I wouldn't have seen otherwise. It was partially hidden by scary trees, so contorted and shriveled, our mango tree back at home paled in comparison. I couldn't see any other traps, but now I knew they would be there.

Yaye went ahead of me, silently indicating the spots I had to avoid putting my feet on. We slowly crossed this minefield that way, in the dark, given that the moon refused to light up this wretched place.

It was 5 a.m. by my watch when the decrepit door appeared within sight, but Yaye pulled at my sleeve, motioning me to stop. She buried her hands inside her satchel before taking out her powders, stuffing a small quantity of them into her pipe and lighting it. She inhaled the fumes deep into her lungs, then with a shiver she turned the pipe over to me.

"There's no way I'm smoking that," I whispered. "What if it's drugs?"

"*What if it's drugs,*" she said mockingly. "These are just magically enhanced herbs. Besides, I crushed them myself, don't worry."

"That's what a low-class drug dealer would say."

She rolled her eyes and shoved the pipe into my hands. With a sigh, I inhaled the strange smoke, which smelled of dried basil and kola nut—a surprisingly balanced combination. Then the strangest thing happened: it was like lightning bolts ran through my veins as though raging steeds, starting from my neck all the way down my limbs. I coughed, my eyes stinging from the smoke, and what could only be magic running through my body.

"What we just inhaled will protect us against any curse that goat could throw at us," Yaye said. "But I'm gonna need you to do something."

She murmured instructions into my ears, and my shoulders tightened, beads of sweat tickling my upper lip. The consequences of her strategy could be dangerous, but I knew that to get my son back, I was ready to risk everything. We both were.

At last, she took out her ceremonial knife, a rusted blade, its handle covered with several strips of red cloth and centered by a single cowrie shell. With it, she drew a cross in the air, and I distinctly heard the sound of fabric being torn. Without a second's hesitation, she busted down the door, and we walked in.

The air inside the hut was stale and overwhelming, making my skin itch. The light of a fire with dancing greenish flames allowed me to discern the configuration of the place. The first thing I saw was my baby, who, thank the Heavens, looked unharmed. He was lying on a shabby bed in the corner of the room, the edges of its sheets way too close to the fire for my taste. There was an entire section of the wall in front of me covered in wooden statues, representing unknown deities with long, eerie faces and protruding abdomens, side by side with stylized animals. A chill went down my spine when I realized that blood still crusted some of them.

My inspection only lasted a few seconds before the owner of the premises, rummaging in an antique, iron chest, noticed our intrusion. She was short and seemed frail, younger than I expected, although her constantly scowling face didn't make her look any better. She wore an ankara dress that had seen better days, and her ashy feet were bare.

When she saw my mother, she screamed, veins popping out, and hatred in her eyes.

Good, because I too had hatred to spare. That woman abducted my baby, and judging by the various sharp instruments at the foot of the bed, she was about to hurt him. It took every ounce of my willpower not to immediately rush to my son, but I had to trust Yaye to dismantle the situation quickly.

Like an angry goat, the woman jumped at my mother's throat, sending a trail of stinking smoke in our direction. Yaye shrugged it off and advanced on her opponent, but I instantly fell to the floor, motionless. As useless as I was, I could only watch as the two women argued, blood ready to spill.

"Give me my grandson back, Ciré," my mother warned, promises of ghastly murder exuding from her voice, "and I might consider breaking only a few of your fingers."

"You're in no position to negotiate!" Ciré said in a grating tone. "I will suffer no interruption; your turn will come soon enough after I'm done with the baby."

I hissed at the mention of my son, and the woman gave me an unfaltering, dismissive glance. "What were you going to do with him, huh?" I managed to say.

"His blood will reveal all your mother's secrets to me, and I will curse her whole bloodline, until the last descendant. The only thing that remains to be done is for me to harvest the first ray of sunlight. At dawn, Yaye Awa Diedhiou, you will be done for!"

"That's low, even for a powerless crone like you," my mother spat as she wielded her pipe, which transformed into a gnarled, full-sized staff. "This folly ends now."

"Not so fast. Didn't you hear? I have a new friend now." Green flames illuminating her gaunt, demented face, Ciré brandished what looked like strands of hair: glossy, purple locks held together by a scarlet string.

"Djinné hair," my mother gasped as the woman blew thrice on the locks, stepping back with an evil grin. Not a second later, the air in front of Yaye rippled as if we were seeing it from underwater. A great gust of wind blew across the room, heralding the approach of something otherworldly, and my baby began to cry.

A shadow appeared before my eyes, its curves becoming clearer and clearer. It was a female being, more than seven feet tall, with dark, naked skin and broad shoulders. Her bulging eyes were surmounted by hirsute eyebrows, and her luxuriant hair was so long it trailed on the dusty floor, matching the locks Ciré had in the palm of her hand.

Ciré had perverted that sad but beautiful tale my mother told so long ago by doing what she did, and I didn't need to be a master in the old arts to know what. And in that moment, I heard my mother's voice in my head.

"That vixen thinks the world revolves around her, so just pretend to have been thrown out of the equation, even though you're magically protected. She's working with dangerous forces above our reach, so you'll have to be the one who takes her out. All her attention will be focused on me, so I'll *be your distraction. Just trust me and wait until the right moment."*

"Because of you, I never had anything in this world," Ciré was ranting. "Everyone turned away from me and looked up to you, their precious pupil. Now, I have the upper hand, and *I* say this ends now."

Pointing at my mother, she howled at the djinné in a strange language of cackles and hoarse sounds. Seeing the last spark of sanity leave the woman's eyes, replaced by sheer madness, I knew what those words meant.

As instructed, the djinné charged my mother, lifting her off the ground as easily as a twig. Yaye struck it with a resolute blow of her staff, aiming for its flank, but it only bounced off its thick skin. The djinné growled at my mother, baring fangs very much like those which its offspring had sunk into me. There was no going back from what was about to happen, and the djinné buried its claws into Yaye's right flank.

My mother cried out, and I felt for her, as Ciré's eyes lit up with ferocious delight—but I'd awaited the right time. And now it was.

I dropped my act and hurtled towards Ciré, the only thing she saw coming was my fist right in her face. I heard a satisfying crack when my punch fractured her nose, sending blood flowing down her face, though my knuckles probably broke in the process.

I ignored the stinging pain and pulled the locks of hair out of Ciré's grip, oblivious to her cries of pain as she held her face. The djinné dropped my mother to the ground to confront its mistress's new assailant, but I threw the locks into the impatient green flames. They were immediately consumed, breaking the bond enslaving the demon.

With a roar of triumph, it leaped on top of Ciré, piercing her chest with its claws. Both of them vanished, just the way it came, leaving nothing but Ciré's shrieks of terror fading on the sudden wind. Then it, and they, were gone.

Entirely drained, I struggled to get up and help my mother, the same way she helped me just a few hours ago.

"Go see to your son," she muttered through clenched teeth. "I'll be just fine."

I nodded, tears of relief streaming down my face as I got up and ran to my baby. He was breathless, eyes puffy from all that crying, and right now I was no better. Calming myself by slowly inhaling his sweet scent, I tried singing the lullaby Yaye used to sing to us when we were upset, and I heard her chuckles when I shamelessly butchered the dioula words. Fortunately, it worked, and he fell asleep between my arms.

Yaye got up, residues of the healing powder on her fingers and her bloody clothes.

"Are you alright?" I asked.

"Takes more than a couple of scratches to overcome me, girl. We need to get out of here, it's dawn."

I frowned, realizing that it would be complicated to carry my baby through the uneven path back to our home. But as always, Yaye was one step ahead of me. Without a word, she pulled out the bedsheet, for lack of anything better, and tied the baby securely against my back.

"That, little toubab, is how it's done."

We exchanged a smile as we got out of the hut into the rising dawn. It was incredible how just a little more light could make a place look less frightening, and the way back was nothing like the hellish track we'd had to face earlier. The forest was awakening, and listening to the reassuring sound of birds chirping, it occurred to me that people back in town would be awake too, women pounding millet and sweeping courtyards.

Not once did we turn around to look at the old hut, but we were both thinking about Ciré.

"What do you think is going to happen to her?" I asked, as we sneaked behind houses, careful not to raise too many questions about my disheveled look and Yaye's bloodstained clothes.

"She messed with the wrong forces, and now she's paying the price," Yaye said, her voice saddened. "Djinné are proud creatures, and this one sounded way too eager to claim retaliation. We may never see Ciré again."

I was expecting that answer, yet I didn't feel sorry for her, not in the slightest. She had an awful ending, but she brought it on herself. That's where a life of hatred led her, and evil could only appeal to evil. I knew my mother felt remorse about what had happened to her, even if she wouldn't admit it. It wasn't her fault though, and neither was my son's abduction by a bitter, vengeful woman. It would be unfair of me to still blame her, especially after she put her life on the line to save my baby.

When we finally got home, Astou was clearly relieved to see us back in one piece—to a certain extent—and she immediately tended to my mother's wounds, assuring me that they were not severe.

She also told me that my husband had left me a text message, saying he had landed safely and would be here in a few hours. He arrived in the early afternoon and found us all seated in the living room.

Yaye, smoking her enigmatic pipe; Astou, making tea while humming around whatever mbalax song was trending at the moment; and me, breastfeeding our baby as if nothing had happened.

It was only in that moment, when Ismaïla held us both close to his chest, his eyes tired but gleaming with all the love he had for us, that I allowed myself to ignore the decaying scent prowling around our home.

Because there was one side to the stories that my mother never told us before, and that she finally revealed to me right when we arrived at our doorstep, dirty and exhausted.

"Once a djinné gets a taste of your blood, my little toubab, it will never stop coming after you, not until he drinks it all. One day, that little djinné baby will return to feed again.

"But when that time comes, we will be ready."

A MASTERY OF GERMAN

by Marian Denise Moore

Somewhere in the world, there is a man, seventy years old, a native New Orleanian who has never left the city except for the occasional Category 5 hurricane. He has a sixth-grade education but has always held some type of paying job. However, if you ask him a question in German, he will answer you without hesitation in an accent reminiscent of the region around Heidelberg.

I still remember watching one of our Belgium-born board member's eyes widen in shock as Victor—that's his name—responded to a question in German. The executive immediately asked Victor where he had served in the army. No, he did not serve in Germany, or anywhere else for that matter, for as I said, he has rarely left the city and has never actually left the state.

Victor Johnston was sixty-five then and secure in his position as an elder, so he laughed in the manager's face. If asked, Victor could have also told the manager what it felt like to be an eleven-year-old girl and how it felt to have your period start thirty minutes before you left for school. But the executive did not ask those questions. Their conversation was brief, so the manager didn't notice that Victor's vocabulary was stuck at the level of an eighteen-year-old girl, my age when my family returned to the United States after my father's third tour of duty.

He turned to our second trial subject and missed the problem and the promise of Engram's newest spotlight project. That was exactly what I planned.

"We need a win, Candace," Lloyd said. He pulled his hand through his sandy hair, got up from his desk and checked the door to his office which I had already snicked closed. The move disguised his need to pace. I had struggled when describing him to my father. He was tall, but with too much nervous energy to be a golfer. I had decided on a retired track star who had graduated to the coaching ranks. He stood beside the desk now, too high-strung to sit down. Despite the chill of the room, his jacket was slung over the back of his chair.

We need a win. Translation: "I need a win." No difference. Lloyd was my supervisor. If he won, I won.

"I thought you wanted me to hang back and shadow Helene?" I asked.

"Yes, well. About that"—Lloyd sat on the edge of his desk—"I need you to take over one of Helene's projects. She's taking leave early."

"Before June? Before the bonuses are calculated? Isn't one of her projects on the spotlight list?"

I watched the flicker of annoyance cross Lloyd's face. Poor Lloyd. Saddled with two women to mentor—even if one of them did bring him plenty of reflected glory. I was willing to become a second star in his constellation. I had moved to New Orleans because of the opportunities presented by a new and hungry company.

"Doctor's orders," Lloyd said. "Nevertheless, she says that she will be checking in occasionally. That should be enough to keep her from losing out on a bonus because her baby decided to raise her blood pressure." He took another nervous pace to the door and back.

"I want you to take the Engram project," he said. "It's not on the company bonus timeline. But I need you to either kill it or bring it to some sort of conclusion. The technical lead is giving Helene the runaround."

"I've never heard of an R&D project named Engram," I said uncertainly.

"Because it is more research than development, I suspect," Lloyd said, frowning. "You need to talk to the lead. I think he told Helene that he'd gotten approval on human trials."

Lloyd hailed his computer and directed it to send me the project plan. I felt the phone in my pocket vibrate as the new task jostled itself into my short list of responsibilities. 'Kill it or bring it to conclusion' sounded like an execution order.

I should tell you what type of company Engram was at that time. For one thing, Engram wasn't the name. The name of the company was QND, named after Quinton Nathanael Delahousse, a MacArthur-recognized geneticist from LSU. QND was renamed Engram when it became the most successful product. When Lloyd handed me the Engram project, QND was five years old and still a startup as far as the tax laws of Louisiana were concerned. Some of the founding staff wagged that QND stood for "quick and dirty" because most of the projects were out the door faster than any other pharmaceutical company. During the first five years, most of our products were generics of existing drugs. None of them was the fame-making formulations that the Delahousse name seemed to promise. The spotlight projects were the high-risk, high-yield portfolios that QND hoped would support them after the state tax credits expired. Helene's spotlight had been underway since the company's founding and was finally coming to a close.

I weaved my way through the alleys of cubicles on my way back to my desk. Pausing, I poked my head around one of the seven-foot walls of textured fabric. Helene looked as busy as I anticipated. She was on the phone, firmly rehearsing the steps of some procedure or another. Her voice was level, but I could see the lines around her mouth deepen as she became more annoyed. The desk was full of folders, no doubt one for me. Helene was famous for killing trees. She'd had a presentation crash and burn because of a hard drive failure one day before an implementation review.

Glancing up at me, Helene nodded and tapped a cream folder on the top of the stack. "Yours," she mouthed.

I took the folder and retreated to my own austere desk. I dropped Helene's folder into an almostempty desk drawer where it could rattle around with the one pencil and a cheap ad pen. I promised myself to check it for notes in Helene's handwriting before I shredded it.

I tapped the keyboard embedded in my desk and brought up the project timeline that Lloyd had already sent me. Within ten minutes, I kicked my chair away and stood over the wavering image of the project plan. Pages of bullet points were followed by empty spaces. Months of deadlines blinked in red because the dates had passed with no input. Pushing the display back into the desk surface, I leaned over it and silently cursed Lloyd, Helene, and the entire board structure of QND.

I was still standing when triple raps came on the metal frame of my cubicle wall. I looked up from my angry notes to see Helene. She pulled my rolling armchair toward her and lowered herself into the padded seat. Helene was 'all baby' as my elderly aunts would say. Her arms and legs were toned and model thin from years of yoga—she was always inviting me—and her face was the polished nectarine of a southern aristocrat framed by frosted blonde hair. The baby had concentrated all of its gravitas to her middle, and she sat solidly in my desk chair with one hand perched protectively on the beach ball protrusion above her lap. Do I sound jealous? Maybe I was. It didn't matter that it had taken four years for her to become the yardstick by which I was now judging myself.

"What do you think?" she asked, pointing through me to the display on the desk. "I suggested that Lloyd give you this project," she added before I could answer.

"There are a lot of empty spaces in this plan," I said carefully.

"Yes, I know." Helene's eyes seared the surface of my desk pointedly. "There's more in the folder that I gave you. Desmond's not fond of filling out status reports. I have to drag information out of him every week. Maybe he will respond better to you."

I felt my back tense, but I retained my casual posture. And why would he respond better to me?

"When is your last day?" I asked instead. "Lloyd said that you will brief me on the project. Why is it so open-ended? That isn't QND's standard procedure."

Helene flipped her wrist over and examined her watch. "My schedule won't allow that," she said. "Desmond is in the downtown office today. You should introduce yourself. Ask him to brief you." She flipped an errant strand of blond hair away from her face, and I saw the sheen of sweat.

Leaning over, I thumbed down the heated fan that sat beneath my desk. Immediately, the chill of the air conditioning rushed into my cozy enclave. When I checked the caged thermostat that morning, someone had managed to set the temperature to sixty-five degrees. I wasn't the only one on the floor wearing a sweater, but Helene was not one of us.

"Tell me about the team lead then," I said. "You said that his name was Desmond?" I wanted to sit down, but I didn't want to sit in the lower visitor chair. "The team lead isn't a geneticist?"

Helene looked at her watch again. "Desmond is Dr. Desmond Walker," she said. "I've known him since—" she shrugged. "Before QND. He and my brother were at Jesuit together. Delahousse was impressed with his research work at Hebei University in Shijiazhuag." Her tongue stumbled over the Chinese names. "I believe that his medical degree came from Meharry in Tennessee. Have you heard of Meharry?"

Only one of the best medical schools in the HBCU universe, I thought, but I only nodded.

"I have never heard of it," Helene said. "Dr. Delahousse was very effusive. I say this only so you understand—Desmond is a favorite. He has had results; I've seen the animal trials. Give me your phone?"

Helene fiddled with the calendar function and announced finally, "Desmond has an opening in two hours. I will add you to his schedule, and you can get your questions answered. This should be easy. Let Desmond continue his research while you fill in the paperwork to appease Lloyd. I would have done more, but"—she patted her burgeoning belly—"this afternoon I have to review the press conference release. And then there's the review of the drug insert that we negotiated with the FDA." She began to rise.

"You'll come with me for the initial meeting," I said quickly.

"You can do this," she said frowning. "All you have to do—"

"I would rather if he doesn't know that I'm his new PM immediately," I said. "You didn't include that in the meeting invitation, I hope?"

"You should not ambush Dr. Walker."

Oh, he's Dr. Walker now, I thought. "I don't plan to," I said. "I want him to explain the project without the expectation that I know anything. I'll read your notes." I pulled the slim folder from the desk drawer and slid it over the recessed keyboard. "But I don't want the type of canned rosy explanation that is created for a new boss. I want to really understand."

Helene sighed, but I knew she was conceding. "We'll both be working through lunch in that case," she said. "Pass by my office in two hours and I'll take you down and introduce you."

Desmond Walker's office was a surprising modern emulation of Victorian clutter. Almost every surface was covered with personal effects. An electronic frame displayed a selection of cruise photos of his wife and two young sons at some Caribbean-looking location. There was one tall bookshelf on which some books were neatly arranged; others lay on their sides, titles obscured, and edges stained from use. Framed awards lined the walls, their lettering too small to read from my chair. Instead of focusing on them, I kept my hands in my lap as Helene ran through a brief introduction. Keeping her promise, she informed Dr. Walker that I was being introduced to all of the technical leads in Lloyd's division.

And why had that never actually happened? I wondered as I watched Desmond Walker's gaze shift from Helene to me with some wariness. He was tall, barrel-chested, and—as I had surmised from his choice of college—black. He was darker than I expected and probably in his late forties; but I was constantly fighting my expectation that all elite Black New Orleanians—the ones who could afford private schools like Jesuit—were Creole and the expectation that all Creoles were light-skinned. His hair was cropped as short as my father's, even though he had grown up in an era when dreadlocks were the cultural standard. But one could hardly carry dreadlocks into one's forties, I told myself.

"You've been here six months," Dr. Walker said slowly. "Have you worked in biotech before?"

Meaning, I thought, 'You're young to be in management. What experience do you have?'

"No," I said. "I worked four years at BASF in Germany, two years at Exelon in Chicago, and two years at Tenet in Dallas. When I interned at BASF, I realized that I was more interested in the process of seeing a project to completion. I found the political juggling for resources exciting; most people find it infuriating." I gazed firmly into his eyes, silently willing him to be impressed.

Out of the corner of my eye, I could see Helene frowning at her buzzing wrist. Oh really, I thought. Did you arrange for a phone call just to get out of this meeting? Then my phone rang.

"Sorry," I said and turned the sound off without checking the screen.

Five minutes later, one of the framed paintings on Dr. Walker's wall faded to grey and lights began to chase around the frame's edge. Dr. Walker glanced at Helene and tapped the answer button on his desk.

"Walker!" Lloyd's voice barked from the pewter surface. "Is Helene there? Her intern thought she was meeting with you. I haven't been able to catch up with her."

"It's on speaker," Dr. Walker said sotto voce and nodded to Helene.

"I'm here," Helene called. "Sorry, Lloyd. I was introducing Candace—"

"Have you seen outside?" Lloyd said. "Walker, turn your screen on. I'm sending you a feed."

The leaden display changed to a confused video of figures clad in jeans and pullovers shouting at men and women in business suits. The targets wore lanyards; each one zigzagging around the protesters, badging the lock quickly, and slipping through the office doors. Occasionally a member of the office staff had to throw up an arm to deter some demonstrators from following them inside.

"That's right outside," I blurted.

"What is this?" Helene asked.

"They say they're here for your press conference," Lloyd said.

"The press conference isn't scheduled until the end of the week," Helene said. Knowing her habits, I was certain that the notes for the event were probably printed and filed at her desk. "I haven't announced it yet."

"And yet, there they are. To oppose the Nil-facim project, I suppose."

"Who the hell protests a cure for malaria?" Helene grumbled, her voice roiling off the walls of Dr. Walker's office.

The video feed did not include sound. I watched the protesters organize themselves into a chorale that shouted at the glass doors of our office. I assumed there must be a news team outside of the view of the cameras. Curious tourists were pausing, folding their arms and listening to the newly organized demonstration.

"Obviously, some people find it fun to protest a cure for malaria," Lloyd said, his voice tight. "Do you have someone to send down to them?"

I felt Helene's gaze land on me for a minute, but I didn't turn to meet her face. I kept my eyes on Dr. Walker and the camera feed.

"No," Helene said finally. "I'll go down."

"You don't need that type of stress now," I interjected without turning. "You might … you might invite some of them up to the office. One of the protesters and one of the newsmen, preferably one with a science background. A meteorologist?"

Walker snorted behind his desk, but I saw Helene's initial smirk morph into something more thoughtful.

"It might be useful to separate the leaders from the followers," Helene said, rising. "You should stay, Candace. Desmond, could you run through your project parameters with her? It would be better if she got it directly from you. Is Lloyd still on the line?"

Dr. Walker looked at the indicator on his desk and shook his head. "He must have dropped off after you said that you'd go down."

With a curt goodbye, she was gone. Desmond Walker looked at the organized chaos displayed outside for a moment longer and then returned the screen to an indefinite southern landscape of oak trees dressed in Spanish moss.

He hummed thoughtfully, leaned back in his chair and asked, "What do you want to know about Engram?"

"All I know is that it is some type of research on memory enhancement or memory retrieval. I looked online but the closest that I could find were some studies done around 2010. Some researchers taught rats how to run a maze and then found that their descendants were able to run the same maze without training."

"Did you find anything else?"

I grimaced. "Five years later, some researchers were saying that the experience of American slavery was passed on to the descendants of the enslaved via the same process."

"Yes," Dr. Walker said. "That's one of the few follow-ups to the research at Emory University."

He swung his chair around, pulled a book off the shelf, and thumbed through it. "There hasn't been much research on that angle since 2015."

"Does your research indicate that the effects of slavery can be edited out?"

"The people downstairs are protesting our plan to edit one mosquito genus to remove its ability to carry malaria," Dr. Walker said wryly. "What do you think they would say if I proposed to edit human genes to remove anything, let alone edit African American genes? Tuskegee is always at the back of everyone's mind."

He tossed the book back on the shelf and stood, stretching. "At any rate, QND is willing to do diverse hiring, but they are not looking to solve problems unique to African Americans."

"I'm not a diverse hire," I said.

"I didn't say that you were." He considered me silently for a moment. "You have memories and talents that are unique, no doubt. Your time in Germany, for example. You speak German?"

"Of course."

"Suppose I had a client who needed to transfer to Germany in a month. No time to study the language. Your knowledge would be priceless."

"A knowledge of anything? What if I needed to know how to waltz for a Mardi Gras ball?" I countered.

"No. Dancing is mainly a physical ability. A waltz or a foxtrot has defined steps; physical coordination is critical. Language is a better fit, though I think that it would be difficult to transfer the knowledge of a language like Xhosa to someone accustomed to a Romance language like Spanish." He frowned as if the thought had brought up an avenue for consideration which he had overlooked. Leaning over the desk, he tapped notes into his desk surface.

"How are you going to get my knowledge of German into someone else's head?" Candace asked. "Write it on a chip?"

"Injecting silicone into people has an atrocious history," Dr. Walker said. "No, I am looking at a biological emulation of a human neural network." He glanced down at me from his six-foot height. "Despite what I said about editing human genes, I am proposing editing in, not editing out. I would be giving you explicit access to memories you have already inherited."

"I could give German to my children, but not to anyone else?"

"Not yet," he said. "Was that a sufficient explanation of Engram?"

"Yes." I looked at my phone and pretended to find something on my schedule. "And I do have another tech lead to meet, even if Helene isn't around to make formal introductions. Thank you."

Dr. Walker nodded, tapping on his desk again. He had already half-forgotten me. I edged out of the office. *Get a resolution or kill it,* Lloyd had said. Engram with its limited application certainly seemed ripe for killing.

"Hey, baby girl!" a gravely male voice bugled from my phone. I quickly squelched the phone to private mode.

I had the project plan and a spreadsheet open on my desk trying to find any pathway for Engram to be profitable. I was working on the scantiest of input from either Helene or Dr. Walker. Sooner or later, I would have to contact Walker.

"Hi, Dad. You know I'm at work, don't you?"

"Yeah—but I was wondering if you wanted to do dinner tonight?"

"Are you in town?" I asked. "You came to New Orleans and didn't tell me?"

My computer was insisting that I needed to take a break. I locked the machine and headed for the staircase. I was ten floors from the lobby. The staircase was private and a good way to burn off some of my aggravation.

"Nah," my father said. "I'm in San Antonio. I have this wall-sized screen in my hotel room. I figured that I'd order in. You order in at home. We share a table virtually." I could hear the humor in his voice. "You can invite Brad-slash-Juan-slash-Phillipe-slash-Tryone to the meal if you like. Introduce me to your latest beau."

"You're crazy," I said.

One floor down, a door opened, and someone pushed past me in a hurry to reach the next floor. I moved closer to the cinder-block wall to give the rushing worker room. "Are you still working off Mom's script?" My mother had died two years earlier after a long illness. I inherited my organization abilities from her, according to my father.

"Yeah," he said. "I still have the script with a few changes. Should I ask about a girlfriend? Want to invite Zawadi instead?"

"Not gay either, Dad."

"Not married either," he retorted. "We left you all of those great genes, when are you going to spread them?"

"That was actually on her list?"

"Yes. First: ask her about work," he recited. "So, how is work?"

"Challenging," I said as I reached the next landing. "They haven't figured out what to do with me."

"Neither have I," he said. "Second: ask her about her relationship status," he continued. "And you said none. Surprising. Troubling. But I've checked that off. Third: are you happy?"

"I don't remember that question," I said.

"I usually let you vent about work," he responded. "That could go on for hours, especially while you were in Chicago. I'm glad you got out of there."

"So am I," I said.

"So, dinner? You can tell me if you're happy over dinner."

"I have piles of data to read, Dad. And a decision to make."

"That sounds ominous." His voice was a pleasant baritone saxophone.

"As they say, that's why they pay me the big bucks."

"So—no dinner? You're not taking a break at all?"

"Dad, why are you in San Antonio? What are you chasing in Texas?"

"Your great, great"—I imagined him counting out relations on his fingers—"great, great, grandfather. The census says he was a stonemason."

"In San Antonio?" I paused on another landing. "Do we have people there?"

"No," he said. "Wouldn't that have been something? I was stationed here for years after we got back to the States. It would have been nice to have family here to show us the ropes."

"Dad—why this sudden interest in history? You always taught me that it's easier to run forward than backward."

"Dinner," he said. "That's a dinner discussion."

I sighed.

"Make your decision tomorrow," he continued. "Does it need to be today?"

"No, I guess not."

"Good, we're in the same time zone for once. So, eight o'clock. Please don't bring pizza again. I expect to see a real meal on the table in front of you."

He broke the connection, and I trudged back up to the tenth floor. There was little sense in putting off the revelatory call to Desmond Walker any longer.

...❖...

"Dr. Walker?"

There was a burble of voices on the other end of the line. Like most people at QND, Dr. Walker had disabled the built-in camera of his computer—which is why Lloyd had needed to ask whether Helene was present earlier. It's a team meeting, I realized. Of course there's an Engram team. If I closed down the project, I would have to consider what to do with the team. QND employees would have to be reassigned. If there were contractors, their agreements might require renegotiation.

"Ms. Toil?" I heard Walker's baritone voice ring over the cacophony. "Did you have additional questions from this afternoon?"

"Yes," I said, "but I see you're in a meeting. We can talk tomorrow."

"Tomorrow I will be in the lab. In fact, I'm leaving for the lab shortly. If there is something quick ..."

"This will take some time. I'm going over Helene's notes and the project plan. I am trying to reconcile the numbers for Lloyd."

"You should talk to Helene," he interjected.

"I will. However, you know she's taking an early leave, don't you?"

"For the baby, yes, of course," Dr. Walker said in a level voice. "But she will be back. There is no need for you to worry over the details of this project. I know you want to understand everything—"

"Dr. Walker, Lloyd has asked me to take over management of the Engram project." I could hear the chatter die on the other side of the line. "I am the new project manager," I said, realizing that I was emphasizing the news for an unseen group. I needed to be as clear as possible. "I want to start going over the project plan when you're available."

The line was silent. "Dr. Walker?"

"You should come to the lab tonight," he said finally.

"Actually, I have a dinner engagement tonight."

"The lab is on the Westbank—on the other side of the river. I am messaging you the address now." I heard a murmur over the phone line. "I'll be certain to update the system so that it'll let you in." The connection broke.

Well, shit, I thought. I should just let him sit there and wait for me. But on the other hand, I was considering shutting down the man's team. I should give him the chance to make his case. If I got there early, maybe I could still pick up a decent meal somewhere and be home by eight for dinner with my dad.

QND's lab was an odd pair of buildings on the west bank of the Mississippi River, still within New Orleans city limits. I parked, carded myself in, and paused to wonder in which of the two buildings was Desmond Walker's office. He had sent 201 as his office number, but both buildings had a second floor. I parked myself in front of the elevator in the first building, punched a button and listened as the antique mechanism inside woke up.

The first floor was dark, but I could hear voices. I soon spied a pair of figures, one pushing a mop bucket, both deep in conversation. The lights of the hallway connecting the diatomic buildings activated, flickering on and off, creating a virtual spotlight as the two walked. The elevator car arrived at the same time they did. Both men were vaguely Hispanic. The first nodded to me; the other ignored me, ranting instead about some local sports figure.

"I'm looking for Dr. Desmond Walker," I said. "He's supposed to be in room 201, but he didn't mention that there were two buildings."

"You're in the right place," the darker man said. He was the one who had acknowledged my presence earlier. "No one's in building two."

The men trailed me into the elevator and punched the button above my second-floor selection.

"I'm sorry if I'm keeping you here late," I remarked, noting the skipped floor.

"Dr. Walker always works late," the second man said. "Him, he has his own man to clean that floor."

I noted the severe look that passed from the first man to the second. The second fell silent and stared at the elevator console.

"You not the reason we still here," the first man countered. "It's a big office—two buildings and all." The elevator shuddered to a stop.

"201's at the end of the hall," the second janitor said. "Ignore the other doors. It's all one big room, but Professor Walker will be closer to the last door."

"Thank you," I said, stepping out. Both men avoided my face as the door clanged shut, and I turned to the brightly lit hall. Despite the '60's exterior, the interior had obviously been gutted and redesigned. I was met with a gleaning hallway of glossy white tile, banded by polished steel and glass. As the janitor had mentioned, there were doors on my left leading into the workroom; the only door that was open lay at the end of the hall. I could hear the muffled sound of jazz music from the local favorite station, WWOZ, echo off the hard, ceramic walls.

Desmond Walker had altered his office attire slightly to match his current environment. A white coat replaced the suit jacket that hung on a nearby clothes tree. His tie had been loosened. He didn't rise to meet me but twisted around from his perch on a lab stool to watch me enter. Unlike his work office, this workspace was sparse, the stark image of efficiency. The worktables held only computer interfaces and electronic equipment that I assumed were microscopes.

"Maybe you want to start by telling me why you didn't mention that you were the new PM this afternoon," he said.

"I've worked on projects where every morning the PL sent a smiley face to the PM as a status report," I said, ignoring his lecturing tone. "That's not what I wanted." I pulled a nearby stool closer to me and gritted my teeth at the grinding sound of its metal legs on the tile floor. "Was there anything you would've preferred to say?"

"I might have given you more time," Dr. Walker said.

"Lloyd gave me the project two hours before I spoke to you. I tried to read what I could before our meeting so that I could ask semi-intelligent questions, but …" I shrugged. "The project plan was skimpy to say the least. Helene's notes don't mention epigenetics at all." I looked across at his stern face. "Did Helene never ask? Or did she not care?" I didn't voice my more unwelcome fear—that he had spent QND money on his own dream project without consulting anyone.

Maybe my fear showed in my voice because he leaned over the worktable, thumbed a virtual keyboard to life, and began pounding the keys with fury.

"I am forwarding you the research papers I've published," he said. "They go back to 2020."

"Wait—QND has only been in existence since 2037," I said.

"My research is why Delahousse brought me in," Dr. Walker said tartly. "Didn't Helene tell you that?"

"No—wait—yes—maybe. In her own way." I peered over the images of papers on the embedded screen. "I will need someone to explain this to me. My degree was in chemical engineering, not biology, and certainly not genetics."

"Why should I waste the time of one of my team to explain genetics to you?"

"Because Helene may have been indulgent, but she reports to Lloyd just like I do," I answered. "His directive was to bring this project to conclusion or kill it. Neither of which means that you get to run a pure research project that has no commercial application."

He started to protest, but I raised a hand. "Yes, I know—I could pass my knowledge of German down to my kids. There are cheaper ways to accomplish the same thing. I can't see QND continuing to pay for this unless you have something more." I paused. "Not unless you tell me that you have Delahousse on speed dial and can bring him in. Everyone gives me the impression that he started QND and then disappeared except for the annual board meeting."

Dr. Walker was shaking his head.

"No? There's a story there, I'm sure. Listen, I'm willing to go to bat for you with Lloyd, but you have to give me something!"

Dr. Walker was silent for moment and then brought up another file. "Sit down, I'm going to give you a genetics lesson."

I groaned. "I don't have time. I have dinner tonight with my father." I was immediately angry at myself for being so specific. Walker didn't need to know anything about my personal life. I needn't have worried, for he ignored my outburst and continued talking.

"Do you know what a haplogroup is?" he asked. I shook my head.

"No?" he continued. "You've never taken a DNA test?"

"That's my father's thing," I said. "I think that he had me do one of those cotton-swab tests. He has the results."

"Well, a haplogroup is just a name of the group of genes that you inherited from your parents. Your father can show you your results. Over dinner." So he had heard after all. "Since the 2000s most people do DNA tests to find out where their family originated." He displayed a chart. "You know that homo sapiens originated in Africa. Therefore, every human on Earth descended from one woman in Africa."

The chart was shaped like a tree with a trunk labeled L0-Eve.

"If she's Eve," I interjected, "why is she L0? Not A0? Or even B0? Is it L0 because of Lucy?"

"Lucy was not in the homo sapiens species," he said. "The labels were assigned in the order that the homo sapiens gene groups were discovered." He clicked on the trunk of the displayed tree and highlighted two branches.

"Then let me guess. They started in Europe. And then, oops! Discovered that L0 was actually the oldest."

I think he chuckled even though he hid it well. "No, but it doesn't matter. L is a letter as good as any other. As my last paper indicates, I can give the memories of anyone on this line, say the L1b mutation, to another person with that same mutation."

"Helene said that you were ready for human trials," I said.

"That paper was written two years ago," he said. "Those trials have been done."

I sat back down on a nearby stool and stared at him. "So when you said that you could give my knowledge of German to my kids, you meant now. Not, maybe after additional study."

"Yes, now."

"Then what are you working on now?"

There was a clatter in one of the darkened areas of the lab. I watched lights spring to life at the far end. Dr. Walker waved briefly. "That would be Victor. He cleans this floor."

"One of the janitors said that you had your own man for this floor," I said.

"Yes, well," he paused. "It's better when the team is deep in development that they aren't disturbed by the cleaning staff." He looked back at the screen. "You asked what I was working on now."

I nodded even as I noted his odd sidestep about requesting one particular person to clean his floor.

"You're African American. Your primary haplogroup is probably one of the first branches of the L0 group." He expanded one of the tree branches on the display. "If it were L1b, I could certainly give your memory to another one with that haplogroup. Right now, the team is verifying that it is true for every mutation down the line: L1b1a, L1b1a1'4, L1b1a4, and so on."

"Why?"

"Excuse me?"

"Why is that important?"

"Because you're right. Passing your knowledge of German down to your descendants is not commercial. But everyone on Earth is a descendent of L0. If I could give your knowledge of German to anyone, that would be commercial."

I felt cold and suddenly sick. "Does QND have a company ethicist?"

"What?"

"Ever since Henrietta Lacks, I thought that every pharmaceutical company had some type of ethicist or lawyer or someone to vet their work."

"QND was not set up like a normal pharmaceutical company, but I'm certain that we have lawyers. However, I don't see the problem."

"Shit." I rubbed my temples, remembered my makeup belatedly, stared at the traces of mahogany foundation on my fingers, then looked up at him.

"Can you separate my memory of learning to drive, or German, or walking into this building this evening from anything else I know?"

"Not as yet," he said cautiously.

"I didn't think so. And if I agreed to sell you my German, how much are you going to pay for the other stuff? Learning to drive, the memory of my mother's death, my first sexual experience? Because I sure as hell am not going to give you those for free!" I kept my voice low, aware of the figure moving around at the other end of the long room. "My memories are me after all. You're proposing to sell me."

Desmond Walker's jaw was tight as he turned and closed down the screen display. "So you will close down the project," he said.

"No." I shook my head. "I'm going home to have dinner with my Dad over a video screen." I stood up. "I'll even ask him my haplogroup as you suggested. I need to think what to do."

"... And all of that history was sand. Easy to sweep away and ignore by the next generation."

"What?" I looked up from my plate where, deep in thought, I had been pushing a meatball around the swirls of red sauce.

"Oh, so you are still with me," my father said. "I wondered if you had rigged up a video loop like one of those crime capers that your mother loved."

I stared up at him. Thanks to my new video screen, it looked as if I had punched a hole in the kitchen wall into a neighbor's opulent bedroom. My father was centered in the window, but behind him hung a tapestry of an improbable frieze of two women in flamenco outfits standing in a plaza surrounded by market vegetables. It had taken two years, but he could finally mention my mother without his normally rich voice wavering like a mourning blues melody. He stood out from his lavish surrounding, a slim, dark man with grey hair cut as short as it had been during his army days. He was dressed in a black polo shirt and khakis.

"Are you still mulling over that decision you needed to make at work?" he asked.

Smiling, I touched two fingers over my mouth.

"Yes, I know you can't talk about work. But I saw something about your company on the news this evening. QND is GMO-ing mosquitoes. That isn't your project, I hope?"

"No, but—" I decided to give in to my curiosity. "What did they say?"

"Depends on who you listen to. Some say QND is releasing a genetic menace; some say that the company is a social-justice warrior promoting a project that benefits Africans more than Americans."

I shook my head as I pushed my plate away. "There will be a formal press conference later; but no, that's not my project. I did hear most of what you said earlier. You found Josiah Toil. You talked about the buildings that he probably worked on. You said that you had reached a dead end. What does that have to do with history written on sand?"

A smile split his face and he laughed. "My multitasking daughter!"

Joining his smile, I got up and tossed the remains of my take-out dinner. The meal had been a little too good. I would have to hit the gym the next day. "Well?" I asked.

"Josiah had three daughters and two sons. The oldest son died in a Jim Crow prison." My father frowned. "The girls just disappeared after adulthood. Do me a favor and don't change your name when you get married." I ignored the prompt, and he continued. "You women are hard to find after marriage. I wish that Elene had insisted that we hyphenate our surnames. She had no brothers. So as far as I know, you're the last of the Tolliver line."

"Is that why you asked me to do the DNA test?" I leaned against the granite counter and poured myself a shot of sparkling water.

"Part of the reason. The gene company tries to find matches for you. The Toil genes passed to you from me, and the Tolliver genes passed to you along the matriarchal line."

"And all the way back to Eve," I mused aloud.

Dad raised an eyebrow that the video caught perfectly, and I grinned.

"One of my coworkers tried to give me a genetics lesson today. He said that some genes go back to the first human woman, Eve." I bowed elaborately. "Where do the Tollivers hail from? My coworker said that DNA tests tell you what country you originate from."

"Oh, you are old, Candace," my father said. Reaching behind himself, he pulled a laptop from beneath papers and flyers stacked on the bed. "Haplogroup L1c."

My hands tightened on the glass. I had not expected to get my question answered so easily.

"From central Africa around Chad, the Congo, or Rwanda. Home of the original humans." He looked up. "Sorry, that's still a wide area. That's where your shortness comes from. You were right to blame your mother's genes for that. I can send you the results if you want."

"Send it on." My own laptop was still in my briefcase. "And the sands of history?"

"Candace, I was just trying to wake you out of your funk," he protested. I watched him pour a sliver of bourbon into a shot glass. I insisted on an answer.

He looked away, sipped his drink once, twice and then looked back at me. "I hit a wall; this always happens. Josiah Toil was just a Black laborer, so his work wasn't recorded. Every generation," he paused, "like Black Wall Street, like all of the Black towns after the Civil War, like the Black miners at Matewan."

"We know all of that," I said quietly.

"No, we rediscovered all of that. It gets wiped away and then two generations later people say 'we were kings and queens in Africa.'

Well, sure. But we were city planners, architects, engineers, bricklayers, and professors here in America."

"And Army officers," I said.

He chuckled. I was glad to hear real laughter after his bitter tirade.

"You can help me with a puzzle at work," I added. "Why would someone insist on his own cleaning staff for a lab? He says he's afraid the normal staff would disturb his team."

"And you don't think that's enough? Is he afraid that his work would be stolen?"

"The guys that I met worship the ground he walks on."

"Does QND have a policy against hiring relatives?"

"Sort of. They don't want spouses or relatives to have to do performance reviews on each other. But I think the cleaning staff are contractors."

"You can ask, you know."

"I doubt the guy who runs the lab—"

"No, the janitor. I doubt that your guy thought to swear his janitor to secrecy. He's probably proud of the job. Ask him."

Lifting my glass, I toasted my father.

"What's a *parian*?" I asked, tossing myself into a chair in Desmond Walker's office two days later. Not for the first time I wondered why a project leader had an office with a door that closed while I had a cubicle. Open-door policy, Lloyd had said.

Desmond Walker made an elaborate point of putting his keyboard to bed and turned to me. "I think you know that it means godfather. Victor called me after you talked to him. He was worried that he'd done something wrong."

"Did you ask the contract company to hire him?" I asked.

"He works for QND," Walker said simply. "Contract companies lay their staff off whenever there's a downturn."

As I sat back in the visitor chair, I considered how to approach the real reason I had come down to Walker's office.

"You're not going to tell me that's an infraction? Victor isn't related to me," he protested.

"No, Victor Johnston was only a puzzle that I wanted to solve. However"—I leaned forward—"I'm willing to bet that you know his haplogroup." Walker stiffened, and I smiled. "Humor me, Dr. Walker."

"L1c," he said, and I felt relief spread through me like a wave. "Why does it matter? You gave me the impression that you were going to close the project."

"I really don't want to. Lloyd needs a dog and pony show. We"—I emphasized the pronoun—"need to give him a reason to continue your funding." I sat back. "I'm still going to insist on an ethicist to help us draw up conditions of use. I'd like to see families have access to their memories before they are exported and sold to others." Especially Black families, I thought, and shivered at the thought of accessing the memory of Josiah Toil seeing his son vanish into a prison that reproduced the slavery that he himself had escaped from.

"You are the one who pointed out that the ability to share a memory along one haplogroup was not commercial."

"I'm certain that every haplogroup would pay for their ancestral memories," I said. "Everybody imagines themselves the descendants of kings and queens. Every magnate wants to pass his genius directly on to his children."

I stood up full of nervous energy. Suddenly aware that I was patterning myself on Lloyd, I stopped and gripped the back of the visitor chair. "I'm not asking you to stop your research. Eventually, it will occur to them that if you could share across one close genetic group, you should be able to do so with others more distantly related. They will remember that we are one human family." I took a breath. "When that happens, I want standards in place for such sharing. And remuneration for the memory donor."

"It sounds like you have a donor in mind."

"I considered asking you. Or Victor. But your memories belong to your children. I'm proposing that you give my memory—my ability to speak German—to Victor. He would be the more dramatic demo for Lloyd."

I saw a wave of anger mixed with—what? guilt?—cross Desmond Walker's face. "You're asking me to experiment on my family?"

"Victor and I are in the same haplogroup: L1c," I said. Releasing my grip on the chair, I seated myself again. "You said that your human trials have been done. I suggested Mr. Johnston because he's such a strong character. He would charm the board with his stories in English; he would certainly do so in German. But, if you have another subject I will accept that. Mind you, I want to meet the person that you propose to give my memories to before you do that. There are other options." I paused and ticked them off for him.

"Second: if you tell me that you are ready now or even next week to transfer a L1c haplogroup memory to an IJ haplogroup subject, I would jump at that." I saw his surprise at my naming one of the European haplogroups. Yes, Dr. Walker, I did my homework, I told him silently. "Third: if you want me to go to Lloyd and tell him to give us two years and we will have that same demo for him, I'll do that."

"You don't think he'd wait," Dr. Walker said.

"No, I don't," I said.

"When do you want a decision?"

"By the end of the week," I said. "That will give me time to float the idea with a lawyer and discuss what type of protection we can offer the initial subject." I saw the word 'protection' enter Walker's consciousness and wondered what machinations had been needed to have QND hire Victor Johnston directly.

I didn't ask. Four weeks later, I watched with others in the lab building as Victor Johnston regaled that board member with his memories second-lining with his krewe on Mardi Gras morning. His German was as colloquial as a native teenager. Standing in the back of the meeting room, I clutched the legal documents that would guarantee Victor a position until he retired and a pension afterwards. As the memory donor, I had only insisted that the memories attached to my genes be given to no other person. I have frozen that moment in my mind: Victor regaling the board members after the formal test was completed, Lloyd smiling and nodding his head at my success, and Desmond Walker carefully defining the current commercial opportunities of his work and emphasizing the future possibilities.

I don't know where Victor Johnston is now. Eventually, he tired of being a guinea pig; he tired of having that "bougie Black girl," as he called me, in his head. No use explaining that I could not be extracted. He disappeared, and Dr. Walker would not tell me where his godfather had moved. I could have queried human resources and found out where his checks were directed, but I respected his wishes. I moved on; I listened to my father and started to date again. The Toil and Tolliver family chart is waiting for another entry. I may be the last generation to pass down my story the old-fashioned way.

ARE WE OURSELVES?

by Michelle Mellon

Every night, before I went to sleep, my mother would recite "My People" to me. She'd whisper that poem like it was a lullaby. Like Langston Hughes himself sat on the other side of my bed, leaning in to hear if she did his words justice. And after a while, when I'd memorized the words too, my mother and I would chant them together in a soft duet.

Those are my happiest memories—among the scattering I know are truly my own. I have few other memories of my mother. I know she worked for the government. My father told me she was a neuroscientist and had been working on consciousness transfer technology long before things went bad. But she saw the early signs. She made the connections. And even though her warnings fell mostly on closed ears, the ones who *did* listen took her away.

I especially cherished that nighttime ritual with my mother in those empty years between her disappearance and when I was put into service. I kept my room as she'd last seen it, hoping one day she'd return to sit on my comic book comforter. She'd place my stuffed bunny next to me as I wrapped my hands in her braids and we'd cuddle, forehead to forehead, and say those words together.

I knew better, even before the linens had grown shabby and the doll decrepit. By then, I was old enough to recognize our special time for what it was. A safeguard, of sorts. To help me remember who I am. Because even in those early days, my mother knew that soon it would be too late to hold onto what made us real.

Soon, it would be the beginning of the end for us.

THE NIGHT IS BEAUTIFUL

Always read the fine print. Isn't that how that old saying goes? Oh, the great irony that the fine print of the United States Reparations Act of 2119 essentially sold the recipients and descendants of those payments back into bondage. Five hundred years after the first slaves were brought to the United States, the Act was hailed as the official beginning of a post-racial America. Proven descendants of slaves were offered payments stemming from a complex formula of passage, labor, land, psychological suffering, and systemic discrimination. Like the lottery, recipients could receive their funds in one lump sum or paid out over the course of their or their children's lifetimes. In return, there was a clause requiring unwavering loyalty to the principles and administrative actions deemed necessary by the government.

At the time, of course, the clause was just a symbolic show of fealty. So, my grandfather claimed his share. And the bill didn't come due for another two generations. No reasonable person could have predicted everything to follow. Apparently "duty to the greater good of the country" meant giving up ownership of your body when it was deemed "vital to the survival of the republic." My mother's conjectures lived outside of the world of politics. She had merely connected some dots between what we'd done to the world environmentally, and our efforts to escape the repercussions. Some legislative wonk had discovered how to use USRA2119 to conscript Black Americans into playing experimental hosts and, when that experiment panned out, The Reparations Act put the final nail in our coffin.

What held true for centuries past still held true—where the United States led, other nations followed. Those that had the resources but no significant Black population of their own to harvest (or legal means to do so), turned the African continent into a tacitly sanctioned source for human trafficking.

As James Baldwin once said, "People are trapped in history and history is trapped in them."

SO THE FACES OF MY PEOPLE

As I stood over his grave, they told me I looked like my father. The aunties and uncles who at some point must have meant something to me, were, in my grief, just extras murmuring meaningless condolences. I wasn't grieving *him*—he died the day the government took my mother away. I was grieving the lost opportunity to one day break through his wall and get him to tell me more about her. And them. And us.

I thought I found her once. In my head, outside of that bedtime routine. A warm memory of a familiar silhouette in a dress with an apron, arms spread wide on the porch of a yellow farmhouse with a bright red door. And me, running across a newly shorn grass field until I pull up short at the bottom of the steps.

Because I've never been to a farm. I spent my entire childhood in a second-floor walk-up in the city. This woman is not the comforting color of hot chocolate—no milk—with strong hugging arms and the lingering scent of sandalwood soap. This woman has auburn hair—no braids—and looks delicate, like straw. She is not my mother. This is not my memory.

Yet I can't help feeling sad, somehow knowing only a few years stand between this woman and the smell of hospital disinfectant drowning out the country perfume of honeysuckle and manure and the sweet sweat of a loving son.

WHEN THE LAST OF THE BIRDS AND THE BEES HAVE GONE ON

by C. L. Clark

After "Girl" by Jamaica Kincaid

Practice your aerial drills Mondays, Thursdays, and Saturdays, even if it's raining—you think you'll never have to fly in the rain?; do calisthenics and sword drills on Tuesdays and Fridays; don't fly bare-winged into a thunderstorm's static; cook your crag deer steak just till they're hot-brown outside and warm-red in; soak your hunting clothes right after you take them off; blood draws blood; never pinion your own fool self with your own clothes; memorize the width of your wing protrusion points; salt your extra meat and hide it; is it true you were letting the Wingless into the crags on Sunday?; always eat your food like you know where your next meal's coming from; if you didn't hunt the deer yourself, cook it until it's hot-brown all through; on Sundays, walk strong like your training's made you, not like you can barely hold your wings up; don't let strangers into the crags; don't speak to the Wingless, not even to give directions; all of this is their fault; drop a little food when you walk because crag mice will follow you, and they make good snacks; *I never bring strangers into the crags, only my friends, and never on training days*; this is how to clean a wound; this is how to suture the wound you just cleaned; this is how you widen and hem the holes in your shirts so you don't pinion your own fool self with your own clothes; this is how you guard your wingmate's back without getting tangled; this is how you guard your wingmate's underside without getting tangled; this is how you gut the crag deer—far from your nest because blood draws blood and fresh meat draws false friends; when you attack from above, don't get fancy and spin, or else you'll get vertigo and lose your sword; this is how you choose a gender; this is how you cast one off; this is how you mark your own nest; this is how you mark the borders of the crags; this is how you hold your wings near someone you don't like too much; this is how you hold your wings near someone you don't like at all; this is how you hold your wings near someone you like completely; this is how you set up camp as a scout; this is how you set up camp as a wingsquad; this is how you set up camp for someone who outranks you; this is how you set up camp before a fight; this is how you set up camp after a fight; this is how to hold your wings in the presence of the Wingless, like your training's made you strong enough to drop them off the crags like they deserve; sun your wings everyday so that you don't get mites or wingrot; don't climb everywhere—you're not Wingless, you know; don't pick the crag flowers—the bees might come back; don't throw stones at crag birds because they've been gone for decades and we want them to come back; this is how to make a nest; this is how to line a nest; this is how to make medicine for wingrot; this is how to make medicine to throw away a fledge before it becomes a fledge, and don't tell me you won't need it—we learn things that help other people, too, you know; this is how to catch a fish from the air; this is how to throw back the perfect fish so that the crag birds have food when they come back to us; this is what Wingless gunpowder smells like; this is how to bully the Wingless; this is how the Wingless bully you; this is how to choose a nestmate; this is how to love a nestmate and this is how to touch their wings; this is how to do an aerobatic loop if you feel like it and this is how to steady yourself so you don't get vertigo; this is how to stretch crag deer meat through lean summers and leaner winters; this is how you dispose of bodies you can't eat; *but what if my nestmate has no wings?* You mean to say that after all that you are really going to be the kind of person who won't lift them up with your own wings?

THE GOATKEEPER'S HARVEST

by Tobi Ogundiran

The wind shrieks its displeasure as it rattles the house, rattles it like a child in the throes of a tantrum, and we, little gnats in this container of brick and mud, tumble from our huddle by the table. The awful shriek reaches a peak of fury, and within it I hear the abominable voices of Eleran's children.

Ebun buries her face in my breasts, breath hot and moist against my skin. "I'm scared, Mama."

I'm scared too. I'm scared of the wind and what it means, the dark and what it brings. I'm scared for the last bit of wood in the oven and how quickly it burns, the smoke thick in the air like an oppressive blanket, smothering us and smelling strangely of goat.

We all hear the sound: the frantic scratching of nails (or hooves?) on wood. Ebun stiffens against me, Teju's eyes grow wide in his skull, and as one we swivel towards the door.

"It's me. Open quickly!"

Ebun has squirmed out of my arms and is bolting for the door before I recognize the voice.

"No! Stop her!" I yell.

Teju dives for Ebun as she races past him, tackling her to the ground in a tangle of limbs and bellows.

"Quickly!" says the voice. "I've brought help, like I promised. Open the door, we don't have much time."

Ebun is sobbing in the corner. I want to sob too, will give anything to curl up in a ball and join her. But I'm her mother, and what is a mother's job if not to protect her children, to put on a brave face and make them feel as safe as possible?

I turn to the door, forcing a cheer I'm lacking into my voice. "Hello, Yomi. Are the elders with you?"

"Yes! Now open the door." More scratches on the wood. Frantic. Mad.

"Use the key, Yomi."

Silence. Even the wind has quieted somewhat, as though it too were listening in.

"What?"

I look up at the charm dangling over the lintel, a small cylindrical bundle dark with dried blood. So long as it's there, we're safe. It doesn't matter how hard the wind rattles the house, how awful those screams sound, the things out there cannot get in unless I open the door. Unless I invite them in.

"The key," I gasp, heart thrumming in my ears. "You said never to open the door for anyone—especially anyone who sounds like you. You have a key, Yomi."

"Oh yes, that's true!" says the voice. (Is it Yomi? Please let it be Yomi.) "And I'm happy you remember all I've told you. But I've lost my key—"

A deep, demonic wail drowns out his voice. Ebun screams and buries her head in her lap, and Teju rushes over to comfort her. My hand reaches for the bolt. That is Yomi out there and I can't leave him alone. Yomi is still talking, voice warping into something else, strained from terror, from desperation—or is it all an act, a clever ruse? I never know what they can do, the children of Eleran, but Yomi told me explicitly to never ever open—

The door bulges in its frame and I leap back as Yomi starts screaming. "OPEN THE DOOR! PLEASE! THEY'RE—!"

The thunder of hooves drowns out his voice, and I can't tell if it's the wind still screaming or him.

"Do you think that was Yomi?" Teju asks.

We're crowded in the upstairs bedroom, that little room the kids shared before Teju decided he was now a man and couldn't share a room with a girl. He doesn't look much of a man now, his worried eyes searching mine for answers, for reassurance. How will I tell him that I don't have the answers? That I also need reassurance? That I wish someone were here to make it all go away. That I wish I hadn't killed that goat.

"I don't know," I say.

Ebun is curled beneath the covers, thumb in mouth as she sleeps off her fright while Teju and I hunch protectively over her. Her baby face is crinkled, as though the terrors of the night have followed into her dreams. And is it me or does her halo of hair seem flatter, shinier? I shake my head, rub my eyes. The wind no longer rocks the house in attack, but the silence is even worse, unnatural. And then there are the boarded-up windows which plunge the house into perpetual darkness, which doesn't allow us to see outside, see *them*. The house feels like a coffin.

"That wasn't Yomi," Teju says, trying for bravery. For conviction.

We sit there listening to Ebun breathe, watching the lantern grow dim.

I'm in the large barn, tying freshly harvested yam tubers in neat rows for storage. It's hard work. I'm caked in dirt, and my forearms bear deep bloody grooves where unruly yam stalks scratched me. The things terrified me as a child, the way they grew like the antennae of some chitinous alien creature, purplish and twitching. Now they are nothing more than nuisance to be clipped off the tubers before they are stored away.

Old hinges squeak in protest as the barn swings open, followed by a blast of hot air from the blazing noonday. The cool barn, specially built with adobe and oak to preserve the tubers as long as possible, is being eroded by hot air. I expect to hear the squeak of hinges as the barn door shuts, but it never comes; the doors are left open for the hot afternoon air to rush in. And I know it's Teju and his ne'er-do-well friends up to some mischief as usual. The hurried scuffle of feet on the wood-shaving-covered floor confirms my suspicions, and I take a deep breath to yell at them when I hear the bleat.

"Ah ah—"

I drop what I'm doing and hurry through endless rows of yams towards the sounds—bleating and more hurried scuffle on the wood shavings—turning round the bend to find five munching goats.

The goats, skinny beyond comprehension, have somehow managed to unravel the rope binding a stack of tubers—the fraying end of the rope where they gnawed at it lies limp like a ripped artery. For a moment I stand, grossly stupefied, staring at the animals as they go to town on the tubers, jostling each other around, crunching into the yams, jaws shifting in that weird animal side-to-side way as they masticated.

In all my years in this town I've never seen a goat. Oke-Aanu is a town of farmers and potters and carpenters. But no one keeps livestock, not even birds; if you want meat, you hop in the truck and travel two hours to Maraba where the mallams try to cheat you out of as much money as they can for one kilo of stale meat. And yet here are five black goats, munching with abandon on my hard-earned harvest. A harvest which is unusually dismal on account of that strange rot.

"Shoo!" I scream, flapping my arms. "Go away! *Away!*"

It's as if I'm not there, as though they can't hear me; the goats continue to feast with abandon. One spares me a look, and in its black eyes I see nothing but contempt.

"Go away!" I yell again, kicking at them. They bleat in protest, moving lethargically, bumping stupidly into each other, dancing around the ruin of yam tubers. But they don't run for the door, only avoid my flying feet as they continue their feast. The nerve. The disrespect. They're hideous things, these goats, these intruders, and they infuriate me.

A rake rests on the nearby shelf next to a sea of rusted farm tools. I grab it by the toothy end and swing for the cluster of invaders.

There's a satisfying crack as the long handle connects with the rump of a goat. It squeals, a sound eerily human in its agony, and bolts for the door.

The goats scatter. Bleating, climbing over each other in their bid to escape the sweeping rake.

"That's it!" I scream. "Run, you little shits, and don't come back here."

I chase them to the barn doors where an old woman stands, resting against a herding stick. A single fading ankara piece drapes across her torso. The goats hide behind her like petulant children, peeking out and bleating in different octaves. It almost feels like they're telling her exactly what happened, communicating their discontent.

"What's this?" I pant. The little exercise has me short of breath. "Are these your goats?"

"My children," she says.

"What?"

"These are my children."

The goats circle the woman's feet, scuffling for the place closest to her, almost like … children. And all the while their black eyes never leave me, baleful stares weighing down on me as if to say, you're in trouble now.

"Well, madam, your—*children*—broke into my barn and were eating my yams. Shouldn't you be—I don't know—watching them?"

"They're hungry."

I open my mouth in indignation, then close it. Try again. "So you led them here deliberately. To eat my yams?"

The woman stands well away from me, so I only just notice the faint wisps of coarse black hair on her lips and chin. There's something not quite right about her face. Too angular, perhaps, or too disproportional … I can't place my finger on it.

"My children are many," she says. "They number in the thousands. They're always hungry."

Something about her tone, the words themselves, sends a chill down my spine.

She moves suddenly, brushing past and startling me into immobility. When I regain myself, she is already in the barn, disappearing round the corner.

"Hey! You can't just—"

I hurry after her, growing increasingly flustered with each passing moment, unable to shake the feeling that something is seriously afoot. I find her in the bend where her goats (children) had been violating my hard-earned harvest. And lying like an offering among the mess of half-eaten tubers and wood-filings, is a dead goat.

"You killed my child."

"What? No!" That's when I see the blood on my hands, thick and clumped with tufts of goat fur on my forearms, my dirty jeans, the old leather of my apron. "Th—this is—"

The strength expires from my arms, and the rake drops to the floor, teeth bloody with the proof of my guilt. How did this happen? "No! I didn't do this!"

The four black goats cluster around their fallen sibling (*where did they come from? I didn't see them reenter the barn*). There's something organized and *un*animal-like about their movement. I want to scream, but something has eaten my voice.

The woman bends and scoops the dead goat into her arms, scoops it as lovingly as a mother with her dead child.

"A goat for a goat," she says, then turns and walks away, her children scuttling in her wake.

···❖···

I wake to the sound of screaming. It takes me a moment to reorient, to register the cramped space of the children's room, the dim lantern, the cords in Teju's neck as he screams.

I leap off the rocking chair, fall to the floor as my stiff muscles spasm. My eyes water with pain, still I manage to gasp a, "What's wrong?" For one wild moment I'm convinced the house has been breached—Eleran and her thousand young flooding the house. But Teju is looking at the bed, eyes wide with horror and confusion, as he gabbles and points at a sleeping Ebun.

"What—"

Ebun is curled fetal, chest rising and falling as she sleeps, completely oblivious to the ruckus. She looks the same, but for the two spiral mounds poking out of her tangle of hair, black and shiny and—

Goat horns.

The blood flows in patterns down the cracked basin drain as I wash my hands. There is so much blood. But where did it all come from? I never killed that goat. I know I chased them, hit them with the handle of the rake. *But I didn't kill that goat.*

A soft knock raps on the door as I step out of the kitchen. I hastily wipe my hands on my apron and open the door.

Yomi is standing on my front porch. He's not much to look at, a plain-looking young man, really. But he has come visiting twice every week ever since my husband passed away. He's especially good to Ebun, and never fails to delight her with little treats and trinkets whenever he comes calling. Though he's never explicitly stated it, I know his intentions are to woo me. And while he's too young for me, lately I've been feeling stirrings, catching myself staring longingly at the path that leads to the farmhouse, hoping to see him coming. Feeling an embarrassing teenage flush at the sight of that crooked smile.

He's not smiling now. He looks like he's seen a ghost. And just like that, I know he knows what's happened. "Tell me," he says.

"There were goats in my barn."

Yomi winces. "They're not goats. Did you feed them?"

"She …" My throat clinches with fear. "I chased them away—I … one of them, I don't know how it happened but it—died—"

Yomi's eyes nearly bulge from his head. *"Died?"*

"She s—said I killed it. But I didn't! I swear—"

"Oh no." Yomi's shaking his head side to side like a dog trying to get rid of flies. "No, no-no-no-no."

"What's wrong? What's happening?"

Yomi massages his neck as if he's choking, runs a hand through his hair.

"Yomi … you're scaring me."

"Sorry," he says. "It's just you don't know—"

"Tell me."

"No, it's best I—"

I grab him by the front of his shirt. "Tell me. *Please.*"

"Alright, alright," he says, prying my hands from his shirt. "This entire area used to be a rocky desert. The story goes that this town was founded back in the fourteenth century by a family of exiles. From where they were exiled, we don't know. But they came down from the mountains into this land, starved and near death. The patriarch decided he could not watch his family die, and in desperation called out in the wilderness for help. For three days and nights he called out to anything—anyone—who could help them. And on the third night, something answered."

"The Goatkeeper," I whisper. "Eleran."

"One of its many names." Yomi shudders. "The patriarch, he pleaded with this being for food for his family. Food for all of them, so that they may never lack, so they may survive out in the desert. Desperate, the gasps of his dying family in his ears, he made a Pact with this being—the first fruits of his harvest in exchange for bountiful harvest. For as long as we dwell in this land, and we left the first fruits of our harvest for Eleran and her children, we would never starve."

I remember now all the times my husband set out a few tubers of fresh harvest. I never understood why he did it, but I never continued the tradition. And I've paid for it ... with the unusual rot of this year's harvest, more than half the crops spoiled ...

Almost as if something had been angry.

"He never told me," I whisper, wringing my hands. "My husband—why didn't he tell me?"

"Only the men know of this, and only when they come of age," says Yomi. "As it's the patriarch who made the Pact, it's the burden of the men to hold it through the generations."

"It's why you've been coming here these past three years," I say. "Helping with the farm. You've been setting out the first fruit."

"I was assigned to you." Yomi looks at me through his long lashes. "I'm so sorry. This is all my fault. I should have been here to help with the harvest. I got stuck in the city—"

"What are we going to do?"

"I don't know," he says, standing. "But I'll go fetch the elders. They'll know what to do. In the meantime, gather the children and cover up all the windows. And keep the door locked."

I'm too petrified to speak. I only nod.

"I'll need a key for when we come back," says Yomi. "Whatever you hear—do not open that door, even if it sounds like me. *Do you understand?*"

I give a shaky nod, handing over a spare key.

He pauses for a moment, then reaches into his pockets and produces a small bundle caked with dried blood. "Hang this over your door. It'll keep them out."

Teju backtracks, eyes wide and rolling like a spooked horse's, then turn and flees from the room. I hear his footfalls pounding down the stairs, but I can't chase after him. I have eyes only for my daughter, that tiny loveable creature now sprouting horns.

"Mama." I start, hastily blinking the tears from my eyes when I see Ebun looking at me. Has she been awake all along? "Will you hold me?"

"Of course, my dear, of course." Silently I slide into the narrow bed. As I pull back the covers, I'm hit by an overpowering wave of animal stink. It stings my eyes and gags my throat, but I don't recoil as Ebun folds into my embrace, as her horns poke me in the ribs.

I can hear Teju raging about downstairs.

"I feel sick," says Ebun. "Am I going to die?"

"No." Not if I have anything to say about it. But those are empty words, empty thoughts. I don't know what to do, and that scares me to death. "Yomi'll come, and you'll be fine." But where is Yomi? An unbidden thought blossoms in my mind: what if that had been Yomi earlier? What if he had really lost his key? What if I left him out there to Eleran and her children?

And yet another thought rises in my mind. Yomi abandoned us. Locked us in the house to save his skin.

"I'm hungry," says Ebun.

"Of course," I say, wiping my eyes. "There's still leftover eko from the morning. I know you like that—"

"No," says Ebun. "I want yam."

"Yam?" I will have to go down to the barn to fetch a suitable tuber, peel it, wash it, dice it. "Do you want it boiled or—"

"Raw." Ebun shifts, stares up at me with hungry goat eyes. "I want it raw."

That's when I know I've lost her.

The wind starts to rattle the house again, followed by that abominable wail. I can hear hooves like drumbeats over the roof—are there goats on the roof? But they're not really goats, I know that now. And they're not really children. They're something else.

I make my way through the house, the lamplight searing through the dark, casting things into vision. I feel like there are shapes lurking at the edges of the beam, skirting away from the light.

Down the stairs, past the living room, through the narrow corridor that leads to the barn. There are things growing through the house, searing through the cracks in the floorboards and the spaces in the walls, snaking like roots. Purplish and large and twitching—

Yam tendrils. Except I've never seen tendrils grow so big, and they're ripping through the house, tearing it apart.

The barn door has been ripped off its hinges, and beyond is a forest of chaos. What before were neat rows of tubers, is now a barn-sized tangle of hairy roots and tendrils (*tentacles*), tubers trapped like insects in the web of their squirming growth.

Swallowing, I reach into the thicket and pluck the nearest tuber. It comes surprisingly easily, and I tuck it in my armpit as I hurry back to the bedroom and my transforming daughter.

The living room is a nest of vines. Fat, fiendish things curl across the walls and floor and door which is cracked halfway open.

The yam drops as I start pushing the door, pushing it shut. A gust of chilly air blows through the crack and I see—

I see the Goatkeeper, standing in the field in front of the house, silhouetted against a purple sky of perpetual twilight. She's not the stooped figure I saw in the barn, but she stands in her true form.

Eight feet tall, dressed in a black dress which snaps about her hooves. Her goat head grows into what should be a woman's body, but is something else. A mockery. An aberration. And though she's several feet from me, I know she is looking at me.

As I watch, black spectral wings unfurl like sails behind her to form a canopy over the gathering goats at her feet. The goats, where they were skinny and emaciated when they stole into my barn, are now robust, furcoats shiny, eyes bright with hunger. They simply stand there. Waiting.

A goat for a goat.

The scream rips through the house, and I jolt, tearing my eyes from the Goatkeeper and her children, staggering through the alien growths as I hurry up the stairs and to the room.

"Teju! What are you *doing*?"

For one crazy moment I think Teju is defiling his little sister: he's straddling her as she squirms and writhes in the sheets, the bed rocking with the force of their movement—or the house's movement? It's only when I look closely that I see that she's lying prone on the bed, both arms pinned beneath Teju's knees, head yanked back by one of her horns (now as long as my forearm), as he tries desperately to saw it off with the crude saw from his father's toolbox.

"Come help me, Mama!" Teju pauses long enough to look at me with bright, mad eyes. "Hold her. If I can cut it off, she won't—"

"Stop it, boy! Stop—she's in pain!"

But Teju has no ear for me, instead grunts with each stroke of the saw. "We—have—to—"

I dive for Teju, but he has always been big. Big boned like his Papa and Grandpa. Lights explode in my eyes as he backhands me, sends me reeling for the rocking chair. My ears ring with the clatter of hooves, the wail of wind, Ebun's screams of agony which already do not quite sound human.

I sit up, spit out a stream of blood and a loose tooth. The saw is already bloody, and for a moment I think of the bloody rake. Beads of sweat fly off Teju's arms as he attends his morbid duty, sawing with the singular commitment of a butcher-mallam in Maraba. I don't know what has come over him; he's deaf to my pleas. But that is my daughter there, even if she smells awful, even though I can clearly see that there's now a fine layer of black fur covering her skin, even though she's no longer screaming but bleating.

I throw myself a second time at Teju, hanging onto his neck, pleading at him to let his sister go. Eventually he lets go. Let's go long enough to snarl doglike at me, long enough to punch me full in the face—

A searing pain washes over me as I come to. My face hurts. It feels shattered, the bone fragments cutting into soft tissue with each errant movement. For a moment I expect to hear Ebun screaming, to wince at the horrible screech of a hacking saw. But the room is silent.

Save for that wet, sucking sound.

I open my eyes and come face to face with Teju. My first instinct is to cower. (When and how have I come to so fear my son?) But he's not snarling; his face is the same smooth boyish face I know and love. And there is no mad glint in his eyes—there is nothing in his eyes, just the glazed look of a dead stare.

A massive beast is on the bed: a six-legged goat, black fur shining in the wan light, powerful horns twisting out of a shaggy head which is lowered, burrowed deep into the bloody torso of my dead son.

That's when I scream.

The goat looks up, snout glistening with red, red blood. Its lips peel back to reveal impossible rows of sharp teeth, then it lets lose a long, abominable sound. The sound is echoed back twofold, threefold, tenfold—a thousand guttural bleats blended in demonic harmony. The goat rears on its hind legs, and I duck as it leaps over me, the sound of its heavy hooves tearing through the house and out the front door.

BABA KLEP

by Eugen Bacon

The sky is a royal blue and dappled with pillows of cloud, white as baby ghosts.

Today, Clyde's cleft lip palate is excruciating. His face is aflame. He's sweating agony. It's always a bad omen when pain happens, but he tries not to overthink it. The last time he felt the lip wrench—stars and shards ripping into his face—was two years ago—his father, a vigorous baby boomer who bowled like a pro, clutched his chest. He was still clutching it in a casket two days later.

Revita understands the pain. She grips Clyde's hand through it, finally smiles when he returns to himself. "Your mama will have a fit when you bring home a black woman," she jokes.

She's tucked behind a seatbelt, stretching across a belly that's beginning to show. Her hair is long and elastic, unlike others of her tribe. She's wearing the natural glow that accompanies a pregnant woman.

Clyde's lip hurts with his smile. He looks into her chestnut eyes that go deep into his soul. Her own cleft lip is beautiful on her face. She wears it like an ornament. It's her defining feature. Hers doesn't hurt like Clyde's.

"Will you talk about my mother's fit 755 kilometres to Nairobi?"

"It's only an hour and a half of it."

"Perhaps we should have driven."

"I can't even ..." But she's smiling.

Wells, the pilot of the UN chartered plane, roars with laughter. "Sure," he says with his rasp voice. "You should have driven. All ten hours and some, all the way from Kigali. Save me a trip."

He's a tall good-looker. Tan skin, grey eyes. A mouth you totally want to kiss. Revita said as much when she first met the young pilot.

Clyde caresses Revita's bump. "You know I'm goofing, right? Mother will admire your intelligence. Once I tell her all you did for the people of Kigali."

"And what good would the skills of installing, maintaining, and repairing irrigation systems do in London?"

"Like teach wannabee volunteers for Africa."

"Very useful," she says. "I could also teach our munchkins when they start popping out."

Clyde's face pulls in pretend shock. "There's more than one in there?"

They're still laughing when the four-seater suddenly rocks. Now they're swallowed in a cloud, the light plane in a seesaw. The overcast clears into a yawn of thin blue, as the sky reappears. Suddenly more cloud and the plane jerks.

"Darn," says Wells.

"Hell's going on?" asks Clyde.

The turbulence cuts whatever answer Wells is planning. It's worse than a rocking horse. Revita's eyes close. Her fingers are clawing the armrests. Clyde is reaching for the airsick bag in the seat-back pocket when the plane judders. It tilts to the left, to the right. Now it's climbing in a tremble. Suddenly it stalls. Time is suspended. Wells is cursing like a trooper. Clyde feels, more than sees, the plane's nosing down in slow motion. Someone is screaming, and Clyde suspects it might be him. The downward rocket at full acceleration hurls his stomach up his throat. His ears are tearing. Revita is slicing his arm with her nails. He has a moment to curse the darn lip before the boom and blackness.

Groan. Clyde comes to. *Groan.* It's Revita.

She's upside-down beside him, still strapped in her seat. The air is cloudy, filling with smoke. He tries to move but is hemmed between metal and his seat. His last memory is of hands, helping hands. Then he blacks out again.

Next he comes to, someone is dragging him. Strong arms supporting his shoulders, walking, dragging, along, along.

"Wells ..."

"Revita is safe," says the white East African in his rasp voice. "But we must move away from the plane. Sorry we had to hard land. But she's smoking and there's fuel."

He gently lowers Clyde next to Revita.

Clyde looks around. It's bleak. Hoary dust and ash everywhere. Charcoal rock and piles of ruin.

"The hell happened here?" croaks Revita.

"Not the plane, I promise," says jovial Wells. "The good news is we didn't crash into Lake Victoria."

"We're in the middle of no place," spits Clyde.

"The flight path suggested we were nearing Entebbe when—" Wells looks around at the desolation. "But this? What world is this?"

A burst of ululation cuts into his words. A group of children in loin cloths rushes at them. Something round hits Wells on the side of his head and knocks him out. He crumbles to the austere dust. Clyde sees the new rock's soar but is too slow to protect Revita and her head. A sound like a sigh escapes her lips. She goes limp on the ground.

A child pulls from the group, comes forth a few steps. He aims with a rock. "No, no!" Clyde raises his arms to ward off the blow. He sees too late. It's not a rock. It's a coconut.

The second time he comes to, it looks like a village. There's a scatter of cinder-licked huts. They look like they endured a grave torrent of ashy rain. Grey fog in the air. Rocks and debris in piles everywhere. Something terrible happened here, and the clean-up is a long-term commitment. You can see the effort. But the place looks like shit.

The children are talking in a strange language of clicks and clacks. They're animated about something. Now they're dancing and ululating around a bundle. Naked girls and babies peer from the huts. A few toddlers step out to observe the spectacle.

Clyde is roped back-to-back with someone. He knows without seeing it's Revita. Her soft smell of bergamot. He feels her nylon hair on his neck.

"Clyde?" she says. Her voice is small.

The toddlers flee at the sound of it.

"We'll talk to them. Sort out this mess," he says. "We'll tell them we're in the UN. Good people with kind hearts. That I'm a doctor and you're an irrigation expert. We can save this ghastly place from whatever doom that befell it."

"They've taken Wells."

"Wait until I get my hands on those little rascals—"

"They're not children, Clyde."

"What?"

"I think they're a tribe of little people."

A dance of the tribe parts to reveal Wells bound on the ground. He's naked, his mouth and eyes covered with leaves. His cries are muffled. He's trussed up like a pig on a bamboo pole. It doesn't need a genius to figure it out.

"Put him down. At once, you brutes!" But there's fear in Clyde's voice. "Stop it. I said now!"

The tribe ignores him. They click and clack as they shoulder Wells away.

Revita's cry pulls from her toes, surges to the sky. It is like the howl of a hound.

The cleft lip suddenly attacks and tears out Clyde's face. It's possible that he faints. He stirs as the pain settles. A sweet aroma of roasting meat seeps into the air.

They come for him at dawn. It's still fog in the air, but a light grey one.

Clyde is in shock or despair. He doesn't struggle as they uncouple him from Revita, as they haul him with a tug of rope to his feet. But Revita is livid. She's fighting with every inch of her living. She's snarling and thrashing, scratching and biting. Any part of her body is a weapon. Her heel connects with a jaw.

Clyde wonders how long through a roast before you die? Or do they knock you unconscious with a coconut. He's heard of superstition about albinos, how pieces of their limbs are meant to bring luck. If the tribe thinks his whiteness is albinism, will they chop something off for some mythical power before they cook the rest of him? What will they take? His arms, legs, ears, or genitals? But Wells was trussed whole.

He has much to say to Revita, to their unborn. He'd like to think of them as twins. He's never doubted Revita, not from the moment he saw her cleft lip in a room full of United Nations people. The connection he felt. It's like the lip reached out for her. She stood out like an African protea, radiant and thriving, regal the way she moved. She was the first woman he ever saw who never hid from a cleft lip. He thought of the Greek god Proteus, prophetic, exploratory ... Clyde knew he would ride a chariot with Revita to any sun.

But she transitioned like the god, was elusive to his interest, avoided him like a turd. One day in the canteen, as he stuffed sweet potatoes and beans into his face, ravenous after a long morning of diagnosing and treating typhoid, pneumonia, and malaria in babies only weeks old, Revita clapped her tray of rice and goat meat onto his table. She sat opposite him and proceeded to eat. She pulled his heart with her chestnut eyes, and he could only stare in adoration and astonishment. Finally, she said, "Your eyes and your work—they suggest you're a people lover. It so happens I'm altruistic too. But what I'm wondering is this: Are you going to propose or what?"

Now these imbeciles, unschooled carnivores, they would bloody dare to eat her and his—

Something stirs in him. He leaps with a roar. He headbutts the first one. Leaps and stamps on the next. A torso slam takes out another of the tribe. Clyde's arms are still bound behind. He flips, now on the ground. His bare feet knock out a few more shorties. The ropes give. Now he is locking with his elbows. Pulling eyes, strangling. He'll teach the half-sized philistines before they make a broth of him.

A coconut knocks him cold.

When he comes to, Revita is kneeling beside him. She's wiping his face with bark cloth. The little people are clicking and clacking, bowing and bowing, as if in reverence.

"The hell?" Clyde sits up with a start. Members of the tribe in the room fall away.

"Look, Clyde," says Revita. "Look at their lips."

Only then does he notice. Each one has a cleft lip. Unsealed like his and Revita's.

And they are still clicking and bowing, when two women sashay in with an offering. It's a fresh roast in a calabash, some rib or thigh. Clyde and Revita are too hungry to question it.

On the last swallow, a tribesman with ash hair—perhaps an elder—appears. He claps his hands, gestures wildly.

"I think he wants us to follow him," suggests Revita.

The elder hurries out of the hut and walks in half a trot. He keeps the distance from Clyde, as if petrified. Everywhere is ruined. It's like walking on cold lava in the dawn of a mountain's fury. They tread across bleak soil and all that fog. Now the elder is pointing at a charcoal-black statue climbing from the ground.

Revita peers long and hard at the effigy. "I have to agree, the resemblance is uncanny."

The gargoyle has an opening from its lip to its nose.

The elder is clicking, bowing.

"I don't know," says Revita. "But I could swear he's worshipping."

Clyde laughs. "What will they do when I start doctoring? When they see some true healing?"

"You're totally a god. It saved you from being dinner."

And so it was that Clyde and Revita lived with the tribe in no place. On the days he wondered about his widowed mother in London, how she might be doing without knowledge of her son's fate, Revita consoled him with the intensity only a person touched by the profundity of the Greek god Proteus understood.

Something else happened. Like a twist of fate. He first panicked when his cleft lip brought him to the ground in agony, but it only heralded a plague of locusts that fed the village for a month. When the lip hit his face like a hammer, a murder of crows appeared from nowhere. Nothing a well-aimed coconut couldn't fell.

As he found crude ways to cure without proper medical supplies, trusting the power of the earth and nature to restore a burn, break diarrhea, assuage acid from gout, Clyde began to associate the agony in his lip with blessing.

So he wasn't astounded when he woke up with anguish on his face, and Revita went into labor that same day. She gave birth to one boy, not twins, and the child was cleft-lipped. Next, Clyde's lip wrenched all the way to his guts, the tribe clicked and clacked, and he clicked and clacked back. It was like a miracle of Babel uncoded by a holy spirit. Suddenly he understood everything they said.

Thus, in clicks and clacks, the tribe unravelled the story of the cataclysmic event that happened before Clyde and Revita tumbled from the sky.

Two days after a millet harvest, a big bird, giant like the one that brought Clyde, Revita, and the tasty one, soared in the sky. But this bird did not cartwheel to the ground. It opened its mouth and vomited light. After the light came a hiss. After the hiss, came a bellow that felled people—they died clutching their heads. When it boomed, people scattered, bits of them everywhere. A few villagers survived the bellow and the boom. Some collapsed to the fire that ravaged nearly everything. Survivors looked around, saw dust and ash everywhere. A grey world full of stumps and rock.

The branding on their face, when it happened, started without warning. One day someone noticed their lips were beginning to crack, forming a split that ran from mouth to nose. In no time, everyone was branded. It was then that they understood. The flash and boom were the work of the great god of the sky. Now He had marked them as His chosen. What they didn't understand was why He set fire to the cows and goats, sheep, and cockerel. Even the maize, peas, cassava, bananas, beans, sweet potatoes, and millet were gone.

Villagers fell back when they faltered into the statue. The god of the sky had lodged Himself in their midst, reincarnated as a boulder. To appease him and continue their ancestry, for indeed they would perish if they ate nothing, they sacrificed and dried the meat of newborns that arrived without a split lip.

Imagine their gratefulness, clacked the little people, when the god rewarded them with a great big tasty one from the sky. Clyde thought of the white East African's generosity, how he pulled them from the wreck.

Imagine their happiness, when it was light and they saw that the god of the sky had appeared to them in true flesh, but they were astonished He had chosen to reincarnate with no skin. They apologised completely for binding Him. Did He see how they did not harm the woman with slippery hair? Despite her charcoal face, she was made in His likeness, shaped from His ribs.

The only time they killed a tribesman with a broken lip, they clacked, he was one of them, but he was also the one who struck the god of the sky with a coconut. They served him as a fresh roast to the god, if He generously remembered.

Revita by now also understood the click language. She clicked her message to the tribe. *The god's name is Baba Cleft Lip. He's no longer angry with you.*

No? they clacked.

No. And He has absolved all your babies from sacrifice. From now on, you are not to kill or eat anyone born without a broken lip.

But, but ... clicked the tribe. *What does Baba Klep suggest we eat?*

Coconuts aren't just for knocking people out, clacked Revita. *You can crack them like this. Drink their water and eat their sweet white meat.*

But, but ... we can't live on coconuts alone, clicked the tribe.

Ah, yes. Baba Klep has also blessed your land, clacked Revita. *And I will show you.*

Clyde needed no convincing that, between the two of them, his wife was the brain, most shrewd. She taught the tribe to listen for water by following locusts and birds. She taught them to dig up the poison in the soil and separate it in latrines. To mark and dig trenches. To make pipes of bamboo poles, create crude but resourceful irrigation systems. Before long, the land was lush with maize, peas, cassava, bananas, beans, sweet potatoes, and millet. It also appeared that either the air chose to cleanse itself or the fog that wrapped around the land had fled.

The villagers thanked Baba Klep for His goodness.

He dispersed them to scout what was left of the big bird. They returned, hauling or balancing on their heads, cartons of towels, gauze, painkillers, antimalarials, gin, beef jerky, and bars of chocolate. They pulled apart the light plane and upgraded their irrigation pipes.

Pain colored Baba Klep's vision, fireworks everywhere. Revita birthed the second child. It squealed out of her womb like a banshee, no broken lip. She suckled the tot with a mother's poise, her world never bleak or grey.

As the sun ebbed from the birthing bed and night brooded in, a sputter of his mother's face crossed his memory, a broken image on a trembling screen. The shape of her jaw, the cast of her gaze, fleeting like a chapel ghost, waiting, waiting, then she was gone. And there was just his wife and newborn. He wondered if he'd ever know that he'd stayed too long, and when that happened if he could ever leave. He stared at the facts, the taste of a muddy river in his mouth.

DESICCANT

by Craig Laurance Gidney

The Bellona Heights Apartments were run-down. The pavement of the open semi-courtyard had cracks; concrete wounds that oozed out moss and straggling weeds. An old fountain, spattered with bird droppings, was filled with stagnant rainwater and trash. The first-level beige brick had graffiti, obscene words, and nonsense shapes scrawled across it. The balconies that faced the courtyard were over-stuffed with plants, bicycles, and rusting lawn furniture. The cornices were crumbling. Hip-hop and reggaeton blasted from open windows.

Tituba shuddered in revulsion. But she had no choice, did she?

You get what you pay for, she thought, and a one-bedroom in Bellona Heights was what she could afford. At least she'd found a place to live on such short notice. Her sister's new boyfriend, Vaughn, had threatened to change the locks one too many times. Tituba loved her sister Leah, but her choice in men was terrible. At least Juan, the last one, didn't misgender her. Yes, this place was below her standards, but, she reasoned, the lease was only for one year. And surely, she could find a more suitable place by then?

Inside the building, Tituba saw worn linoleum and the chipped paint on the walls. She picked up her keys at the office from a sullen clerk who couldn't pull her eyes away from a game on her phone and rode the old gear-grinding elevator up to the fourteenth floor. Phantom odors drifted down the hallway: weed, old fried fish, and of course, boiled cabbage. Boiled cabbage was the smell of despair and deferred dreams.

1412 was semi-furnished with a futon/couch frame and dresser drawers. It was on the other side of the building, so there was no balcony. The window faced the alley, which was full of dumpsters.

At least it was clean, for the most part. The only visible flaw was the discoloration right outside the air-conditioning vent. Carmine smears dribbled from the grate. Tituba touched it before she thought better of it. She felt a powdery dust on her fingertips, surprised to find that it was not dried paint or even worse, blood.

Fabiana was late, as she always was. Tituba had been sitting at the café for a good fifteen minutes. She entered the space with a dramatic flair, her face wrapped in a bright-orange scarf, and wearing bejeweled sunglasses. Her hands were encased in some silvery gloves. Heads turned, whispers came up from the other tables. She always wanted to be noticed. While Tituba had her moments, for the most part she wanted to be left alone.

Fabiana air-kissed her and then ordered an Americano and a low-fat blueberry muffin. She ignored both of the items.

"How's the new place? And when's the housewarming?" Fabiana asked her as she removed her sunglasses, revealing violet-colored contact lenses.

"The place is ratchet, so there will not be a housewarming party. Leah and that scrub Vaughn practically tossed me out into the street."

"I thought Leah had your back," Fabiana said.

"She usually does," Tituba said, "when she's not dick-a-matized. Vaughn pitched a fit when one of his boys asked him for my number. He threw around the words, 'she-male,' and tranny, and accused me of flirting. Leah didn't stop him. She became a whole other person. Meek and useless."

"Girl, if he had called *me* those names, I'd have sliced him up. I still carry my knife in case anyone is fixing to get smart with me!"

"Trust me, it got ugly. He was all, 'What type of crazy name is Tituba?' Frankly, I was angrier at my sister than I was at him. I felt betrayed."

"I'm so sorry for you," Fabiana said. "Do you want me to do something to teach this dude a lesson? I know some people."

"No," she replied. "I guess this is part of my journey. I thought I'd lucked out and wouldn't have to go through people around me rejecting who I was."

"I don't blame you," Fabiana replied. She finally ate a bite of her muffin. A tiny bird bite. "You sleeping alright?" she asked.

"No … why do you ask?"

"Them bags under your eyes, child. You know what will fix them? Hemorrhoid cream. It tightens the skin."

"I am not about to put ass cream under my eyes!" Tituba said. Both of them laughed loudly, causing the other café patrons to glance in their direction.

Fabiana said playfully, "Keep it classy, bitch!"

Tituba swatted at her hand. "Oh, hush. Seriously, though. Falling asleep isn't the problem. Hell, *staying* asleep isn't, either. I sleep, but I wake up tired as if I had a tough workout at the gym or gone a few rounds with a boxer. And when I wake up, there's always some weird reddish dust on me. And it's not just me. My neighbors all look … drained. One day, I saw a kid at the bus stop and his collar had stains of that red dust."

"Huh," said Fabiana. "Have you heard about Sick Building Syndrome? It's a place where all the occupants get headaches and permanent sniffles. And fatigue. I think the *Post* did a series about it—one of the buildings owned by the EPA had it, and they had to close it."

"The *effing* Environmental Protection Agency had a 'sick building?'"

"You have to get out of there," Fabiana said, "Or, you need to get all *Norma Rae* on the building supervisor!"

Dust! Miles and miles, dune after dune of rust-red, as far as her eye could see. A red that was the color of old blood, slowly changing from crimson to brown.

She stood knee-deep in the middle of a valley, surrounded by mounds of the stuff. The sky above was hidden, obscured by a veil of red powder. She was sinking under, unable to get purchase on the feathery ground. The clothes she wore were reduced to blood-stained rags. It looked like she was shedding a membranous skin, like a snake. Her skin had abrasions, a network of thin cuts that were crusted over and flaking.

She must move on, before being swallowed whole by the wavering ground. If she didn't move, she would drown and die, forever preserved beneath a beautiful mummy noone would ever see. She must move, or else she would die.

She lifted one foot clear of the squelching redness. And the wind began to blow. Dust rose into the air, into a corrosive mist that erased her body. Soon, she could not see anything. All was lost in the simoom.

Tituba woke up coughing. Her body shuddered with the fit. She could feel something rattling in her chest, as if her body were a percussion instrument filled with dry rice or sand. After the fit was over, she got up and switched the light on. Her tongue was heavy in her mouth, so she stumbled to the sink and drank two full glasses of water before she felt relatively normal.

She put the glass in the sink, checked the time. It was 3:30 a.m., early enough for a second shift of sleep. But she was too wired to get back into her bed. And, it seemed that she wasn't the only person up at this hour. The floor above her creaked with footsteps. Bellona's paper thin walls revealed activity on either side of her apartment, coughing on the left, the plaintive voice of a distressed child on the right.

Tituba knew that falling back to sleep would be difficult, so she pulled her phone from its charging port. Her headphones were on the ottoman next to her futon. That's when she first noticed the red dust. It was all over her mattress and futon, a fine sifting of rust-colored powder. She touched it. It didn't feel of anything. It was not coarse or smooth. It was feathery and insubstantial, even though she expected it to have a gritty feel, like sand or salt. Then, it moved. An infinitesimal slither through her fingers, a blur of micro-movement. Reflexively, Tituba shook the stuff off her fingers and headphones.

It wouldn't come off. There was a slight disturbance but then the powder-dust settled back. It clung to the curve of the headphones, the whorl of her fingertips. Tituba rubbed at the dust, hoping to dislodge it with friction. That did not work. Her fingertips were stained.

She muttered a curse word or two under her breath. She ran water over the stubborn stain at the kitchen sink.

A piece of dried skin, embossed with a fingerprint, fell off her hand, leaving behind tender new skin. She watched as the opaque, red crinkled skin settled in the sink.

The powder-dust plumped up with the water. Fat with sudden moisture, the flakes began to rise upward, as if buoyed by an unfelt breeze. Red drops of old blood hung in the air, hovered. Then, they burst open.

Tituba screamed.

The office door was locked, as it had been for the past two weeks. Tituba had stopped by the superintendent's office before and after work, on the weekend, but the door had always been locked. The emails she sent were unanswered, and the phone calls went straight to voice mail.

She didn't know if she'd even seen him during the time she'd been in Bellona Heights. Her neighbors confirmed that he was elusive and unreachable at the best of times. Everyone she'd spoken to had given her a 'why bother' attitude. When she told the residents in the mailroom or lobby about the mysterious, weird dust she'd seen, they just shrugged, as if defeated.

One time in the laundry room, she asked Phylis, an older woman who lived on the same floor, if she knew anything.

Phylis had been folding a child's clothes when Tituba entered the shabby basement with a week's worth of dirty clothing. Phylis had grudgingly given her a greeting when Tituba broached the subject.

"Yeah, I've seen it," Phylis had said, dripping with attitude. "Folks made a stink about it back in the day. Nothing happened."

"But it must be unhealthy. So many people here have respiratory problems."

"And?" Phylis said, as she went to unload a dryer that had just buzzed. "Ain't nobody who owns this glorified flophouse care about our health. This ain't Northwest."

Tituba purposefully ignored the bitterness dripping from Phylis's voice. "Maybe not. But the dust isn't natural. I hear it rattling in the vent, like tiny ants. Like it's alive ..."

Phylis stopped folding the laundry and threw it into the basket. "You're a fine one to talk about 'unnatural' things," she announced as she headed to the door.

Tituba said, "Excuse me?"

But Phylis was already out of the room.

Now, she stood in front of the office door for the umpteenth time. She jiggled the lock, even though she knew there was no point. Maybe Phylis was right, and she should leave well enough alone. But she couldn't. Tituba's entire existence had been full of struggle, starting from birth, and it didn't look like it was going to get easy anytime soon. The dancing dust was just one more obstacle to overcome.

Tituba went to the mailroom instead. She found the tiny room full of packages and guessed that some of them were nebulizers and humidifiers. All week long, residents had unboxed the machines in the room, leaving a pile of broken-down cardboard boxes. She had toyed with getting one herself, to combat the dryness in the building.

Fabiana was right. Bellona Heights *was* a sick building. Ever since she'd moved in, she had been plagued with low-key headaches that threatened to grow into full-on migraines. Her stomach was unsettled, and food tasted weird. Walking down a city block easily winded her. And she began to notice discolorations on her skin: darkness beneath her eyes, and white spots on her arms. Most of all, she was always thirsty. She would drink bottle after glass of water or juice, but she could never be satisfied. She didn't pee often, for the amount she drank. Where did it all go?

She passed by the superintendent's door in futile hope.

"Warren not in again?" said someone behind her. It was Ty, who also lived on her floor. He was around her age and height, with a muscular, lithe physique. His skin was dark and velvet-smooth, his bald head glowing with head wax. At least, that *had* been his appearance. Now, crow's feet and forehead wrinkles marred the smooth expanse, and the lustrous blue-blackness of his skin was dried out to a leathery brown.

"Apparently not." Tituba looked away from Ty, hoping that he didn't notice her shocked reaction.

He jiggled the doorknob, as if to verify. Then, he glanced at Tituba and gave her a conspiratorial wink.

"Desperate times," he said, and he pushed against the door with his shoulder. The door quivered with the pressure, and after a few more aggressive pushes, it popped open.

Ty and Tituba were immediately hit with a wave of stale air that had a slight cindery taste. They simultaneously began coughing in response. There was also another smell beneath that one—a smell of turned meat and the coppery tang of old blood. A haze of carmine simmered in the room, thick enough that they both had to wave it away. The shades were drawn, so it was dim in the room.

"Oh, my god," Tituba said, after her eyes adjusted to the gloom.

There was a body slumped over a desk. She knew it was a corpse. The angle of the head looked too uncomfortable to maintain, and the visible eye was open. She switched on the overhead light and immediately wished that she hadn't. The older gentleman was in a grey mechanic's suit, his mouth opened in a grimace. Dust pooled around the open mouth, onto the desk. It was embedded on his skin, in his hair, and she could see flecks of it in the whites of his eye.

Ty walked around the desk, reached out to touch the body.

"Leave it alone," Tituba said.

Ty lowered his hands, and reached for his cellphone instead, presumably to call for an ambulance.

Tituba saw the wrinkled flesh, fold upon fold of thin skin, some of it so dry that the pigment had leeched out. It didn't look like skin. It was papery, cracked like old parchment. And in the folds of skin, remnants of the red dust gathered. His mouth was open, and a crumbled pink tongue lolled out past black, cracked lips.

"He looks like a mummy," Ty said after he finished speaking to the emergency operator. "I wonder how long he's been here."

Tituba heard him, but she was distracted by the thin trail of red dripping down from the HVAC vent.

Whatever lived there had drained the superintendent, had turned him into a husk. His skin had the same color and texture as a tamarind. She could only imagine the poor man's innards, the pulp toughened into sponge and coral.

"He's been sucked dry," Tituba said. "We're gonna end up like him."

With tweezers, Tituba scraped the red residue into an old nail polish bottle she had cleaned out. Something was in the vents, something that left behind this weird substance.

She brought the bottle with her to dinner at a restaurant.

The first thing Fabiana said when she saw Tituba was, "Girl, you look ashy and worn out!"

"I know," she replied, waving the comment away. "Listen to me. You were right. Bellona Heights *is* a sick building. Some kind of virus or something *lives* in the vents and gives everyone who lives there breathing problems!"

"Last week, one of the other residents and I found the superintendent dead in his office. His body was dry. Bone dry. Desert dry. All of the moisture had been sucked right out of him."

Tituba pulled up a picture on her phone and handed it to Fabiana.

Fabiana shrieked. "Put that thing away!"

Tituba complied.

Fabiana said, "I don't think I've ever seen anything so terrible. Poor dude. He looks like one of those apple-head dolls."

"I asked the EMTs if they were gonna do an autopsy to determine the cause of death. They ignored me."

Fabiana sucked her teeth in sympathetic dismay. "They always do. And we end up dead because they won't listen!"

Tituba dug around in her handbag until she found and pulled out the nail polish bottle.

"Look at it, Fab. Look closely."

"Look at an empty bottle of Carolina Beet lacquer?" Fabiana cautiously picked the bottle up and peered into it.

"Stop kidding around, girl. Tell me what you see."

Fabiana stared at it for a long moment, still looking as the server refilled their wine glasses with rosé.

Finally, she said, "That dust moves."

"I'm glad you saw that too! I thought I was going crazy!"

Fabiana still held the bottle close to her eye. "I don't think it's dust, Tituba. I saw one fragment of whatever-it-is, apart from the others, move on its own. I see wings. Tiny, infinitesimal scarlet wings. The wings of a moth, not a butterfly. The straggler eventually joined the rest of the swarm, I suppose. And it looked like a swirling dust."

"You think it's insects?"

Fabiana shrugged in response. "I don't know. All I *do* know is, you have to get the hell out of there!"

...❖...

Tituba was unlocking the door to her apartment when she heard the scream. It came from down the hall. She found herself running there and knocking on the door until Phylis, the grandmother who lived there with her daughter Krystle and grandson Kendrick, opened it.

"What's wrong, Miss Phylis?" she asked.

Miss Phylis was wild-eyed and apoplectic, apparently unable to speak. She gestured weakly to an opened doorway off the L-shape of the apartment. More screams came from there, mostly Krystle saying, "Lord, lord, lord!" Tituba left Miss Phylis behind to look in the doorway.

She tried to make sense of the bizarre scene. This was obviously a child's room, full of Thomas the Tank Engine paraphernalia, the google-eyed train's face on toys and curtains and posters, its frozen smile stretched across the face. The walls were splattered with moving constellations that came from a projector lamp. Tituba saw little Kendrick being cradled by his mother, in what looked like a grotesque parody of the Pietá, his limp body draped over her lap. His eyes were closed and fluttering, as if he were fighting to keep them open; some nightmare thing wouldn't let him wake up. Things moved on his unconscious body. Scarlet specks, a tide of them spilling over his pajamas, arms, and face. The tiny little blister-colored things vibrated as they moved. And they moved with purpose, heading for his nostrils and slightly opened mouth. She imagined the minuscule things coating his nasal passages, flurrying in the chambers of his sinuses, ricocheting and embedding themselves in spongy alveoli as they drank up the mists of the boy's body, drying out mucus membranes, turning plasma into dust. She heard Kendrick begin to wheeze, heard the raspy rattling in his chest.

Those creatures have done the same thing to me, every night, she thought. She recalled her dreams about Martian-red deserts and dust storms.

She switched on the overhead light. The stars became invisible. The moth-things slowed down, and lazily detached themselves from the child's body. They drifted upward, red motes of dust, heading toward the ceiling, heading toward the grates of the vent. More of them dribbled from Kendrick's nose and mouth. It looked like a twinkling river of blood. Tituba dug around her purse until she found a bottle of spray lotion. She spritzed the red-speckled air with the thick mist, saturating it. A clump of the things fell from the air, a worm-like wriggling ball of red paste with the consistency of snot. The coagulated mess fell on the floor with a wet splat. Tituba, Krystle, and Miss Phylis watched with disgust at the wet wings flexing in globules of oily lotion.

Tituba said, "Quick! We have to get the rest of the stuff out of Kendrick! Wake him up and make him drink water. Maybe that will flush them out."

Krystle carried Kendrick into the kitchen, where he blinkingly woke up in the harsher light. They got the confused child to slurp down a couple of glasses of water. Then he began coughing, body-wracking spasmodic coughs. His mother patted his back, calling Kendrick her little angel, her sweetheart, her precious boy.

Then, he vomited.

Out of his mouth came a stream of red paste. They saw the fragments of wings and waterlogged pieces of something drip onto the floor. The swarm of dust-insects was decimated. But more lived in this forgotten, neglected building full of brown and black bodies. Were these tiny, mothlike vampires conscious of what they did as they fed upon sleeping bodies, draining the moisture of breath, crawling down throats? Perhaps they weren't malevolent, these winged specks of decay.

Bellona Heights. More like Hellona Depths.

Back in her apartment, Tituba blocked the vent with a piece of plywood. It was a temporary measure. She thought of black mold, or Legionnaires bacteria brought to life with some dark magic. She thought about contacting the press or an exterminator. But people ignored the superintendent's death, and the complaints brought by the other residents. It was unlikely that anyone would listen to a black trans woman.

She would have to fix this on her own. Survival was in her DNA. Survival, and its importance, was why she chose her name. Titus, her birth name, had been meek and a victim of the church, his family, and society. Titus would have succumbed to the dust-moths and been one more epidemiological statistic to be ignored.

Tituba, however, would fight. She would survive, like the historical woman she'd named herself after.

As she lay down at 4 a.m., exhausted from saving Kendrick's life, she heard the scarlet moths skittering around in the blocked vents, banging against the plywood barrier.

"I dare you," she said.

And she began coughing. Violence was in her lungs, her chest, her throat, her head. She coughed so hard that black spots appeared before her. *Some of those things must've found their way into me.* The malevolent red moths were attacking her, with clear intention. It could not have been a coincidence. They had heard her issued challenge, and now they responded.

If—*when*—Tituba survived this assault, she would destroy miniature dust-demons. She would kill them *tonight*.

DISASSEMBLY

by Makena Onjerika

Eighteen years ago, Ntinyari takes her heart out of her chest for the first time. It is a frightened bird in her hand. An ugly thing, slick with fat, and slippery and loud, *kugu kugu kugu*. She squeezes it, willing it to still for just a moment and let her hear herself. Mother finds her fallen over, a marionette in a heap. Her heart has rolled under the bed.

"Why would you do this?" Mother asks, jamming her heart back in place and shuttering her chest. "I have given you everything."

Ntinyari tries to remember she has no right to unhappiness, but she cannot help occasionally taking out and cataloging her parts: kidneys, lungs, vagina, eyes (those she puts back in immediately; watching herself from the table is disorienting), lips, spleen, uterus, nose, stomach (it sloshes with undigested breakfast), pancreas, ears, tongue, intestines. Everything is present, she thinks. Everything is present. Not a single part is missing.

Why then doesn't laughter escape her in puffs of yellow, pink, and blue as it does the other girls at her secondary school? Could she not be as possessed of saccharine happiness? Or at least be at the center of some frivolous rebellion—going without a bra, for example? Anything to make her more than a well-mannered, if awkward, blob of excellent grades.

...❖...

They meet at a nightclub they are both a year too young to be in. Together and drunk on fruity cocktails, Kiku and Ntinyari own the deserted floor, vanishing and reappearing among the colored strobe lights, each feeling secure because the other is there. They shout introductions over the licentious dancehall music and are soon grinding buttock to pelvis, because they can, and because it makes men stare greedily. A few hours later, they are bent over a sink, united in vomiting and the best of friends.

Kiku's love for nail polish, makeup, and perfume soon permeates Ntinyari's bedroom. Mother approves: Kiku is just the kind of influence Ntinyari needs to smooth out her edges.

"Ask her what she is doing to her skin," Mother says.

Ntinyari's hand goes to her cheek. A new pimple is sprouting there, hard and stubborn. Her forehead is a constellation of rashes and black spots. Nothing she does seems to stop her pores from secreting thick, greasy sebum. She feels poisonous. If only she could slip into Kiku's skin.

At their next sleepover, she presses against Kiku as they lie on their bellies watching a bootleg DVD on Kiku's laptop. Kiku's face is wet from all the crying she has done along with one of the movie's characters.

"I can't help it," she says every time Ntinyari witnesses her osmose other people's emotions.

And this is why they are friends. Ntinyari gets off the bed and slips out of her skinny jeans and T-shirt, then her lacy panties and bra.

Kiku hides behind her hands. "What are you doing?"

"I need to show you something."

Ntinyari reaches her hand to her back and feels for a zipper. She draws it along the rail under her skin. It splits her open halfway across her neck and then down through her chest. Her ribs peer out, visible through muscle. She is almost unzipped to her navel when Kiku punctures through her shock—and screams.

Then come years of endless falling. Ntinyari is a bottomless pit, an unpunctured exclamation, a darkness imperceptible to the human eye. Under a microscope, she finds that her nerve cells have tails like mucus pulled out of a child's nose. Her blood cells could be doughnuts, her muscle cells worms, her bone cells spiders, her skin cells blocks of gummy sweets stuck together. And yet, nothing is out of the norm here. She pulls away from the microscope and rubs her eye with her fist. A dull pain creeps up her back between her shoulder blades.

She is twenty years old, and behind her, on a laboratory's cold slab, lies a cadaver. His face and chest are hidden under a blue sheet, as if that could shield him from the indignity of what is happening to the rest of him. She and the other first-year medical students have been picking him apart for four months, stripping him down to his essentials, naming him by his pieces. After every session, the pain in Ntinyari's back escalates into a smoldering spot of lava.

"Sometimes, I dream I am him," she says to Brother-on-a scholarship-abroad.

With each conversation she feels she is regurgitating her brokenness into the world, soiling it. Brother squints into his video-chat window, trying to make out the seams along which she is coming undone, but even he cannot tell her what hurts or why.

"You scored an A, Nti."

"He's dead. He feels no pain."

He does not understand that she is a composite of mismatched parts: too-large eyes; a short, rounded nose; arched eyebrows; a too-small mouth; and ears flattened against her head. She is God's left-over pieces.

They chat once a week, but she does not settle. What is murky about her does not fall to the bottom and leave clarity that she can decant and inhabit. She grows more turbid. She fails her exams that semester. She drops out of medical school. And all who know her shake their heads and lament wasted potential.

At twenty-five she swipes right on a dating app.

"Architect," he says over what he insists are the best burgers in Nairobi.

Ntinyari hides her disappointment at having to pass a first date in an open yard, among rough-sawn benches, chairs, and tables, while all around, expats smoke pungent marijuana. But slowly she relaxes into his world. He nods his head to music she has never heard before. He calls out the names of artists and soundtracks.

"This is the real stuff," he says.

She is envious of his confidence, his firm belief that he belongs—a sticky kind of envy that forms a lump in her throat. His gestures are wide, his posture straight yet relaxed. She is ashamed of her inability to be as large, to saturate every space with her own contentment. Mother's words return to her: you have everything. She smiles wider and wider as he talks. She could choke on that smile.

When he calls asking for a second date, Ntinyari is scared. How soon before he realizes she is broken? Date after date, she works hard at being interesting and nodding intelligently.

"You are so different from anyone I've been with before," he says after date five.

Her insides liquefy with gratitude. She settles into this warm feeling. She deserves it. A month later, she is sharing her secret, and he is listening intently, beer can midair on its way to his mouth. She knows this will be different from Kiku. And it is.

He is not afraid. When she pulls off her leg to illustrate, he puts his hand out for it. She lifts it up to where he sits on his car's bonnet, as though making an offering to a god. He gives it a light toss and takes another gulp off his beer can.

Ntinyari sips wine in kisses from her place on the picnic blanket. He has brought her to Karura forest for date twelve, to the twitter of birds and the rustle of leaves and an air so fresh that she feels slightly dizzy. In her mental checklist, she has ticked "romantic."

"Can you pull off the other one?" he asks.

As he examines both legs and notes that there is no blood, his expression—his bewilderment—makes her feel proud, as though this coming apart is a gift, and she is special.

He drinks from his can and considers her closely. When he speaks, his voice is cold and exact: "Now come get them."

Not even the realization that she is terrified makes Ntinyari demand that he give back her legs. She tries lifting herself up onto the car bonnet. He is testing her, must be testing her. Sometimes, this is the way to love and be loved. She laughs as she struggles. She laughs and he laughs.

"I will break you," he says when he leaves her a year later.

"Look," she pleads. "Look, no pain."

She pulls off an arm. It is as easy as breaking a Barbie doll apart. *Klack!* She could throw her head against a wall to make him stay and make her lovable again.

At twenty-nine, she has climbed to the significant position of team lead at an advertising agency, which means she is often sitting on the bad side of her boss's desk. Everyone in the open-plan hall beyond the woman's glass office can see Ntinyari squirming as she waits for the boss to finish typing out an email. When the woman shuts her laptop, Ntinyari feels herself crinkle under her gaze, like foil on a fire.

"This job is too big for you, Ntinyari. Don't you agree?"

Pain is the cheekbone-chiselling bob cut her boss wears and its stark red highlights. Against the light of the window in her office, she looks aflame.

"Have you considered looking for something you can actually handle?"

There has been an email from Ntinyari's nightmare client, the bank man in charge of the agency's largest contract. He regularly shares briefs at 5 p.m. and expects work delivered by 8 a.m. the next morning, forcing Ntinyari and her team to work overnight.

"We are trying our best. It's just not possible to work on his ..."

Boss Lady jabs her finger at Ntinyari. "Excuses. Excuses. How long are you going to live like this? Doesn't it bother you to be so mediocre?"

Ntinyari does not dare to let the door bang on her way out. She walks back to her desk under a deluge of stares and whispers. In that soup of 24/7 office-wide music, advertising jargon, too many hugs, and endless brainstorming sessions, she stands out for her inability to dissolve. She lacks a certain *je ne sais quoi*. Spontaneity, she's heard someone say, or perhaps just more life than a rock. She's heard worse things whispered about her, and a few of these have made her lock herself in a toilet stall twice this past year.

Laughter explodes from one corner of the office. It's Maina, her team's social media strategist and perpetual latecomer. Today he arrived at eleven o'clock, but is now seated on someone else's desk, telling what must be a funny story for all the laughter it's causing. He's a creative, he says, and his ideas need time to percolate, so no, he hasn't yet worked on the Christmas campaign proposal the client wants to see tomorrow, and she should buy him time, because that is her job, isn't it?

She has a First Class Honors degree in Marketing, but it is only a piece of paper in the face of office politics and client ass-kissing.

"You will keep running away when things get tough and then discover you have wasted your life," Mother said when Ntinyari quit medicine nine years ago.

For entire weekends she lies in bed afraid of something she cannot articulate. Something gaseous and amorphous. She is trapped in her bedding. And when her undrawn curtains darken again and a whole day is gone, guilt takes on a tangible form and becomes her companion in bed, cold and cutting, insistent on cuddling.

In September, she is passed over for a promotion at the agency. Two mornings after, she cannot find the big toe of her left foot. On another, her eyeball hangs out of its socket; she cannot quite get it back in. And on yet another, she has only one breast. Then she comes home from work one night and stumbles upon her hand still clasping a dirty teacup on the kitchen counter. How did she not notice all day? She sits staring at it for a long time, knowing that she has crossed a certain dangerous line.

Yet she experiments. She detaches her lower jaw and sits disfigured through meetings. She hops around the office on one leg. She walks blind into walls. She leaves her buttocks on a chair in the kitchenette area. She stands by the water dispenser with her intestines spilling out of her in twisted, visceral knots. No one looks at her twice. No one says more than a dry, hurried, "Hi." She has vanished from the world.

She weeps with upraised arms. She sways in the slow, melancholy music the choir members foment in the depths of their despair. Ntinyari is broken before the Lord. Pastor David bellows into his microphone and reverberates off the walls: "Receive the healing." If the Holy Spirit descends, He only descends on other people. To them go grace and renewal. Ntinyari swallows her bitterness and sings louder.

One Saturday morning, while sitting on her couch, she has a maddening itch in her scalp. She attacks it with the lid of a pen, then the point. It multiplies and spreads, as angry as a thousand ant bites. She plucks off her head, sets it between her knees, and gives her scalp a thorough scratch. Thus, with ten fingers aggravating her itch, she alights on an idea: the thing that is wrong with her is inside her head, the only part she has never broken down. It must be.

Self-help books tell her to picture what she must excavate: a malicious, black ball nestled between the lobes of her brain. She finds a screwdriver. She tries to coerce the seven screws in her skull out of their holes. Hours or years later, one flies off and cracks her TV screen. Alas, the other six are bolted down tight. All is futile. Nothing can be mended.

On her bedroom floor of cold brown tiles, she uncouples her feet from her ankles, her toes from her feet, and her nails from her toes. Piece by piece, she lays herself out on the floor in the lazy parallelograms of sun falling in through the window. She is thirty-one years old. She can no longer hold together; she has never known how to hold together. She decouples hip from torso, thigh from hip, knee from thigh. She watches herself from where her head lies on its side. Even now, nothing is missing.

Life seems a row of glass windows on which she slides, leaping, reaching, appearing, and disappearing. She is a mere reflection. She does not die; or perhaps she does.

Dr. Oduor is a cliché: a white head, thick spectacles on the bridge of his nose, and an array of framed certificates on his wall. His greeting is flat. He mechanically tracks her movements from the door to the chair. All he will do is lecture her, as others have done since she woke up at the hospital, all of them whispering because she committed a crime and could be arrested if discovered. A peppering of allusions, here and there, to the value of life and the importance of talking about one's problems. Even her doctor and the nurses had to pretend she accidentally swallowed a boxful of paracetamol.

"Do you want to live?" asks Dr. Oduor.

Is it so simple? Wanting or not wanting? She looks away.

A lonely, dwarf palm is trapped in a pot in one corner of his office. A laden bookshelf is sagging in the opposite corner. Above a hand basin is the painting of a nondescript stretch of beach in which wanders a bare-chested, black boy. Ntinyari imagines him looking over his shoulder at her.

"You just wanted attention," he would say.

When she does not respond, the doctor jots down something on his pad. If she were to begin trying to scratch off her face, would he be forced to lock her away in a psychiatric ward forever?

"Do you want to live?" he asks again.

So irritating. She could scream luminous colors onto his ugly, off-white walls. She could crack thunder and flash lightning. She could burn his books and dance around the fire naked. But she is just a body in a chair, and tired, so tired.

"Do you think it was easy?" she asks.

Now he has no words, staring out of his silly glasses. He sits back in his chair, retreating behind defenses. He is going to tent his fingers and attempt to cower her. She glares all her anger at him and forces him to break eye contact first.

"I am not your enemy."

She fills up like a glass under a tap of cold water. Her voice is dissolving when she speaks: "Who is my enemy? Who is doing this to me?"

Does he not see that she is in too many pieces, and some have been lost? He passes her a box of tissues before she realizes she is crying.

"Look, Ntinyari. Depression is treatable, but you must want to be treated."

She has not wanted to accept that word. Depression.

All that she has suffered summarized in a single word. Depression.

The feeling of being constantly submerged in dark waters. Depression.

How can such a large thing be so neatly delineated?

He puts a rough hand on hers. She nods.

But this will be a long journey. Ahead are years and years of pills and therapy. Ahead are days when she will wake up a confusion of parts. Days so small, so hard, so gnawed upon. Bruised, ugly days when she will almost fail at putting herself back together. Ahead is the gigantic impossible task of lassoing and pulling down an intangible, ferocious beast.

But then, at last, the day will come—surely it must come—and a golden day it will be, when Ntinyari no longer disassembles.

THE RIVER OF NIGHT

by Tlotlo Tsamaase

The river of night settles in my thighs waiting for your tongue. It knows your patterns, your timings, knows the hour is always seeking you.

You cum at the witching hour—*always*, a booty call is my body to collect the spam of your illicit desire to be with someone. Your satisfaction is always the end credits. Hush. The buzz of a cigarette, a mosquito, a fly, technology humming in our veins—an eye in our room. I sit huddled, knees tight to my breasts. Today, the air doesn't know I'm human. You tell me I'm only good for your exhales. I'm your lit joint, you've licked me, sealed me good so I don't flee.

"Did I get you high, baby?" I ask.

"Not high enough," you say. "Again," you instruct me. You flick the lighter and burn me into your firework. Tonight, every night, I'm your zol, I'm your jol.

I'm the drug you hide from your wife.

"Leloba," Matshwênyêgô says, and I hate the way she tosses my name across our open-plan office desks. "Aren't you sick of this dead-end job? I mean, sure, you're an editor, but it shit-sure doesn't feel like it sitting here. No windows, just a bloody jail cell. Plus"—she taps her manicured index finger counting one of the many reasons why I shouldn't be here—"no one treats you like you hold a senior role. Look, everyone here thinks you're small, that you're inconsequential. They know that you're not made for this job. What if you get fired? How will you pay the rent? Where will you live?"

It's all my fears tumbling out of her mouth. I didn't study journalism or creative writing, instead I'm self-taught, and the imposter syndrome is a daily claustrophobic suit I'm unable to take off—it's my skin.

"I still don't get why you're punishing yourself," Kakanyô says, spinning in her swivel chair. "Go back to architecture, fam."

I shrink into my seat. The twins know me more than I know myself.

It's creepy the way they emit my thoughts. But they're right. I let people walk all over me; my body is a basic welcome mat for assholes. I committed the foulest career change: five years after studying architecture plus eight month's stint of dabbling through architectural firms, I quit my profession as an architect-in-training to being a sort-of architectural journalist-cum-proofreader-editor. Everyone thinks architects make millions on their first job. My job paid me peanuts. I worked weekdays and weekends raw into the night. I was on the hem of death, sewing my nerves with alcohol. To save myself, I had to quit. I am now living the consequences of it: a failure.

"Right now, you'd be a registered architect with your own firm making millions," Matshwênyêgô whispers. "Words don't make money, designing buildings does. You'd be like a fucking STEM woman, a lot of opportunities out there for you, ja."

"Not just that. You're a Motswana woman. There are a lot of cards you can play. Black. African. Poverty. Female," Kakanyô adds as she leans on her desk ignoring her article and its impending deadline.

"That really doesn't sound genuine," I say.

"Well, is being genuine paying your bills?" She raises her finger to shut me up. "Barely. You can't just survive life; you need to live life."

"Success takes time," I say.

Matshwênyêgô scoffs. "Ja. Sorry, but I don't want to start living life when I'm a septuagenarian. Then what's the point of living?"

"You wasted such a good opportunity; you wasted your life," Kakanyô adds in agreement. I wish they'd keep their voices low. I don't need everyone knowing I'm a failure.

Fortunately, a notification beeps of an incoming article I need to edit. I drown out their conversation. We continue punching out stories, interviewing sources, editing and working painlessly at some forgettable media organization.

Kakanyô is my colleague-slash-roommate who has a streak of negativity, so does Matshwênyêgô, who's an over perfectionist. She analyzes every scenario or domestic hygiene. If she's not worrying about the state of the kitchen, she's worrying about my future, whereas Kakanyô picks at everything about me, from my abilities, to my dreams, to my choice of boyfriends. But living with them makes life less lonely. Every single day they wake before I wake and press a warm cloth to rub the sweat of nightmares from my forehead.

We've been Siamese—not literally but in the sense that we're stuck in the same job, the same house, same age, like orbiting planets in the same womb circulating an identical lifestyle.

I find it so hard to differentiate them. Sometimes they disappear on the weekends. I never see them leave, I just wake up and they're gone. They return days later, and I wonder how they're able to go over their leave days. I don't want to fuss over how they lead their lives, they're grown-ups. They've no family ties, no standing status, and are okay with it. I wish I could be as confident as them.

"The landlord is on my back," I say out on the office's balcony, the only respite from the "jail cell" for fresh air, daylight, and quiet. I take a bite of my chicken sandwich and in between chewing, I add, "You two need to put in your half of the rent."

"You're our half of the rent," they say, breaking into giggles. The joke's lost on me. They always have these inside jokes, making my isolation more prominent. The combination of our salaries was meant for one person—not three. Each time, during my appraisals at work when I bring up the idea of a raise, my manager hushes me with, "The company is currently undergoing financial difficulties. Once we overcome the adversity, we will look over your contract." It's been three years and no dice. So sharing the one-bedroomed servant's quarter's rent was the most economical way to go.

I don't look forward to home though: the nocturnal twin-sisters and I sleep in the same room, but sometimes the proximity is too close: it feels as if they sleep in my body, in my mind. I. Just. Can't. Breathe.

...❖...

The evening traffic is slow. I stumble into my home and throw my clothes off. I can breathe now. I can exhale the ennui of work from my bones. I can bloom today. I can—my cellphone flickers a neon light, clingy, calling me back. I unlock it. A notification. A childhood friend across borderlines, many rungs above the corporate ladder, with towers of beauty and charm. How beautiful she looks. How glowing her brown skin is. She's engaged. A romantic getaway in the Maldives. This is who I'm supposed to be. The light from my phone gobbles my face whole. My life is blatant today. It reeks in this small servant's quarter, in the old walls, the leaking tap, the broken skin.

I am nothing.

Five years as an employee, a sheep. What have I been doing with my years? Where did I stack them? A knock. The landlord. I'm consuming too much electricity. The rent has gone up. I only have one income. Where the fuck is the rest supposed to come from? The room is too cold. There is no ceiling, only the bones of the exposed rafters. There is no one home to kiss me, to ask me how my day was, to tell me I'm beautiful. I can't see myself anymore. I can't feel my skin. Where are my lungs? The dark has taken my eyes. Again. Oh, no. It's happening. Again. If I hold my breath, this will subside, and I will be fine. I will see myself again. I will catch my sight. In my home, even I am invisible. Each second shaves me into invisibility, each thought dilutes me with the acid of its torment, of its fervent belief that I do not mean to exist.

I have my own pet, Keletsô, but the twins have an insidious pet, Manyaapelo, they keep locked up in the wardrobe or under the bed. People who visit our city are confused at this breed of evil some of us talk about. I always wonder if it is jubilance or horror that will meet me. Manyaapelo always waits for me at home, waits for the shuffling of my shoes across the welcome mat, the key turning in its hole. Once I close the door, this creature, Manyaapelo, leaps onto my back. Sometimes it lives in the body, hanging on the spinal cord of your last hope. But those who don't experience it love to discredit it, as if it doesn't exist.

"But how is it born?" a colleague once asked. "What does this creature look like?"

"It shape-shifts from moody to ecstatic joy," I say. "It has many mouths. It has many voices, so you can't focus. It makes you feel like you're drowning in your own body. It comes unexpectedly. We've tried to burn it with muti. Nothing vanquishes it. Sangoma hands can't bury it. Its terror lives as long as its owner."

They shake their heads and laugh like we're crazy.

Kakanyô steps out from our bathroom, watching me envy my childhood friend's fortune.

"Your years are passing you by," Kakanyô says. "Your age mates are married. You're letting your degree collect dust. Just what are you doing with your life?"

I sigh. "I was working Monday to Sunday. I wasn't sleeping. I was stressed. I was going insane. I didn't know what happiness meant anymore—"

"Is this what happy means?" she asks, circling my bachelorette pad. "Living in this dump. Living paycheck to paycheck starving—for what? Wake up, man. You've no savings. What you going to do next year? What you gonna do if you lose your job? Like, is this your life?"

"Cut me some slack," I shout.

"A devil could put better use to your body."

"This is not working out. I'm going to look for a place and move out."

She laughs. "Good luck getting rid of me, babes. Easier to get rid of your skin than me."

The many mouths of Manyaapelo reiterate her: You are useless. You will lose your job. They will find you're an impostor. You don't deserve your job. You don't deserve to live. The words, the syllables, are so meshed into each other I can't single out individual statements; my heartbeat senses the language of terror and dwells into the sludge of negativity.

Kakanyô pulls Manyaapelo by the leash from my wardrobe. I could ask her why she's doing this to me, but it could either be her or me, and she's choosing herself. Standing on the tall feet of anger, of shock, of this miserable life, Manyaapelo seeks to possess me. My knees buckle. The creature spins me around, working a web around my form with its teeth. It drags me into bed, heaving and panting. Its tooth is strung into my neck; the blood in me, the life in me is siphoned hour upon hour.

When daylight returns, I wake up. It is morning. The creature's web is gone. I stand on shaky limbs and sprinkle sweat all the way to the bathroom. Cramps crawl up and down my legs. My period must have started. My pupils are still alive. I hate going to work on my periods; the first three days consist of a tsunami of pain down my thighs. Pain medication helps barely. My mind is always hazy, scuttling unsteadily all over the place, making my hands jittery. Appearing stable and normal is an exhaustive task. But I have to get ready for work and rely on changing every hour.

The mirror shows me the caves and convex planes of my face. The creature left no flesh behind. Dark prints stand beneath my eyes, turning them bloodshot. I just have to eat and I will be fine. My hands tremble as I splash my face with cold water. Eight hours of work ahead of me. I haven't even started the first hour and I am a zombie lugging the corpse of me around. How am I going to trek through the apocalyptic eight hours of this job I hate? How will I maneuver the misogynistic jokes that light fire to my body?

Matshwênyêgô's reflection appears in the mirror. "*Leloba*, if you don't go to work, you'll get a bad report, a warning. You'll lose your job. You have no money, no savings. Nothing to live on."

"You could ask to work from home today because you're unwell," my pet says, stretching its back against the wall.

"Haven't you seen how the other editors stare at me when I request something?" I say. "I don't want to be any more difficult. They'll replace me with a less difficult person. And I need this job."

It purrs. "Well, if you fed me, gave me—"

"Don't start. Not today." And I shut the bathroom door on my pet.

Today at work, the male editor is jostling around with his ego. He's eagle-eyed and scanning the office, wanting to pin someone and watch them scuttle under the burning gaze of his jaunts. I tend to ignore him, so I'm not his favorite victim. This morning, as usual, his target is Tshiamo, a twenty-year-old intern, who's been here for three months plus. She places his morning coffee, phaphatha, and gizzards by his laptop as he remarks something about her outfit. She stirs uncomfortably. She's not on payroll. It shows in the fading quality of her clothes. A work-for-free exposure and experience, they say.

I check my phone to set an alarm that will notify me in an hour to change, before I stain myself. It's happened before; being under the onslaught of articles to edit, time just flows by and suddenly your pants are stained, and everyone stares at you like a freak, an alien, when you're really just a person who's a woman. I'm wearing thick underwear, a pad, and a tampon, the former two serving as backup plans, and I hate it because it makes me feel like a baby wearing a nappy; I'm overdosing on pain medication which tends to blur my eyesight. So much armor, all for the purpose to survive the day.

"I'm still waiting for your article," the male editor says, leaning onto his elbows.

"Eish, sir, I have an issue," Tshiamo says. "My source invited me to his place. At night. I told him I couldn't; now he's dodging my questions."

"He plays an important role in your article. Why didn't you go to his place then?" he says, a laugh tickling his lips. "Sometimes you have to do everything and anything to appease your source. You women have it easy. If I had your body"—he catches me staring—"if I was a woman, hell, I'd get away with anything."

I hate his crude jokes. It's his conversation filler that blitzkrieg the dignity of any woman.

"All fun and games, I suppose," Kakanyô says. "It's just a joke. Take it easy."

"Find an alternative source," I say, "and please send me your article soon."

Sighing in relief, Tshiamo hurries out to her cubicle. The editor, displeased with my interruption, mumbles something. The editor and I both have senior roles, except we're separated by two decades or so of years. I'm a young woman, so all these factors, plus me "cockblocking" his attack, is covered silently under his vibrating ego, a land-mine awaiting any unaware footsteps. He continues staring at me, but I do not buckle. In this office place, you must always be on your guard.

Besides writing articles, I proofread articles for the other newspapers and radio. Now some of these newsreaders-cum-journalists can't string sentences together, and don't know the language of writing enough to play with style, as they're used to working with speech in radio content. It was the only way for the media organization to keep costs down: turning newsreaders into journalists. But they fuck with typos and grammar. I want to throw the articles out. They need to be rewritten. But my job is to proofread ASAP and send the stories to the graphic designers. There's no time to rewrite their articles, and I'm not getting paid enough to be motivated to do so. So every deadline day consists of myself and the male editor calling in the journalists to question them about what they're trying to convey, to ensure that, as we're editing, we aren't misconstruing their intended points to the reader. So that involves educating the journalists on content writing and how to approach sensitive material. As usual for demonstrations, the other editor enjoys using me as tinder for his fire.

This morning, the crime journalist stands by the editor listening to the developmental edits of his story, which is missing some significant content.

"Imagine if Leloba is raped," the editor says jovially. I freeze, caught off guard by the casual approach of this subject.

"Imagine if Leloba is raped," the editor repeats, a smile creeping at the edges of his lips like a snake.

I am paralyzed. I am Leloba, and right now they are imagining this terrifying thing happening to me.

The editor continues his visual elaboration, "Imagine she is assaulted. Imagine her clothes are being torn ..."

The testosterone in this room is chloroform placed to my lungs. My voice is muzzled. It takes a span for my mind to wrap itself around this. This is happening. I am literally in a small room where two men are imagining me getting raped, imagining me naked, *casually* having a conversation about it. There are other ways to illustrate his teachings. Just not this. I look down, and all my clothes are gone. I am naked. I yank my laptop bag, conceal myself as I run to the toilet and beg the cleaners to buy me clothes from the shops on the lower ground floor. As I wait, I wash my skin in shame. I run my nails against my neck.

"You just don't joke about shit like this," I shout to myself, staring at my reflection in the mirror, replicating into three people. I blink to ease the blurriness of my eyesight.

"If they're so casual about it, then there's nothing wrong," Kakanyô says, touching my shoulder. "This is the norm, you have to keep reminding yourself of that instead of becoming overly emotional about it. Your voice doesn't matter in this place—only your labor matters."

That's what words are in this place: they are not just empty things floating listlessly around; words have arms and weapons to do as they please. People who migrate to our city don't understand the concept that words turn into objects, they turn into thieves, they perform the purpose of its statement. It's a highly acceptable patriarchal part in our society, and everyone moves around with no opposition against them, so I have too as well.

Words have power. And that day, the editor's words undressed me. His words abused my thighs.

I'm trying to move on, but trauma sits on my back, making it difficult to walk. When I get home, my pet welcomes me with a wagging tail and a hungry stomach. I got my pet shortly before I started first year in university. I lived with it in my dorm room as I worked on coursework, before feeding it. Every time I walked in, it'd wag its tail, looking brand new and fresh. Now it's looking old and frayed, with a little sparkle in its eyes. During a span of overwork and exhaustion, it caught rabies and faced a near-death experience when I started my first job and spent nights and weekends at the office.

In the kitchen is a small round table where I unpack the groceries I bought.

"What's that on your back?" my pet asks.

"Nothing," I say.

"You can't keep letting them get away with this." My pet hops onto the counter. "You know if you feed me once in a while, I could grow into something. We could get out of this crappy place." It wags its tail in the direction of the ceiling-less kitchen. "You could live in a place with a garden, a view—an interior with good aesthetics. If you fed me, you wouldn't have to worry about the rent being too high, about waking up and forcing yourself to shit, to get to a job only to kiss ass to earn a living. You could have dignity, you could travel, work on your own schedule, get yourself something pretty. And laugh once in a while."

I stroke its fur. "But how long would I have to feed you for?"

It tilts its head as if shrugging. "Days, months, years. I don't know. I'm no fortune teller. I'm just here because there's something in you—a talent, an idea—that you want to get out. And the world needs that."

"I'm inconsequential in this universe of ours."

"Just feed me. You got me this far, didn't you?" It purrs. "I know it doesn't matter to people like you who have a law that protects their lives. People give birth to us, their passion. But then they forget about us, which aborts us. I'm dying here. If you take care of me, I can take care of you."

I dish food into its bowl. "Here you go then."

"What is this," it asks, sniffing its bowl.

"Tinned cat food," I say.

"This looks like someone's vomit." It pushes the bowl away with its paw. I try to avoid eye contact, so it leaps onto the counter with a glint in its eye. "You know what I consume."

"I don't have time, I'm tired."

"Take a nap then. It's only 7 p.m."

"I have a long day tomorrow."

"Excuses, excuses. You're slaving away at a job you hate, yet you can't slave away for yourself."

"You can't keep nagging me every time I come home."

"I'm starving. I. Am. Starving." It licks its paw. "Please." I lean against the counter and crumble into tears. "Now, now," it says in a soothing voice, patting my shoulder with its paw.

A week later, my period has stopped, and things feel slightly lighter. It's no surprise you call to meet me, for I am finally useful to you when I'm no longer "leaking from your vagina," you once said jokingly as if that lightened the blow.

"You are a slum," Kakanyô says when you pick me up at the office. You wait outside like a delivery man come to collect a package. You check the sparkle of your watch and can't hear the whisper of my hello.

You are a slum.

(she repeats when I enter your car)

You are a slum.

(she continues when I wrap your seatbelt around me)

You're a place stray things can't even call home.

In times like this, the signal to my pet connects, and its message transfers to my mind: "There are people who walk into your body with promises. There are people who see the value in you, who scrape inside you, trying to break you, trying to steep themselves in pleasure and in power. They empty you to fill themselves. Why do you let this happen?"

You. Are. A. Slum.

I shut my eyes to cancel the noise in my head.

"I can't stay for long," you say, breaking my attention from Kakanyô's words.

I nod. Your wife can't know of the drug you smoke away from the house, the drug that sleeps in my vagina.

You drive through roads to somewhere isolated from humanity. I am your vagina-on-call. I lay back, thighs around you, feet pressed to the ceiling of your car, and wait for the end. I do this to murder my loneliness, only I'm lonelier than ever. I'm fucked in the bundus, in hidden-away spots in the village areas. At first, it's different, adventurous, and spontaneous. "You're not like other girls," you say, admiring me. Then I realize how cheap it is, how cheap I am, like ordering a fuck like take-away from a street vendor.

I'm a take-away fuck.

This is what I do to murder my lonely, but I murder myself.

Maybe if I were like those beautiful girls, like my other friend Dikeledi, I'd ask you to start paying me, buying me things, paying my rent. But it's not me as much as it's who they are. We go again. As usual, you come at the witching hour, it jilts me, the moon slashes its eye in half, it spills on my thighs, a luminous light, and you rest back, panting, uncaring of my pleasure. *What about me?* I think. Every week I see, and I know this is all I will ever have.

You take me home.

Insomnia wraps around my feeble body. I wake up in the middle of the night paralyzed. The creature, Manyaapelo, growls into my ear, *You are nothing.*

Outside my window, the night sky is covered in my scars instead of stars.

In the morning, there is a piece of sky and foliage out my window. The birds sing, sometimes I'm too deaf from stress to hear them. Today I hear them and pray for hope. I sit in the bathtub and wash the nightmare clung to my skin. It's Saturday. A break from work. You're back again, nerves unwired, wishing for a quick high. I wish I could say many things, like, stop pumping false love into my womb if you mean to destroy it. If you mean to use it to let it cuddle

your desire

your swag

your masculinity

I wasn't taught what love is.

They say anger is made of your body. You're lean, broad-shouldered. You have a lisp, a buzz cut. You ask me if lunch is ready. I stare at my pet, Keletsô, sitting hunched back against the wall, whinnying.

"I need to feed my pet," I say.

"Who's your pet?" you ask.

"My Dreams is my pet," I whisper.

As you get up you slap my butt, I think, no, this is not love. "You look hot, baby girl," you say. "You just need to put on some fat. You're so skinny."

Kakanyô catches me in the kitchen, shaking her head. "There's a reason why they all cheated on you. Now you're dating married men." Then: "You're a slum."

"I need to feed my pet," I wearily add.

"Feed the man in your bed," Matshwênyêgô says. "There's no point to that pet of yours. You're wasting your time with it. Just kill it. Kill the damn animal."

When I return to bed, you are gone. You've done your job. I'm alone.

I need to burn muse on the fire, feed it to Keletsô. But I'm too hungry. My starving pet enters the bedroom. "Matshwênyêgô and Kakanyô are wrong you know. You deserve better. You don't need someone to feel less lonely. You mean something."

"But why won't anyone love me?" I ask.

"Because you won't love yourself." My pet and its brutal honesty. "They treat you how you treat yourself, because they know you'll still be there for them. No matter how cruel they get, they know you'll still stick around, because you've lowered your self-esteem for them. You fear being lonely, yet the thing you fear is the thing you feel with them: lonely. What difference does it make if you leave? Because one, they ignore your messages, your calls, your needs. So it'll still be the same if you walk away from them, except this time you'll be choosing yourself. Being single is not the end of the world. You can't continue to be this person; kill this person you're becoming to save yourself. Be a snake and shed that skin, sis."

I sigh and pick it up, wondering, where do I start?

"What do you want to do?" it asks.

I stroke its fur, so fluffy, so full of yarn, so soft. "I want to start a business."

"What kind of business?" my pet asks.

I mutter incomprehensible words.

"Remember," it says with teary eyes, "if you kill me, you kill yourself. You won't let me die, right?"

I swallow. "I'm just a bit tired today. How about I feed you tomorrow? I promise."

My pet slips from my grip, grunting. "I wasn't going to resort to this, but if you don't take care of me, I will go to someone who will."

"You're threatening me? You're my idea! I gave birth to you!"

"Everyone births ideas, it doesn't mean they belong to them."

"Fuck you!"

"Some people turn those ideas into something great, some let those ideas linger like strangers, others turn them into cheap products. Execution makes them their property. *You* have done nothing. Your promises are just graves waiting for bodies that will never come."

There's a new girl at the office. She's pretty. Her makeup makes her melanin glow. Her Peruvian hair weaves down her back. Her eyelashes and eyebrows are poetic ballerinas. She has a beautiful accent. Her body is the right shape. It makes me stare at myself in the public toilets. I am jealous. The guy I like drools, cocooning her with his fantasies.

"Don't you think you should fix your hair?" Kakanyô whispers as I walk by to make some coffee. "It makes you look … unkempt."

I pat my Afro as if it did anything.

"She's right, eh," Kakanyô says. "And you wonder why the girls at the office have rich husbands, cars, and homes. They look better than you. I mean, for instance, how can you go to work without makeup, not even high heels, brah. No one will ever be interested in you."

"But it costs money I don't have, money I'd rather save," I whisper.

"What was that?" they ask.

I look down at my hands. "Nothing."

That's the day I stop rising from my seat, the day I stop protruding from the field of cogs like a weed. I hold my piss, I hold my hunger, I hold my thirst until everyone knocks off.

Today is the day for the big chop.

It is dark. The night has broken through the doors; it has dragged the light away, its nails screeching through the abyss. It is time for the killing. I stare at my Afro, my child that I have watched grow for years. The memories of its youth, of its glory, of its misbehaving, of its birth, flood me. Before, I remember my relaxed-hair days. If I had on a weave or braids, I had to account for the time to undo them. Then, I'd have to pay someone at the salon to relax my hair. After two weeks, my hair would break and turn frizzy, and I'd have to braid it. Expenses. Expenses. My hair controlled me, and now it continues to control. I will control it now. "Chop it all off," I want to scream to a barber, except I'm too broke to go to one. My Afro was born as a buzz cut that grew into a halo of growth. Today, its voice is too strong for me.

"What the hell are you waiting for?" Kakanyô asks. "Do it now." She hands me a pair of gleaming scissors. "Go on, butcher it."

"Please, don't make me do this," I say. "I promise I'll keep her quiet."

Kakanyô jams the scissor and the clipper into my hands. "It is time for the killing." She hands me a weave. "Bury it."

I tell my Afro to, "Sit still, be quiet. Damn it, stop moving!" I tie it down in tracks and tracks of lines on my skull. "Shut up, damn it!" I maim its voice with glue and stitching. I veil it with the Peruvian weave and it waters to my shoulders, an ocean on my backbone, a tickling shoreline of waves to my elbows. Beneath this ocean, my Afro is hog-tied. Closure seals its voice. I pick the shovel, exorcise the old me, drag its body into the old garden, and start digging. I bury the old me. I bury the old me. I bury the old me.

I am a new me. I twirl and ask the mirror, "Am I pretty now?" My reflection repeats itself in many more mirrors. The mirror is translucent waters. I am a fish gliding through its waters, clones of me are reposted in many mirrors, many homes reflecting their comments back to me: *You are fire, baby girl,* the mirror says. *But you can do better.*

My clones are lost in the mirror world.

I stare at my bank account. My credit card bill for the weave is high. I ogle the other purchases I made—designer clothes, perfumes, shoes. The costs can pay my rent and spare some change for groceries for the month. What am I going to eat this month? How am I going to pay the rent?

Kakanyô lifts my chin, my sight to the mirror. "It's worth it to starve for beauty."

I slip back into bed, lie in it as if it's my coffin. I will not crinkle my hair, I will not crinkle myself, nor my skin. I have to be perfect for tomorrow.

*AmIPrettyNow?

I startle to the glaring hour that's broken by dawn.

"I am perfect!" I shout. It is morning already. I am perfect. Yet I am unhappy in this new body of mine. The streets are soaked in a static of ignorance. My movements cut through passersby. I'm a stranger even to myself. I am sunbaked dirt. My bones are jail bars. My breasts are barren cells, my thighs are wounded soldiers. No one sees this jail cell walking through the streets, a tower of heels, expensive labels, through the malls.

But I am a beautiful scent; bees follow my trail, flowers bloom and die in my breaths, perfumed of a desperate want. My skin is tautly wrapped around my skeleton, the skeleton of my dreams. I see them, strangers, men, women, children, staring at my smile, how even it is, how beautiful I am. My teeth are crossbars to the words I want to say, the words I could say, don't say. Words that lie in the tombs of my gut.

No one noticed my new hairstyle today, nor my new clothes, my new look. Sure, some said I looked hot. I paid all this money, and no one really notices me. *Fashion your body with your personality,* my pet said, *that's what makes you real. That's what attracts joy and good things.* I stare at my desktop screen wondering how I can wear my personality.

"Yo, ain't you going home?" my colleague asks. "You always stay late, it's not like you're getting overtime."

"I'm afraid to go home," I say.

She laughs. "Is the landlord on your back too? This place gotta stop with this shit of delaying our salary, man. My landlord wanted to kick me out this morning."

I sink into my chair. "No … it's not that. Don't you …"

"Hey, if you're going through something, you can talk to me, ja."

"I can't sleep. No, it's not insomnia, because I'm in bed, my eyes are closed, but my body is not resting. How do you handle the terror when you get home?"

"Terror?" Her eyes widen into panic.

"That animal that waits for you at home, waiting to terrorize you. It threatened me last time, said it'll follow me everywhere now."

She slinks back, a shadow preferring the embrace of the norm. "That's silly. Africans never had these things in their home. It was brought by the oceans."

Brought by the oceans from other worlds. "But I feel it, and it is real," I say. Can I really trust her and tell her about this thing that terrorizes me nightly?

"That *thing* leaps onto my back and sinks its teeth into my neck. It spends the whole night feeding on me."

"Why don't you just fight it?" she asks matter-of-factly.

"It ties me down."

"Before it ties you down, why don't you just fight it?"

"You can't fight it," I say, sighing with exhaustion.

"We all get sad, but it'll pass. I'd invite you over … but … I hear it's bad luck to mix with this thing, not that I believe in it, you know. I can give you a ride home though."

Give me a ride to hell. She thinks what I have is infectious. I see it in her eyes. She was only being kind by asking, she didn't really mean that I spill my thoughts to her. Is that what friendship is?

Home. The darkness is dust-sullen. I wade myself through it, swim through it, but it is heavy. There's no power. I've no candles. I use my phone as a candle. My presence—the trigger—awakens the sleeping creature; a shark smelling the blood long escaped. It lifts from its haunches, grunting its smoky breath. It circles me. Ruffles its muzzle against my leg, sniffing me. My soul is a cacophony of fright. The creature's paw drags across my back. "You should've been home an hour ago. You wouldn't want me following you out there ..." Its paw jabs my shoulder, and it clambers onto me, alchemizing with the trauma on my back. I heave to my knees.

My pet purrs and strolls by. "You've been ignoring me. If you feed me—"

"How can you ask that of me when this is happening?" I say. The creature's hoof stabs into my back. "Help me!" I reach out to my pet, but it stares down at me.

"Procrastination is the murderer of your dreams," it says. "I warned you. You've chosen them over me."

"Them?"

"You know, Kakanyô and Matshwênyêgô are just thoughts. They're not real people; they're your fears and thoughts manifested into real life. And they're coming to kill you."

I clamp my hands to my ears, screaming, and the hooved monster claws my back.

The twins appear from the dark of the bathroom, clothed only in skin. "Unfortunately feeding the pet destroys us. We can't have that," they say.

My pet steps back onto its haunches. "I told you it'll be too late one day. They were once unreal, but you fed them the flesh on your bones." It disintegrates, fur falling to ground like cloth, bones clanking in their hands like jewels.

Kakanyô and Matshwênyêgô and their creature move forward in unison, their gait not so human. I'm famished, sight weak, astonished. Kakanyô and Matshwênyêgô have the shape of breasts, no nipples or vaginas; they're brown sleek mannequins.

I can't breathe, and I don't want to probe and ask how they pee—do they even have an anus? I hardly see them eat, yet they pack normal weight on their bodies, appearing soft. Their heads are Afro-tinged, eyes like impalas—a liquid black. Their ears like antennas scanning frequencies, catching gossip out in the world, reading into mannerisms and people's secrets. They have the same features as me, except today they're skewed with slanted long necks, high foreheads, sharp jawlines like shoulder blades of a black crow.

"We're born like this," they mime. "An accident in the womb."

They close in around me. Their sharp-metal tongue bends my spine, spills my blood.

"Let me go," I cry.

They laugh so loudly it hurts my ears, almost as if it's coming from inside my head.

Matshwênyêgô kicks at my chest, at my head, at my body, until I'm breathless, panting. My mind is her church, every day it's at her sermons. My unstable appetite hobbles to my hunger with a machete and hawks it into a bloody mush.

"What did you expect anxiety and depression to look like?" the say in unison, smiling. "All your worrying, your negativity, so self-deprecating. *You* allowed us into the world. Gave us the power to breathe. But we can't just feed off oxygen. We need more to live."

They need me to be alive for their torment.

Tensions lull in the air, a midwife to my terror. The din inside my mind grows, and no one can hear my screaming. My eyes are windows I bang against. Outside the glassy opaque eye of my body, I am a prisoner. The river of night settles in and around me, filling this pit of depression and anxiety, burying me. Kakanyô and Matshwênyêgô—they know my patterns, my timings, know the hour is always seeking to drown me. My skin is a straitjacket clung to my bones; I can't escape them; my skin has us all locked in. I stare up into the night, a heavy breath against my neck. The lone light of the moon stares me down as my soul is nulled by its head.

EGOLI

by T. L. Huchu

Stare up at the infinite stars through the port window of your hut and see the passage of eras. The light has traveled millions of years, and you are directly looking at the past. You are unable to sleep despite the undlela zimhlophe the herbalist prescribed. It's the dreams, the very lucid dreams, the herb induces that scare you the most—you've already seen so much in this world. Your eyes aren't quite what they once were, but you see well enough to make out shadow and light, the pinpricks in the vast canvas that engulfs the world before sunrise. You are old now and don't sleep much anymore. There will be plenty of time for that when they plant you in the soil where they buried your rukuvhute; right there under the roots of the msasa and mopani trees where those whose voices whisper in the wind lie patiently waiting. Your grandson Makamba messaged you yesterday and told you to look south to the heavens before dawn. This window faces east.

Your bladder calls out urgently, so you grab your cane and waddle out, stepping round your sleeping mat, and opening the door outside. Once you had to stoop to get under the thatch. Now, you've lost a bit of height, and your bent back means you walk right under it with inches to spare. Your pelvis burns, and you're annoyed at the indignity of being rushed. It seems that time has even made your body, which has birthed eight children, impatient with you as you go round the back of the sleeping hut, lean against the wall, hitch up your skirts, spread your legs and lighten yourself there. The latrine is much too far away. The trickle runs between your calloused bare feet and steam rises.

"Maihwe zvangu," you groan midway between relief and exertion.

When you are done, you tidy yourself, carefully step away from the wall, and patrol the compound. Each step is a monumental effort. It takes a while before your muscles fully wake and your joints stop complaining, but you know the drill now, how you must keep going before your body catches up. Young people talk slow when they address you, but they don't know your mind's still sharp—it's just the rest of you that's a bit worn out. That's okay too; you remember what it was to be young once. Indeed, you were only coming into your prime when the whole family was huddled around Grandfather's wireless, right there by the veranda of that two-roomed house, the one with European windows and a corrugated zinc metal roof that was brand-new then, and the envy of the village. Grandfather Panganayi was a rural agricultural extension worker who rode a mudhudhudu round Charter district, working for the Rhodesians until he'd made enough money to build his own home. You remember he was proud of that house, the only one in the compound with a real bed and fancy furniture, whose red floor smelled of Cobra, and whose whitewashed walls looked stunning in the sunlight compared to the muddy colors of the surrounding huts, just as he was proud of the wireless he'd purchased in Fort Victoria when he was sent there for his training. Through his wireless radio with shiny knobs that no one but he was allowed to touch, the marvels of the world beyond your village reached you via shortwave from the BBC World Service, and because you didn't speak English, few of you did, the boys that went to school, not you girls, Grandfather Panganayi had to translate the words into Shona for you to hear. In one of those news reports, it was only one of many, but this one you still remember because it struck you. They said an American—you do not remember his name—had been fired into the sky in his chitundumusere-musere and landed on the moon.

And so, you looked up in the night sky and saw the moon there and tried to imagine that there was a mortal man someplace beside the rabbit on the moon, but try as you might you could not quite picture it. It seemed so foolish and implausible. You thought Grandfather Panganayi was pulling your leg; that these nonsensical words he had uttered were in jest, and that perhaps was what he did all the time on those nights you gathered around his wireless listening to those crackly voices, the static and hiss, disrupting the quiet. But you kept this all to yourself. What could you have known? You, who then could neither read nor write, you, who had never been to Enkeldoorn or Fort Victoria, let alone seen Salisbury, you, whose longest journey was that one traveled from your parents' kraal, fifteen miles across the other side of the village to come here when you got married. The wedding—now *that* was a feast! The whole village turned up, as they do. So Grandfather Panganayi was really your grandfather-in-law but you cared for him as much as your own, because the bonds of matrimony and kinship *meant* everything here.

One day when you were young, much younger than on the night of that insane broadcast, only a little girl really, you sat on the floor of the kitchen hut. Yes, that one at your parents' homestead that looks exactly like this one over here, the one with the black, treated, cow-dung floor with a fireplace in the center and benches on the fringes. The one with thatch darkened by smoke and a display unit with pots, pans, calabashes and gourds. One of which held the mahewu that Grandmother Madhuve, your real grandmother, offered to you in a yellow metal Kango cup, and you clapped your hands like a polite little girl before you received it and said, "Maita henyu, gogo." Then you drank the bitter, nourishing brew. It was on this day she told you about her people, who were not your people, since you were your father's child and therefore of his people, just as your children were not of your clan, but of your husband's, an offshoot of the Rozvi, whose empire had ruled these savannah plains back when people wore nhembe and carried spears and knobkerries. Long before the time of wireless radios and the strange tongues that rang out from them.

You stop and rest against your cane, because the dog has barked, and it is now running towards you from some place in the darkness. The sound of its paws against the bare earth tell you it is coming from the grove of mango trees near the granary to your left. It growls, then slows down seeing you, wags its tail, and comes nearer. There's no intruder to fight.

"Kana wanga uchitsvaga mbava nhasi wairasa," you say, as the mongrel brushes affectionately against your leg.

A firefly sparks bioluminescent green against the darkness of the compound. You don't need a light, you know every inch of this ground well. Careful now, there are fissures where rainwater has run towards the river, eroding the soil. See the dwala rise up just ahead. That's it, plant that cane in front of you and tread lightly. Then you remember the story Grandmother told you about the Rozvi emperor Chirisamhuru, because ... his name meant *the small boy who looks after the calves while the older boys herd cattle*, or, less literally, *one who minds trivial things*, and his parents must have understood his true nature even as a child, because once he found himself master of the savannah plains, he set his mind towards nothing but his own comfort and glory. Wives—he had plenty; meat—he ate daily; beer—was his water. Still, none of the praise the poets and the flatterers that overflowed his court could satiate his incredible ego.

And so Chirisamhuru sat, brooding in his kraal, the gold and copper bracelets he wore bored him, the silver adorning his spear meant nothing, and the comforts of his leopard skin nhembe were no longer enough to make him feel great, neither were the caresses of his beautiful wives, for he needed his subjects and the world beyond the tall grass kingdom to know he was the mightiest emperor who'd ever walked the Earth. His advisors, seeing their lord thus filled with melancholy, deliberated for many days until they had a plan. Those grey-haired wise men, representing all the clans in his empire, came and crouched before Chirisamhuru and presented their proposal.

With his leave, the Rozvi would plunder the heavens and present to their emperor the moon for his plate. So that when the peoples of the world looked up into the moonless night, they would know it was because the greatest emperor was using it to feast on. When Grandmother told you this story, you were at the age where it was impossible to discern fact from fiction, for such is the magic of childhood, and so you could imagine the magnificent white light radiating from a plate, just like the Kango crockery you used at your meals.

Here you go over the dwala. Turn away from the compound and carefully descend down the slope, mindful of scree and boulders, for your home is set atop a small granite hill. Now you carry on past the goat pen. You can smell them, so pungent in the crisp air. The cock crows, dawn must break soon. The others still aren't up yet. *Only witches are abroad this hour*, you think with a chuckle, stopping to catch your breath. It's okay, your children have all flown the coop or you have buried them already, so now you live with a disparate caste of your husband's kinsmen, rest his soul too. The three eldest boys left one after the other, following the railway tracks south across the border to Egoli where there was work to be had in the gold mines in Johannesburg or the diamond mines at Kimberley, just like their uncles before them. There they toiled beneath the earth's surface, braving cave-ins and unimaginable dangers. None of them ever came back. Not one. All you got were telegrams and letters containing the occasional photograph or money that they remitted back to you here in the village to support you. You would rather have had your sons than those rands anyway. What use did you have for money in this land when you worked the soil and grew your own food; here where the forests were abundant with game and wild fruits, and berries and honey, the rivers and lakes brimming with mazitye, muramba, and other fish. Their father, rest his soul, drank most of the money at the bottle store in the growth point anyway and still had enough left over to pay lobola for your sister-wife sleeping in one of those huts yonder. You did alright with your four daughters, they married well, finding good men with good jobs in the cities. The youngest boy you buried in that family plot there, since he could not even take to the breast. At least there are the grandchildren, some who you've never seen, and the precious few you seldom see.

In the meantime, you linger—waiting.

Adjust your shawl, the nip in the air is unkind to your wrinkled flesh that looks so grey it resembles elephant hide, though with none of the toughness. You forgot to wear your doek and the small tufts of hair left on your head give you little protection. You really ought to turn back, go to the kitchen, light a fire, and make yourself a nice, hot cup of tea. After that you can sit with your rusero beside you, shelling nuts until the others wake. But you're stubborn, so on you go—mind your step—down towards that cattle kraal where the herd is lowing, watching your approach. The wonderful scent of dung makes the land feel rich and fertile. No one need ever leave this village to be swallowed up by the world beyond. Everything you could ever want or need is right here you think as you stand and observe the darkness marking the forest below, stretching out until it meets the stars in the distance, there, where down meets up.

Come on now, this short excursion has worn out your legs. Gone are the days you were striding up and down this hill, balancing a bucket of water from the river atop your head every morning. That's long behind you.

There you go, sit down on that nice rock, take the weight off. Doesn't that feel nice? The dog's come to join you. Let him lie on your feet, that'll keep them warm. Oh, how lovely. Catch your breath—the day is yet to begin.

You reach into your blouse and search inside your bra, right there where you used to hide what little money you had, because no thief would dare feel up a married woman's breasts, but now you pull out a smartphone. Disturbed, it flicks to life, the light on the screen illuminating your face. So much has changed in your lifetime. The world has changed, and you along with it. You were a grown woman by the time you taught yourself to read—can't put an age to it, the exact date of your birth was never recorded. You pieced out the art of reading from your children's picture books and picked up a little English from what they brought back from Masvaure Primary and then even more from Kwenda Mission where they attended secondary school. Bits and pieces of those strange words from Grandfather Panganayi's wireless became accessible to you. Now even old newspapers left by visitors from the city to be used for toilet roll are read first, before they find their way into the pit latrine. You are not a good reader, but a slow one, and if the words are too long, then they pass right over your head. But you still like stories with pictures, so when your granddaughter Keresia introduced you to free online comic books, you took to them like a duck to water—the more fanciful the story, the better.

You were ready when your second son, Taurai in Egoli sent you this marvel, the mobile, and it changed your world in an instant. Through pictures and video calls and interactive holograms you were able to see the faces of the loved ones you missed and the grandchildren you'd never held in your arms. They spoke with strange accents as if they were not their father's blood, but from a different tribe entirely, yet even then you saw parts of your late husband Jengaenga in their faces and snippets of yourself in them. With this device that could be a wireless radio, television, book, and newspaper all in one, you kept abreast with more of the world outside your village than Grandfather Panganayi ever could. More importantly, you harnessed its immense power, and now you could predict the rainfall patterns for your farming. They no longer performed rainmaking ceremonies in the village, not since Kamba died, but now you could tell whether the rains would fall or not, and how much. Now you knew which strain of maize to grow, which fertiliser to use; it was all there in the palm of your hand.

You've lived through war, the second Chimurenga, survived drought and famine, outlasted the Zimbabwean dollar, lost your herd to rinderpest and rebuilt it again, have been to more weddings and funerals than you care to recall, seen many priests come and go at the mission nearby, and witnessed the once-predictable seasons turn erratic as the world warmed. All that and much more has happened in the span of your lifetime. Indeed, it is more useful to forget than it is to remember, or else your mind would be overwhelmed, and your days lost to reminiscences. And if you did that, then you would miss moments like this, just how stunning the sky is before dawn. While you wait for Nyamatsatsi, the morning star, to reign, some place up there in Gwararenzou, the elephant's walk that you've heard called the Milky Way, you can still find Matatu Orion's Belt, or turn your gaze to see Chinyamutanhatu, the Seven Sisters, those six bright stars of which they say a seventh is invisible to the naked eye, and there you can see Maguta and Mazhara, the small and large Magellanic Clouds seemingly detached from the rest of the Milky Way. You know how if the large Magellanic Cloud Maguta is more visible it means there will be an abundant harvest, but if the small Mazhara is more prominent, then as its name suggests there would be a drought.

Yes, you could always read the script of the heavens. They are an open book.

But now you look down and check your phone, because your grandson Makamba is traveling. He said on the video call yesterday if you looked south you might see him. There's nothing there yet. Wait. Fill your lungs with fresh air.

Now you recall Grandmother's tale of how the Rozvi set about to build a great tower so they could reach the sky and snatch the moon for their emperor. It is said they chopped down every tree in sight for their structure and slaughtered many oxen for thongs to bind the stairs. Heaven bound they went one rung at a time. For nearly a year they were at it, rising ever higher, but they did not realize that beneath them, termites and ants were eating away at the untreated wood. And so it was the tower collapsed, killing many people who were working atop it. Some say, as Grandmother claimed, this marked the end of the Rozvi Empire. Others, like Uncle Ronwero, say no, having lost that battle, the Rozvi decided instead to dig up Mukono, the big rock, and offer it to their emperor for his throne. But as they dug and put logs underneath to lever it free, the rock fell upon them, and many more died. A gruesome end either way.

There it is, right there amongst the stars. You had thought it was a meteor or comet, but its consistency and course in the direction Makamba showed you on the holographic projection can only mean it is his chitundumusere-musere streaking like a bold wanderer amongst the stars. You follow its course through the heavens, as the cock crows, and the cows low, and the goats bleat, and the dog at your feet stirs. Makamba said he was a traveler, like those Americans from the wireless from long ago, but he wasn't going to the moon. He was going beyond that. These young people! He'd not so much as once visited his own ancestral village, yet there he was talking casually about leaving the world itself. So you asked, "Where and what for?" And he explained that there are some gigantic rocks somewhere in the void beyond the moon, but before the stars, and that those rocks were the new Egoli. Men wanted to mine gold and other precious minerals from there and bring them back to Earth for profit. Makamba was going to prepare the way for them. If he had grown up with you, maybe you could have told him the story of the Emperor Chirisamhuru and the moon plate, and maybe that might have put a stop to this brave foolishness. First the village wasn't enough for your own children, now it seems the world itself is not enough for their offspring. In time only old people will be left here, waiting for death, *and who then will tend our graves and pour libation to the ancestors?*

You watch in wonder the white dot in the sky journeying amongst the stars on this clear and wondrous night. Then you sigh. You've lived a good life, and there is a bit more to go still. Let your grandson travel as he wills. When he returns, if he chooses to make the shorter trip across the Limpopo, through the highways and the dirt roads, to see you at last in this village where his story began, then you will offer him maheu, slaughter a cow for him, and throw a feast fit for an emperor on whatever plate he chooses to bring back with him from the stars. But he must not take too long now. If he is late, he will find you planted here in this very soil underneath your feet, and your soul will be long gone, joining your foremothers in the grassy plains.

"Ndiko kupindana kwemazuva," you say. The horizon is turning orange, a new dawn is rising.

THE FRIENDSHIP BENCH

by Yvette Lisa Ndlovu

The young woman is driven to my Healing Hut by a question. She doesn't need to ask it. Everyone who seeks out my services comes here as a last resort.

As soon as she closes the door, the floor beneath her sneakers morphs into a meadow. She inhales sharply, realizing that she now stands in grassland awash in the afternoon's yellow glow. She turns back frightened, looking for the door she entered through, but finds nothing.

I wave at her from the bench under the shade of a jacaranda tree. The purple jacaranda petals occasionally fall onto my greying afro. The Friendship Bench looks like any other classic park bench, yet the girl hesitates to join me. I wave and smile. It does the trick to remind her that I look like I could be anyone's grandmother. Good. She'll bring me closer to my quota.

Her name is Khaya. She has come all the way from America. Her life flashes before me like a collage of photographs the moment she steps into the Healing Hut.

"Are ... are you the N'anga?" she asks in broken Shona. "Makadini zvenyu."

She struggles through the greeting.

"You can call me Healer, if you like," I say in English.

Khaya exhales gratefully. She chooses to sit as far away from me on the bench as possible. Most people do.

I know what's troubling her. I see the two branches of her family tree. An African American father and a Zimbabwean mother. Other people have generational wealth, but for someone like Khaya, all she has inherited is pain. The pain is a centuries-old, pallid, undulating mass sitting on her shoulders. It is no wonder she slouches so much.

A memory floats in the air as she shifts uncomfortably on the bench. A fight with her father the night before she boarded the plane to Zimbabwe. Her father is part of the anti-Friendship-Bench movement.

"It is running away from your problems," her father had said vehemently as she packed her bags. "Don't you see that it makes you forget your pain? Your history? It makes you forget the truth of this world. It makes you live a lie."

"Maybe I just want to breathe sometimes," Khaya had shot back. "Maybe I don't want to shoulder all this grief. Maybe I just want a life where history means nothing to me!"

The memory disappears with the wind.

"What is troubling you, my child?"

Memories inundate the air, casting a shadow over the bench. The mass on her shoulders bellows at me, sinking its talons deeper into the girl's shoulders.

"I want you to unburden my soul."

"Very well."

Her eyes widen. "Can you do it? Can you take it all away?"

"Every emotion and sensation, good or bad, that you feel is energy," I say, assuredly. "A Healer's duty is to turn the energy that burdens you into something ... more pleasant."

I extend my palm. Khaya peers at the device in my hand as if it is a treasure beyond her reach, like window-shopping at an upscale boutique.

"This is a shock absorber," I say with a smile. "I will implant it into your temple. The device will absorb your pain, converting it into a new energy called an aura."

Her fear and doubts prickle against my skin. "First you must choose an aura."

The menu of auras is listed outside the Healing Hut's door. It is the first thing one sees before they enter.

"I ... I ... don't know," Khaya says. "Can you explain what each aura will do to me?"

"If you choose Euphoria, each time you feel sad, angry, or hurt, the shock absorber will turn it into a state of intense excitement and happiness," I say. "Laughter will make you laugh off every trauma. Patience means you will always keep your cool. With Resilience, you will still feel the pain, but it will make you stronger. If you choose Apathy, you will be indifferent to anything that happens to you."

Khaya bites her lip. She can hear her father's voice warning her about the evils of the Friendship Bench. *Don't you see that it makes you forget your pain? It makes you live a lie.*

Another memory escapes from her mind and fills the space between us—Khaya watching the grief eat away at her father, grief that could have easily been taken away by this simple procedure.

"What do you recommend?" she asks.

"I cannot make that decision for you." Her shoulders droop lower at my words. "Most people choose Euphoria," I offer.

Khaya turns over the options in her head. Apathy is very tempting, even resilience, but she sees no joy in them.

"Euphoria," she says, finally.

I lean toward Khaya, tucking her braids behind her ears. I gently insert the device into her skin through the temples. All she feels is a slight pinch. When I'm done, the top half of the device sits behind her ear. "All set," I say, leaning away.

The mass on her shoulders blanches until it fades away, melting into a warm sensation. Only one memory remains. Her father teaching her to ride a bike. Khaya falls and scrapes her knee. Her father is by her side immediately.

"You know why your mother named you Khaya?" her father says in a soothing voice. "It means 'home.' No matter how far you go, no matter how far you fall, you will always have a home."

Khaya smiles for the first time since stepping into my Healing Hut. She has the most dazzling smile of all the people that have sought my services.

"I wish you all the happiness," I say, watching her leave.

The meadow wanes with her receding footsteps and completely vanishes when she is gone. I deposit the cold memories into a jar. My hands tremble more with each new patron, but I can't stop. One more patron and the masters will be pleased. And I'll be free.

FORT KWAME

by Derek Lubangakene

Two hours passed before Jabari Asalur acknowledged his dread. His chest felt hollow, and a damp stillness was lodged in his gut. If he had any breakfast left in him, he would've fallen to his knees, stuck a cold finger down his throat, and let the exploding bile jar his senses. Anything was better than the endless waiting.

Two hours, something was definitely wrong. Naleni hadn't made it. Their rebellion had failed. She was probably dead. He regretted letting her go back instead of himself. *Asalur, you stupid, clumsy coward,* he chastised himself. If he hadn't been such an Asalur and messed up the charges, she wouldn't have had to risk herself cleaning up after him. Naleni and he would've already joined the others and been miles away from danger. Instead, he lingered here on this blue-tinged cryocrater, their rendezvous point. There was no point in waiting for her, he knew this, but he couldn't leave. He owed her that much.

To distract himself, he laid down the four control units flat against the ice. One had gone off okay, but the other three still glowed red. He suspected their fuses had come loose. He didn't account for that earlier. Naleni should've fixed the fuses by now. But no, the control units still glowed red, not green. Even if they finally turned green, he wouldn't detonate them until she was with him. She was his only green light.

"Come on, Naleni. Come on," he whispered.

He glanced once more at the biomonitor on his wrist. It blinked a steady amber light. The declining power blurred his vision, turning his mask's optic visualiser cloudy like a Harmattan haze. He had maybe forty, fifty minutes of breathable air left. It was already too late, but he couldn't leave. Not without Naleni. He didn't want to believe all he had done—all they had done—was in vain. No way.

He crouched beside his Kunguru and waited.

An hour later, he checked the control units, two of the three had turned green. All three would be great, but two was enough. If only there was a way to communicate to her. He would've told her to get out of there. Perhaps she already had. He had no way of knowing, but he wouldn't detonate the charges until she had returned to him. He ignored the sense of urgency. Even when his biomonitor light turned red and the temperature dropped a dozen degrees,

Jabari double-checked his thermskin's isothermal functions. They were at eighty percent. The wireless receptors between the Kunguru's backup isothermal reservoir and his thermskin suit still worked. Hypothermia proved a distant threat. Around him, the cryocrater remained silent, save for the frozen ice shelf cracking underneath the porous bedrock. That and the rumble of distant thunder medleying with the howling winds. As the landscape steadily sluiced into dusk, Jabari's panic rose. In spite of his thermskin's capabilities, no amount of training would save him once dusk fell. No amount.

He glanced afresh at his surroundings, hoping to see Naleni stumbling down the glacial outcroppings. Hard luck. Only the winds replied to his anguish. Theirs was a dialect of misgiving. A language he now knew too well.

The Kunguru's comms, connected to his mask, implored him to climb aboard and recharge his thermskin.

Jabari ignored the warning. He knew the moment he hopped inside, the Kunguru's A.I. interface would supervene his manual override and fly him someplace dry and safe. Not that such a place existed. Not for miles in any direction. Fort Kwame was one of a few embers in a growing darkness. The last frontier against the creeping chill.

"Come on Naleni," this time his whisper was a prayer.

He knelt, figuring this would conserve power. Perhaps a few fractions of a percent. Perhaps a little more. His movements were the least pilferers of his standby power. He figured the beating of his quailing heart probably consumed enough to excavate a sinkhole by himself. Probably more. He shut his eyes to even his breathing. A vain endeavour.

I could just go back for her, couldn't I? Nah, Jabari dismissed the idea. It was impossible. From the cryocrater, eighty klicks away, he recognised the slick, oil-spill hue of the intrinsic shield-glass doming Fort Kwame's orbit.

Everything had gone according to plan. Well, except for his clumsy mess that had sent Naleni scurrying back.

Despite the intrinsic shield going off, Jabari believed Naleni made it out somehow. She had to.

The gravity of what he had done, helping the water dwelling Jo'Nam destroy Fort Kwame, didn't undo him. Not yet anyway.

By sunfall every Civic Centre in every Orbital City from Old Cape Town to New Cairo would hear of Fort Kwame's fate. They'd hear of the meltdown of the nuclear reactors, the cracking gas hydrates, and the sinking tonnes of metal and bedrock. They'd hear it all. Jabari and Naleni would join the rest of the Jo'Nam exodus and resettle in the colonies west of Fort Kwame. They'd be closer to their real home. The ancestors weren't pleased, and none of this thawing would cease unless the Jo'Nam returned home—well, what was left of home.

He checked his biomonitor, then lowered his breathing, and waited …

The last perfect day Jabari remembered was the day he crashed his Kunguru in the thermokarst lake below the pylons which held Fort Kwame aloft. It was also the last time he saw the clockwork methane flares storm across the intrinsic shield. The methane flares burned blue and fiery, turning the intrinsic shield into an opalescent canopy wherever they hit. He loved the way the shield absorbed the flares then radiated their fire outwards. It always made him feel the tiny perforations press against his thermskin's polyethylene fibre. They used to call these goosebumps. Back when the language allowed for the acknowledgement of involuntary body functions. Now every inhabitant, from sentry cadets to frontier explorers, and the glaciologists and anthropologists, everyone was taught to master their bodily functions. It was the only way they could survive.

Back then, Fort Kwame lay in the trajectory-spray of one of those volcanic hydromethane archipelagos. Now, who knows? Geological faulting constantly shifted their bearing. For now, as of this morning that is, Fort Kwame was anchored to the subglacial mountain ranges entombed beneath Antarctica's solid ice sheet. Many other Orbital Cities were likewise anchored to whatever floating landmass not yet completely inundated. What remained of humanity was incredibly lucky to have survived rapid polar amplifications and permafrost thawing which raised water levels to diluvian heights. Subsequent nuclear fallouts in the twenty-second and twenty-fourth centuries disrupted subduction patterns and the evolution of tectonic plates. Chunks of continental bedrock now floated freely on hot asthenosphere, crashing into each other like a bad game of bumper cars.

It's why no one else marvelled at the methane flares. Jabari wasn't everyone else though. He was an Asalur. His ancestors descended from cattle-rustlers; back when East Africa still had a Rift Valley; he knew a thing or two about living dangerously. Not that that had anything to do with methane flares. He loved reminding himself and others that he was an Asalur. The Asalur were the first Frontier Explorers. They traversed the unstable globe, searching out new landmasses to anchor Fort Kwame. Jabari's baba had led the last exploration trip. It was yet to yield reports. He was lost, presumed dead. Jabari wasn't surprised. The vision of Frontier Explorers like his baba once ensured they had a tomorrow, even at the cost of their own lives. The ice sheet wouldn't hold them forever. Jabari was poised to step into his baba's shoes, but by his own actions today, he had spurned his Asalur legacy, and damned them all. They would say it was cruel fate. The baba builds, the son squanders.

Jabari, like a thousand other cadets, had patrolled one of five Fort Kwame sectors, and often assisted the glaciologists in their expeditions beyond the darkening ice sheet. Sometimes, they'd escort ethnolinguists attempting to re-create "ethnic blueprints" based on the passed-down oral ciphers of the Jo'Nam. Ciphers about dwarf pyramids in ancient Nubia, two-faced, two-sexed gods, myriad orishas, and water dragons named Nyami Nyami, Ninki Nanka, the Mazomba, and Grootslang. It was mildly amusing, but delusional in the face of near-certain extinction.

Jabari's regiment patrolled Sector Five. Sector Five was nothing but a lingering abyss. It was the dark netherworld beneath the Orbital City's flatform. A site often attacked by Jo'Nam terrorists. Though Jabari was being fast-tracked to become a Frontier Explorer like his baba, he had to prove himself in Sector Five.

On the day he crashed his Kunguru, he had lost a wager to his roommate Bakida Okol and had to pull a double shift. Though exhausted, Jabari's pride wouldn't allow him to put the Kunguru on autopilot. The crash surprised no one, least of all himself. He would later learn that Bakida led the search party. Like his baba, Jabari too was presumed dead. His return, having spent six months in the company of the Jo'Nam, surprised everyone. They seemed to have all moved on. Bakida had even given away Jabari's family heirlooms.

The bastard was six inches taller than Jabari. His combat and analysis scores were the highest in their sentry graduating class. Bakida never ever regarded Jabari with the respect his family name deserved. For this, they often duelled. Much to Jabari's disfavor. Now Jabari had the ultimate "leg-up" on the bastard.

Fort Kwame was made of colonies stacked on lead pylons twenty thousand feet above permafrost. A hodgepodge of largely desert or river-basin cultures—Nilotic, Bantoid, Amhara, Mande, Nuer, even some Nubian—now banked on immense concave flatforms. Polymerised solar panels and pressurised water nuclear reactors powered Fort Kwame's ever-expanding colonies. The colonies widened in inverse proportion to their population. This, another thorn piercing at the heart of the Jo'Nam, fueling their dissent. Jabari now agreed with the aspersion that these colonies intended to grow so large their flatforms would lock together in circular mosaics and form a new lithosphere, ultimately forging a roof over Jo'Nam world.

The Jo'Nam, just because they lived almost entirely in the taliks and meltwater, weren't mermaids or men with gills. Evolution, after all, takes millions of years. Their hands and feet were webbed though. Some clans at least.

When the ice sheets first started melting and submerging continents, the coastal towns migrated inland. The then Allied African Union—well, what remained of it—decided that the Orbital Cities were the only way to survive. Much like Noah's Ark. Only, they wouldn't take two of each. The migrants who proved useful, those coastal tribes whose parents and ancestors had taught them to make dhows and ships, spear fish underwater on a single breath, and work heavy, wet machinery were retained. They became the Jo'Nam. The Cities were small to start with. Those fortunate enough to afford placement up in the City survived. The rest fended for themselves or joined the Jo'Nam working the City's pylon-anchor mechanisms like symbiotic organisms, in the hope of seeing their children ascend to the Orbital City. Radiation, drownings, accidents were common, and the advisors in the Orbital cities estimated that the Jo'Nam would slowly become sterile and die out. But they thrived instead. And Jabari wouldn't have known better if he hadn't crashed his Kunguru a year ago.

He never regretted it though, even now, even lying on the ice, anchored by the weight of his betrayal. For if he hadn't crashed, he wouldn't have met Naleni.

Naleni, his lithe, dark-skinned goddess. Hair braided and eclipse black. Eyes bright like a methane flare, her lips full and thick. She looked ageless, despite the ritual scarring on her cheeks. Her skinsuit was an emerald color that changed shade with each flicker of the waves when they went exploring sinkholes. She was the most beautiful thing he had ever seen.

It's always an accumulation of little things that undoes a man. Not Naleni. She undid Jabari all at once.

The day his Kunguru crashed, Naleni said there were unexpected oscillations. Like the Haboob winds of ancient Sahara, except these oscillations traveled vertically and burnt a cold, fierce fire. Naleni claimed these oscillations were water-djinns mating; an adapted myth from the people of the Libyan Desert who considered siroccos to be desert-djinns mating.

Naleni described how Jabari's Kunguru rattled with each swelling jet stream and eventually struck the pylon before crashing into the lake and killing four Jo'Nam.

She never ever took credit for pulling Jabari out of the sinking wreckage, but for stopping her kin from gutting him. They spent many days together trying to repair the comms unit of his Kunguru. She was competent with her hands. Her baba worked on the pylons and always went with her whenever they could manage it.

The six months he spent as her captive passed like a blur. He never would've believed he lived through it, if not for the memories on his skin. They say the best affairs leave scars. He bore the marks of her tiny teeth on his neck. That's from the day he told her the elders who dwelt in the hollow Conch of Enlightenment had chosen him to betray his own people. She wouldn't let him do it unless she came along. The Jo'Nam couldn't defeat Fort Kwame from without, so they chose to strike from within. Jabari didn't mind the taint of treachery. Not for her. Now here they were; he, dejected, failed; and she, missing, probably dead.

A kick, blunt as entropy's glacial teeth, woke Jabari.

Wincing, he roused to see a wavery figure solidify in front of him. His vision struggled to adjust to the glare of a hovering Kunguru right above his resting ground. He trained his vision at the figure and recognised him by his musky scent. It was Bakida.

"Bastard," Jabari cursed.

Bakida drew near and towered over Jabari. "I always knew you were spineless," he said. "But not this spineless." He threw something which cluttered against Jabari's mask.

Jabari picked it up and held it to the light. It was one of the fuses for the time-delay control unit. The fuses Naleni had volunteered to replace. The bastard had her. Jabari tried to scramble for the control units, but Bakida kicked him again. This time hard enough to snap a rib. The pain blurred Jabari's already strained vision. His power was too low. Otherwise his thermskin should've absorbed the impact of Bakida's boot. Jabari regretted not having worn the tensile armour-suit. This camouflage suit was good against the cold, but not much for impact resistance.

"Get up, traitor." Bakida loomed over the floored Jabari.

Jabari glanced at his biomonitor. Its broken face told him, with or without Naleni, he should've left this wet rock hours ago. He should've rejoined the Jo'Nam exodus and continued east to the nearest colony. He glanced at the control units and saw that Bakida had stomped on them already. They were broken.

Thaw now blunted the ridges around the cryocrater. Its solid footing now soggy. Gas hydrates from afar, burnt readily. Their pale, luminous flame, spotlighting the backdrop. The ice no longer cracked but vibrated. The cryocrater was warming rapidly. Jabari's Kunguru steadily sunk into the ice shelf. No wonder Bakida kept his hovering.

Bakida's presence in *their* sacred place—his and Naleni's—undid Jabari.

Jabari wondered how Bakida could've tracked him here. He searched around and saw Naleni tethered to Bakida's Kunguru.

"Naleni?" he cried.

"I have her," Bakida dropped a pair of cuffs beside Jabari. "Come quietly or I'll serve you swift justice right here."

Jabari stared at Naleni a long while.

"I wouldn't be too hasty." He turned to Bakida and held up the two fuses Bakida flung at him. "You broke four control units, but only three charges are accounted for."

Bakida tapped his mask and his visuals cleared. He snarled and came to grab Jabari, but Jabari lunged for his foot. A poor plan. However hard he strained, he managed only to make Bakida flail for balance. Bakida settled, stooped down, and cracked Jabari's bloody breathing mask with one blow.

Whooooshhh, Jabari's mask hissed. The rushing methane displaced what little oxygen Jabari had left. Jabari clawed at the mask clumsily until he unclasped it from his face.

From his disadvantaged point of view, Bakida looked massive. *No matter, titans can be toppled,* Jabari thought. His body relaxed. He braced himself on his elbows. Rose but his feet slipped a moment, his thermskin running on so little power as to fulfill the basics. No matter, Jabari took a deep breath. Methane wasn't all that noxious. Besides Naleni's people had taught him to adapt to its lightness. Anyone else would feel quite heady. Jabari squared his shoulders, appeared larger.

Bakida offered a diabolical grin.

Jabari rammed into Bakida's gut, and wrestled to unsteady him, but the bastard stood firm. His boots wouldn't slip, but their reinforced traction forced the ice to crack. Both Jabari and Bakida sunk into the freezing water underneath.

In the water, Jabari was no longer prey. Bakida's thermskin had power enough, but Jabari now knew how to hunt like the Jo'Nam. With his thermskin's camouflage properties, he moved like he had a hydrostatic skeleton.

So much for calling me spineless, Jabari gloated. He twirled and torpedoed at Bakida's core with stealth and precision, like ancient jengu. Bakida's tensile armor-suit allowed for little flexibility.

Bakida gasped and floundered like an eel in quicksand. He grappled to hold onto Jabari, but Jabari evaded him. Bakida sank deeper.

Jabari didn't linger to enjoy the satisfaction of watching Bakida sink. He knew Bakida's suit would adapt quick enough. He swam for the surface. The ice they'd only a moment ago stood on seemed to melt rapidly. Jabari kicked furiously, pumped on adrenaline. Naleni was in danger.

"Naleni?" he shouted as he swum towards solid ice.

"Jabari?"

Jabari swam towards the direction of her voice. His lungs burned, but he kicked harder and harder. He could see her.

She looked smaller. Fragile. Broken, somehow.

Jabari pulled himself to out of the water, but he was on the wrong end of the solid ice. He had to swim around or dash to her. The latter a risky idea, considering the loose traction of his boots.

Bakida crawled out of the water using a grappling hook. He stumbled towards Naleni and grabbed her by the neck. He palmed her mouth so she wouldn't speak. The Jo'Nam never wore any breathing masks. Not down here at least. Naleni bit Bakida and he pulled his hand away.

"Help me," Naleni shouted.

Bakida restrained her in a half nelson. She tried but couldn't squirm away from his hold.

"Lover boy," Bakida said. "Your plan is foiled. Give up now and there'll be less pain to trade." Bakida's tensile-armor suit had a viselike grip. Naleni would never break free.

"Jabari, don't let her pay for your treachery." Bakida's voice carried a crisp note against the howling wind.

"I'm here. Let her go." Jabari walked towards the pair. His isothermals were slowly failing. He felt the cold creep in but forced himself to ignore it.

···❖···

The shadow beneath the Flatform didn't lift. Mist covered the pylon like a grey caftan over some mythical titan's stump of a leg. It was solid and dull against the faded light. Jabari's Kunguru, in autopilot, flew Naleni in front of Bakida's craft. The bastard had set coordinates for the large hangars in Sector One. ETA, thirty minutes.

A portion of the intrinsic shield split open to allow their Kunguru to pass. Behind it closed all hope of escape.

Their climb proved slow and ponderous, despite Bakida dribbling his fingers against the control panel. Jabari didn't bother questioning this impatience. Neither did he regret getting himself here. Thoughts of justice and retribution didn't bother him, but hopelessness clouded his heart. He now doubted the righteousness of his actions.

In any case, Bakida would never understand Jabari's motives. Jabari wasn't sure he understood them himself anymore, but what was done was done. It wasn't enough though. It wouldn't set things right. His rebellion would never even the scales of Fort Kwame's injustices. Everyone Naleni knew had lost family members to radiation leaking from the pylons. This was the unfortunate legacy of the scramble to survive in a broken world. Its victims had bloated, rotting skin, and bled from their orifices. Jabari had looked upon this misery feeling like a voyeur of private grief. Their dim and dwindling lives touched him. This was death's ultimate kingdom. When the Elders approached him, despite his pride and everything he'd been told, he agreed to betray his name.

"Three minutes to docking," Bakida said. He kept his eyes steady on the ring of glowing gas flares guiding their descent onto the flatform.

Bakida steadied the Kunguru and released the landing gear. Jabari's Kunguru hovered low as Naleni climbed out. The hangar was a flurry of activity. Cadets scampered here and there in response to the charge which went off earlier. None of them seemed to notice the two Kunguru.

Naleni's eyes darted around, seemingly afraid and exposed.

Jabari struggled against his restraints. He worried about her. The strangeness of the air, and the regiments assuming battle formations, was an otherworldly sight. Their laser canons glistened in the weakening light. It felt like the end of the world, and Jabari and Naleni seemed the only ones caught by surprise. Had they been triple-crossed? This wasn't how things should've gone.

"I'm not surprised, honestly," Bakida said. "Like your fallen baba, you're the only one naive enough to think you could save the Jo'Nam."

Their airlock opened up.

"Just kill me already. Don't bore me to death with your vindication."

Bakida stepped out, circled backwards, and undid the cuffs on Jabari's limbs. They walked towards Naleni, whose hands were bound behind her back. A hundred paces away, the five Sector Commanders marched towards the three.

"Release her. Please," Jabari pleaded Naleni's fate. Her skinsuit had turned translucent as though externalising her fright. To her, the ionised air must've felt like complete sensory deprivation.

"It's not too late to reverse what you've done," Bakida said.

"It's too late to reverse anything," Jabari said.

"If that were the case, I wouldn't have bothered bringing you back," Bakida said. "You both." He nudged his chin in Naleni's direction.

"You touch her and I'll—"

"I won't, but they might," Bakida pointed to the Sector Commanders marching their way, a squadron of hard-jawed sentries following behind. "You've a chance to save not only her. But all of *them*, and us too." He paused for effect.

Jabari said nothing. His attention drawn towards Naleni.

"Asalur, where's the remaining charge? I caught her with two fuses, but here we have four control units. Where is it?" Bakida had carried the control units from the cryocrater.

"Let her go," Jabari answered. He was resolved to his fate.

"There are teams scouring the reactors right now, but you could speed it up by telling us where they are. If you don't. We all die. Right now, a legion of *her* people is marching to bludgeon the pylons."

"Good, that way they'll finish what I couldn't," Jabari snarled. He knew better than to fall for Bakida's manipulations. As far as he knew, the Jo'Nam exodus was miles away from the blast radius. He and Naleni should've been there with them also.

"If we fall, they fall too, don't you realise this?" Bakida said.

Jabari sneered. "They'll rebuild from our ashes. They'll rebuild a better, fairer society than this one. The Orbital City network will be better for it."

"You fool! Haven't you ever wondered why your baba never returned? We lost communications with all the other cities years ago. There's no refuge anywhere else. This is the last Orbital city. Destroying Fort Kwame condemns us all." He ambled closer to Jabari. His tone almost plaintive. "You've been misled. Help me before it's too late."

"I was in awe of you earlier," Jabari said. "But now I see you didn't bring me here to face the poetic justice of dying with Fort Kwame … I'll indulge your sadism, just let her go."

"She's not worth destroying Fort Kwame for."

Jabari smiled in self-derision. He couldn't save himself, but he would see her safe at least. Besides, there was a chance the last charge could still go off. Bakida had secured only two of the three charges. Naleni was clever enough to foil their plans. He'd see the deed done; he just had to find out if she had at least fixed its fuse.

"You'd destroy Fort Kwame seven times over if you'd seen the things I've seen. This is justice, long-overdue justice."

"It's foolishness, that's what—"

The Sector Commanders arrived right on cue. They formed an arc around Bakida, Jabari, and Naleni. The Kungurus hovered in the background.

"Haai." The burly Afrikaner from Sector One regarded Bakida. "Okol, sit-rep." His direct, unnerving gaze pierced through Bakida's stoicism like a laser.

Bakida stood at attention, but before he could speak, Jabari cut in.

"I'm the one you want. If you let her go, I'll tell you everything."

"*Jammer*, we know everything," the Afrikaner said. "*Verder*, don't shake the chicken. You're in no way entitled to assume leverage. If not for your mate's graces, you'd be dead as the cryocrater you sought shelter in." He turned to Bakida, "Hand the meisie over."

Bakida did as commanded. The Afrikaner outranked all the other SCs.

The Afrikaner knelt Naleni by his feet and drew his weapon to her brow. "I won't count to *drie*. Go on, let the baboon out of your sleeve."

The SC's actions froze Jabari.

Naleni didn't put up much of a fight. Bakida had disabled her mask's comms. She was mute to everything.

"Jabari, tell him," Bakida said.

"Let her go," Jabari stood up to the SC. "There's more than one charge left, and if you want what I have, you'll let her go."

The SC turned to Bakida. "How many charges did you recover?"

"All but one," Bakida answered.

"But you'll never find it," Jabari said. "And yes, the Jo'Nam have secondary control units. They must've already realized something isn't right and will blow them any time now. Let her go, and I'll help you."

The SC chewed on this a moment. He didn't like the taste but signalled Jabari to approach.

Jabari obliged him. He braced Naleni to her feet and activated her mask's comms.

"I'm sorry," Jabari addressed Naleni. "I shouldn't have left you alone. I won't leave you now."

She clung to him.

"I will get you away." Jabari spoke low, and in the little Jo'Nam he could speak. "Please tell me you fixed the last charge."

She shook her head. "I couldn't find it. I looked and looked. The tall one cornered me before I … I dropped the fuse." She clutched his shoulder tight. "Jabari, we—"

"It's alright. They don't know this."

"They know." She no longer spoke the Jo'Nam tongue.

"They don't," Jabari insisted.

"Tell them where the charge is," she said.

Jabari pulled back, stunned.

"They lied to us. You have to help your people."

"You're my people!"

"Help them, or we all die."

Jabari, baffled, held her at arm's length. "What have they done to you?"

"Nothing. They speak truth. There is no other city to run to. We were wrong. The Elders don't know this. They are making a mistake. They will destroy the only hope we have left."

"You've seen the charts. Naleni, there are over a dozen orbital cities. We will rejoin the others as planned."

"Those are old charts," Naleni said. "Your friend showed me Fort Kwame's recent charts. The eastern colonies have sunk, and our passage to the old continent is gone. This is the last Orbital City. My people want justice but will damn us all with ignorance instead."

Jabari looked to Bakida for confirmation. He got it. Bakida was many things, a deceiver not one of them.

"If this truly is the only City of Tomorrow, we are already doomed." His shoulders deflated.

"Asalurs; stubborn as ever. No problem," the SC said. "I won't appeal to your sense of duty, but I'll call on your honor. On the name you used to take so much pride in."

"Your trust in my honor is grossly misplaced," Jabari retorted.

"Yah, that might be so. But your heart is what I can finally count on."

With that, he shot Naleni in the foot.

Well, grazed her skin in fact. But the way she screamed in pain, and the way Jabari fell by her side, spoke otherwise.

None of the other commanders encircling them reacted.

Jabari's eyes filled with rage as he rose, fists balled. But the SC pointed the weapon to his temple. Bakida who had rallied to pull Jabari away, backed off on his own accord. Naleni lay wincing on the ground.

"Hah," the commander exclaimed. "My aim is worse than I thought. Will you allow me try again?"

Jabari, though still seething, raised his hands in surrender.

"Tell me where the charge is?"

Jabari snarled, but he had no leverage. His ruse had failed. And once again he put Naleni in harm's way. Glancing at her, he sighed.

"The cooling tower. Reactor six." Jabari said, exhaling the words reluctantly.

Jabari crawled to Naleni's side.

The commander barked an order to one of his underlings. The collective air of tension dropped.

"Uh-uh, up, up," the commander urged Jabari up. "Your dues aren't fully paid up. Hop in your Kunguru and tell the Jo'Nam all you've learnt in the few minutes prior. They damn themselves in damning us. We believe many things about the water-folk, but we do not believe them to be suicidal maniacs."

Jabari wouldn't leave Naleni.

The Afrikaner motioned to Bakida. "Tend the meisie's wound."

Bakida knelt beside Jabari. "Go. I'll look after Naleni."

"You'll pay for this," Jabari said.

"I don't doubt that, but you won't get your vengeance if the Jo'Nam destroy Fort Kwame."

"The Jo'Nam rally a few klicks from where Okol apprehended you," the Afrikaner said. "There's no exodus. We know they intend to attack at the very spot you crashed your Kunguru. If they attack, there will be great loss on either side. Them more than us."

"I won't do your bidding." Jabari said.

"A shame. All this will have been for nothing." He came and raised Jabari to his feet. "It's not just my bidding you do. But hers, and theirs most of all. They still believe in the City of Tomorrow," the Afrikaner pointed to Naleni.

"You may be a cold bastard, Asalur, but not cold enough to bathe in the blood we will shed if you don't act."

Jabari said nothing.

The Commander tilted his head. "Hmm. Yes, I'd be scared too. They might kill you, thinking you a double-crosser—"

"I'm not scared."

"Of course. You've survived their capture once before. Do what you did then."

Jabari stared at Naleni but couldn't bring himself to ask her to risk her life again.

The Commander noticed his look and smiled. "Okol, help the meisie to his Kunguru."

Bakida hesitated a moment but obliged. He had finished dressing Naleni's wound.

Jabari asked for the charts Bakida had showed Naleni. Bakida fished a copy from the nearby Hangar offices and returned to watch Jabari assist Naleni up into his own Kunguru. No words were shared between Bakida and Jabari, nor between Jabari and Naleni.

Jabari fired up the Kunguru and hovered away as the SCs and the rest of the squadrons readied themselves for the Jo'Nam, should he fail.

Bakida lingered, his expression wary and full of suspicion. Jabari met his gaze and felt somewhat reassured. There Bakida was, yet again, sending Jabari off on a mission they both knew Jabari couldn't pull off. But unlike the Kunguru crash a year ago. Jabari had a lot more invested in the outcome. Not that that tilted the balance in his favor, but it was a starting point. He was an Asalur; a starting point was more than he deserved. He squeezed Naleni's hand and keyed in the coordinates for the cryocrater.

WE COME AS GODS

by Suyi Davies Okungbowa

First, we come as servants. Who we were before this is not important: not the wars we may have fought in or ran from; not the academies we may have attended or not; not if we were once master or slave. All that matters, in the beginning, is that we are a people's people, that we may stand in the midst of a crowd and be indistinguishable. On our heads lie the same hair as theirs, and on our feet the same sandals. We are simply one and the same, isn't it obvious?

Next, we come as heroes. Shining armor, arms unafraid to swing, tools of mass destruction that fit in the palm of our hands. We invoke the gods of our people, and they descend and stand beside us. The people see their hands outstretched upon our shoulders; their eyes shut in blessing. Godly garments turned inside out so that all of the bloodstains they bear, vestiges of their pasts—we can smell the red wetness of them, this close—may stain their skins, but the fore of their garments, that which is in view of the people, glisten white. That is not for us to judge—these bloodstains were earned in battles like this, after all, long, long ago. Too long, faded from common memory. Of what use is such old knowledge to today's people? Let them worry about today's problems. So we keep the eyes of those before us from straying too far, keep them on today's prize. *For our freedoms!* we scream, and we strike down mercilessly, bolstered by the bloodthirsty cheers of our kin.

Then, we come as saviors. People line up in the streets to cheer our victory. They bear our names and battle cries on their banners, on their tunics, on their hats, in their hearts. They radiate a hope not long witnessed in this land. There are more hopes, too, clung to by others, but those are distractions. Some hopes are more important than others. We let the songs of praise wash over us, drown out any voices of discord. Today is a day of victory, and there will be room for nothing but that.

Afterwards, we come as merchants. The people need a firm hand to represent their interests, to protect them from alien forces of disrepute. We rip what we can from the land for collective gain, but first, we must shell it out to whoever will fork out the most. We must do this to satiate the endless pits. No, not of our bellies—there are no pits in our bellies; who would think such?—but in the hearts of those we serve. Pits so endless they have become an abyss. But no matter. There will always be something to be sold, something to feed back into that abyss. There will also be enemies, within and without, who remain unsatisfied with this good work, but again—no matter. We shall hunt them down and remand them. They shall rot alive until they call out to their gods. Our gods. And yes, they do answer, our gods, and they descend again—not with outstretched hands of blessing this time, but with questions we cannot answer. We tell them just so, and they understand because they, too, did not have answers in their time. So they leave us be, and we continue to fight for the people. We decree laws. We impound, incarcerate, protect. Their cries are hysterical, but we silence them with the good solutions we know are best. We keep our people safe and secure. We keep our people. We keep.

In time, we come as ghosts. In the moments after we bite off the final poisoned apple—that which banishes us to a life outside of this one—we are besieged by Death's messenger. He comes to our door in our moment of failing and stands there, staff in hand. Silent, watching. We go berserk, call for our household, tell them, *Can you not see?* But they hold up their hands, say, *Are you going to leave us like this?* They blame us for our sickness, yet in the same breath, inquire about where we have placed our bounties. So, it is with relief that our bodies surrender, that we escape the sting of tears and anger cast our way. Only

Death's messenger remains to taunt us as we exit, saying: *You and I are the same. We are the harbingers of something that ends all in its path, yet we may not always deal the striking hand.* He never leaves, Death's messenger, even after we do, lingering on for the next, and the next, and the next.

In our final days, we come as gods, just like those who once stood beside us. They invoke us now, the people, praying us to bless their new hero preparing for battle. Now we stand beside this hero, our arms outstretched, garments inside out so that the white is clear, and the bloodstains from our conquests remain invisible. The red wetness presses our garments to our bodies, causing an itch we cannot scratch, and a smell we cannot escape. But no matter. The people sing our names anyway. They want this hero, just like they once wanted us. Soon after, they will want another again. So long as they live and we exist, they will always want another.

And so, we oblige. We stretch out our hands and bless.

AND THIS IS HOW TO STAY ALIVE

by Shingai Njeri Kagunda

BARAKA

Kabi finds my body swinging. I watch my sister press her back against the wall and slide to the ground.

My mother shouts, "Kabi! Nyokabi!"

No response.

"Why are you not answering? Can you bring that brother of yours!"

My sister is paralyzed, she cannot speak, she cannot move, except for the shivers that take hold of her spine and reverberate through the rest of her without permission. She is thinking, *No, no, no, no, no.*

But the word is not passing her lips, which only open and close soundlessly. Mum is coming down the stairs.

Pata-pata-pata.

Slippers hitting the wooden floorboards in regular succession. In this space between life and after, everything is somehow felt more viscerally. Mum is not quiet like Kabi. Mum screams, "My child . . . Woiiiiii woiiii woiiiiiiiiiiiii! Mwana wakwa. What have you done?"

She tugs, unties the knot, and wails as I fall limp to the ground. She puts her ear on my heart. "Kabi. Call an ambulance! Kabi—I hear his life; it is not gone, quick, Kabi quick."

Kabi does not move; cannot move. She is telling herself to stand, telling her feet to work but there is miscommunication between her mind and the rest of her.

Mum screams at her to no avail. Mum does not want to leave my body. She feels if she is not touching me, the life will finish, and the cold will seep in. Death is always cold. She wraps me in a shuka. It does not make sense, but she drags my body down the hall to the table where she left her phone. "Ngai Mwathani, save my child." She begs, "You are here; save my child."

She calls an ambulance. They are coming—telling her to remain calm. She screams at them, "Is it your child hovering between life and death? Do not, do not tell me to stay calm!"

She calls my father. When she hears his voice, she is incoherent, but he understands he must come.

The hospital walls are stark white. There are pictures hanging on one wall, taken over sixty years ago, before our country's independence. White missionary nurses smiling into the lens, holding little black children; some with their ribs sticking out. This is what fascinates Kabi—she cannot stop staring at the black-and-white photos. The doctor comes to the waiting room area and Kabi looks away. She knows it in her spirit; she cannot feel me.

It is not until my mother begins to wail that the absence beats the breath out of her. Kabi feels dizzy. The ground comes up to meet her, and dad is holding mum, so he does not catch Kabi in time. The doctor keeps saying, "I am sorry. I am sorry. I am so sorry."

For Kabi, the sounds fade, but just before they do, somewhere in her subconscious, she thinks she will find me in the darkness. Yes, she is coming to look for me.

But I am not there.

Funerals are for the living, not the dead. Grief captures lovers and beloved in waves; constricting lungs, restricting airflow, and then, when and only when it is willing to go, does it go. Kabi tries to hold back tears—to be:

Responsible
Oldest
Daughter

Visitors stream in and out. She serves them tea, microwaves the samosas and mandazis that aunty made, then transitions into polite hostess.

"*Yes, God's timing is best.*

No, as you can imagine we are not okay, but we will be.

Yes, we are so grateful you have come to show your support.

No, mum is not able to come downstairs. She is feeling a bit low, but I am sure she will be fine.

Yes, I will make sure to feed her the bone marrow soup. I know it is good for strength.

No, we have not lost faith."

But sometimes; sometimes she is in the middle of a handshake or a hug or a sentence when grief takes her captive;

binding her sound,
squeezing her lungs,
drawing her breath.

She holds herself. She runs to the bathroom or her room or anywhere there are no eyes, and she screams silently without letting the words out …
her own private little world out.

NYOKABI

"Wasted tears." The lady, one of mum's cousins—second? Or third?—clicks and shakes her head. How long has she been standing there?

I am confused by the question; have no time for old woman foolishery. Already there is Tata Shi shouting my name in the kitchen. "Yes?" I answer because I must be:

Responsible
Oldest
Daughter

Always in that order. No time for my grief, no time for mama's cousin—second? Or third?—to sit with and dismiss my grief. The first "yes" was not heard, so I shout again, hearing my voice transverse rooms. "Yes, Tata?"

And the response: "Chai inaisha, kuna maziwa mahali?"

How to leave politely, because respect; to mumble under my breath something about going to make tea for the guests.

"You have not answered my question."

I sigh, in a hurry to leave. "What was the question?"

"Gone, child—these terms that talk circles around death; gone, no longer with us, passed away, passed on—what do you think they mean?"

"NYOKABI?" Tata is sounding irritated now, she is trying not to, but you can always tell when she is.

"COMING!" I scream back, and to the woman in front of me, "Gone is … not here."

"Aha, you see, but not here does not mean not anywhere."

This woman is talking madness now. I mumble, "Nimeitwa na Tata Shi, I have to attend to the guests now."

She smiles. "I know you are trying to dismiss me Kairetu, but here, take this."

She slips a little bottle into my hand just as I widen the door to leave. She says, "A little remedy for sleep. There are dark circles around your eyes."

I slip the bottle into the pocket of my skirt and run to the kitchen, no time to look or to ask, no time to wonder or to wander, no time to be anywhere or to be anything but the:

Responsible

Oldest … only?

Daughter

BARAKA

This is how to not think about dying when you are alive: look at colors, every color, attach them to memory. The sky in July is blue into gray, like the Bahari on certain days. Remember the time the whole family took a trip to Mombasa, and Kabi and you swam in the ocean until even the waves were tired. Kabi insisted that you could not go to Mombasa and not eat authentic coast-erean food, so even though everyone else was lazy, and dad had paid for full-board at White Sands Hotel, the whole family packed themselves into his blue Toyota and drove to the closest, tiny, dusty Swahili restaurant you could find. It smelled like incense, Viazi Karai, and Biryani. Are these the smells of authentic coast-erean food?

This is how to not think about dying when you are alive: take note of smell, like the first time you burned your skin and smelled it. The charring flesh did not feel like death; in fact, it reminded you of mum's burned pilau; attach feeling to memory.

"Tutafanya nini na mtoto yako?" dad never shouted, but he didn't need to.

"What do you mean? Did I make him by myself? He is your son as well." Mum was chopping vegetables for Kachumbari.

"Yes, but you allowed him to be too soft."

Her hand, still holding the knife, stopped midair, its descent interrupted, and she turned around to face him, her eyes watery and red from the sting of the onions.

"Too soft? Ken? Too soft? Did you see him? Have you seen your son? The fight he was involved in today ... he can barely see through one eye. How is that softness?"

Baba looked away, mum's loudness overcompensating for his soft-spoken articulation.

"Lakini Mama Kabi, why was he wearing that thing to school?"

She dropped the knife. "Have you asked him? When was the last time you even talked to him Ken? Ehe?"

Quick breaths. "We went to the church meeting for fathers and sons. I spend time with him."

"Ken, you talk to everyone else about him, and you talk at him, but you never talk to him. Maybe if you were here more ..."

"Don't tell me what I do and do not do in my own house, Mama Nyokabi. Do I not take care of the needs of this house? Nani analipa school fees hapa? You will not make so it looks like I do not take my responsibilities seriously. If there is a problem with that boy, it is not because of me!"

Smoke started rising from the sufuria. You reacted, pushing yourself from behind the door, forgetting you were not supposed to be in such close vicinity to this conversation. "Mum, chakula chinaungua!"

She rushed to the stove, turned off the gas and then realized you were in the room, looked down, ashamed that they were caught gossiping. The smell of burned pilau.

This is how to not think of dying when you are alive. Move your body; like the first time you punched Ian in the face.

Whoosh!

Fist moving in slow motion, blood rushing through your veins, knuckles-connecting-to-jawline, adrenaline taking over: alive, alive, alive, alive, alive. This is how to be alive. This is how to not think about dying when you're alive.

Of course, this was right after Ian had called you shoga for wearing eyeliner to school and then said, "Ama huelewi? Do you want me to say it in English so you understand: F-A—

"Go fuck yourself!" You screamed and punched simultaneously. And of course, this singular punch was right before Ian punched you back and did not stop punching you back over and over and over, but God knows you kicked, and you moved, and you were alive.

NYOKABI

On the night before the funeral,

I am exhausted but I cannot sleep. There is shouting upstairs. I close my eyes as if that will block my ears from hearing the sound. A door is banged. I hear footsteps shuffling down the stairway.

I should go and check if everything is okay, but I do not want to. I cover my head with my pillow and count one to ten times a hundred, but I still cannot sleep.

I switch on my phone: so many missed calls, and "are you okay?" texts. I see past them, my mind stuck on a thought. Could I have known?

Google: *How to know when someone is suicidal*

Offered list by WebMD:

- Excessive sadness or moodiness
- Hopelessness
- Sleep problems
- Withdrawal …

Things I have now, things everyone has at some point. I can hear them whispering in the hallway. The main lights are off, so they do not know I am in his room. Mum has been looking for every opportunity to pick a fight with anyone and everyone since Baraka …

I switch on the bedside lamp, look around the room, and feel the need to clean, to purge, to burn; everything reminds me of him. I notice the skirt I left on the dark brown carpet, tufts fraying in the corner of the fabric, a bottle peeking out—bluish with dark liquid, and I remember the old lady; mum's cousin—twice removed? or thrice?—what have I to lose? I pick at the skirt, unfolding its fabric until I get to the bottle stuck in the pocket. It is a strange little thing, heavier than it should be. I try and decipher the inscrutable handwriting on the white label. One teaspoon? I think it says, but can't be too sure. I open the lid, sniff it, and wrinkle my nose. The scent is thick, bitter; touching the sense that is in between taste and smell. All I can think is I am so very exhausted, and I do not want to wake up tomorrow. Can I skip time? I throw my head back, taking down a gulp. Its consistency is thick like honey, but it burns like pili-pili.

At first, nothing. I close the lid and drop the bottle. I should have known, probably nothing more than a crazy lady's herbs. Could I have known? I should have known. I should have bloody known. I punch the pillow and fall into it, exhausted.

TIME

And this is how it went. On this day that Baraka came home from school with a dark eye and a face that told a thousand different versions of the same story, on this day that mama Kabi burned pilau on the stove, on this day I begin again.

They wake up on different sides of the same house with different versions of time past. Kabi, with her head a little heavy, feeling somewhat detached from her body, hears singing in the shower and thinks she is imagining it. Her bed, her covers, her furniture. "Who moved me to my room?"

Smells wafting from the kitchen, and mum is shouting, "Baraka! You're going to be late for school, get out of the shower!"

Has she finally gone mad? Hearing voices ... a coping mechanism? Two minutes later the door is pushed in, and there he is with a towel around his waist, hair wet, and the boyish, lanky frame barely dried off.

"Sheesh, Kabi, you look like you've seen a ghost! It's just eyeliner, what do you think?"

She cannot move, and she thinks this is familiar, searching her mind for memory and then she thinks this is a dream. Closing her eyes she whispers, "Not real, not real, not real, not real,"

"Kabi, you're freaking me out. Are you okay?

Kabi?"

He smells like cocoa butter. A scent she would recognize a kilometer away, attached to him like water to plants on early mornings. She opens her eyes, and he is still there, an orange hue finding its way through the windowsill, refracting off his skin where the sun made a love pact with melanin, beautiful light dancing, and she makes a noise that is somewhere between a gasp and a scream.

"Muuuuuuummmmmmmmmmm! Kabi is acting weird!"

"Baraka, stop disturbing your sister and get ready for school, if the bus leaves you ni shauri yako. I am not going to interrupt my morning to drop you!"

He walks towards the mirror in Kabi's room and poses. "Sis, don't make this a big deal okay. I know you said not to touch your stuff, but I don't know, I've been feeling kinda weird lately, like low, you know? I just thought trying something different with my look today would make me feel better."

She croaks, "Baraka?"

He looks at her, eyes big and brown, outlined by the black kohl, more precious than anything she has ever encountered, and she wants to run to him, but she is scared she will reach for him and grab air, scared that he is not really there. So instead, she stays still and says, "I love you." Hoping the words will become tangible things that will keep this moment in continuum.

He laughs. Their 'I love you's' are present, but more unsaid than said. "I guess the new look does make me more likeable."

"BARAKA, if I have to call you one more time!"

"Yoh, gotta go, mum's about to break something, or someone." When he reaches the doorway, he turns around. "But just so you know, nakupenda pia." And then he is gone.

Okay, she thinks, looks at her phone, notices I am different from what she expected. The thoughts running through her mind, *okay*, she thinks, hopes? Maybe Baraka dying was just a nightmare? And this is what's real, but no, too many days went by.

She collects herself and moves, taking the steps down two by two; she almost trips, steadies herself on the railing, and reaches the last step just in time to catch the conversation taking place in the kitchen.

"Not in my house!"

"Ayii, mum, it's not that big a deal!"

Mama Kabi, never one to consider her words before they come out says, "What will you be wearing next? Ehh? Lipstick? Dresses? If God wanted me to have another girl, He would not have put that soldier hanging between your legs."

Baraka is mortified. "Muuum!"

"What? It is the truth." She sees her daughter lurking. "Nyokabi, can you talk to this brother of yours? I do not understand what behavior he is trying."

—And how small this detail is in the scheme of everything. Does she know he was dead? Will be dead? But how can she know?—

"Sometimes I swear God gave me children to punish me. Mwathani, what did I do wrong? Eeh? Why do you want my blood pressure to finish?"

Baraka did not expect her reaction to be positive, but he expected … well, he does not know what he expected, just not this, not the overwhelming despair this reaction brings up inside of him; if he had just slipped by unnoticed—but he didn't slip by unnoticed, and they are here now, and he knows with his mother it is a battle of the wills, so he tries to reflect strong will on his face, but his eyes are glistening.

"Wipe it off."

"But …"

"Now!"

Nyokabi takes the chance to intervene. "Mum, maybe …"

"Stay out of this, Nyokabi!"

Kabi works her jaw, measuring her words. "So, you only want me to speak when I am on your side."

Their mother gives her a look, and she goes silent.

When he is gone, the black liner sufficiently cleared off his face, another tube stubbornly and comfortably tucked into his pocket, saved for the bathrooms at school, the unfinished conversation hangs in the air between the glances traded back and forth.

"Usiniangalia hivo, I do it for his own good." Mama Kabi looks at her daughter, about to add something, but changes her mind, busies herself with clearing dishes, signalling she is done with the conversation.

Kabi thinks of the words to tell her, to explain what is happening, but they do not come. How to say—*your son will die by his own hand, and I know this because I found his body hanging from the ceiling in the future*—

Something clicks. "Mum there is a lady, your second or third cousin, I can't remember her name, but she has long dreadlocks and big arms."

She is distracted. "What are you talking about? Kwanza, don't you also need to go to work, Kabi?"

"Mum, LISTEN! This is important!"

Mama Nyokabi looks at her daughter hard. "Nyokabi, you may be an adult, but you do not shout at me under my roof, *ehh!* Remember, I still carried you for nine months. Umenisikia?"

Nyokabi restrains herself from throwing something, anything. Deep breaths. "Okay, I just need to know how to find the lady?

Mum?

She's your cousin, the one who always carries cowrie shells."

Mama goes back to cleaning the counter, silent for a moment and then, "Are you talking about mad-ma-Nyasi?"

"Who?"

"Mad-ma-Nyasi. Well, she is named Njeri, after our Maitu; we started calling her Ma-Nyasi, because after her daughter died she left the city for up-country, went to live in the grass, and started calling herself a prophetess of God."

For a moment Kabi's mother is lost in thought. Does she know? And then she remembers she is in the middle of conversation. "Anyway, why do you want to know about her?"

"I just, I just do. Can I get in touch with her?"

"Ha! Does that woman look like she is reachable? I'm even surprised you remember her. She only comes when she wants to be seen, but that is probably for the best. She carries a bad omen, that one. Anacheza na uchawi."

The dishes cleared, she wipes her hands and moves away. "Anyway, I have a chamaa to go to, and I suggest if your plan is still to save enough money to leave this house eventually, that you get to work on time."

And when the house is empty, Kabi texts in that she is sick and sits in front of her computer, researching Google:

Potions to go back in time?
Can you change the past?

Skips articles offered by:

Medium:
How to Change the Past Without a Time Machine: The Power Is Real

Psychology Today:
How You Can Alter Your Past or Your Future—And Change Your Present Life

The Philosopher's Magazine:
Sorry, Time Travellers: You Can't Change the Past

Over and over again, unhelpful papers, essays, conspiracy theorists until she stumbles on:

Time in Traditional African Thought

I take as my point of departure for this paper the thesis of Professor John Mbiti that in African traditional thought, a prominent feature of time is the virtual absence of any idea of the future .... Time is not an ontological entity in its own right, but is composed of actual events which are experienced. Such events may have occurred (past), may be in the process of being experienced (present), or may be certain to occur in the rhythm of nature. The latter are not properly future; they are 'inevitable or potential time' (3). Consequently, time in African traditional thought is 'two dimensional,' having a 'long past, a present, and virtually no future.' Actual time is 'what is present and what is past and moves "backward" rather than "forward."'...

—John Parratt

And more and more she reads until she thinks she knows what she must do and then she starts to feel tired, so, so tired, and she rests her head, closing her eyes, thinking, *it is possible, not tomorrow, not after, only yesterday and now.* But I dare say the "what if" cannot always exist in the same realm as the "what is."

And somewhere on a different side of the city the "what is" is a boy, is a blessing, a blessing moving and breathing and feeling and loving and punching and suffocating and choosing and chasing after what it means to stay alive.

BARAKA

This is how I felt it: for a moment during the night Kabi was not here and I was not fully here either—wherever here is for those who exist after life but before forever—and I cannot remember how or where, but we were together. Me in death and her in life, met somewhere in the middle of time where the division had not taken place. And maybe this is why, on this morning before my body is to be lowered into a casket, she sleeps with a half-smile on her face. Baba finds her in my room and gently taps her; there are dark shadows on his face and under his eyes, but I do not feel guilt or pain for him. "Kabi, sweetie, we cannot be late. Wake up."

Half still in sleep, she asks, "Late for what?"

"Today is the burial."

She yawns and stretches. "What? Which one?"

He clears his throat and repeats himself, "The funeral, mpenzi. We need to get ready to leave."

The expression on her face shifts, she shakes her head. "No, no burial, he is alive."

Baba is terrified, does not know what to do when his strong, collected daughter loses her reason. "It's okay, baby, we all, *uhh,* we all wish he was still alive, *uhm*, but today"—he places his palm at the back of his head, rubbing his neck compulsively—"Today let us give him a proper send-off, ehen?"

"No baba, he is alive. I saw him. He was alive."

He holds her, rubbing her back, "Hush,

Tsi

tsi

tsi,

Hush.

It was a dream, mpenzi. Be strong now, you have to be strong also for your mother."

Nyokabi's face turns bitter. "That woman can be strong for herself!"

"Ayii yawah, daughter, don't say things like that. I know things have been hard, but she is grieving."

"No, she is the reason Baraka was so unhappy. She always looks for a reason to be angry, disappointed."

"As much as I wish I could blame anyone more than myself, Nyokabi, that is just not true. Your mother's responses always have a valid justification."

"That is just her trying to get into your mind. She is always blaming everyone else but herself …"

"Nyokabi, enough."

"And do not think I did not hear her shouting at you. Aren't you also allowed to be in mourning? You are a grown man! No one, least of all you, should be taking her shit."

"I said enough, Nyokabi!" His voice barely raised but firm. "You will not speak of my wife that way in my house, okay? I know you are angry, but today is … today is a day for us to come together. Not to fall apart."

Kabi's jaw hardens. "You want to talk about coming together, but even you, you were a problem. You and mum both." She shifts her body up, not making eye contact. "You never let him just be himself, everything that made him—him, you had a problem with. You were afraid he would be one of those boys you and the other fathers gossip about, the ones that bring shame"—her voice cracks—"and now somewhere inside of you there is a sense of relief because you never have to find out."

Whoosh!

Rushing of air, palm-on-cheek.

Baba has never touched Kabi before today. How dare he? She holds her face where it is hot, and he gasps at what he has done. "Kabi, baby. I'm sorry." He moves to hold her tighter, but she pulls away. "You just ..." He lifts his hands in exasperation. "You're saying that I wished my son dead. Do you think any parent wishes this for their child? *Ehh?*"

Kabi does not look at him.

"I would do anything to bring him back, Kabi, believe me—any and every version of him. I didn't understand him but ... but God knows I loved him."

"Just," she whispers, head down, "he was alive." Her eyes well up. "I could have saved him, but I didn't."

Baba stands up. "Darling, we all could have saved him, but none of us knew how." He walks toward the door. "Get dressed, I expect you ready in thirty minutes." He sighs. "I know it doesn't feel like it right now, mpenzi, but we will get through this. Somehow, we will get through this."

When he is no longer in the room, Kabi drops to the floor, on her hands and knees, frantically searching until she finds it.

As she tips her head back, her hand stops midway, and she rethinks her decision. Bringing the bottle back down, she dresses in her black trousers and cotton shirt and places the bottle discreetly in the corner of her pocket. She fiddles with it all the way to the service.

NYOKABI: EULOGY

"Baraka used to say that one of the reasons we are here, is for here and now. He advocated for fully living in the present moment, and I ..."

Can't finish. The tears closing my throat come out in a sob on stage in front of this collection of friends and strangers. I've been better about holding my tears, keeping them for when I am alone but,

"I just, I just can't talk about the here and now without talking about yesterday." There is mucus running from my nose, and I feel the weight of this grief will bring me to the ground. It is not pretty. I look at mum, and she does not look at me. Her eyes are hidden behind dark shades, and even though I can't see them, I feel her gaze elsewhere. My hands are shaking almost as much as my voice. I can't talk. *"I can't talk about the here and now without talking about the absence that exists in tomorrow."*

Yesterday tomorrow, yesterday tomorrow, yesterday tomorrow. I close my eyes, and he is there behind my lids in the darkness. I see him, and I curse him, and I want to say, "How dare you make me write your eulogy?"

But instead, I say pretty words, *"God's timing, and Baraka means blessing, and I . . ."*

Can't finish. And suddenly there are arms around me and I think it is him but I open my eyes and it is Baba and I fall into him and I stop pretending that I have the energy to be strong and I wail into his shirt and he takes the half-open silver notebook in my hand and reads on my behalf and I am led to a chair to sit and I close my eyes and I count to ten times one hundred, fiddling with the bottle in my pocket, and I remind myself how to breathe and I open my eyes and wish I didn't have to, so I draw it up to my lips and swallow. It is more than halfway gone; let me go with it. This time I can save him, I know I can. This time he will stay alive.

BARAKA

This is how to not think about being alive when you are dead: Do not watch the living. Do not attach memory to feeling. Do not attach memory to feeling, but of the things that reminded you what it means to be alive:

Music. Sound and rhythm interrupting silence, taught you how to move; you learned, even the most basic beat,

ta tadata ta-ta

ta tarata ta-ta,

ta-tarata-ta-da.

Do not attach memory to feeling but remember the time Kabi surprised you with your first Blankets and Wine concert tickets, and on that day in the middle of April when the clouds threatened to interrupt every outdoor plan, you prayed.

And you didn't pray to be different and you didn't pray to be better and you didn't pray to be other, and all you prayed is that it wouldn't rain and all you prayed is that you would get to listen to Sauti Sol play. And sometimes prayers are like music, and sometimes someone listens and is moved, and this time the sun unpredicted, teased its way out of hiding and this time the grass was greener on this side and this time you stood with Kabi out under the still partly cloudy sky and sang

Lazizi word for word at the top of your lungs and this time you let the music carry you and you took Kabi by the hand and she said, just this once, and you laughed, and you danced until even the ground was tired of holding you up.

Do not attach memory to feeling, do not watch the living, but as you watch her swallow the liquid that burns her tongue, you think, *she is coming to find me, somewhere between life and after, in the middle of time, she is coming to find me.*

TIME

And this is how it went. On this day when Kabi first became paralyzed with a grief she had never thought possible, on this day when Mama Nyokabi screamed at a paramedic on the phone, and screamed at God for more of me, on this day when Baraka decided to die, I begin again.

They both wake up with different memories of time passing. The clock: a tool, tick-tocking its way into later, vibrates and Kabi opens her eyes. He is singing in the shower, and now she knows she is not imagining.

"Baraka!"

THE FRONT LINE

by WC Dunlap

My ass sticks to the thick, hot plastic seat of a waiting room chair that is unable to accommodate the spread of my hips. The AC groans with effort. It's 68 degrees in here, but my body runs hot. I squirm in discomfort, inadvertently pushing my shorts up my crotch. My thighs pop out like sausages heated to bursting. Thick with sweat, their dimpled roundness lays bare for the judgmental stares of those seated around me. Leaning to my side, I lift a butt check and ungracefully dig the shorts out of my crack. It takes longer than it should. I glance around nervously, but no one's looking. I'm just another big girl whose body has become armor.

"You weren't wearing panties," the officer replies impassively.

I don't sleep in underwear, so I don't answer, but the unspoken accusation hangs in the air. This was my fault.

That was two years and two hundred pounds ago.

There are three other women in the waiting room, only one like me. She is nearly my size and wraps her arms self-consciously around her belly. Legs too thick to cross, she presses her knees together. She'd be more comfortable if she'd just spread 'em, even in these tight-ass chairs. I smile in commiseration, but she looks away. She will learn to take up space, or she will die.

"Monique Renée?" The nurse calls my name.

I roll myself out of the chair, and the nurse tries not to stare.

Instead she says, "That's a really pretty name."

"That's why I chose it," I answer, squeezing past.

"Were you conscious when it happened?" the investigator asks.

"I was awake," I answer.

"Did it hurt?"

"Yes."

"Any idea why it chose you?"

I shrug. "Because no one cares what happens to a Black woman's body?"

I sit in another white room now, flat on my back, legs spread, pelvis tilted. The top of the doctor's head is barely visible below my belly.

"Your BMI is high," the doctor says as she scrapes and swabs. "You need to lose weight."

"Uh huh."

"There are other health implications ..." She prattles on, and I zone out. She doesn't understand. If I shrink myself, I will be crushed.

"Well, things seem normal enough down there," she says as she emerges. "They say that once the initial trauma passes, women like you can live quite normally with ..." she hesitates to find the words, "... the remnants," she concludes.

Women like me?

I want to grab her and shout, PLEASE, I'M A SUPERWOMAN! But I bite my bottom lip instead. None of this feels like superhero treatment. I promise to walk every day and drink more water. I dress quickly and head across the street for a venti iced mocha latte, extra whip.

There are five people in line when I arrive. A young Black boy, maybe fifteen, struggles with large hands to dig coins out of skinny jeans.

The barista sighs impatiently. "Five fifty. You got it?" Her name tag reads "Brandy."

The boy digs deeper into his pockets, pushing the tight denim farther down his ass, revealing more of his crisp white boxers. There are sneers of disgust from the other customers.

"You don't have it." Brandy cancels the order and gestures for the next customer.

I step forward. "I can pay for him …"

"I said I got it, bitch!" the boy shouts at the barista.

Brandy gasps.

At that moment, two cops enter the coffee shop, and a stillness descends.

"What's your name?" I whisper to the boy, eyes planted on the officers.

"Dante," he responds.

"Dante, baby, please take your hands out of your pockets now. Slowly."

The officers' hands hover over their guns. They take in the frightened, nervous faces of the patrons, the baristas nervously ducking behind counters. It doesn't matter that they are the ones creating the fear. Their eyes hone in on Dante.

Dante stares back, wide-eyed but defiant. "You gonna shoot me over some coffee?" he challenges.

Brandy tries to speak. "It's okay …"

I push the boy behind me.

Patrons and staff drop to the floor.

The first bullet hits like a punch to the gut. It slams my liver into my lungs. Belly fat absorbs the impact and enfolds the bullet before it can pierce my skin. I double over as breath is pushed violently from my body. My knees crash against the hard linoleum, threatening to shatter. The second bullet hits my shoulder blade, and the impact sends me sprawling across the floor. The bullet bounces away and is lost in my mass of hair. I crawl towards Dante to shield him with my body. But I am slow, and I am tired.

Two shots later, the trigger-happy cop is restrained by his partner. The echo of gunfire rings in my ears, joined by the screams of frightened bystanders.

"You feared for your life," one cop coaches the other.

Dante sits frozen, back against the counter, shaken but unharmed. I reach him and wrap my arms around his trembling body.

The officers notice me now. "Shit, how are you still standing?"

"I'm unarmed," I respond.

"She's one of those," scoffs one.

"No paperwork," the other replies with a shrug. They shove me out of the way to cuff the boy.

As they drag Dante away, he looks at me, perhaps for the very first time. "Hey, lady, I don't even know your name!"

I know you don't.

Not for the first time, I watch cops stuff a teenager into a squad car, decidedly better than a hearse. As they drive away, I help myself to a cup of drip before staggering home for a bubble bath and some Ben & Jerry's.

I pass the thicc sistah from the waiting room. She gasps at the bullet holes in my clothing, the scent of gun smoke and death dripping from my pores.

"I'm off duty now," I tell her. "You got this?"

She doesn't answer.

PENULTIMATE

by ZZ Claybourne

There was power in her pen, but she dared not use it. There were stories in her head she dared not say. She walked the Earth stealing pens from hotels and banks, writing no more than three words at a time on slips of paper here and there, tucking the parts of a story meant to be discovered long after she was gone: into books, between the cushions of bus seats, cracks in trees, and—very specifically—the tables of lovers looking for something to be rekindled, looking to be reborn.

She'd been born seven times within one year once, always with that pen nearby. A fountain pen. Casing black with white dots like random stars, the nib as golden as first light, the band the gold of a ring. She was born married to the pen. She was in love with its hidden stories.

She had forgotten their strength once.

A long time ago. She can't remember any of the people's faces although she'd loved them and knew them. The pen was an odd thing. When she'd found it in the lee of a tree and touched it, everyone went away. Everything went away. The world was changed ... except her.

What had been a field, now contained structures. Huge buildings and noise all around.

She'd dropped the pen to immediately return to her world, the pen at her feet. She was relieved to find that birds sang, that insects struggling beneath her tickled the soles of her bare feet, and in the distance were people, people whose conversations flowed as though never interrupted.

No one was dead. Nor had anyone noticed she was gone.

"I want to stay," she told the pen, hesitantly bending for it.

It obeyed. It was patient with her. Memory was sometimes tricky.

In the earliest days it showed her there were more uses for a pen than lists. It gave her new words; the words became stories; the stories became ... reality? Sometimes it was hard to know which dream was hers and which belonged to all the world.

She would write, then glance around, and notice things had changed. Small things. The arguing lovers across the way, now kissing. A hornet prepared to sting, now content to laze among the many flowers that grew uninterrupted.

One day she got bold, very bold; she wrote a tale of new love, designed specifically to change.

Which it did.

She unwittingly wrote everyone out of existence.

Even the world: gone.

She looked for her hands and they weren't there. Her body consumed stars as a galaxys-wide nebula thrust into the universe mere seconds after the Big Bang; she was the first touch of consciousness and wonder and delight and fear and wanting ever to exist.

She was love.

It had taken a huge effort of will to pull herself together. Billions of years. In that time the world re-formed, people returned, life evolved on track.

And the pen lay nearby.

She didn't fear it. She picked it up, willing everyone and everything to stay.

They did.

She knew the story of love. It involved destruction, tearing, rebuilding, reimagining, becoming—all things the world wasn't designed strong enough to hold in its hands for very long.

It was a story to be told in whispers, in slips, in sudden findings.

In epiphanies or words stopped solely by kisses on lips.

After several lifetimes she realized she was not separate from the pen; it was not separate from her.

She hadn't found it. She'd forgotten she'd created it, knowledge which created a nomad of her. As she walked the Earth pretending to be smaller than anyone ever truly was, for the world, the stars, the universe was a story of love, a tale which erased entire existences to rebuild them anew, she felt more emboldened at leaving parts of the mystery much more often in full view.

She remembered loving the summer, the sounds of lovers, intertwined stories erasing solitude, erasing separation.

Strips of paper on the wind, blowing toward you.

LOVE HANGOVER

by Sheree Renée Thomas

That night disco records weren't the only things that burned. I lost someone irreplaceable, a creature that lived off blood and music, the life force of a people, but a creature that was also my friend.

Delilah brings it, and I mean she brings it one hundred percent! Delilah Divine! Sang, girl, sang!

Delilah teased death the way she teased her fans. Her voice, an odd constellation of sound.

She had tasted death and knew she would always live, in one form or the next, like the singer resurrected in the record's groove. Every night was a different club, one after the other. Sixteen on a hi-hat, four on the floor, two and four on the backbeat, that was the sound that announced her arrival and all of disco. Like Delilah Divine's voice, the music was sweet water finding its own way home. It was going to get through, just a matter of time. The challenge was finding a way to listen and not get drenched. With Delilah you drowned.

The first night I met Delilah, she danced on a speaker box. Bianca Jagger rode by on a white horse, her black locks shining ebony waves, but all eyes returned to Delilah. To say she was a vision is to insult the very nature of sight. Beauty is internal and eternal, and Lilah's beauty came through in her songs. Motown, funk, soft Philly soul and salsa.

It wasn't what she said. Not the lyrics nor the music with its lush orchestral arrangements, her soaring vocals with reverb. It was the story that was beneath her words and music, the message she carried within.

The message was about freedom. That's what the sound was and the movement. We danced to be free. Candi Staton sang from her heart and that's why we loved her songs, too. I had no idea how true her lyrics would be.

Self-preservation is what's going on today. Delilah started off singing jazz, Top 40 hits. When deejays arrived in clubs carrying crates between sets, she and the other vocalists sang for their own survival. And sing she did. I loved the way I moved when her music was on, the way we dove and split from our old selves into something sensual and new. The way the dance floor took us in, wet and holy in its mouth. We were all glitter and steam, blurred blazing bodies spinning in the music's light. If I turned away from the hypnotic rhythm and the beats, from Delilah's seductive song and dance, I could have saved myself and a lot of dead people a whole lot of trouble. Heartache was Delilah's last name. Nothing else was fitting.

Young hearts just run free. Delilah only had time for the young and none of us, not a single soul could run away or leave her embrace. She was like Diana's song. *If there's a cure for this, I don't want it, I don't want it.* I thought about Delilah all the time, and she gave me and all her fans the sweetest hangover. When Delilah got into your bloodstream, she controlled lives, heartbeats. I practically lived in the clubs just to see her.

The club's appeal was that the ultimate rocker lifestyle was available to anyone who could manage to get in. When I first met Delilah, it seemed like she was always in the club, as if she emerged from beneath the parquet floors fully formed. Dressed in slinky, silk dresses that wrapped her curves in silver-tinged moonlight, Delilah was a vision. You could not turn away from her and believe me, many tried, only to find themselves in her thrall.

Music was her spell. Deejays played with minds. Stories told with songs seeped into your soul. Walk through a door in the forest. No confidence at all, but in music spirits take shape. I became who I wanted to be, what I needed. Dancing with Delilah Divine was like that.

Five a.m. when the club was closed, most others would stumble their way home or fall into the faded booths of a diner. Delilah wouldn't want rest or breakfast. She wanted to be near water. Delilah would sit next to the ferns and bulrushes. She said unlike the clubs, the green life formed a wall of kindness. She would bend her ear to the waves that lapped up against the shore, whispering to voices I could not hear. I tried to reach her with a joke, some laughter, or a bit of gossip, anything that might hold her attention, pull her from the faces, the arms I could not see. But she was lost in the waters, in search of depths where she could drown her weight of years. What she sought to drown was not a name but her history. Sometimes she spoke as if she lived beyond her twenty-odd years.

Lilah lived for the rust of songs, for the scars and cutting parts of choruses, the hooks that dug in your soul and made you cry from recognition of depths. She wanted to laugh with the joy of it, and dance and dance until she could reach the gray vaults of sea. She said her sisters waited for her on the other side, but she could not swim her way back to them. Said she was already drowned. Each night at the club I watched her struggle to breathe. They played her songs before I knew they were hers. String sections and synthesizers, syncopated bass lines and horns, and that voice, that incredible voice. She danced as if the music was a stranger. As if the songs were notes that came out of another's throat.

"Where did you learn to sing like that?" I asked. She looked at me with dead fish-eyes that should have run me away, but I was already hers before the first time we even touched or danced.

"From the throats of a thousand, thousand men and women. But the children," she said, closing her eyes as if the memory pained her, "their voices are too sweet. I cannot bear the taste of their songs."

I thought she was high. I'd seen her with blow and biscuits, poppers and whippets—whatever made the music and lights, the dance and the tempo last longer.

"What do songs taste like, Lilah?"

"Like ambergris and champagne."

She spun around, eyes staring straight up. "They've come back." She pointed. The disco ball was the largest in the studio. It reflected the jewel tone beams of the strobe lights. "We used to party with these in the '20s, back in Berlin."

"Berlin? Lilah, you are only twenty, if that. How would you know how flappers partied then?"

She stopped spinning with a shrug. "Saw it in a movie," she said. "Mirror balls. *Die Sinfonie der Großstadt, Die Sinfonie der Großstadt!*" she shouted, then repeated her spinning-top dance.

Her nipples brushed the sheer fabric of her teal, jewel-toned dress. I forced my eyes from staring. Instead I watched her sleeves flutter and float, gossamer moth wings. Lilah favored dresses that made her look as if at any moment she could fly away. She was always so restless, like a hummingbird, a kind of lightning flowed through her, even without the drugs. She was never fully present. Her eyes, her mind, the random stories—her memories, she claimed—would burst from her at any moment. And the voices no one heard but her. I thought she was schizophrenic and mentioned it to a doctor friend, a shrink who frequented the clubs. "No," he said, after chatting with her, drink in hand. "Frankie, that one's very clear."

Lilah was like standing on a hill with the weeds and the wildflowers. The wind blowing through me. If I wasn't so determined to pretend that I didn't imagine her breasts in my mouth, the soft curve of her belly beneath the silk skin, I would have seen the telltale signs of the monster she really was, the creature she hid.

The garage on 84 King Street became our paradise. The club was like church. More than gospel piano riffs threaded through twenty-two minute extended versions of songs. There we had chosen family. Delilah was mine. I didn't know who I was until I came here. Then I found out I was everybody. Everybody was me. No judgments, everyone enjoying themselves. Love, peace, unity, unforgettable happiness, and then there was blood.

Though I wanted her more than my own disappointing life at the time, Delilah never wanted me. She said there wasn't enough music in my blood to sustain her, not enough firelight and smoke.

"You've made up your mind to die young, Frankie," she said one night, after we left the dance floor, having spent hours studying the power of sweat. She would dance with other bodies, take one or two back into the VIP rooms, but she always found her way back to me. When she returned, she was uncomfortably clear, her edges more precise. Before she disappeared with her various lovers, she was like a channel on the television or radio dial that you can sort of see and hear but doesn't quite come through. You would try to turn it left or right, experiment with various degrees of movement, but there was always a kind of distortion, a slow rupturing of meaning, of sound—and feeling.

Lilah was mercilessly blunt.

"It's your choice, of course," Delilah said, no judgment or pity, just straight no chaser with Delilah the Divine, "but if you do, you'll never find your song then, Frankie. They've run out of music on the other side," she said. "And I ought to know." The sadness that shadowed her eyes deepened as she spoke. "Sorry, but you've got to *live* a while longer," she said, throwing her head back. "Until then, there's nothing there to take from you."

She didn't want my heart, so I offered my body. She laughed.

"No love, I like you fine, Frankie. There's just not enough song in that stream of yours to make it worth the while," she said slowly, as if explaining to a very small child. "As they say, you couldn't carry a tune." She stroked my collarbone. Her touch felt like red streaks of fire. I wanted to kiss her and never, ever stop but her eyes were a warning. I thought her obsession with musicians was weird but nothing my musical inability couldn't allow me to overcome. "Ironically," she told me later, "your lack of talent, my friend, saved your life that night and every night since. So, don't feel so bad. It's a blessing in disguise."

Mother said I looked sad in childhood pictures because I was an old soul.

I looked sad because I knew what lay ahead.

The first time I saw Delilah's true form was an accident. It was the only time I was grateful I'd stayed conscious during those dry-bone English lectures in college. It was Ovid and Hyginis who said the original sirens were friends of Persephone, the poor soul snatched up by Hades, forced to spend a season in the underworld. Ovid assumed they were good friends, loyal women turned into halflings. Transformed, they wore the head of a woman and the body of birds. The wings were gifts to help set their abducted friend free.

But Hyginis had a darker vision. He said the transformation was a punishment. That the grieving mother, Demeter, cursed the jealous girls for not protecting their friend, her daughter during the abduction. She blamed them for the rupturing of her family and cursed the women to spend their lives as half human, half serpent, or fish. From some craggy island in the middle of the Mediterranean, halfway between Africa and Europe, the legend of the sirens was born.

But I was following the wrong legend. Delilah was something else, something more ancient.

Delilah wanted a drink. When I returned to our spot under the balcony, she was gone.

I went searching. I know it's not attractive to be possessive of what was never yours and never would be, but that night I did not feel like being evolved. I wanted to find her, so she could drink the bourbon before the ice melted, the drink I stood in line to get. I wanted to find her so she could bless me with a smile, approval, any kind of sign that I would be in her company again.

When I stumbled into the storage room, a wet, panting sound drifted above the music's dull thud.

"Delilah?"

I walked in and a sharp iron scent assaulted me. I strained to see. The walls bled red. Claw marks covered the wall. His or hers, I could not tell. The strange metallic scent I smelled was that of someone dying. There is honesty in murder.

"It doesn't have to hurt," she said. The bearded man was slumped beneath her, his eyelashes twitched until they stopped. Lilah's lips were stained as if she'd been eating strawberries. "Doesn't even need to be blood." She stared at me. "I just like the taste." Horror must have flickered in my eyes. She offered a wry smile, a lifeless explanation. "My sisters would not approve."

Fear gripped me. I concentrated to slow my breathing, to make my vocal cords work.

"Is that why you don't see them anymore? Why they went away?" I managed.

"Creative differences," she said. Her voice steely. "You could say we broke up. Like the Supremes. I'm the star now."

I had the feeling that she always was. Even as she drained whatever melodies and harmonies she could from the man's throat, the deejay played her song. She finished wiping her mouth then joined the chorus, adding impossible runs that no record label had ever recorded.

"You can't give them everything," she said, smiling. "Got to save some for you." A berry-sized crimson stain rested above the mole on her chest. She sniffed. As far as anyone knew, could have been a nosebleed. She rose and adjusted the glimmering halter top. Her golden harem pants shimmered around her hips.

"Don't look so mournful, Frankie," Delilah said. "Yes, Simeon was talented, but he was on his way out." She held up his limp arm. Track marks and cuts like jagged railroads all along the stiffening flesh. She reached for me and I recoiled. I couldn't forget the young man's face. She took the drink instead. Blood and lipstick stained the highball glass.

I watched her, frozen. Unsure if I should run or stay.

It was not the blood that killed them. It was the heartbeat, the life force in it. Delilah took their first music, the heart drum, that unique rhythm we are all born with, and then, she took the last. All of it. She told me later that she had stopped stalking churches and choirs. "Too much practice," she said. "Never-ending rehearsals. Hollow hallelujahs." She stalked amateur nights, but they brought too much attention, so she settled on nightclubs.

Satiated, Delilah's face switches textures and tone. First she is a diamond, now her face is the shape of the moon.

"I need water." She doesn't wait to see if I will follow her.

Looking at the budding singer's lifeless body, I knew then why nightclubs were her favorite haunting grounds. Anonymous hookups and no real-world connections. She could feed and still have time to dance until her feet went numb. And of course, vanity. The deejays played her record on constant rotation with the most popular beats, Donna and Diana. They called her the *Never Can Say Goodbye Girl* because Delilah could dance all night. She shut the club down with her rhythm and song. Killed it every time.

Hers was a visceral music. The kind of hard-won grace that came from speaking across elements, living across time. She opened the door. When a cone of light revealed the second body slumped in the corner, I knew I needed to get away. After spending most of the night with her, I was running out of time. But she leapt on me. The glass crashed to the floor. My arm felt as if she had wrenched it off. Her breath was overly sweet, the opposite of rot.

"Just because I can't feed from you doesn't mean I won't kill you," she said.

I could feel her hunger across the stale cigarette air. Her angled bones pierced the darkness, paralyzed me where I stood.

She was on my throat before I could cry out. Her hands burned me. She released her palm, leaving me rubbing the slightly blistered flesh. "We will get along fine, Frankie, as long as you do what I say. I don't want to hurt you. Let's keep this cool." She nodded her head toward the door.

"What about them?" I stammered.

"A bad trip. Won't be the first."

It wasn't the last.

We walked past men grinding in the strobe and black lights. Their hips were all shadow and sound. The whole scene was raw and delicate. Pressed bone to bone, each breathless body swelled into a wave of desire. Red lips, eyes pretending to be flowers. That night on the dance floor, she held me like I had never been held, as if my every movement was necessary. She made me forget the dead eyes hidden in the darkness. We danced on until I was delirious. Her laughter rang through me. Finally, Delilah hurried out of the club, just a few steps from sunlight. I avoided my reflection in the mirrored hall. Guilt betrayed by my own ravenous glare.

After that night the mood was different. It wasn't about dancing but feeling the energy of the place so it could stay with me forever. The sound that could not be replicated, the lights. Being with Delilah, as dangerous as it was, became its own intoxicating drug for me. She made me feel powerful, glamorous, seen, needed in a way I had never been before or since.

But some friendships eat you alive. Some love is stolen by water, carries you away, except for the bloodied hands that held you.

Avenues emptied hours ago, the sidewalks wrapped in secrets, we skulked along in silence until we reached the great steps that led to the water. We were in Battery Park, the southernmost tip of the island. Delilah said the Atlantic was a gray bowl of sound and need. That there were layers of want and memory. She said if she wanted she could strike its rim like a singing bowl, call her sisters and they would return to her. Said she could still hear them singing, not through blood but in water. The sound of grief made her wish they never came here.

"Where did you come from?" I asked. The air was cold against my face. Her eyes look tear-stained, scabs falling from a wound.

"A place I am not sure I can return to."

"Why don't you want to be with your sisters?" I asked again. She usually dodged this question. Her answer surprised me.

"I'd rather die than meet their judgment," she said. "They take the joy out of this cursed life, what joy there is."

"Can you die?" Delilah did not answer. She took so much from life. I wondered if death was something she even feared. The white bolero on her shoulders trembled like moth wings. She ripped the garment off and leapt into the ocean.

"Lilah!"

She disappeared under the water. Moonlight stripes raked the ocean's surface. I held myself, shook, my jaw locked from shock. Her absence triggered a strange withdrawal in me, a separate grief that broke free. Who was I without the shroud I wore, the bodies I carried? Delilah was the shadow who walked with me, the valley I feared and could not escape. I called her name a few more times then turned to go. I had no destination in mind. Wherever I was going I had already been.

Behind me a keening sound erupted, water churned. Something burst from the ocean's floor.

If it wasn't for the expression in their eyes, *defiance, oblivion*, I would not have recognized the creature that rose from the waters. Stories tell of ships and men dashed against the rocks, but what I saw that night was the nature of stone itself. Hard, iridescent metallic scales covered what used to be toned brown skin. Gone were the delicate bones under soft flesh. Water droplets dripped from long golden feathers. Neither an angel nor a demon, they were another creature for which I had no words. The wind howled as they rose. Wings, scales, the twin-tailed serpent, not fully dragon, not fully fish.

I knew it was Delilah from the way the creature hovered over me. I wanted to scream, but no sounds emerged, just the choked silence that comes when fear takes over your body, even your breathing. When she surfaced from the waters I wanted to look away, but she was like a sun forever rising. She reflected her own light. There was a wholeness in her irregularities. The oddness was better than beauty, how she chose traits from species found on land and sea. Her birdlike mouth was shaped as if she wanted to say something but there was nothing to be said. I knew Delilah was a monster. I saw her monstrous appetite for reaping talents she never sowed. But when she took another shape, so did my fear.

I watched her circle the air, the night filled with music culled from the centuries, from the lives of other humans I could never know. She sang as if she had ten throats instead of one. I covered my ears. The weight of what was stolen crushed me, the songs these long-dead voices never sang, the strings never plucked, the drums of gods forgotten across time.

Delilah wanted a witness, an accomplice, but her eyes told me that she wanted something else, too. She had revealed her face to me but not her real motives. She came from deep ocean or dark cosmos. There was no way to be sure and she would not tell. It wasn't until later when I realized what Delilah wanted was a stooge.

Radiant plumage full and thick, she extended powerful wings. She still wore the guise of a woman's body, but her arms and breasts were tattooed with golden symbols I could not read. She held each of the two-serpent's tails up in her hands as if they were long braids and hovered over me. Her eyes flashed, daring me to follow, then with an impossible note, Delilah screeched and disappeared behind the clouds.

Terrified, I was afraid to move. I waited, my whole heart in my throat and wondered how she lost—if she had ever known—the meaning of kindness. She took so much. Generous isn't a word anyone would use to describe Delilah Divine. But she had a seductive charm, charisma. Being with her was like being all the things you knew you would never be.

How did I ever believe that she cared for me? But believe I did. My thoughts churned, chaotic as the first waters. Frozen in fear, I waited for her to emerge from the clouds. Waves upon waves crashed against the walled park, the sound ominous. I shivered. No sign of her disturbed the parting clouds, the moonlit sky. I exhaled, hoping it was safe to go. When my mind gave my body permission to move, I *ran*.

Dancing shoes aren't made for marathons, but I didn't care about that. I pounded the pavement as if my whole world depended on it. Remembering the look in her eyes, I knew it did. I tore past the huge gray granite pylons that dotted the plaza. I never spent much time in that part of the city, and I knew if I survived that night, I wouldn't want to return again. The park was deserted. The wisps of trees made strange shapes across the night, but when I ran headlong into the shadow of giant wings, I nearly had a stroke. Unlike Delilah, this bronze eagle remained still, perched on its huge black-granite pedestal. I wiped my eyes and continued running out of the lonely park until I finally reached State Street. Gasping for air, my lungs burned in my chest. I stumbled past an overturned trash bin, looking for the subway when I heard a familiar voice up ahead.

"Don't move. Sing for me."

Naked, her body glistened, still wet from the ocean or her transformation. I could not tell which, but the fear on the suited man's eyes was unmistakable. Delilah held him by his throat with one hand. Her hair dripped down her back. A briefcase was tossed on the street. Another man, his companion, held onto his arm, weeping.

"We don't have any money!"

"Did I ask for money? I said sing." Delilah's voice was low, menacing. The skin on her back rippled, remnants of the golden fish scales shimmered in the night. I tried to will my breathing to stillness. It was the first time I did not want her attention.

"But I can't sing. I don't know any songs," the suited man said, coughing. He struggled to speak over Delilah's iron grip.

"Then you better think of something quick," she said.

The poor man began to hum out of tune. "What a fool believes ..."

"Please don't," the weeping man cried.

"... no wise man has the power ..."

Delilah's fingers tightened around his neck, pressed at his windpipe.

"No!" the other cries and sobs. "... to reason away what seems to be ..."The sobbing one's voice was frightened but sure. His notes more solid and confident than his lover's.

Delilah pushed the suited weeping man away and held the sobbing one's throat. "Tolerable but ..." He faltered, stops, tries again louder this time, the notes crack under Delilah's crushing vice grip.

She takes his neck and squeezes it until his voice is a sieve. All the pain he feels, and his lover's, seeps into the air. There was no music worthy enough for Delilah to take, but she took this man's life anyway. I want to close my eyes and unsee the way his body crumples to the ground, a lifeless doll. Unhear his lover's scream. I want to walk through the shadows and streetlights to a night that is all mine. A night without Delilah.

She takes the dying man's jacket from his body, even as he lay in his lover's arms. The sobbing man keeps rocking him back and forth. "Why? Why would you do this?" She strokes tears from his cheek. He cringes. She loosens his tie. Unloops the dark, silk fabric from around his neck. Takes it. Ties it around her throat.

"Because I can."

When she rises to walk away, she turns and looks straight at me. Hidden in shadow, behind thick undergrowth and bushes, my heart stops.

"Time to go, Frankie."

The sound of my name on her tongue made me recoil. I stumbled out of the darkness and left what remained of my courage in the night's mouth.

Night after night I returned. From 54, the Garage, GG's Barnum Room to the moving sets of Xenon and my pre-Delilah favorite, Infinity, where it all came to a fiery end. How could I have known? When she returned from feeding, her mouth slick, eyes glazed, almost giddy, she never questioned what I did to take my mind off the murders. As long as I helped cover her tracks, made the straight lines look crooked, the zigs zag, I thought she didn't really care about what I did. So, I danced with many partners and took more drugs than I ever had. She wasn't the only one wearing a tiny canister on a ring of gold around their neck. I needed a little more each time I cleaned up after her "bad trips." I had no idea how much music was stolen from our world, how many futures. I did not have the stomach to count them. I wondered how long Delilah had plundered the world, stealing the songs that might heal whole nations. And for what? She sang beautifully, but why should her voice be the only one? Wasn't the world room enough for multitudes?

With each new rising star snuffed out by her insatiable appetite, her voice became even more astonishing. She had depths that came from having lived and devoured many lives. I found myself seeking solace elsewhere. New partners to erase the horror I witnessed. Each night we danced as if time was our servant. Like Lilah's beauty, I knew it was a lie. Tomorrow morning could never save us.

I had just tucked a number in my back pocket when I heard her unmistakable voice behind me.

"So, this is who you've been hiding."

Thierry, my dance partner looked confused. Just another lonely soul looking for absolution. I knew Delilah did not love me, yet she had begun to watch me as if she did.

"Let's go," she said.

"But I'm just getting started." I didn't want to be alone with her. Not now. Not anymore if I was honest. She frowned. I returned the hat I'd borrowed from my new friend and watched them escape to the dance floor. There was always another dance partner waiting. Everyone looked happy except for Delilah and me, locked in a dangerous dance.

She watched Thierry disappear in a cloud of smoke.

"This place is dead. I need some air, water."

I hailed a cab, and we rode in silence all the way down to the river. Traffic was light, still early yet. The sky over the Hudson looked foreign on the other side of the dark window. Sirens swept by, but Delilah didn't even blink. We'd all become numb to them. As she leaned against my shoulder I tried to disappear into the corner of the cab. The cool glass felt good against my skin.

Clearly I had listened too closely to her music and yet not close enough. The night she found me lost in another body's symphony, her interest shifted. She knew I had once loved her, as inexplicable and unrequited as it was, but the monotony of murder had dulled that ache.

Was it now Lilah's turn to wait for the words that end affairs, break hearts? She knew better than most that speeches begun with words of love ended in heartbreak. How many times over the years had she pretended? Like any killer, Delilah needed to feel good before she tore your heart out. But a monster like Lilah didn't need a ruse to be let off the hook. She was the hook.

Anger sliced through the cab's cigarette smoke-filled air.

"I'm just here for the music!" I cried, fear and shame rolling down my cheeks.

"The music I gave you," she sneered. We stepped out of the cab and walked along the boardwalk, beyond an abandoned pier that had collapsed in the river. The Hudson rolled silently past us. On this side of town, the piers were our only beaches. There was no other major place to get sun. Now the normally crowded boardwalk looked deserted. The few lights from the Jersey side twinkled faintly, muted like distant stars. Lilah kicked off her heels and sat on the weathered planks, holding her knees. I couldn't tell her how I hated the curve of my own back, how I could barely hold my head up now that I had felt the weight of bodies, devoid of life, the ones I carried and tossed in the dumpsters, in the waters that she sat, meditating by. One day the truth of my own crimes would wash back on shore to haunt me.

I thought I could dance with a demon, that the only thing that would burn would be the hot music branded into skin. Now my skin bore the mark of the damned. Old and new pains stained my face. I didn't have any more music inside me than when I first met her.

A fetid scent of decay and mildew blew across the waters. My foot slipped on moss-covered, rotten timbers.

Delilah rose without looking. I knew what this night meant. *Goodbye*.

I resolved that whatever rage she contained, whatever music I hid within, she would not steal my soul's last song.

Human muscle gave way to ancient inhuman bone. Skin stretched and twisted, turned into scaly flesh and shimmering feathers. Eyes steely, I waited for the rip of flesh, the acrid scent of my own blood. But without a sound Delilah leapt into the darkness. She flung herself into the wind and was gone.

Heart pounding, the veins in my neck strained from tension. After that first deadly night with Delilah, I'd started grinding my teeth. I trudged toward the street. I almost made it when I heard a ghostlike whipping sound, its source felt more than seen. I looked up. A fedora hat floated down in a spiral and landed on the cracked sidewalk before me. My new friend's hat, Thierry's.

I doubled over, sickness filling me. When I opened my eyes again, Delilah was bending down to pick up the hat that was still spinning like a top.

"I feel like dancing," she said and placed the fedora atop her head. The brim dangled at a rakish angle, covering her eyes.

I grabbed her elbow, forced her to face me. "Where did you get it?" I yelled.

"Want to come and see?"

The thought of seeing Thierry tossed away in some alley as if their life never mattered ... I wanted to scream, wanted the sound to be more than hurt rising to the surface. I wanted Delilah to feel some of the pain she only expressed in song. Defeated, I shook my head 'no.'

"I didn't think so," she said. "Aquarians make the worst companions. Come."

"Where are we going?" I asked, my voice hoarse.

She smiled showing all her teeth. "Infinity."

The 600 block of Broadway in Soho was home to a few warehouses where artists could live and work without needing a trust fund. 653 Broadway had an old, vaulted reputation. Originally Pfaff's Beer Cellar, Walt Whitman and others descended a set of stairs to drink pints. Later it became an envelope factory and then a nightclub. Like Whitman's unfinished poem, the weekly parties at Infinity were more intimate and never seemed to end. With its black walls and ceilings covered in neon lights, banquet tables of fresh pears and ice-cold water, the atmosphere in the block-long nightclub was for true-blue partiers, those who came strictly to dance and release.

But Delilah wasn't there to dance or to see *the bright eyes of beautiful young men* as Whitman had penned. She came to teach me a lesson, something about possession, about what it means when you can't—or won't—break free. Engaged in our own battle of wills, neither of us had any idea that hundreds of miles away a mob would gather in a baseball field, intent on breaking every Black record they owned. A bonfire had been set up, a disco demolition, by a twenty-four-year-old disgruntled rock deejay. He was angry that the music we loved, pioneered by mostly Black and Latino gay artists, had taken over the airwaves. His airwaves. The music provided a powerful platform for those who were often invisible.

We, the misfits, the invisible would-be superstars, and all those in-between were drawn to its irreverent rhythms and pulsing beats, the hypnotic cymbals and sounds. Disco even changed the way we moved. The dance floor was no longer restricted to just couples, straight or otherwise. Stemmed by a series of epiphanies and communities, the experience became *en masse*, a group high where love was the key. It was all about love in the beginning, being in love, spreading love, the very act of creation, breathing new life into something that did not exist.

That last night offered its own epiphany. It was already crowded beyond belief when we walked through the club's infamous black double doors. The last shift was in full swing. Both the front and back bars were packed. Vincent, the bartender flowed back and forth behind the long, oak bars as if he was rolling on skates. Blondie's "Heart of Glass" blared from the sound system, and I had no idea it was Valentine's Day until I saw all the pink neon and red-clothed dancers crowding the floor.

Delilah took my hand, and I flinched. She offered one cutting glance as she led me past the giant white columns that guarded the dance floor, ancient sentinels from a forgotten era. Even Debbie Harry's icy vocals couldn't pierce through the deepening sadness I felt. The revelers danced on, oblivious to the threat that threw her head back, lipstick on her teeth as she swayed among them. Nonstop energy pulsed through the music and the lights. The neon illuminated the heart-shaped confetti that suddenly rained down from the ceiling.

"Come on, dance! Frankie, you used to be fun." She pulled me close but the thought of her kiss, the same mouth that drained my friend and so many nameless others, repulsed me. What I once thought was inner beauty, her incredible energy was just endless hunger, a gaping hole of want. She had all the makings of a god but none of the love, no mercy. Whatever light drew her to our world was snuffed out long ago.

She stroked my face. Her touch felt like hot razors against my skin. We navigated the mass of bodies that danced around us as if they feared no tomorrows. Under the confetti shower, her body poured into mine. Squeezing ever tighter, her fingers made it known she could snap my neck and spine at a moment's whim. Time passed under the flickering lights. Nothing was the same as it was before. Infinity was the place where I came to know myself, the club where I once felt most free. Lilah took that. She made me a stranger to myself, a witness and accomplice to terrible deeds. What I knew now was loss. Whatever music I once had was drained out of me.

"You … make … me feel … miii … ighty real!" Delilah sang as she spun around. As soon as Sylvester's falsetto pumped through the speakers a roar went up. The crowd came alive, lit beneath the swirling constellations.

"When we get home darlin' and it's nice and—"

Delilah froze. Sweating bodies swayed around us. Spinning colors, beautiful fabrics, shimmering lights. Something was different about her. An emotion I hadn't seen before. Fear.

"Frankie," she said, her voice low. She turned me slowly so that my back now faced the back bar and her back faced the front doors. "Do you see that one there?"

"Who?" I asked, confused. Who was Delilah hiding from? Infinity was a New York City block long. The club was packed, a throng of fashionable bodies dancing each other under the tables. You could get lost just going to the restroom. Too bad if you were new and got separated from your friends. Might drift in the void for a while. I peered over Lilah's shoulder, unsure who I was looking for and then I saw her.

A woman so serene, she exuded radiance. She walked with a kind of assured calm and peacefulness amidst the pheromones, chaos, and noise. A being so ethereal she could not be from this world at all, a being so magnetic that it could only be one of Delilah's infamous sisters.

Dressed as if she had just arrived from the equator itself, she danced her way through the crowd.

"Yes, I see them," I said, matter-of-factly, trying to mask the satisfaction in my voice. Delilah had once said that the only thing she feared was her sisters' judgment. I didn't know who Delilah had once been, but I did wonder what this long-lost sister would think of her now.

"Where is she going?" Delilah asked, her voice a whisper. Her nails dug into me. Could she actually be afraid? I had seen Delilah emote before, a persuasive performance to lure her ill-fated lovers, but I never thought fear was within her range. The novelty of the moment got the best of me.

"I think she's heading this way," I said. "Third column."

Delilah's eyes widened. Sweat beaded on her forehead. "No." She pulled away. "Follow me!"

She pushed through the crowd without looking back, weaving in and out of the jubilant dancers. I watched the mysterious woman stop at the DJ's booth. Heads bent, she and DJ Animus, the latest phenom passing through, were deep in conversation as the music swelled. Surrounded by vinyl-filled crates, they held each other with the warmth and intimacy of old friends. She kissed him, her wrap dress hugging her curves. Clearly seduction ran in the family, but there was a genuineness about this other sister. She held her friend with a sense of caring that showed in her slightest movements. There was no malice there.

Adrenaline with the ever-present sadness filled me as I turned to shadow Lilah through the nightclub. A few of her fans greeted her, but she waved them off.

She ran all the way to the back, stilettos stomping past the couples hidden in darkness. Concealment was key in places of nocturnal revelry. The ends of cigarettes burned in the shadows, unblinking red eyes. When she reached the off-limits area, a bouncer moved to stop her. She fingered the canister on the gold chain around her neck. With one hand on her high-slitted dress, she smiled at him. I knew that smile.

"Oh," he said, recognizing her. "Miss Divine, go 'head." She didn't have to whisper a code name like the patrons from the past. He frowned at me but waved me through. She didn't wait for me as she strode down the dark narrow hall. We descended a rickety flight of stairs, down a ramp. Here, the four-on-the-floor, constant quarter-note bass beat was muted. I had never been in the club's labyrinth. I half-expected a minotaur to emerge from the shadows, but the only real monster there was Delilah.

We walked past several old, dusty oak barrels. The hoops were rusted, the lettering on the heads faded. She sidestepped the barrels outside a wide, heavy door and ducked into a vault-like room.

"What is this?" I asked. She shrugged, tossing Thierry's fedora and taking a seat on a velvet couch. "Backroom deals need back rooms, no? This used to be a speakeasy." She adjusted the strap on her dress. I moved to sit with her. "No," she said. "I need you to go back up. Come back when she's gone." For the first time her voice was shaky. None of the dazzling diva confidence that fueled her flight. She looked pensive. The room's primeval green walls cast murky dark shadows over bronze skin. She looked almost ill. "Light?" She held a skinny joint up.

I pulled a lighter out and lit it, eager to leave. Fragrant smoke floated in the air, a halo around her face. She closed her eyes, not offering me a hit. She sighed and tossed the roach on the floor. I watched as she opened her cannister. Whatever family reunion lay ahead, Delilah wasn't ready.

"And Frankie?" she said.

"Yes?"

"Bring some ice."

I left her fingering her necklace, the canister empty now as I wondered what awaited me outside. No sooner than I reached the top stair, the stench hit me.

A scream rose from black clouds as I stepped out. "Fire!" The guard that waved us into the labyrinth was gone. Panic-stricken dancers reached for each other, knocking over the swivel-back chairs and stools.

"What happened?" I screamed at a passing couple. They shook their heads. I couldn't see the flames at first, but I could feel the heat. On a good night the club was smoldering. This was hellish.

As the giant neon lights that spun around the columns began to flicker, the overhead lights dimmed. Instinctively I ran back through the hall, down the stairs. When I made it to the vault, the image of Thierry's fedora hat haunted me. Delilah had taken a life she didn't need. She did so to punish me.

I had been a loyal, faithful friend, never revealing her dark secrets, even when loyalty and faith were the last things Delilah deserved. Going back down into the maze beneath the club could cost me my life. Did I still believe being with Delilah was worth it?

I stood outside the heavy door, silent, thoughts lost in the corners of the past. Labyrinths were designed to generate chaos and confusion. Like magic, this labyrinth manifested clarity.

"Frankie?" Delilah's voice on the other side of the door was a tentative question. I held a barrel by its spigot and awkwardly rolled and wobbled it over, propping it under the door's handle. "Hello?" I kicked the other oak barrel on its side and rolled it to the door. The handle shook slightly but did not move.

"Who's there? Open this door!" she cried. She pounded but the door held.

I backed away. My feet felt heavy as iron, as if I was bolted to the ground.

"Hello? Is anyone there? I'm stuck. The door is stuck. Let me out!" she screamed.

Panic set in, but also resignation, and now the screams reached a fever pitch.

I could run or I could unroll the stone sealing the tomb, but I knew this was no messiah coming back.

I ran, running into one of the other barrels that lined the hall. "Damn," I cried out, my knee throbbing.

"Frankie?" she screamed, incredulous.

I ran, but two partiers emerged from the narrow hallway, startling me.

"We've got to get out," I said, breathless. "There's a fire."

"What?" Confusion flashed across their faces, then panic. We fled as fast as we could, up the ramp and the rickety stairs. When we reentered the main floor, the room was plunged in total chaos. Black clouds of smoke filled the air. I tripped over a high heel shoe, coughing up half a lung. Even in the panic, the tears and fear, my ears strained. I could hear Delilah over the din. That voice, that incredible voice, the throat that sounded like ten. The sound was a keening, weeping. I paused in the darkness, shame and guilt knotted in my chest.

I was the monster now.

Then I heard it, not weeping but laughter. Her voice, that remarkable otherworldly voice rising above the echoes of terror and dismay. Faced with being burned alive, Delilah Divine laughed.

A chemical, plastic scent began to fill the air. Smokey fingers reached for me. I bolted, banging into a cocktail table, tumbling over an upturned chair. Whatever grace I once had was gone, too. Vinny from the bar waved me on.

"What are you waiting for, get out! Drag anyone else you see. Infinity's going to blow!" He pulled up a man who had fallen down, his ankle twisted. They hobbled away.

As I ran, slipping over the slick, drink-stained floorboards, the piles of pink confetti, I couldn't tell if the pounding I heard was the pounding of my heart or the pounding of the music's beat. No one stopped the music. The DJ booth was empty. Crates of vinyl sprawled across the dance floor. If Delilah's sister had come looking for her, she was gone now.

I reached a bottleneck near the fourth column. Neon pulsed and flickered above our heads. An explosion from the left then a screech somewhere behind us sent us scrambling.

"¡Ay bendito!" someone cried. "What is that?" People shouted, pointed.

Just like Orfeu, I knew I shouldn't look back, but I had already stared into the abyss. Only a narrow strip of sky separated us, so I turned to see.

Golden scales, impossible wings. One, no, two serpent's tails bursting through the flames. A song so loud and wretched, it sounded as if the whole sky's throat opened to sing.

For some, cautionary truths, though known, must be lived. Others can see the signs before the symbols emerge and still they fall head in. I was the latter. I saw but didn't want to see. I wanted the dream. When we look in the sky to watch the stars, we are seeing them as they once were. But bright suns give the most light when they are leaving you.

Transfixed we watched as the creature circled the high, vaulted ceilings of Infinity. Brilliant flames, great flickering tongues of fire and heat, rushed through the nightclub engulfing the black walls. The crowd moved, eyes wide, coughing, wailing, mouths flung open, but it was as if all the sound was turned off. It felt like I was running against a great, hot wind.

"This way!" The guard from earlier guided people out of a side door that led to an alley. Relieved, we bum-rushed the door, one person getting jammed before the screaming crowd pushed us all through.

"El fiesta se fue al garete!" a woman in a glittering emerald gown yelled. "The party went to hell!"

Standing outside shivering in zero-degree weather as fire trucks descended, I had to agree.

The night Infinity burned was the night Disco nearly died in me. But even though the nightclub burned, the fire couldn't burn my memories. I had gone to the discos in search of strangers, anonymous partiers who on the dance floor became my friends. Instead of love and solidarity, I left with unclean hands, a stained shirt, and enough disparate memories to haunt me for years.

I could hear the last notes of Delilah's song, a scream as if every star in the night was afire. The notes scatter like broken teeth across the smoke-filled air. What was tender in the notes, the soft, the thrumming, came from a thousand other heartbroken souls like me. That night I stood in the crowd with those who were still in shock. We watched as the firemen worked to control the six-alarm fire, grieved for the loss of our shared home. I blink back tears, covered in ashes, but when the day rises and the sky clears, there is only the burned-out building, its gaping windows, and the outline of the sun. I walk away, but only make it a few steps when something falls from the sky and drops in front of me. A melted canister. I pick it up. Misshapen, it's still hot to the touch. Like her love, a smoldering wild thing.

RED_BATI

by Dilman Dila

Red_Bati's battery beeped. Granny flickered, and the forest around her vanished. She sighed in exaggerated disappointment. He never understood why she called it a forest, for it was just two rows of trees marking the boundary of her farm. When she was alive, she had walked in it every sunny day, listening to her feet crunching dead twigs, to her clothes rustling against the undergrowth, to the music of crickets, feeling the dampness and the bugs, sniffing at the rotten vegetation, which she thought smelled better than the flowers that Akili her grandson had planted around her house. Now, she liked to relive that experience. With his battery going down, he could not keep up a real-life projection and, for the first time, she became transparent, like the blue ghost in the painting that had dominated a wall of her living room. Akili's mother had drawn it to illustrate one of their favorite stories.

Granny laughed at the memory. "That ghost!" she said. Her voice was no longer musical. It was full of static.

He could not recharge her. He had to save power, but he did not want to shut her down because he had no one else to talk to. He did not get lonely, not the way she had been: so lonely that she would hug him and her tears would drip onto his body, making him flinch at the thought of rust. She would hug him even though she complained that his body was too hard, not soft and warm like that of Akili. He did not get lonely like that, but Akili had written a code to make him want to talk to someone all the time, and he had not had a chance for a conversation since the accident, twelve hours ago.

He had resurrected her after her death, while he waited for a new owner. He used all the recordings he had made of her during their ten years together, to create a holographic imitation of her so he could have someone to talk to. It was not like walking with her in the mango forest or sitting at her feet on the porch as she knitted a sweater and watched the sun go down. Technically, he was talking to himself; but it was the only chance he had for conversation.

"I would have enjoyed being an astronaut," she said, floating a few feet in front of him, her limbs kicking in slow motion, the way humans moved in zero gravity. She was careful to keep behind the shelves, out of sight of the security camera. "This is the—"

She stopped talking abruptly when white-cell.sys beeped. A particle of ice was floating about like a predator shark. If it touched him, he would rust. He jerked, like a person awaking from a bad sleep, though the ice was ten meters away. Steel clamps pinned him onto a shelf. He could not get away.

The half-empty storage room looked like a silver-blue honeycomb. They had dumped him in it after the accident ripped off his forearm. The captain had evaluated his efficiency and, seeing it down to 80 percent, tagged him DISABLED. They could not fix his arm on the ship, so they shut him down and dumped him in storage until he got back to Earth. Entombed alive. Left to die a cold death.

"You won't die," Granny said, laughing. She sat on a fuel pod in a cell on the opposite shelf. "It's just a little ice. It's not even water."

He had lived all his life dreading rust, watching his step to avoid puddles, blow-drying his kennel every hour, turning on the heater all the way up to prevent dew from forming. He knew it was irrational, for his body, made of high-grade stainless Haya steel, was waterproof. He never understood his aquaphobia. Had Akili infected him with a program to ensure he stayed indoors on rainy days? Very likely. Granny liked playing in the rain as much as she liked walking in the mango forest. Yet every time she did, she got a fever, sometimes malaria. Akili might have written a code to force Red_Bati to stay indoors on rainy days, and so Granny, who used him as a walking aid and guide, stayed indoors too. Red_Bati could have searched for this code and rewritten it to rid himself of this stupid fear, but he did not. He loved it, for it made him feel human.

"I'm not worried about the ice," he said. "It's the temperature."

He was in Folder-5359, where temperatures stayed at a constant -250° C to preserve fuel pods. Technically, the cold would not kill him. He had a thermal skin that could withstand environments well below -400° C, but it needed power to function. Once his battery ran down, he would freeze and that would damage his e-m-data strips. Though these could be easily and cheaply replaced, he would lose all his data, all the codings that made him Red_Bati and not just another red basenji dog, all his records of Granny. He would die.

"That won't be a bad thing," Granny said, chuckling. "If you were a true dog, you'd be as old as I am and wishing for death."

He was not a dog. He was a human trapped in a pet robot.

Granny chuckled but did not say anything to mock him again. She watched the ice and tried to touch it, but it passed through her fingers and floated upwards. It would not touch Red_Bati, after all. He relaxed. If he had flesh and muscles, this would have been a visible reaction. Instead, white-cell.sys reverted to sleep mode, the red light in his eyes vanished, and his pupils regained their brownish tint.

His battery beeped, now at 48 percent for white-cell.sys had used up a lot of power in just a few seconds. In sixteen hours and forty-three minutes, it would hit zero and then he would die.

"You're not a human in a dog's body," Granny finally said, still watching the ice as it floated towards the ceiling.

"I am," Red_Bati said.

"Humans have spirits," Granny said. "You don't."

"I do," Red_Bati said.

"You can't," Granny said.

"Why not? I'm aware of myself."

"Doesn't mean you have it."

"Why not?"

"You're not a natural-born."

Red_Bati wanted to argue his point, to remind her of things that made him human, like agoraphobia; to remind her that he got consciousness from a chip and lines of code, just as humans did from their hearts and brains. He was not supposed to be conscious, much less super intelligent; but Akili had wanted Granny to have more than just a pet, so he installed Z-Kwa and turned Red_Bati into a guide, a walking aid, a cook, a cleaner, a playmate, a personal assistant, a friend, a doctor, a gardener, a nurse, and even a lover if she had wanted. She could live her last years as she pleased rather than suffer in a nursing home.

After she died, Akili had put him up for sale along with all her property and memorabilia. For a moment, Red_Bati had feared that Akili would remove Z-Kwa and wipe his memory, but Akili contracted a cleaning firm to get rid of Granny's property and either forgot or did not care to tell them about the chip. Red_Bati was too smart to let them know he was more than just a pet. Nor did he show it off to the people who bought him, Nyota Energy, an asteroid-mining company that, rather than buying miner-bots, found it cheaper to convert pets into miners. They gave him a new bios and software, a thermal coat, X-ray vision, and modified his limbs and tongue to dig rocks. They did not look into his rib-cage cabin, so they did not see Z-Kwa, otherwise they would have removed it. When they shut him down after his accident, Z-Kwa had turned him back on, aware that if his battery drained, he would die. He had self-preservation instincts, just like any other living thing with a spirit, and he wanted to tell her all these things, but she was draining his battery.

"Sorry," he said. "I have to conserve power."

"That's okay," she said.

He blinked, and she vanished. His battery life increased by two hours.

He examined the three clamps that pinned him to the cell. They had not expected him to wake, so they had not used electronic locks. With his tongue, he pushed the bolts on the clamps, and they snapped open. He could escape. The room had only one camera, at the front, to track crew who came in to pick up fuel pods. If it saw him, the ship would know he had awoken and service_bots would pounce on him and remove his battery. To hide from it, he needed the identity of another robot.

He checked the duty roster he had received before the accident. He did not expect the fuel roster to have changed since his accident only affected the cleaning roster. The next pickup was due in an hour, a karbull dragon-horse. It would not do. Six hours hence, it would be a tomcat, and then in thirteen hours, a robot that looked like him, a basenji dog. He wrote an identity-stealing app and hibernated.

He awoke ten minutes to time. His battery was down to 35 percent and would last for another ten hours. He slipped out of the cell, staying behind the shelves to hide from the camera. He floated to Shelf-4B and hid inside Cell-670, where he could see Cell-850, which had the fuel pod to be picked up next. He heard the outer door open and close. Then the inner door opened. The two doors ensured the temperature of Folder-5359 stayed at a constant -250° C, while the ship was a warm 16° C.

The basenji floated into view, riding a transporter tube. It saw Red_Bati but did not raise any alarms. It adhered strictly to its programming and ignored anything out of the ordinary, assuming the ship was in total control. Astral-mining companies stopped sending self-aware and self-learning robots many years ago after a ship had developed minor engine trouble and its crew, seeing their chance of returning safely to Earth had dropped to 99 percent, landed on an asteroid and refused to move until rescue came. Fearing to incur such needless losses, the miners resolved to send only "dumbots" incapable of making vital decisions without human input.

For a moment, Red_Bati wondered what had happened to the owner of this basenji. Its jaw was slightly open, its tongue stuck out to imitate panting, a design that little boys favored. He hoped its owner had only grown tired of it and had not died. He did not feel empathy the way Granny felt whenever she saw a dead ant; she felt so terrible that she would bury it. Granny had thought a dead child more horrible than a dead ant, and Red_Bati wanted to feel as she might have felt.

He waited until the basenji turned its back to him as it positioned the tube to suck the pod out of the cell. He turned on his X-ray vision to see the basenji's central processor and the comm receptor chip, both located just below the backbone, and on which the basenji's serial number and LANIG address were respectively printed. Two seconds later, his app was ready.

It would take ninety seconds for the pod to enter the tube, and in that time, Red_Bati had to take over the basenji's identity. He aimed a laser beam at the other dog's left ear, which was its comm antennae, to disable it. He activated his comm receptor at the same moment that he fired the laser beam. There would be a delay of a thousand microseconds between the basenji's going offline and Red_Bati's assuming its identity, but the ship would not read that as strange.

Red_Bati went into hover mode which consumed a lot of power but allowed him to move quicker. He tapped on the power button at the base of the basenji's tail, and the basenji shut down in three seconds. He grabbed it by the hind legs, guided it into an empty cell, and clamped it.

He raced back to the carrying tube and ten seconds later a beep came. The pod was inside the tube. He pushed it to the door. The tube had a temperature-conditioner that kept the pod chilled at -250° C to keep it from decaying. If a decayed pod ended up in a fuel tank, the engine's temperature would shoot from 80° C to a blistering 300° C within fifteen minutes. Fire would break out in the Ma-RXK section while there would be explosions in the Ma-TKP section. With eight engines, the ship would not stop if one was damaged, though its speed would drop. But fire in the engine made the ship vulnerable to hijacking.

Red_Bati turned a dial on the tube, turning off the temperature conditioner. It would take two minutes to reach the fuel tank, and by then, though the tube's temperature would have dropped by only two degrees, the pod would have decayed.

The ship was logged onto the tube, so the moment decay set in, the ship would be alerted and service_bots would not allow the pod into the fuel tank. Red_Bati had written an app to fool the ship into thinking the pod was still good. Hiding from the cameras, he had secretly fixed a finger into one of the tube's data rods to infect it with his app.

Stealing the ship, his calculations told him, was a very bad idea. The asteroid-mining companies would not rest until they understood why a ship suddenly went dark. They would send probes to all corners of the solar system, and Red_Bati would be running for the rest of his life. The other option, to hide until they reached Obares, an asteroid in the Kuiper belt rich in kelenite, did not seem possible. He could not hide his missing arm from the ship's cameras for the next two years of the journey. If he managed to, and got on the asteroid, he could sneak away with enough supplies, a tent, machines and spares, and he could use the sun to recharge; but that would mean growing old alone, with no one to talk to other than a holograph.

The ship was worth the risk. It had enough resources on board to sustain robot life for eternity, to create even a whole new world. It had VR printers that could give birth to new robots, who would be conscious like Red_Bati. Nyota Energy could have printed for him a new arm, but the cost was equal to buying another secondhand basenji, so they reserved VR printing to fix critical damages to the ship and to replace worn-out engine parts.

Once he had the ship under his control, he would take it somewhere far from human reach, maybe beyond Earth's solar system. He could hop from one asteroid to another, mining minerals to make fuel and VR cartridges, until he found a place big enough and rich enough to be a new home. The VR printers could give birth to new robots, to other VR printers, and even to new spaceships. He would not be lonely anymore.

Red_Bati kept his body close to the tube to hide the missing arm from the cameras, opened his mouth, and stuck out his tongue to imitate the panting basenji. The storage section was on the lowest level and the engines were in the midsection at the back of the ship. He followed tunnel-like corridors and did not meet other robots until he neared the engines, and the three he passed did not notice him: their eyes were focused in the distance. If they were humans, he would have exchanged nods with them in greeting, maybe even a cheerful, "How's it going?"

He reached Engine 5 without raising any suspicion. The fuel tank was in the first room. Its floor looked like the swimming pool which Granny had in her backyard. Things that looked like purple ice cubes swirled in a mist in the pool, under a glass lid. Red_Bati placed the carrying tube on the edge of the glass and pressed a button. The tube opened, the glass parted, and the pod slipped into the pool. The moment it touched the mist, it broke apart and thousands of ice cubes floated about. They were not a deep shade of purple like the others: they looked desaturated, but the ship would not immediately pick this up, because the steam swirling above the pool gave the cubes fluctuating shades. It relied entirely on the tube to alert it of a decayed rod.

Red_Bati hurried out of the engine, still shielding his body with the now-empty tube. When he reached the Supplies Folder, he did not shelve the tube, for he needed it to hide his missing arm. He settled in a corner, and five minutes later got the first message from the ship, which had noticed that he was not going to Docking for his next assignment. The message had a yellow color code, indicating low-level importance, inquiry only. If he were any other robot, he would have auto responded by sending the ship an activity log and system status, and the ship would have analyzed it and notified the captain to take action. Z-Kwa blocked his Comm_Sys from sending the auto-response. The ship sent another message two minutes later, with a blue color code and an attachment to auto-install a program to force a response, but Z-Kwa deleted the attachment. The ship waited another two minutes and then sent a third message, in white color code. It had notified both the captain and Nyota Energy on Earth about his strange behavior, and it had told them that two service_bots were on their way to take a physical look at him.

Before they could reach Supplies Folder, the ship sent a message in red color code to every bot: *A Red-Level event has occurred in Engine 5.*

Red_Bati could not hear the explosions. The ship was silent as though nothing was happening. The ship would know that decayed fuel was responsible and would associate Red_Bati's strange behavior to the crisis, but all service_bots would be needed in the engine to contain the disaster, and none would come after Red_Bati.

The first sign that the ship had become vulnerable to hijacking came in the next red message, hardly ten minutes after Red_Bati got the yellow message. *Kwa-Nyota is going into sleep mode.* Once in hibernation, other engines would shut down, all nonessential programs would shut down, all auto functions would cease, and all robots, apart from the service_bots and the captain, would go to sleep, too. Seventy-five seconds after the message, the lights went out.

Red_Bati activated infrared vision and made his way to the heart of the ship, where the data servers glowed in the dark like the skyscrapers of Kampala. When he was sold to Nyota Energy, he had scanned the internet for everything about the company and its spacecrafts. He did not have any particular need for the information but was only responding to a very human instinct: *know your employer*. He had blueprints of the ship, a Punda Binguni model built by Atin Paco, a Gulu-based company that had pioneered low-cost space travel. He had the source code of all its software and its operating system, Kwa-nyota. First, he went to the Comm Control Panel and flipped several switches to OFF, cutting communication with Earth. Now, Nyota Energy could not stop the hijack by sending the captain direct instructions, nor could it track the ship.

The captain would notice that it had lost communication with Earth but would not send a service_bot to check, for all fifty service_bots were in Engine 5.

It took Red_Bati fifteen minutes to write a program to convince the ship to take instructions from him rather than from Nyota Energy. Then he used a jiko data cable to connect physically to the ship's mainframe, making him a part of the ship. It took him another ten minutes to deactivate the security programs and install the hijacker. When he unhooked the cable, he had control of the ship.

All that work had drained his battery down to 8 percent. He had to wait for the service_bots to put out the fire before recharging. He went to sleep again. He stayed in the data room, for the rest of the ship froze during hibernation.

The service_bots spent nearly an hour putting out the fire and stabilizing Engine 5. The ship came out of hibernation and so did Red_Bati. He checked the cameras and saw smoke billowing from the engine, though this was mostly from komaline fire-suppressing solution. Three service_bots were severely damaged and were on stretchers to Storage. It reminded Red_Bati of Granny after her last stroke, as medics took her to a waiting air-hearse. Like the captain, the service_bots had humanoid structures, though their thermal coats gave them an alien skin, and as Red_Bati watched them leave Engine 5, he began to daydream about finally leaving his dog body.

He hurried to Docking where the robots were still asleep and sat on a charging chair. The other seven engines ignited, and in thirty minutes the journey resumed. The robots in Docking woke up. One of them was a humanoid in police uniform, a pet that girls loved. Red_Bati did not want to think about the little girl who had owned it. They had programmed it to be one of the ship's extra eyes. It noticed Red_Bati's missing arm and sent in a report. If Red_Bati had a face of flesh and skin, he would have smiled at this cop. Instead, he blinked rapidly and made a happy, whining sound. Granny would have known he was laughing at it. Red_Bati sent all robots a message, stripping the cop of his powers, and the cop stopped looking at him.

Once the ship was running again, the captain checked its inbox for new instructions. It could not maintain speed, now that it had lost one engine. It could not reach Obareso on schedule. The ship needed a new schedule. Every bot needed a new schedule, otherwise their systems would hang up in confusion. The captain found only one new message which, when opened, auto-installed a program and changed its coding and instructions. The captain immediately changed course to another asteroid, Madib Y-5, a flat rock ten miles long, seven miles wide, right in the middle of the asteroid belt, with generous supplies of kunimbili, from which they could make enough fuel pods to take them beyond human reach.

Granny flashed on, no longer bothering to hide from the cameras. With his battery now at 60 percent, she looked real. Her smile was full of teeth. It surprised him because she never used to smile like that. She did not like false teeth and thought the few teeth in her gums made her ugly.

"Good job," she said.

He shrugged only in his mind, because his body was incapable of shrugging.

"I don't see the point," she added. "After you land on a bare piece of frozen rock, what will you do with your life?"

Nothing, he wanted to say. I'll be alive. I'll start a new world. Then he saw what she meant: robots sitting on frozen rocks, basking in the sun like lizards, looking out at the emptiness of space, enjoying the brightness of stars that shone around them like a giant Christmas tree. Just sitting there and not looking forward to anything. The VR printers would give birth to more of his kind, but they would not grow like human children. They would be fully functional adults at birth, with almost nothing new to learn because they would have all the knowledge that forebots had gathered.

Would exploring for new worlds and searching for new matter give their lives meaning?

Humans needed a purpose to live. School. Job. Wedding. Children. Adventure. Invention. Something that would make them wake up the next day with a cheerful smile, though they knew there was no purpose to it all, and that they would eventually die and all their achievements would turn to dust. What life would his kind have? He could write coding to make them think like humans, to make them fall in love and get married and desire children, to make them have aspirations and build grand cities and spectacular spaceships and desire to travel deep into the galaxy. But they would be self-aware and self-learning and might then wipe off the code. Some might even decide to return to Earth.

He wanted to smile, to tell Granny that that was the beauty of it all. Like humans, they would live without knowing what tomorrow would bring.

"I want to rest in peace," Granny said.

"You are not a ghost," Red_Bati said.

"Am I not?" she said. "Look at me, look!" She walked as though the ship had gravity. She tried to touch things, but she was like smoke. "See? I'm a spirit."

"You are not," Red_Bati said.

"What do you think spirits are?"

He was quiet for a while, thinking of the painting her daughter had made. He could not be sure anymore if it was all code. Humans, after all, imagined spirits into existence.

"You'll be our goddess," he finally said.

She laughed. "That's a beautiful dream," she said. "But I want to rest in peace. I don't want to spend the rest of eternity talking to a metallic dog that thinks it's human."

Red_Bati imagined himself giving her a smile, the polite smile that a human would give a stranger in the streets. Then he shut her down and wondered what had gone wrong. She had never been mean to him. She had never called him a "metallic dog" before.

Maybe he should write new code so he could have Granny again, the Granny who took him for long walks in the mango forest, not this grumpy spirit.

ABOUT THE CONTRIBUTORS

SOMTO O. IHEZUE ("Where You Go") is a writer and filmmaker. He writes because there is beauty in the world and through words, he seeks to show it, explore it, live it. His works have appeared or are forthcoming in *Omenana Magazine, MINDS Africa, Massive, Escape Magazine Africa, Ibua Journal,* and others. In his spare time, he fantasizes about being a High Supreme Witch and falling in love. He tweets @braised_irodney

PEMI AGUDA ("Things Boys Do") is from Lagos, Nigeria. She is currently a fellow at the Helen Zell Writers Program at University of Michigan where her work won a Henfield Prize and Hopwood Awards. She received a 2019 Octavia Butler Memorial Scholarship Award by the Carl Brandon Society for the Clarion Workshop, and a 2018 Bread Loaf Conference Work-Study Scholarship. Her work appears in *Granta, American Short Fiction, Zoetrope: All-Story*, among others. You can find her at pemiaguda.com

RUSSELL NICHOLS ("Giant Steps") is a speculative fiction writer and endangered journalist. Raised in Richmond, California, he got rid of all his stuff in 2011 to live out of a backpack with his wife, vagabonding around the world ever since. Usually set in the near future, his stories revolve around concepts of race, mental health, technology, and the absurdity of existence. Look for him at russellnichols.com

TAMARA JERÉE ("The Future in Saltwater") is a graduate of the Odyssey Writing Workshop. Their short stories appear or are forthcoming in *FIYAH*, *Strange Horizons*, and *Fireside*. You can find them on Twitter @TamaraJeree or visit their website tamarajeree.com

TLOTLO TSAMAASE ("The ThoughtBox" and "The River of Night") is a writer of fiction, poetry, and architectural articles. Her work has appeared in *Clarkesworld*, *The Dark*, *Terraform*, *The Best of World SF Volume 1*, *Strange Horizons*, *Brittle Paper*, and other publications. Her poem "I Will Be Your Grave" was a 2017 Rhysling Award nominee. Her short story, "Virtual Snapshots" was longlisted for the 2017 Nommo Awards. Her novella, *The Silence of the Wilting Skin*, is a finalist for the Lambda Literary Award. You can find her on Twitter at @tlotlotsamaase and at tlotlotsamaase.com

SHEREE RENÉE THOMAS ("The Parts That Make Us Monsters," "Ancestries," and "Love Hangover") is the author of *Sleeping Under the Tree of Life* (Aqueduct Press), named on the 2016 James Tiptree Jr. Award Longlist and honored with a *Publishers Weekly* Starred Review, as well as *Shotgun Lullabies*. Thomas is also the editor of the World Fantasy Award-winning *Dark Matter* anthologies (Hachette), Associate Editor of *OBSIDIAN: Literature & Arts in the African Diaspora* (Illinois State), co-edited *Trouble the Waters: Tales from the Deep Blue* (Rosarium) with Pan Morigan and Troy Wiggins, and recently took on the mantle of editor of *The Magazine of Fantasy & Science Fiction*. Her short stories and poems can be found in *Sycorax's Daughters*, *Apex*, Harvard's *Transition*, *Afrofuturismo*, *Stories for Chip*, *Revise the Psalm*, *The Moment of Change*, *Mojo: Conjure Stories*, *Strange Horizons*, *Mythic Delirium*, *Jalada*, *So Long Been Dreaming*, *Memphis Noir*, and *Mojo Rising: Contemporary Writers*. Find her @blackpotmojo or in Memphis, Home of the Blues.

Born in the Caribbean, **TOBIAS S. BUCKELL** ("Scar Tissue") is a New York Times–bestselling and World Fantasy Award–winning author whose novels and almost 100 stories have been translated into 19 languages. He has been nominated for the Hugo Award and Nebula Award.

INEGBENOISE O. OSAGIE ("Breath of the Sahara") is a Nigeria-based writer and editor whose fiction has appeared in *West Branch*, *Juked*, *T-Gene*

Davis's Speculative Blog, and elsewhere. He hopes to own two German shepherds someday and is still deliberating on their names.

TOBI OGUNDIRAN ("The Many Lives of an Abiku" and "The Goatkeeper's Harvest") is a Nigerian writer of dark and fantastical tales, some of which have appeared in *The Dark*, *Beneath Ceaseless Skies*, *FIYAH*, *Tor.com*, and elsewhere. His short fiction has been longlisted for the Nommo award and been a finalist for the British Science Fiction Association award. Find him online at tobiogundiran.com and @tobi_thedreamer on Twitter.

CHINELO ONWUALA ("A Love Song for Herkinal *as Composed by Ashkernas Amid the Ruins of New Haven*") is the nonfiction editor of *Anathema: Spec from the Margins*, and co-founder of *Omenana*, a magazine of African Speculative Fiction. Her short stories have been featured in Slate.com, *Uncanny*, and *Strange Horizons*, as well as in several anthologies including the award-winning *New Suns: Original Speculative Fiction from People of Colour.* She's been nominated for the British Science Fiction Awards, the Nommo Awards for African Speculative Fiction, and the Short Story Day Africa Award. She's from Nigeria but lives in Toronto with her partner and child, and she's always happy to pet your dog.

MOUSTAPHA MBACKÉ DIOP ("A Curse at Midnight") is a Senegalese author living in Dakar. He is in his fourth year of medical school, and when he's not stressing about finals or hospital rounds, he reads and writes mainly fantasy. Obsessed with mythology and African folklore, he has published an urban fantasy trilogy written in French, named Teranga Chronicles. You can find him at his website, on Goodreads, and he tweets as @riverjengu

MARIAN DENISE MOORE ("A Mastery of German") converted a childhood love of science into a career in computing analysis. She lives in Harvey, Louisiana and works in the city of New Orleans. Her love of literature led to her writing both poetry and fiction. In 1998, she became a member of the NOMMO Literary Society, a writing workshop led by New Orleans writer and activist Kalamu ya Salaam. Her book of poetry, Louisiana Midrash, was published by UNO Press/Runagate in January 2019.

Her fiction has been published in the anthology *Crossroads: Tales of the Southern Literary Fantastic*, the online journal *Rigorous*, and the anthology *Dominion: An Anthology of Speculative Fiction from Africa and the African Diaspora*.

MICHELLE MELLON ("Are We Ourselves?") has been published in more than two dozen speculative fiction anthologies and magazines and is a member of the Horror Writers Association. Her first story collection, *Down by the Sea and Other Tales of Dark Destiny* was published in 2018. She is currently completing her second story collection. For updates on her work, visit www.mpmellon.com and/or follow her on Twitter: @mpmellon

C. L. CLARK ("When the Last of the Birds and the Bees Have Gone On") is the author of *The Unbroken*, the first book in the Magic of the Lost trilogy. She graduated from Indiana University's creative writing MFA and was a 2012 Lambda Literary Fellow. She's been a personal trainer, an English teacher, and an editor, and is some combination thereof as she travels the world. When she's not writing or working, she's learning languages, doing P90something, or reading about war and [post-]colonial history. Her work has appeared or is forthcoming in *FIYAH*, *PodCastle*, *Uncanny*, and *Beneath Ceaseless Skies*. Twitter: @C_L_Clark

EUGEN BACON ("Baba Klep") is African Australian, a computer scientist mentally reengineered into creative writing. Her work has won, been shortlisted, longlisted or commended in national and international awards, including the British Science Fiction Association (BSFA) Awards, Bridport Prize, Copyright Agency Prize, Australian Shadows Awards, Ditmar Awards, and Nommo Award for Speculative Fiction by Africans. Website: www.eugenbacon.com and Twitter: @EugenBacon

CRAIG LAURANCE GIDNEY ("Desiccant") writes both contemporary and genre fiction. He is the author of the collections *Sea, Swallow Me & Other Stories* (Lethe Press, 2008), *Skin Deep Magic* (Rebel Satori Press, 2014), *Bereft* (Tiny Satchel Press, 2013) and *A Spectral Hue* (Word Horde, 2019).

MAKENA ONJERIKA ("Disassembly") won the 2018 Caine Prize for African Writing. Her work has appeared or is forthcoming in *Wasafari Magazine*, *Waxwing*, *Samtiden*, *Jalada*, and *Doek!*, and the anthologies *New Daughters of Africa* and *Nairobi Noir*. She teaches at the Nairobi Fiction Writing Workshop (NF2W) and edited the workshop's first anthology, *Digital Bedbugs*.

T. L. HUCHU ("Egoli") is a writer whose work has appeared in *Lightspeed*, *Interzone*, *AfroSF*, *The Apex Book of World SF 5*, *Ellery Queen Mystery Magazine*, *Mystery Weekly*, *The Year's Best Crime and Mystery Stories 2016*, and elsewhere. He is the winner of a Nommo Award for African SFF, and has been shortlisted for the Caine Prize and the Grand prix de L'Imaginaire. His fantasy novel *The Library of the Dead*, the first in the "Edinburgh Nights" series, will be published by Tor in the United States and the United Kingdom in 2021. Find him @TendaiHuchu

YVETTE LISA NDLOVU ("The Friendship Bench") is a Zimbabwean sarungano (storyteller). She is pursuing her MFA at the University of Massachusetts Amherst where she teaches in the Writing Program. She has taught at Clarion West Writers Workshop online, earned her BA at Cornell University and is a 2021 Tin House Scholar. She was the 2020 fiction winner of *Columbia Journal's* Womxn's History Month Special Issue and is the co-founder of the Voodoonauts Summer Workshop for Black SFF writers. Her work has been anthologized in *Tor.com* and *Fiyah Literary Magazine's Breathe FIYAH* anthology and the *Voices of African Women Journal*. She received the 2017 Cornell University George Harmon Coxe Award for Poetry selected by Sally Wen Mao and is a 2020 New York State Summer Writers Institute Scholarship recipient. Her work has appeared or is forthcoming in the *Columbia Journal*, *Tor.com*, *Fiyah Literary Magazine*, *Jellyfish Review*, and *Kalahari Review*. You can find her on Twitter @lisa_teabag

DEREK LUBANGAKENE ("Fort Kwame") is a Ugandan writer, blogger, and screenwriter, whose work has appeared in *Escape Pod*, *Apex Mag*, *Omenana*, *Enkare Review*, *Prairie Schooner*, *Kalahari Review*, *The Missing Slate* and the *Imagine Africa 500* anthology, among others. Listed as one of *Tor.com*'s new SFF writers to watch, his work has also been shortlisted for the 2019 Nommo Awards best short story, longlisted for 2017 Writivism Short Story Prize and the 2013 Golden Baobab/Early Chapter Book Prize. In 2016 he received the Short Story Day Africa/All About Writing Development Prize. He is currently working on a short-story anthology and his first novel. When not writing or reading, Derek spends his days fundraising for a nonprofit wildlife conservation organization. He lives online at www.dereklubangakene.com

SUYI DAVIES OKUNGBOWA ("We Come as Gods") is the author of *Son of the Storm* (Orbit, May 2021), first in The Nameless Republic epic fantasy trilogy, and the godpunk novel, *David Mogo, Godhunter* (Abaddon, 2019). His shorter works have appeared internationally in periodicals like *Tor.com*, *Lightspeed*, *Nightmare*, *Strange Horizons*, *Fireside*, and anthologies like *Year's Best Science Fiction and Fantasy*, *A World of Horror*, and *People of Color Destroy Science Fiction*. He lives between Lagos, Nigeria, and Tucson, Arizona, where he teaches writing at the University of Arizona and completes his MFA. He tweets at @IAmSuyiDavies and is @suyidavies on Instagram. Learn more at suyidavies.com

SHINGAI NJERI KAGUNDA ("And This Is How to Stay Alive") is an Afrofuturist freedom dreamer, Swahili sea lover, and Femme Storyteller among other things, hailing from Nairobi, Kenya. She is currently pursuing a Literary Arts MFA at Brown University. Shingai's short story "Holding Onto Water" was longlisted for the Nommo Awards 2020, and her flash fiction "Remember Tomorrow in Seasons" was shortlisted for the Fractured Lit Prize 2020. She has been selected as a candidate for the Clarion UCSD Class of 2020/2021. *clarionghostclass. She is also the co-founder of Voodoonauts, an afrofuturist workshop for black writers.

WC DUNLAP ("The Front Line") draws her inspiration from the complexities of a Black Baptist, middle-class upbringing by southern parents, and all that entails for a brown-skin girl growing up in America. Equally enthralled by the divine and the demonic with a professional background in data and tech, she seeks to bend genres with a unique lens on fantasy, fear, and the future. WC Dunlap's writing career spans across film, journalism, and cultural critique, previously under the byline Wendi Dunlap. You can find her writing in *FIYAH*, *Lightspeed*, *PodCastle*, *Christian Century*, and in the upcoming anthology *Whether Change: The Revolution Will Be Weird. Carnivàle* is her first long-form fiction published serially via the Broken Eye Books Patreon, Eyedolon. WC Dunlap holds a BA in Film and Africana Studies from Cornell University. She is the proud mother of a young adult son and two British Shorthair familiars. Follow WC Dunlap on twitter @wcdunlap_tales

ZZ CLAYBOURNE (he/him, also known as Clarence Young) ("Penultimate") is the author of the novels *The Brothers Jetstream: Leviathan*, *Neon Lights*, and *By All Our Violent Guides*, as well as the acclaimed short-story collection *Historical Inaccuracies* and inspirational gift book *In the Quiet Spaces*. His essays on sci-fi, fandom, and creativity have appeared in *Apex*, *Strange Horizons*, and various other outlets. He is currently at work on his fourth novel. Find him on the web at writeonrighton.com

DILMAN DILA ("Red_Bati") is a Ugandan writer and filmmaker. He was longlisted for the BBC Radio Playwriting Competition (2014), shortlisted for the prestigious Commonwealth Short Story Prize (2013), and longlisted for the Short Story Day Africa prize (2013). He was nominated for the 2008 Million Writers Awards for his short story, "Homecoming." He first appeared in print in *The Sunday Vision* in 2001. His works have since been featured in several literary magazines and anthologies. His most recent works are the novelette, *The Terminal Move*, and the romance novella, *Cranes Crest at Sunset*. His films include the masterpiece, *What Happened in Room 13* (2007), and the narrative feature, *The Felistas Fable* (2013), which was nominated for Best First Feature at AMAA 2014. His first collection of short stories, *A Killing in the Sun* (2014), was released during the Storymoja Hayfestival. More of his life and works is available at his website www.dilmandila.com

Printed in the USA
CPSIA information can be obtained
at www.ICGtesting.com
JSHW021902221024
72178JS00001B/2